FALLING IN PLACE

FALLING
IN
PLACE

A Novel by

ANN
BEATTIE

RANDOM HOUSE
NEW YORK

*Grateful acknowledgment is made to the following for
permission to reprint previously published material:* Cherio
Corporation: Lyrics from *Never on Sunday* by Billy Towne
and Manos Hadjidakis. Copyright © 1960 Esteem Music
Corp. and Llee Corporation. International Copyright Se-
cured. All Rights Reserved. Used by Permission. The
Hudson Bay Music Company: Lyric from *She's a Lady* by
John Sebastian. Copyright © 1968 by The Hudson Bay
Music Company. Used by permission. All rights reserved.
MCA Music: Lyric from *Tammy*, Words and Music by
Jay Livingston and Ray Evans. © Copyright 1956 by
Northern Music Company, New York, New York. Used
by permission. All Rights Reserved. Stafree Publishing
Company: Lyric from *Disco Duck* is reprinted by permis-
sion of Stafree Publishing Company.

The author wishes to express her thanks to the Guggen-
heim Foundation for its support.

Library of Congress Cataloging in Publication Data
Beattie, Ann.
Falling in place.
I. Title.
PZ4.B3715Fal   [PS3552.E177] 813'.54   79–3880
ISBN 0–394–50323–6

Manufactured in the United States of America
4689753

FALLING IN PLACE

I

JOHN JOEL WAS high up in the tree, the one tall tree in the backyard. Forget the stick-y lilacs and the diseased peach tree with branches that splayed like umbrella spokes. The tree he was in was a great tree. The robins had left their nest early in the week, so John Joel had his favorite resting place back: the tenth branch up, the one that he could crawl out on, high above his mother's Chevy and the small kidney-shaped pool, now empty, that in previous summers had held goldfish, tadpoles and water lilies, and that now was filled with sticks and leaves no one had cleared out when winter ended.

"Frog face," his sister Mary said. She crossed her eyes and puffed her cheeks in and out. She was coming home from her friend Angela's house, and she had cut through the empty lot between their houses, even though she had been told not to because of poison ivy.

"I hope you get poison ivy," John Joel said.

Mary was going to summer school because she had flunked English. Every morning from nine to twelve she went to school. Then she went to Angela's and listened to the new Peter Frampton album. Angela's mother worked, so no one was home to object.

3

She had her book bag with her, filled with books. The bag had "Peter Frampton" imprinted on it and there were hearts instead of the "a" and "o" of Frampton. Mary was swinging the book bag. Behind her was the field of poison ivy and wild strawberries, daisies and phlox.

"Blaaaaaaaa," John Joel retched, and spit out a glob of saliva.

Mary watched it fall. It landed at the side of the kidney-shaped pool.

"Save the rest to grease your cock in case a skunk comes by you want to screw," Mary said.

She went into the house. She dropped her bag by the door and went upstairs to her room. She looked out the window and saw her brother lying on his stomach along the tree branch. She was glad that he had decided to stay there instead of coming into the house to bother her. She opened the window and pushed her hair back and clutched it in one hand, in a ponytail, as if there were a breeze; then she went to the bureau and got a brush and began to brush her hair. Her hair was damp. It was July. She was wearing powdered eye shadow instead of stick, because her face got so damp. On days when her mother drove her to school, she wore stick. Her mother's car was air conditioned, and Mary didn't care what she looked like getting out of school—just what she looked like going in. She hated summer school and thought it was as bad as jail. It would have been jail, except that Angela had also flunked English, and they sat together. Their teacher was named Cynthia Forrest, and Mary loathed her about as much as she loathed John Joel and a little more than she loathed Lloyd Bergman, who had given Angela a hickey on her tit.

Cynthia Forrest had graduated from Bryn Mawr and she was studying for her Ph.D. at Yale. She had sent around a notice with a drawing of herself at the top and that information, and she had made all the summer school students take the notice home to their parents and bring it back signed, so she could be sure that they had seen it. She really thought she was hot shit. All those mimeographed handouts with the drawings of her turned-up nose and her credentials coming back with names signed at the bottom: Art and Alice Dwyer ("Keep up the good work!"), Marge Pendergast, J.D.O. ("I'm a Harvard grad myself"), Cici Auerberg

("Mrs. Charlie Auerberg"). *Shit.* Let her have her fancy credentials. She was still stuck in summer school like the rest of them.

Imagine: She was having them read Great Books. They weren't reading the entire book, though, because there wasn't time. There wasn't time, and, as Lloyd Bergman said, they were so stupid that they wouldn't understand what was going on anyway, so they were reading parts of books. They had already read "The Pardoner's Tale," Act One of *She Stoops to Conquer* and Chapter One of *Vanity Fair*. Next week they had to read more of *Vanity Fair* and Chapter One of *A Tale of Two Cities*. And *Pride and Prejudice:* They were to open *Pride and Prejudice* at random, and whatever page they opened to, they were to read the whole chapter that page appeared in. The end of the course, the most up-to-date the course got, was—get ready for this—*The Old Man and the Sea.*

Mitch Auerberg had hit a squirrel on his motorcycle and had brought it to school in a plastic bag inside a paper bag, and while Billy Fields distracted Cynthia by clutching his stomach and stumbling away from his desk pretending to be about to throw up in the hall, Auerberg switched the bag with her lunch bag and crammed her sprout salad sandwich—that was really what she ate—into his desk. The day before that he had opened a bottle of ink and poured it in his desk. Not for any reason, just to see what would happen. The ink was still there, and it looked like the same size puddle. As he lowered the top of the desk, the lunch bag began to turn black.

"Is this all a joke, Billy?" Lost in the Forest said to Billy in the hallway. He was heaving with laughter as well as faked nausea.

Mary put on a Peter Frampton T-shirt and went into the bathroom to throw her other shirt into the laundry hamper. There was a quarter on top of the hamper, so she pocketed it. As her father would say, it was important to have money, because if you had money, you could buy the Brooklyn Bridge. She braced her arm on the bathroom sink and leaned forward to look at her blue eyes in the bathroom mirror. They were her best feature. The eye shadow had stayed on pretty well. She went downstairs and got a Tab out of the refrigerator and went upstairs and slipped the curl of metal from the can under John Joel's sheet. On second thought, she pulled the sheet back and put it farther down in the bed, where his feet might get cut by it. Then she tangled the sheets again. He was a pig; he never made his bed. A breeze was blowing through his window. His room got more air than hers. She closed his window. Downstairs, she collapsed in a kitchen chair. It was Wednesday. Her mother was being a do-gooder at the hospital and wouldn't be home for another hour. She went into the den and put Linda Ronstadt on the stereo. She shook her head at how good Linda Ronstadt was.

Lost in the Forest was probably home at her condo—Billy Fields had followed her home and found out that was where she lived, in a yucky condo—and she was probably having—what would she have?—an iced tea, and listening to Vivaldi. She was probably conducting Vivaldi with the tail end of her braid, ordering the musicians around. Certain books were like Vivaldi, Lost in the Forest thought. When she had said this, she had cupped her hand and curved her four fingers toward her thumb, making a little crab-claw. And she had stared at it. It was one of her intense gestures. The other one she used a lot was putting her thumb and first finger between her eyes and pressing the sides of her nose. She had done that after she read the first two lines of "The Pardoner's Tale."

The other thing Billy and Auerberg had thought to do, which was so funny, was to get hold of Anthony O'Dell—he had had to start summer school late because his father died and he had to ride the train with his mother to bury his father in Chicago—and convince him it would be funny if he lisped and stuttered. O'Dell did it, and very well—he raised his hand all the time and did it so convincingly that by the time a few days had gone by, they just wanted him to snap out of it.

The telephone rang, and she took a final swallow of Tab before she got up to answer it.

"Hello, Sunbeam," her father said. "How was school?"

"Suck-o," she said.

"You could at least say something pleasant before you're foul-mouthed. If you have to be foul-mouthed."

"You'd be too, if you had to sit there and listen to her giving a dramatic reading of *Vanity Fair*."

"Never read that one."

"She probably didn't either, and that's why she was reading it out loud."

6

"If you're so smart, how come you flunked English?"

"Because you can only be smart in so many things. Like, I'm really good at knowing how many rows of beans Jack can plant in his garden if his garden is in the shape of a parallelogram and I know the lengths of two sides."

"The reason I called," he said, "is because when your mother called the house during her break there was no answer. She wanted me to ask you to put the hamburger meat out to thaw."

"The retard's up in the tree, doing his tree frog number. He tried to spit on me and missed."

"Did he really try to spit on you?"

"Yeah. What are you gonna do—tear off your gray business suit and glasses in the nearest phone booth and fly in from the Big Apple to deck him?"

"I don't own a gray business suit, and you should try to find a phone booth on a New York street that has a door that closes."

"Navy blue? What color do you own?"

"A fire-engine-red leisure suit, made of Dacron polyester. You think I'm a total ass or something? A gray business suit. Don't tell me you'd like it if your dad was the sort who'd button himself into a vest and stick a pocket watch in one pocket and a Hershey's Kiss for his little princess in the other."

"You're so weird. So you wear a sports jacket. You think that's so different from a suit."

"My Sunshine Girl," he said. "Pretty as a berry, sweet as a dream. Suck-o yourself."

He hung up.

The record ended. She flipped it to the other side. A tiny feather of dust rose off the record and settled on it again. She watched it spin. Too small to cause any problem. She decided not to bother to blow it away.

June. A long time left in summer school, having Lost in the Forest read them things from books at the end of every class. She did it to kill time, probably. She said she was doing it because language was beautiful (crab-claw), and it was very rare that a person knew how to read aloud well. Presumably Lost in the Forest did: She read in whispers and sudden gasps, sometimes slowly, then fast, looking at the book as if there were real movement there, as if characters hardly larger than specks of dust were actually running and quarreling and jumping in the air, while Lost in the Forest stared down at them appreciatively, like God.

There was going to be a true-false test about the first chapter of *Tom Jones* on Monday. There had already been a test on "The Pardoner's Tale," and there was going to be a test at the end of the week on *Pride and Prejudice*. The first test had been an essay, but Lost in the Forest said that they would not have to write more essays; for what she was being paid, she wouldn't consider reading twenty of their ill-expressed opinions again. "I'd worry that you'd tell your parents what I said," Lost in the Forest had told them, "but none of you can communicate clearly enough to get your message across." She had sniffed. A self-righteous Mary Poppins sniff, but she had neither taken off nor landed. She had stood rooted to the spot, and then she had sighed deeply and fumbled in her book bag and read them a poem about somebody falling out of the sky while some other people worked. Then, gazing up at the globe-shaped light in the classroom ceiling, she had said that they could leave, ten minutes early. Auerberg had looked back at the schoolroom and had called their attention to Lost in the Forest, standing at the window, watching them walk away. The ones who saw her had waved dramatically; Billy had bent over as if he were mooning her; Claude Williams had made circles with his wrist, pretending to lasso her.

She had done nothing in reply. She had just stood there, watching them, hating them, and feeling a little sorry for them, and sorrier for herself. She wished that the sidewalk would sink and they would disappear from her life as easily as when you wave goodbye to company, the elevator door closes and they're gone. Oh, maybe a second of joking, when the slightly drunken guests push the "Door Open" button to say a final thank you, and the hostess is caught off-guard, looking blank-faced and exhausted. But then gone, taken away, all over. No: They'd be back the next day, and the next. They'd be there all of July, and so would she. And that lunch bag, thank God she had been able to tell by the weight of it that it was not a sandwich and her little bag of raw carrots. Thank God it wasn't a bomb—that these children were not destructive, just stupid. She had no curiosity about what it was.

"Lost in the Forest, you are such a drag," Mary said to the

8

empty house. She went upstairs. In her room, she took off the Peter Frampton T-shirt and put it on the bed, unzipped her jeans, took them off and her satin underpants, too (a Christmas present from Angela: an upside-down strawberry ice cream cone painted on them, neon pink melting where her pubic hair began, spattering pink all the way to where the pants curved into her crotch).

She went over to her wall. There were six posters of Peter Frampton, all the same. In the posters, he had his head tilted. His hair was very curly and his mouth was pale. His blue eyes were paler than her own. His skin looked as if it had been photographed through a screen. Up close to the poster, you could see the faint lines of the grid marks.

Mary put her cheek to his, rolled her head until her mouth touched his lips. The paper was smooth and cool. She took her mouth away and said two words: "Peter Frampton." "Peter" made her mouth open. "Frampton" made her pucker her lips so that ending the word was a kiss. This was Mary's routine. She did it every day. And every day it was predictable that Peter Frampton would not come to life, that when she said "Peter" and her mouth opened, his tongue would not come into her mouth. No point in hoping against hope for the extraordinary: a small seed exploding into a giant beanstalk; a body falling from the sky. A body falling from the sky?

She had forgotten to put out the hamburger meat.

"Spangle," Cynthia said. "Tell me that I am not actually seeing what I'm seeing."

"You're blind," he said. "You don't see anything. Stumble into bed and let your other senses take over."

"Spangle," she said, "I can understand that I might have deserved a put-down like this if sending this notice around had been my idea, but I only typed it because the vice-principal told me to. So do you think it was a good idea to draw a little picture of me on the ditto master? Do you think that was funny? Did you think I'd like that?"

"It's a good drawing. Besides, those money-up-the-ass parents will love it. They'll think it establishes rapport. You watch: You'll get yourself invited to a garden party."

"You're a real shit. Now I'm going to have to do this thing over."

"No you won't. Just tape a piece of paper over the drawing."

The room was dark except for the frog night light on the table beside the bed. She had left the ditto master on the table when she got undressed and went to take a shower, and Spangle—bored, trying to twirl a Frisbee on his first finger—had picked up the piece of paper and a pen and doodled Cynthia's face. It was not a caricature; it was what he thought she really looked like.

"Believe me," Spangle said. "Watch all the nice notes you get."

"And you're going to go to the garden party with me?"

" 'Can't please everyone, so you've got to please yourself,' " Spangle sighed. "I am going to be on a mission of great importance, retrieving my brother from the mysteries of Madrid. Hoping he isn't already married and that there isn't already an olive-skinned infant and a maid he's two-timing Rosita with. Hoping to get him back to law school. My esteemed brother. Have to be careful not to piss him off, though. I'm almost out of the money the old man left me, but he hasn't run out of his. As far as I know."

"Move over," she said.

"Speak right into the microphone," Spangle said, kicking back the sheet and taking his penis in his hand. "Do you think there are really tankers full of crude oil off the coast that the United States is stopping from making deliveries? Are you angry about gas rationing?"

"Get over," she said, nudging him with her hip.

"Come closer," Spangle said. "The mike isn't picking this up."

"I'm going to have to deal with your neurotic mother all the time you're in Madrid."

"Do you think . . ." Spangle said, raising his pelvis in the air and pointing his penis toward her.

"God almighty," she said. "If you want to play with yourself don't let me interrupt."

She pushed until she had enough bed space to lie down on.

"I'm a tanker," Spangle said, rolling toward her, holding his erect penis, "and I'm steaming in to make a delivery."

"Get off," she said. "I'm not amused, Spangle."

"What's today's date?" he said. "Tomorrow had better be an odd day, because I'll never make it to Bradley Field on an eighth of a tank."

11

2

CYNTHIA DREAMED that she was falling. It was a late afternoon
fright dream. When she took naps after teaching, she often had to
wake herself up in the middle of some nightmare. At night she
slept all right, but when she napped she was likely to have nightmares. It was worth the risk, though: When she slept, she forgot
the students, and if she had a nightmare and shook herself awake,
she was always glad to find herself in her lover's apartment, instead
of at the high school. Her sister had left her the key to her condominium while she was in Mexico for the summer, but Cynthia
found the cramped New Haven apartment more comfortable. That,
and that idiotic Mitch Auerberg—he was older than the rest of
them, and had failed a similar course the summer before—who
had followed her home one day on his motorcycle and gunned it
and streaked off when she saw him. He was probably hiding in the
bushes like Popeye, waiting for her to go out back of the building
in her bathing suit so he could scare her—she did not think he was
capable of worse than that. She went on the assumption that there
was no great malice in those children, and that was what kept her
going to work every day.

She found a joint on the night table and lit it, got out of bed and went into the kitchen. She turned on the window fan and undid her pigtails, putting the rubber bands on the counter. An ant ran around them and disappeared down the crack between the wall and the counter. Her lover, Peter Spangle, would not let her buy any chemical bug killers; his own nightmares were about being at the test site when an atomic bomb was detonated. He was sure that it was the odor of Raid that provoked his nightmares. Raid, he insisted: not all the acid he had taken; not the recent newspaper reports linking exposure to radiation with cancer.

Spangle was in Madrid, trying to talk his brother Jonathan into returning to law school. His mother had paid for the trip to Madrid. She had paid for his brother's trip, too, not realizing that Jonathan had intended his vacation to be a year long. She was afraid, now that Peter was in Madrid, that he would stay too—that the country had some secret power over highly intelligent white American males. She called the apartment often, to see if there was any word on how things were going. She also complained that her new wall-to-wall carpeting was fuzzing, and that as soon as an avocado seed took root, it rotted. When Spangle had been in the apartment and his mother called, she only spoke briefly to Cynthia, to exchange a few banalities. Now that her son was gone and she had no one else to talk to, she sometimes called twice a night. Cynthia was tempted to pick up the phone and say, in her most faraway voice: "This is the spirit of Madrid, and I have captured your sons forever. Don't watch for them in the breeze or in sunlight. I have their power. I have sucked their souls as empty as the inside of a straw."

Enough dope smoking for the day. Strange how hard two tokes could hit. They could wipe you out when you were not yet wide awake.

She went to look in the refrigerator. She settled for leftover hummus and some pita bread and sat on the counter and dipped the bread into the bowl. It tasted like baby food. When she finished eating, though, there would be no one to wipe her chin and put her on her back to admire her while she kicked her legs. Instead, she would go to the laundromat—the one next door to the donut shop, to torture herself for having given up refined sugar.

How could the students not care about the pilgrimage to Canterbury? How could she care that such idiots did not care? How could

Mitch what's-his-name have had the nerve to follow her as she walked to her sister's apartment and then make a twisted face at her, letting her see that it was him? Didn't they care that she could take it out on them later, in the classroom? Didn't they care that they were making such fools of themselves in front of an adult? She would have been mortified not to have appeared sophisticated when she was their age.

But where did sophistication get you? It got you selected for an education at a classy college, and when you graduated, this kind of part-time job was the best thing you could get, and the pay was no good, and your brain—after so much time realizing that she *had* a brain—was now being challenged by trivia. How can I kill bugs without using bug spray? Where is the best place to wash clothes? Should I or should I not go out to the swimming pool in back of my sister's condominium? By the time her education was completed, her brain would be worn down to a little stub, pencil shavings on the floor.

"My hair hurts," Spangle's mother said when Cynthia picked up the telephone. "I had it in a rubber band yesterday, but this is the first time it's hurt, so I don't think it's that. It's Freudian, I guess. It feels like somebody's tugged it."

She was not calling about her hair.

"Tell me without my having to ask whether you've heard from him."

"I haven't. I told you that when he left, he said they'd be back this Friday."

"One little *par avion*, you'd think. Anyway, I'm hoping they're really coming back. I've lost five pounds. It's a combination of worrying and eating nothing but poached eggs and drinking Perrier."

"I was about to eat when you called," Cynthia said. Anything to get her off the phone.

"Don't tell me if it was fettuccine. I love all those coiled pastas, ready to spring into calories: tortellini and fettuccine and all those curlycue things like enchanted snakes."

Heavy breathing. Cynthia would have been frightened if Tess Spangle had done that early in the conversation, before she identified herself.

"Who's meeting their plane?" Tess said.

"Nobody."

"It doesn't seem right. Of course I wasn't invited. I always let myself be taken advantage of, and I won't put myself in the position of being made a fool of, too. Of course, if they don't come on the plane Friday, and I'm there, who would know but me that I was made a fool of again? My shrink would know. I'd tell the shrink. The shrink would try to make it all appear normal. He's insidious that way. 'Why blame yourself for meeting a plane?' "

"I'll let you know if I hear anything."

"If a woman goes to the airport and no one knows she's there, does she still exist at the airport? Do you play philosophical games with your students, or are they too young? How can anyone be young?"

"I see it Monday through Friday."

"Poor dear. Friday the men will come bounding home."

Bounding? Spangle? Pigeon-toed Spangle? He loped, and seemed always on the verge of tripping himself.

Hanging on the kitchen wall was a picture of Spangle that she was very fond of, taken the summer before at Provincetown. He was flying a kite, but all that was visible in the picture was the string. He was photographed in profile, hair wind-whipped, a look of complete astonishment. He had not realized she was there, with her camera, up on the dunes. It had been a very gray day, before a big rain, and there were few people on the beach. She had seen him from far off, and had run to come up behind him. She had time to focus, and that was about all. The picture was a little grainy. That surprised look of his, though—it had been perfectly captured. It was the same look he had when she struggled awake in the dimly lit bedroom to put her face in his and say, "Spangle—stop. There is no fireball."

She saw that it was raining. That meant that she would have an excuse not to go to the laundry. She disliked the laundry next to the donut shop, the closest to the apartment, because a lot of crazies always hung out there. The last time she went in a magician had been there—a magician on vacation from Hollywood, visiting his mother in New Haven, washing his dirty clothes.

"Do you have change for a quarter?" he had asked her.

The change machine was not six feet from where they stood. She had assumed that he was trying to pick her up. Silently, she had reached into her pocket and taken out two dimes and a nickel. He pocketed the nickel and held his hands out to her, palms up, one dime in each palm. Silently, he had closed his hands, shaken them three times, then opened his fingers. There were two dimes in the palm of each hand. She stared at the forty cents. He smiled and pocketed the money. Then he took out one dime, showed her both sides of it, and tossed it in the air. Twenty cents came down. He pocketed that.

"How did you do that?" she said.

"If it wasn't a hoax, I'd be a rich man," he said.

He took a pink sponge-rubber rabbit out of his pocket. He showed it to her, then put it in the palm of his hand. He closed his hand, shook it, and when it opened, there were two pink rabbits. He closed his hand and opened it again. One pink rabbit. He reached in his pants pocket and came out with what looked like the same rabbit, and handed it to her.

"Squeeze hard," he said, "and think of your lover."

What she had thought of, what she had been thinking of as he spoke, was that she had put her red blouse—the one that bled— into the washing machine. Dumping it in, it hadn't even registered what she was doing. Everything was going to have to be bleached. Spangle would accuse her of being stoned. As she opened her hand, she jumped back: Dozens of tiny pink rabbits leaped into the air and showered down onto the floor of the laundromat. The magician bowed, and presented her with his business card.

"Available for parties," he said. "Be in New Haven most of the summer. My routine for adult parties runs differently from this one, as you might surmise. What I need to know is the name of a good dentist."

"I'm sorry," she said. "I just moved here."

"If I don't find a dentist, I'm going to wake up one morning and open my mouth to brush my teeth, and my teeth are going to fly out like little bunnies."

The man's card had a California phone number, crossed out, and a Connecticut phone number written in. She put the card in the pocket of her jeans. When she got back to the apartment, she reached into her pocket to put her change and the card on the

16

table. The twenty cents she could have sworn she did not use in the dryers was not there, and there were two cards with the magician's name and phone number on them. The dimes did not reappear, and the cards did not replicate further.

There was also the time a young woman with a little boy asked her for three dollars so they could buy a pizza, and she had been so taken aback—the woman was nicely dressed, they both were rosy-cheeked—that she had given the woman three dollars. The woman had kissed the back of her hand as she held out the money. And of course there were always the usual crazies: Moonies, or whatever they were, who in exchange for money wanted to give her a paper flag on a toothpick; a drunk who went up to the dryer where her clothes were spinning and began waving his arm in a wild circle, imitating the motion of the machine. It would figure that Spangle would like living in New Haven. Before she knew him he had money and a nice house (anything with more than three rooms was by definition nice), but by the time he met her he had lost the house and the money. He had put up bail money for a friend who skipped the country. He had smoked it up and given parties in restaurants with Peking Duck for twenty. He had bought a Martin D-28 for a musician friend who was broke and who had smashed his own guitar against a cigar-store Indian he used as a coatrack when he broke a high E string for the third time that day. He had paid an ex-girlfriend's thousand-dollar telephone bill so she could calm down and get her head straight. He had given money to the dog pound, bought a sports car and crashed it up, paid high insurance rates when his broken leg healed and he could drive again. Money just disappeared. It went. It was nothing like a handful of pink sponge. Money did not respond to pressure. Squeeze it as hard as you could, and when you opened your hand, there would be less of it. A psychiatrist had taken two thousand dollars of the money to tell Spangle—in part—that he was afraid of money, so he had gotten rid of it. Spangle believed this, but also believed that he and his money were psychically attuned: It had not wanted to stay with him, either. His money had itched to escape into the drawers of cash registers, into the deep pockets of maître d's.

Her sister had introduced her to Spangle when she was eighteen. Her sister worked for the phone company in New Haven, before she met a rich older man who took her on vacations; the price she paid was having her lingerie drawer sprayed with Chant d'Arômes, and their dinner napkins with Norell. She could never wipe away the smell of flowers and ferns because their bath towels were sprayed with Wind Song. Her sister had been behind the counter when Spangle came in, ex-girlfriend in hand, to slap down the phone company's latest threatening letter and to pay, in quarters, the one-thousand-dollar-plus phone bill the ex-girlfriend had run up. They had brought the rolls of quarters in the girl's Save-A-Tree bag. Cynthia's sister had been counting quarters into piles when Cynthia came in to meet her for dinner after work. There were piles of silver all over the counter, and her sister had looked up at her sadly and she had said: "Here's somebody who thinks I'm to blame for the phraseology of the phone company's dunning letters, and that I deserve some shit." Then her sister had stopped counting and said to Spangle, "What did you say your name was? So I can always remember you?"

"Peter Spangle," he had said.

"Cynthia, meet Peter Spangle—a man who knows how to treat a girl who makes three-twenty an hour."

It had ended with all of them cursing the phone company and hunching over the desk to count quarters together. Then they had gone out for a drink. Spangle's ex-girlfriend had left the table after she had two gin and tonics and had tried to call Budapest, but during the ten minutes it was going to take for the call to go through, Spangle caught wise, realized what was happening, and managed to stop her. He had not seen the ex-girlfriend after that night, and the next day he had called Cynthia. Cynthia's fingers were still sore from counting money, and once the effects of the alcohol had worn off, she was not sure that she wanted to see Spangle again. But finally she had said yes, and they had dinner together. She found out that he had once had money, left to him when his father died; he found out that she had been a Bryn Mawr girl. Both of them were unclear about what they were going to be —except lovers, maybe. It was Spangle's belief that, left alone at their typewriters, after a certain period of time—before or after they have written all the great books—eventually monkeys will become lovers.

The magician had been depressed. New Haven was an ugly city, and it looked doubly grim because he had just come East after a weekend vacation at a mansion in Ojai where he had made rabbits pop out of record executives' shirt pockets and hypnotized people to bark like dogs until he had sniffed too much coke to continue. They paid him anyway. His mother didn't have a washing machine, and his clothes were dirty. His mother did not approve of his being a magician, and she was taking it out on him by refusing to wash his clothes. The magician thought that his mother was more childish as a mother than he had been as a child. "Why don't you just flick your wand like Tinkerbell and make the dirt go away?" she had said. So he bundled up the laundry and walked down the street until he found a laundromat. It was small and crowded—a fat lady with eyes that didn't focus, as if they had taken a spin through the dryer, a comatose kid, about twenty, who came out of his trance to lift the lid of the washing machine and talk to the clothes, and several other uninteresting people. Naturally he selected the one pretty girl to show one of his magic routines to. She didn't have a wedding ring on, but she wasn't very friendly, either: interested, after a while, but not friendly. "You don't know how to make a washing machine full of pink clothes go back to their original colors, do you?" she had said. People always wanted things from him that were in no way spiritual. He liked spiritual things, and real surprises: donkey tails sprouting from the seats of people's trousers as they closed their eyes and turned around three times, candles that kept burning after you blew them out. People wanted the errors they had made fixed. They wanted the past to do over again. And of course they wanted money. The one girl the magician had ever loved had had a great sense of humor. She had been a cartographer, and she had been as interested as he was in magic tricks, because they were abstract problems to solve. She had drowned herself when she didn't get a promotion she had expected. No barrel and chains and the rushing white water of Niagara Falls—just a jump from a rowboat into water so cold she died almost immediately from hypothermia. The girl he had met at the laundromat was nothing like her, except that he had a hunch that she was special. A laundromat was a very good setting in which to test people: If you got a strong vibration from someone in a laundromat, chances were that that person was interesting. So he had followed her when she left the laundromat. Awkwardly, because he knew nothing about sleuthing, but he didn't think she had noticed him. If she had, she was being very cool. He had written down her address and put the piece of paper in his pocket, along with the multiplying rabbit and the flower that squirted liquid that looked like blood and a whistle only dogs could hear. He had not had the nerve to say anything more to her that night, but he planned to hang around some other night—just casually bump into her—and then he would ask her to have a drink with him. He had a totally harmless pill that he could slip into her drink, and as she sipped the liquid would form a head like beer and boil out of the glass.

He had always known how to start things, but he had never known how to stop things. The nice thing about the tiny pill was that it would only make a drink foam for fifteen seconds.

3

"DADDY," John Joel said, "she calls me Prince Piss and Monkey Meat."

"Your father doesn't want to be nagged at, John Joel. Forget it," Louise said.

"Yeah," Mary said. "He wants you to be quiet. Go climb a tree and dribble spit. We want you out of here."

"That's enough," Mary's father said.

Under one arm, Mary's mother, Louise, was carrying a Styrofoam cooler filled with hot dogs and Tab and a bottle of Chablis, the pretzels and potato chips piled on the lid so they wouldn't get wet. She held her five-year-old's hand. He pulled on her arm, wanting to pull her, it seemed, to the center of the earth. John, their father, carried a shopping bag with some charcoal, lighter fluid, a radio, a pack of True cigarettes, the late edition of the *New York Times* and a towel.

They were at the park for a cookout. Nobody had wanted to come, except Brandt, the baby. He was hoping that the three-legged dog would be there. The dog could do everything: It could run, swim, fetch sticks. Brandt was half interested in sighting the dog, half interested in seeing if he could pull his mother over.

"Say anything you want to your brother about his ugly face, but lay off about his weight. Understand?" John said to Mary.

Peter Frampton, on her T-shirt, was looking straight ahead. She nodded yes.

"What about here?" Louise said. "That's a nice grove back from the road."

"Closer to the water," John said.

"Daddy—" John Joel said.

"Are you going to start complaining again when I just told you to be quiet?" Louise said.

"What is it?" John said.

"Daddy, how many feminists does it take to screw in a light bulb?"

"That's not what he was going to say," Mary said. "He was going to nag."

"I don't give a shit about feminists," John said. "I don't send my secretary for coffee, I go get it myself. Today I walked down the hall to the machine, and it was being repaired. I didn't say anything. I looked disappointed for a second, I suppose. The person repairing it was a woman. 'Oh, just send your *girl* down in about five minutes,' she said. Very sarcastic."

"Four," John Joel said.

The baby screamed, so he didn't get to say his joke. The baby screamed because his mother had let go of his hand, making him stumble to regain his balance. He knew that if he screamed his father would start screaming at his mother. He had tried to pull her over, and she was stronger: She had almost gotten him to go down.

John didn't say anything. He kept walking. He slapped the back of his neck to kill a mosquito.

"Daddy, it takes four," John Joel said.

"Why does it take four?" John said.

"One to do it and three to write books about it."

"You think that's funny? You should work with women today," John said. "You will. You'll get your chance."

"I think that one thing women don't like is having men generalize about all women," Louise said.

"Women don't like anything."

"Not even nice soapy dishwater and darning tiny little booties?"

"Where'd you learn the snappy comebacks? Exercise class?"

"Pay no attention to me," Louise said. "Women go crazy during their periods."

"At least you're not so crazy you're pregnant."

"I impregnated myself the other three times," Louise said, "but now I've learned my lesson. I won't do that again all by myself."

"Dad, look! Is that a snake? Is that a crushed snake?"

"Look at the shape of it. Does that look like a snake to you?"

It was a squashed frog, with a wasp hovering over it. A bee joined the wasp. The frog had been recently squashed.

"Don't just stand there, John Joel. Come on," Louise said.

"He's too fat to walk anymore," Mary said.

"I got through to you very well when I spoke to you a minute ago, didn't I?"

Mary lifted a strand of hair from behind her ear, stroked it and twisted it around her finger. She wished she had hair that hung in long waves and curls like Peter Frampton's girlfriend's. She had just seen a picture of the two of them at a Hollywood party. Their hair was more noticeable than it might have been because the photographer had gotten so close to snap them that their features had been washed out. It was almost like looking at people without faces, but Peter Frampton's expression, however faint, was unmistakable: the expression on the poster. Peter Frampton and his girlfriend—the paper identified her only as his "lady love"—would have thought that this scene was hopelessly bourgeois. If Peter Frampton went on a picnic, Mary was sure that he went naked, in a speedboat, to some private island at midnight, with the lady love and a bottle of champagne. He wouldn't be seen dead in a button-down shirt hanging out of a pair of baggy jeans, with a bag full of things to have a barbecue with and a wife and three children trailing behind him. On Peter Frampton's picnic, he would want to pour champagne on the lady love's nipples and lap off the sweet, tiny bubbles; he wouldn't want to find out how many feminists it took to change a light bulb.

She had bought a pen and ink and a book about calligraphy so that she could write a love letter to Peter Frampton.

Stupid Lost in the Forest had had a tantrum when nobody had

any idea why Becky had thrown away the dictionary in the first chapter of *Vanity Fair*. "You probably think that getting rid of a book that heavy would just be common sense," she had said. She had threatened to make them write essays called "What I Did with My Summer." Even Lost in the Forest, much as Mary hated to admit it, was probably having a better summer than she was. She was on her own, and if her parents were somewhere having a barbecue, she didn't have to go along. She could stay home and read one of her precious books and understand every word of it. Even reading a book would be better than coming to the park on Friday evening and eating hot dogs, with mosquitoes closing in as it got dark, and nobody with anything to say. Her father was deliberately walking them this far on the path by the side of the access road so they would be tired when they got to just the place he wanted them to be, and nobody would talk, and he could read the paper and listen to the radio. Her mother knew it, too. Her mother was glaring at his back as he walked ahead of them. Brandt was swinging on John Joel's arm, singing "Hooray for Captain Spaulding, the Af-ri-can ex-plorer . . ." He lived with his grandmother, John's mother, and he watched television all the time. He knew a lot of routines from Marx Brothers movies. Last week he had driven everybody crazy by putting one leg up for them to hold, and when they swatted it down, bobbing his leg up again. He was also able to imitate, perfectly, Harpo's eye roll and Groucho's walk. He did it so often that Louise was embarrassed, worried that people would think he was retarded. She was always worried that somebody would think one of her children was retarded. She was also worried that neighbors would see in her windows. Never mind that no neighbors could see through the tall fir trees that bordered their lawn, and that there was a huge lot between their house and the Dowells': The neighbors would see from the road, driving home. See *what*?

John spent the weekends at home. The rest of the week he lived with his mother in Rye, and Brandt and Henri the big black poodle lived with them. John had gone there, in part, because his mother said she had cancer when she didn't. When he found out the truth, he didn't much care: Rye was a short drive to New York, and he hated commuting.

At first he had gone alone, and then he had returned for the poodle. There had been two dogs, and suddenly, when they were both five years old, one of them (at least) had started shitting in the house. Louise had been convinced that it was the poodle. She had always liked the German shepherd better. But an experiment with blue food coloring in the poodle's food had pinned the blame on the shepherd, and the next weekend John had taken the unfairly maligned poodle with him to Rye.

He went to stay with his mother, at first, because she had said she was dying. What she said was cancer was only anemia, though, and now she took pills and cooked in an iron pot, and her anemia was just fine. When he first went to his mother's, Louise was sick with the flu, so he took the baby—partly to relieve Louise, partly to cheer up his mother. When they were both better, Brandt stayed. It was argued about for a year, and then they stopped arguing. For the last two years, they hadn't talked much. The shepherd had been hit by a car.

Mary thought that Lost in the Forest might like to hear how her father came home on Friday evening and left on Sunday night, and about how the housebroken poodle was with her grandmother and her younger brother—all of them together in Rye with the Marx Brothers running amok on the tube. The situation was embarrassing, and Mary wouldn't have minded embarrassing Lost in the Forest.

She wondered with what emotion Lost in the Forest would read the essay: the way she read "The Pardoner's Tale," smiling at every word, or the way she sounded self-righteous, reading "All happy families are alike . . ." That was pretty good. Mary remembered that one. The rest of the book probably fell off, but that was a zinger.

"Daddy," John Joel said, "make him stop."

"Stop," John said tonelessly. Probably John Joel didn't even hear that his father had responded. Mary heard him, because she was walking close behind him.

"Stop it!" Louise said, whirling so suddenly on Brandt, who was pulling his brother's arm, that both John Joel and Brandt stopped walking. "Walk with me," she said to Brandt.

Brandt turned and ran into the road.

John put down his bag and ran after him. He caught him before he made it around the curve. Mary braced herself for Brandt's scream, but John just hoisted him on his shoulders, and Brandt laughed, either because he was relieved, or just because he was enjoying the ride. No doubt about who was the favorite child in the family.

"I'm not carrying this thing another mile to humor you," Louise said to John, when he and Brandt came up beside her. "If you don't want to have the picnic at the next bench, I'm going back to the car."

A car passed them and turned into the next picnic area.

"Not my fault," John shrugged.

"Not that you're not happy they're there," Louise said.

The car bumped over pebbles and onto the grass. As they passed by, music was already playing loudly and two boys were throwing cans of beer to two girls who had gotten out of the car. They were trying to go into the woods, but the beer cans kept sailing at them.

"They're going to explode!" one of the girls hollered. "Stop it."

The beer cans kept flying. Once Mary had seen a comedy routine on television when the comic had thrown balls offstage, throwing carefully into somebody's hand, no sound because there were no misses, and then as he was about to toss another ball, all the balls came flying back, knocking him over. She couldn't remember how it ended.

"Cut it out!" the girl screamed again. The other girl had run into the woods.

Beer cans kept flying at the girl. She was dodging them, after she had caught one can in each hand. She was trying to keep away from them, backing into the woods, backing up because she didn't want to get hit in the back.

"Lovely little bit of Americana," John said to Louise when they passed the boys.

John had put Brandt down, and he scurried away, looking left and right, doing his flat-footed Groucho shuffle.

"Your mother's turning him into a great intellectual," Louise said.

"He's five years old."

"I remember how old he is. Little as I see him, and small as my brain is, I *am* able to store *some* facts away."

"Go ahead and be a bitch," he said.

"Thank you for encouraging me to grow in new directions," Louise said.

Mary passed them. John Joel was lagging behind, panting as they began to go up another hill. Brandt had picked up a stick and was pretending it was a cigar, tapping the top of it, rolling his eyes and talking to himself.

"Mary," Louise called, "why don't you carry this cooler the rest of the way?"

"Because I don't even want to be on this picnic," she said.

"Come here and get it and carry it," her father said. "Please."

Mary stopped and let them catch up with her. When they did, she took the cooler. "I guess I'm not the only one who doesn't want to be on this picnic," she said.

"Where would everybody like to be?" John said. "Just where would everybody like to be? You want a pizza? You want Chinese? What? I didn't hear that nobody wanted to be on this picnic until we were on the picnic."

"This isn't a picnic," Louise said. "This is walking around and getting sweaty. Which is okay, if you're in the mood for that."

"What would you rather be doing, Louise?"

"It doesn't matter what I would rather be doing."

"Just tell me," he said. "Tell me, and stop right here, and I'll go get the car and chauffeur you wherever you want to go."

"Magnanimous," Louise said. "You're only here two nights a week, but it's the *quality*, not the quantity."

"Where?" he said. "Where do you want to go?"

"Oh, maybe you could drop me at exercise class. I like that a lot. I can socialize with Tiffy Adamson and Marge Pendergast and I can wonder along with everybody else what it feels like for Marge to do those stretch exercises with no tits. I can pick up some more smart talk. Or you could drop me at the hospital and I could see if Marlene's father's leg ulcer is clearing up. It's not New York, but there's a world of excitement out here in suburbia. I read in the paper today that a deer got hit crossing the road. We could call the police barracks and find out where the deer was buried and make a pilgrimage to its grave. It was probably escaping from New York when it had its accident."

"Don't kid yourself. Whatever cop pronounced it dead is eating it tonight."

"Well," she said, "it's not entirely civilized out here in the woods. Everyone has to make do."

"I asked you at Christmas if you wanted to get an apartment in the city."

"You're going to put them all in private school?" she said.

Mary was far enough ahead of them so that she didn't have to hear the answer. She wished she had gone to Angela's for dinner, even if it would have meant listening to Angela's father trying to convince both of them to do well in summer school so they could get into good colleges and become lawyers. He wanted everybody to be a lawyer. Angela's mother was taking courses in law at night. During the day she worked selling real estate. Mary wanted to do well in English just so she would never have to read, or have read to her, another book. It was for sure that Peter Frampton didn't sit around reading first chapters of famous books. You could bet that Peter Frampton's business manager didn't bore the lady love by lecturing her about going to law school.

Her parents called to her. Finally, her father had found the place he wanted to have the cookout. Her mother was already sitting at the wooden bench, opening the bottle of wine. If this was like the last cookout, her mother wouldn't eat anything, and she would make a scene if Brandt refused to eat. Brandt liked hamburgers instead of hot dogs. Tonight there were hot dogs.

John threw a match on the coals. Small blue flames spread through the coals. He watched until a streak of flame went up.

"How many men does it take to light a barbecue?" John said to John Joel.

"How many?" he said.

"One," John said. "One supremely confident and competent man. Your dad. Don't forget that Father's Day is the seventeenth."

John Joel laughed.

"They're all as materialistic as you are," Louise said. "They're not likely to forget. They'll have to think hard about what's presentable but inexpensive. Isn't that right, my loves?"

She had started drinking the Chablis. She was staring at the coals burning down.

"The eternal flame blew out at Kennedy's grave," she said. "It does it all the time, but they keep it hushed up." She took another sip of wine. She ran her hand across the picnic table, lightly, so she wouldn't get a splinter. "If there was one thing I could have tonight," she said, trailing her fingertip along the wood, "do you know what it would be? Mister Blue brought back to life. I'd like to be playing 'get the stick' with my dog."

He was standing with his back to the bed, looking out the window. A week ago, looking out the same window—but early in the morning, not late at night—he had seen a robin teaching her six babies to fly. He had taken one of the shells, an indescribable blue, to New York, to Nina.

He knew that Louise was awake, although she was in bed with her eyes closed, and he knew she did not care that he was standing at the window. Or if she did care, it was because it was an opportunity for sarcasm. So many husbands had stood at windows while their wives lay in bed. So many wives had done the same thing. So many people got married and had children and survived it.

Risky to have mentioned the apartment in New York again. What if she took him up on it?

"What did you want?" he said. "Be straight with me. Was it some special kind of food you wanted, or did you just not want to be on the picnic?"

"I love how you care deeply about things late at night."

"Maybe the problem is manners," he said. "Your manners are about as nice as your son and daughter's."

"Sons *plural*. I have two sons."

"You have two sons. You'd like to have three. You'd like to have me be a child, too, so you could be even more rude to me."

"I have quite enough children, thank you."

"You're so clever," he said. "You *really* do have a snappy comeback for everything these days."

"Not everything," she said. "I don't know everything." She turned over in bed. "I don't want to, either. Why don't you stop brooding and go to sleep?"

"You should really see this," he said. "There are so many shooting stars tonight."

"Are you sure it's not pieces of Skylab falling?"

"I'm not sure of anything," he said. "I'm not sure of anything, and I'm tired of your cleverness. You're not going to quit, are you?"

She quit. She didn't say another word, and eventually she fell asleep.

4

"YOU WANT me to always talk to you and tell you what's the matter, right? So I'm going to talk to you: I'm getting tired of hearing about your weekends with your family."

John was standing at the window, looking down on Columbus Avenue. There was a sidewalk café at the end of the block. People were roped in like cattle. Unlike cattle, they had umbrellas over their heads. Water to drink. San Pellegrino, no less. They weren't going to be stunned by being struck on the head and then hoisted and cut and bled. Maybe one of them was; one, encountering some perverted mugger on the way back to his apartment, might later be found hanging by a meat hook in a deserted warehouse, but the chances were against it. The chances were really against it. That you had a good chance never to end up snagged on a meat hook in a deserted warehouse made going into New York five days a week plausible. Nina, the woman he was in love with, helped too. He knew that he should not talk to her so much about his family, but after the weekend he was always depressed, and she was the person closest to him.

She was washing her hair in the kitchen sink. He had started to leave clothes at her apartment, and she had started to wear them. At the moment, she was wearing his jockey shorts and nothing else, cupping her hand and pouring water through her hair. With her hair still wet, they would go out to dinner. At ten o'clock Horton Watson was coming to Nina's apartment. He would stay around for the visit, to make sure she was all right when Horton left—to make sure that Horton did leave—then take a cab to the garage off Third Avenue to get his car and drive back to Rye. Instead of taking the train, he had driven into the city. Once or twice a week he liked to do that: to drive in fast, taking risks, so that some of his hostility was gone before he got to the office. On the days when he did not drive in, he usually went to a health club around the corner from where he worked and played handball during his lunch hour.

"It's hard to picture you at a family barbecue," she said, straightening up and wrapping a towel around her hair. "Do you use one of those three-pronged forks to turn the hot dogs over? One of those devil's forks? You like to think of yourself as a devil—so *bad* for having a mistress. Do you have those barbecues to make yourself suffer for your sins?"

"I loved having barbecues when I was a kid," he said. "The barbecues aren't the only thing I feel bad about."

"Did you know that eating one charcoal-broiled steak puts as many carcinogens in your body as smoking thirty packs of cigarettes?" she said.

He was looking at the broken half of the robin's egg he had brought her from his backyard, holding it as carefully as he had ever held anything in his life. He put it back in the small saucer she kept it in.

"We didn't even have steaks. We had hot dogs."

"Well," she said, hugging him from behind. "That's something to feel very *guilty* about."

She rubbed her hair so that it wasn't dripping wet and went into the bathroom to hang up the towel. She opened a little jar of cream perfume and dipped into it with her index finger. She patted the finger across her forehead. She smoothed her hair back and went into the living room, where her dress was draped over the back of a chair.

He watched her pull the dress over her head and tug at it, and step into sandals. The dress was cotton, like a long T-shirt. It was black, and went to her knees, and she looked perfectly beautiful in it. She was ten years older than his daughter. He could slam balls into a wall for a million years, and it would never get rid of his frustration that he had married the wrong person and had the wrong children. His friend at work, Nick, said that the real killer was when you married the wrong person but had the right children.

"You haven't told me if anybody funny came into the store today."

She laughed. "Those people. They feel like they have to explain everything. Everybody who comes into that place is so defensive, as though everything they do is being watched and I'm going to judge them. One woman came in with twin daughters, about eight years old. She had a bag from Olof Daughters she put up on the counter; and she started apologizing for wanting something she knew we didn't have—cotton knee socks; we didn't have them—and then she started telling me that her daughters were going to Sweden to visit their father, and telling them, while I stood there, that it wasn't going to be such a long flight. She stood in the aisle at Lord and Taylor's for five minutes, apologizing for sending them to Sweden."

"That's okay, but it's not very funny."

"It wasn't a very good day."

"Hungry?"

"I guess I'd better be. We've got to be back here by ten."

She got her big purple canvas bag from the bathroom doorknob and they went out.

"You know what else I've been feeling guilty about? That my daughter's in summer school reading a pile of books I've never read myself. I bought *Vanity Fair* at the bookstore next to my office today. I'm going to start reading it tomorrow, when I take the train in."

A man in a white chef's hat mashed down low on his head passed them, carrying a radio that was blaring Linda Ronstadt singing "Blue Bayou." Linda Ronstadt was way ahead of him; the man just kept chanting "I'm goin' back some day" over and over. Hardly anyone on the street looked at him.

"I saw Carly Simon crossing Fifth Avenue today," she said. "She had one of her kids by the hand. She was pretty."

"Did she stop to say hello to you?"

"She had so much hair. I look bald by comparison. I don't think I know one famous person. I have a friend who knows Linda Ronstadt, and my aunt went to school with Joan Kennedy. A girl who lives in my building once went to a beach party and jumped on a trampoline with David Nelson."

"David Nelson?"

"I thought you were older than I am. Ozzie and Harriet," Nina said, stepping off the curb. "That's who you think you should be, probably—Ozzie. 'Harriet, hon, defrost those four steaks, and I'll flip them on the grill when I've finished reading *Vanity Fair.*' "

"What am I supposed to do, read some Watergate criminal's book?"

"I know somebody who knows Ehrlichman."

They went into the restaurant, and he asked for a table in the garden. There was a barrel by their table with a rose tree growing out of it. There was one large, perfect pink rose on the tree. Above them was a fire escape, with pots of geraniums pushed to the far side of the steps.

"Are you ever going to come live with me?" she said.

The waitress came to the table and put down two menus. "Excuse me," she said. "I just wanted you to know that we have no bluefish, and no soft-shell crabs."

"Okay," he said, nodding.

"Okay?" Nina repeated, stretching across the table to clasp his hand. "When?"

He smiled at her and shook his head. "August, I guess. At the end of summer."

"I hate it that it has to be at the end of summer. That it has to be when something's over, I mean. We'll both be thinking more about what's over than what's beginning."

"I think it's already begun," he said, squeezing her legs between his under the table.

"I'm serious," she said. "I'm talking about how I feel."

"I can't erase my life," he said. He picked up the menu. "I'm so used to complaints that I think everybody's complaining," he said. "I'm sorry. I know what you were saying."

"I wanted bluefish," she said. "On top of everything else, I was thinking about baked bluefish all afternoon."

He was thinking that his wife was going to get custody of Brandt. Although he didn't love his mother, he felt sorry that she would be losing the one thing she had formed an attachment to besides Ming vases.

There was a child wandering around the restaurant who was younger than his son, but who looked like him. He had come by once before, and shyly made eyes at Nina. She had lifted her napkin from her lap and shaken it out and put it over her eyes, slowly lowering it as she winked at the child and raised it again. He must have been two years old, wearing blue corduroy shorts and a shirt with a worm coming out of an apple on the front.

The waitress came back to the table, and they both ordered salmon. He had tried to get John Joel to taste different kinds of fish because fish had fewer calories than meat, but his son couldn't stand the sight or smell of fish. John Joel was still fat and carnivorous; it was obvious that he was sneaking food because he was still just as overweight, even though Louise had put him on a diet. He had a double chin that John often felt like taking hold of to shake some sense into him. John Joel never looked good in the summer: He got blotchy pink, but didn't tan, and the shorts and shirts he wore made his body look worse than his winter clothes did. Up in his tree, resting on the limb, he reminded John of the Cheshire cat in *Alice in Wonderland*.

"I'm sorry I'm grumpy," she said. "I've been in a bad mood all day."

"What's the matter?" he said.

"I didn't have a very good weekend either. I got a letter from an old boyfriend who's over in Europe, and all he talked about was how he'd blown all his money. I'm not very sympathetic to people who have a lot of money to piss away. I was thinking about you out on your three acres of land, and I was feeling very cooped up in that tiny apartment. How can you like that apartment so much? Just because it's so different from what you have?"

"It is small. One of the pillars at the end of my driveway is as wide as your bedroom."

"Are you kidding?"

"Yes. There aren't any pillars at the end of the driveway."

A man was standing beside Nina's chair. "I'm sorry," he said, "but your little boy wandered into the kitchen, and we'll have to ask you to keep him at the table. He could get hurt in the kitchen."

"What?" Nina said.

"He isn't our child," John said.

The maître d' looked puzzled. He turned and looked at a couple sitting at a table in the opposite corner. John looked, too. The woman was talking drunkenly, and the man was paying no attention to her; he was laughing silently and pointing at the maître d' in a parody of the way someone would ridicule another person.

"Very amusing," the maître d' said, without apologizing to John. He went to the corner table and began to argue with the man, who now also looked drunk. The little boy stood with his back to the kitchen door, staring at them. The next person who came through the door was going to trip over him. John sighed and didn't watch. He broke off another piece of salmon and put it in his mouth.

"God," Nina said. "Those people must be crazy. Look at the poor little boy—he's not even going up to his parents' table."

"I hope you don't want kids," he said. "I'm a rotten father."

"I don't think you'd be a rotten father."

"As I said: I hope you don't want kids."

"I'm not the only one in a bad mood," Nina said. She ate a leaf of lettuce with her fingers. "I wish I could see your house," she said. "I'd like to see the pillars that don't exist at the end of the driveway."

"The driveway isn't even paved. It's gravel."

"Ah," Nina said. "You also want me to feel sorry for you. Next you'll give me the line my mother always gives me: that there are great jobs for college graduates, if only they will go out and find them. You know what my mother's done her whole life? Played bridge and gone to the track in the summer."

"How come you were an only child?" he said.

"My father says it's because my shoes were so expensive. He was shocked. They had to be Stride-Rites, with a quarter-inch built-up arch. I was flat-footed." She took a drink of wine. "My mother says it's because my father said my shoes were too expensive."

One of the two men who had just been seated at a table adjacent to theirs was looking appreciatively at Nina. He didn't stop until John caught his eye. The man had long hair and a T-shirt that said "Chicken Little Was Right"; the man sitting with him had on a business suit and a black band tied high on his arm. The fedora on the table belonged to one of them. When John stopped looking, the little boy was walking toward their table, eyeing the hat that rested slightly over the edge.

"My youngest son has the measles," he said. "Have you had the measles?"

"This is very romantic talk," she said, running her foot up his leg.

"Have you?"

"Measles," she said. "Yes. I have had measles."

She really was not in a very good mood. Ordering a bottle of wine instead of a glass had been her idea. If she continued to drink the wine as quickly as she had been, there was no doubt that they would make it back to her apartment with time to spare before Horton Watson got there.

Nina had first introduced Horton to John as "a ghost from the past." "Are you saying I'm a spook?" Horton had asked. It was very odd, Horton's smile. He had false teeth, and they were shiny white and perfectly even. Horton smiled a lot. If what people were saying to him didn't make him smile, he told a joke or just muttered to himself. Horton would only go a few minutes without smiling.

They left the restaurant and walked back to Columbus Avenue. Horton was already there, on the front step, white hat pulled low over his eyes, looking—except that he was tall and thin—like a Mexican taking a siesta. A white puff went up from below his hat. Horton was smoking a cigarette.

"There I was on Park Avenue," Horton said, pushing back the brim of his hat. "Martini cocktail. Nice shiny Steinway piano I could play. Not that the lady would have liked any song I might have selected to play, but I could have gone ahead and played it anyway while she, you know, pretended to really rock to it. No, I said to myself: Horton, a man has got to honor his commitments. Turns out I was a little early—might have banged out a tune or two before I left. 'Course, she was itchy for me to leave. Bad enough her husband knows she smokes. Man doesn't want to come home and see some spook banging out songs on his piano. Business is business, of course, but no reason for the man to see the business. All he's got to see is a neat little box left behind, joints all in a row." They went into the building, and the landlady opened her door and looked at them. Horton grabbed Nina on the stairs, laughing.

"With high-paying business deals like this one, who needs enemies?" Horton said, as Nina put the key in the door and opened it. "Nice lady has no habit at all, doesn't even drink martini cocktails. But you've got to do a thing just for old times' sake. Plus which I have to pass down this street on the way to my dear old mother's anyway. Got to visit her at her bedside. 'Oh, Mother, what big *eyes* you have!' and Mama's gonna say, 'I'm stoned.'" Horton gulped down a glass of water. "Humid night," he said. "What I have is Cuernavaca grown, and quite tasty. Seventy an ounce." Horton smiled. "Moving on up the line to beautiful Annandale-on-Hudson, for a weekend in the country. I've got a bicycle chained to a tree there. Guess I'll do a little business and take a spin on my bicycle. I was such a misfit when I was a boy that I had training wheels on my bicycle for a full year. Took me to become a pothead and then give it up to have my brain get stable enough to have the balance I have today. When I was a child I had no power of balance. Don't things come upon you as you get old, though. This morning I was looking in the mirror and I saw a little cluster of white, up by the temple. Have to get my hair bleached and dyed lavender like some faggot, so I don't get bothered by noticing that."

He took a small bag of grass out of the back pocket of his pants and went into her bedroom and put it in a suitcase she kept pushed under her bed.

"Believe I might move on down the line," he said, smiling.

"Can I fix you a sandwich? There's vodka, if you'll drink anything besides martinis."

"I believe not. I think I'll just take my new-found riches and hide them away, so if some leprechaun is walking down Columbus Av, there's not going to be any temptation—I mean, so's the leprechaun's not attracted to my green stuff. Bad enough the riff-raff you've got to fight off these days." He smiled at Nina. "Seventy even," he said.

He sat down and rolled up his pants leg and pushed down the sock. Underneath the sock was an ankle strap that had a small zipper in it. Horton rolled the four bills she had given him into tight tubes and flattened them with his thumb. He put them in the band, pulled up his socks and stood up. "I hear that at midnight tonight New York City goes on odd-even gas rationing. What times we live in. Glad I've got my feet to carry me. Big as wings, even if they're not quite as powerful. And if they fail, I've got an addict friend up at a station on 125th Street. No problem with my getting off the ground, though. Just thought I might wait till I got to the fine area of Annandale-on-Hudson and unchained my bicycle before I ingested anything. Fine way to spend a weekend in the country."

"What about your music?" Nina said. "Will you be playing with Ray when he gets out of the hospital?"

"Thirty years old, with a hematoma," Horton said. "Think on it. He's gonna bounce back, though. He's thinking real clearly now. Time before when I saw him he was about as flaky as Mama's pie crust. This time he was seeing clear. We'll be back playing music." Horton tossed his hat from one hand to the other. "Everything's on the high sign," he said. "Full moon coming up. Nice gentle breeze out there tonight. It's a fine night to think on those things, and what I left you stands to be a big help." He sighed. "Cuernavaca," he said. "Just turns my head around to think of all the places out there I haven't been. Nelson Rockefeller sure would have liked to keep this man from them, too. Damn shame about Nelson Rockefeller dropping dead." Horton smiled. "Always enjoy conversing with you," he said to John. He put his hat on. "Tip of the hat," he said, tipping his hat on the way out.

Walking toward his mother, John thought: What was it I was thinking earlier today about her new-found health and sobriety? If he were not stoned what he was looking at would be very funny indeed.

He was looking at his mother, who had fallen asleep on the redwood lounge in the backyard. Hating mosquitoes and mortally afraid of bees, she had wrapped herself in gauze before she stretched out. The spotlight outside the back door lit up a circle of light on the lawn, where she sat. For a moment—for too long a moment—he got sidetracked looking at the crazy motion of all the white moths floating and flying in the lamplight. He looked back, and she was still there. It was certain she was drunk, or she would have awakened when he drove up the driveway.

He wondered if the gauze had crept over her in sleep, like the creeping white fungus in Invasion of the Body Snatchers. *He stood very still. A cricket was chirping. There were stars, and Horton was right—or nearly right: The moon was almost full. He rubbed his hand over his face, exhausted. Leave her there or wake her up? She looked like a mummy. She looked like she was dead. Behind*

41

his head, he heard the buzzing of a mosquito. He wanted to be back with Nina, curled beside her. He wanted this not to be happening, even if by the next day he could change things so that it would be a funny story to tell Nina. He felt a wild longing to be back with her, in the apartment on Columbus Avenue, as he stood and stared. His mother was as still as the grass, and more silent than anything else in nature.

5

THOUGH SHE didn't see much point to it, Cynthia decided to do what the administration wanted her to do. What they had suggested, in their memos to the summer school staff, was that they think of ways to get the students involved in literature: There were recordings of writers reading from their work; there were films, which needed to be ordered two weeks in advance; the teachers might have the students read aloud or act out some scenes from the works they were reading.

After sitting up late Sunday night, drinking wine and playing Go with the woman who lived next door, Cynthia had gotten out of bed to face the beginning of another week of teaching with a slight hangover that the memory of having done well at Go wasn't doing much to help. Today the students would be acting out scenes from *Macbeth*. Those mindless, untroubled, silly rich kids would be examining their hands and pacing and raging, talking about the meaning of growing old, feigning shock and horror. Mary Knapp and Angela Dowell and Terri LeBoyer would be standing in a schoolroom, circling a wastebasket, discussing their meeting on the heath with Macbeth (gesturing to the corridors with rows of lockers). Then Billy what's-his-name would pretend to have a revelation. Was it possible that in his life he had ever had a genuine moment of insight? Cynthia thought not. Unless he had realized, say, that McDonald's was serving fewer French fries. Billy what's-his-name would stand beneath the Stars and Stripes, in front of the chalk-hazed blackboard, and looking out at his classmates' uncomprehending, bored faces, tell them that "all our yesterdays have lighted fools / The way to dusty death."

Reaching for her toothbrush, she thought of the beginning of "Howl." She was born the year "Howl" came out, but she still felt sure that she was one of the people Ginsberg was talking about. She always felt sorry for herself on Monday morning. Spangle was taking his time about getting back from Spain, and she had no idea how to get the fan out of the kitchen window so she could turn it facing outward; all that was happening now was that hot air was being blown into the apartment. Nevertheless, when she walked into the kitchen for her morning glass of juice (with a teaspoon of protein powder), she turned on the fan and stood in front of it. Skylab was supposed to fall on the twelfth of July.

When she turned on the car radio, she was in time for the golden oldie of the morning: the Doors, with Jim Morrison, singing "Touch Me." It was followed by a shouted statement that today was an odd day, and only cars with license plates ending in an odd number could get gas. The announcer gave examples of odd numbers: one, three, five . . .

She thought that she did not deserve such a summer job, and that the day was going to be a disaster. She was tempted to follow the NEW YORK signs all the way to New York.

She pulled off into the breakdown lane and sat there, staring straight ahead. The windshield was dirty. Blondie was singing "Heart of Glass." There was no real introduction to that song; it just started, sounding like music from outer space, seeming to be pulsed out instead of played. Cars whizzed by. Monday. Always a difficult day: A lot of people got depressed on Monday. In order to keep her job, it was necessary to get back onto the highway and drive to school and listen to teenagers recite lines memorized from *Macbeth* as they circled a wastebasket. To watch Karin Larsen hold out a hand, her wrist loaded with thin gold chains, to hear her say that there was no way the hand would ever be clean.

The sun went behind a cloud, and she followed the pink cloud as the road curved, a cool breeze blowing through the window.

44

The Merritt Parkway was quite nice. A man in a sports car, passing her, looked over and smiled. She smiled back: They were both whizzing along, it was a fine day, they were both young.

She began to feel better. It was summer, and she was twenty-two, and she had a lover, if he ever got back from Spain. She could call the school and think of something to say. She could call and tell Diana DeWitt, the vice-principal, who wore sundresses patterned with butterflies the size of dinner plates, that driving to school she had realized that she was young. Not silly young like her students, but still young enough to know that she should be in New York today, not standing in a schoolroom that smelled like an eraser. Smiling, she knew not to call. She knew to keep going past the service area where there would be a phone.

From a phone booth on Sixth Avenue, she called Connecticut information and got the number of the school and, with horns honking and a woman singing in a loud soprano as she walked by holding a poodle on a leash, told the secretary in the principal's office that she was in the emergency room, having her stomach pumped. A taxi screeched its brakes and honked long and loud at an out-of-state car hesitating before making a right turn.

She wandered through a store near the phone. Inside were pillows of various sizes, decorated with satin flamingoes and bits of rhinestone and lace. She particularly liked a blue satin pillow in the shape of a half moon, with a pretty lady's face painted on it and curls of angel-white hair along the seam. A man was walking through the store, selling roses from a wicker basket. There was a tiny dog in his jacket pocket, all popping eyes and panting tongue. A woman trying on a pair of black gaucho pants bought a white rose and tapped the little dog on its nose before she stuck the long-stemmed rose through a braid that hung down the back of her head. The moon pillow was fifty dollars. She bought a gumball from the machine by the door on the way out and a parrot on a stand above the machine said "Thank you." A salesgirl with wavy hair and red-black lipstick looked, with no expression, at Cynthia leaving. Her shirt said "God Is Coming and She Is Pissed."

It was actually nice to be in the city without Spangle, because he liked to talk to everybody, and it was hard to make any progress. Spangle would have talked to the man with the flowers about his dog. He would certainly have said something to the salesgirl. He stopped to listen to street musicians and stayed for whole songs, even if the musicians were no good. Putting a quarter in the open instrument case, he would ask questions about their instruments, or just wonder how the day was going for them. Spangle noticed lush trees growing on the roofs of buildings, new editions of books he already owned in bookstore windows, pieces of paper advertising things he always thought would be interesting, six-toed people wearing sandals. He didn't miss a thing. And he was always thinking that he saw someone he knew, most of them people he wouldn't have stopped to speak to if they had been the right people: Mr. Binstock, the man who used to run the good fish restaurant on the Cape; a friend of a friend from Cambridge, 1968, minus beard and long hair. But had that guy worn glasses? Spangle could keep it up all day. In a bar, he'd talk to the bartender, study the jukebox, read the menu even if he wasn't eating. He would go home with a tacky rhinestone pin of a jet plane, what looked like a gnawed Tarot card found on Macdougal Street, a Lyndon Johnson key ring, a perfectly fine pen that had been lying on the sidewalk right in front of him, a record he had been looking for for ten years, an acorn that looked like a peanut, picked up in Washington Square Park. Then, at the end of the day, he would always say to her: "Do you have any idea where I parked the car?" The last time she had been in New York with Spangle he had bought a jacket in a secondhand store that fit him as well as one that had been custom-made. It was made of light-gray wool with nubs of white in it. ("It looks like a chicken picked the threads out of it! I'm going to be some lounge lizard in this one. Maybe I should get some Brylcreem.") Also a copy of *On the Road*, reissued with a new cover, a package of post cards of sporting events in China, a half-pound of chocolate cookies that looked like spun lace, and a roach clip with a little heart-shaped piece of mother-of-pearl inlaid in each side. They had had moussaka for lunch and homemade tortellini in Little Italy for dinner, and a drink in SoHo, and ice cream on Bleecker Street. "I love it," Spangle always said, driving away, "but I don't think I could live there. I mean: When would you *think*?" He would be munching on cookies from Miss Grimble's as he shook his head and the car hit potholes, jumped up, came down again.

She had had a long and very on-and-off-again relationship with

Spangle. When they had not been together for very long, he had left and gone to Berkeley. That summer he wrote to her and she sold her bicycle and some books and bought a one-way ticket to California. Most days they would go to lie in the grass and read in one of the small parks. The first week she was there, a couple had appeared with a cocker spaniel, a doberman and a goat. The goat had taken an interest in Cynthia. Spangle, playing with a Frisbee, had sailed it close to her, and the goat had bolted in terror, almost knocking her flat. Everyone ran to see if she was hurt: the goat's owners, Spangle, the man Spangle was throwing the Frisbee with. And she couldn't stop crying—not because of being frightened by the goat, but because it had occurred to her that she was in Berkeley, California, where she knew no one but Spangle, and that she had been in danger, even if it was just a silly sort of danger. Of course Spangle began to talk to the goat's owner. It was an African Pygmy goat, and it was trained to pee outside; for the other, the woman said, they just picked up the pellets. The woman was a chef; the man had gotten his Ph.D. from Berkeley, writing his dissertation on Turgenev. He was unemployed. They looked familiar to Spangle, but he did not look familiar to them. Squatting beside Cynthia, Spangle had kept saying what a coincidence it was that the book Cynthia was reading was *On the Eve*. The four of them had gone to a coffee shop on Telegraph Avenue and left the two dogs and the goat tied outside. She and Spangle had been about to go to the movies to see *Grand Hotel* when he took a scrap of paper out of his pocket and saw that it was playing the next afternoon, not that afternoon. So they had stayed in the coffee shop for another cup, while Spangle and the man traded lines from *Grand Hotel*. They exchanged phone numbers, writing them down on napkins. They never called each other. A month later, Cynthia ran into the woman walking near the university, and they went for coffee. She gave the woman their phone number again, and the woman gave her theirs; she and Spangle meant to call, but never got around to it. Then, two days before they were leaving Berkeley, the woman called and asked them for dinner. Dinner had been three kinds of cold soup. They were serenaded by a scratchy Miles Davis record coming through one speaker, and later by a fight downstairs which ended with some woman going outside and picking up a rock from the tiny rock garden and banging it against the door, shouting through the open window to the man inside, who had long since stopped making any noise.

At the end of the summer Spangle thought it would be a good idea to drive her back East. They took turns driving, and she made it back to school two days before classes started. In those two days, he worked on her constantly to forget about college and come back to the West Coast with him. She wouldn't. Finally he moved in with her. Their only disagreements were about the West Coast versus the East Coast. That, and Spangle's childishness: He would hide behind doors and jump out at her, or come to the door naked when she had a friend with her. When he was out of the apartment, he would call her and pretend, always convincingly, to be a librarian demanding an overdue book, or someone at the garage saying they had made a mistake fixing her car and under no circumstances to drive it, or someone from one of her classes asking her for a date.

Her family didn't like him. At Thanksgiving dinner he announced his switch to vegetarianism; he wouldn't laugh at their jokes; he was seven years older than she was. She lost touch with him in 1977, when he left for nine months to get his head straight. He became a lifeguard at a country club pool in Hyannis and, in the winter, a copy editor in Boston. Then he came back as though he had hardly been gone, gradually easing himself out of Valium and back to grass. All of this—even Berkeley—was after the time when he had money. They had been together again for two years, and if he came back from Spain, they would still be together.

She looked in her wallet and saw that she had more money than she had thought. She got a cab and went to Battery Park and stood in line to buy a ticket for the boat ride to the Statue of Liberty. In spite of the sign posted to the left of the ticket window saying how long the ride was, the women in front of Cynthia kept debating whether it was a long ride or a short ride. One wanted to take the ride no matter what, but the other was hesitant. One wanted to stand in line, and the other didn't know if they weren't wasting time. Both looked at their watches. They had the same conversation twice before they got to the window and began to question the ticket seller. Going away with their tickets, both looked at their watches.

There was hardly any wait. The line was forming, the boat was there, and she got into the crowd. A lot of people had cameras. Cameras and children. On one of the benches a man in a Mouse-keteer hat sat playing his guitar and singing an off-key version of "Who Knows Where the Time Goes?"

On the boat, she went to the upper deck and sat at the far end of one of the benches. When the boat began to move, she got up and leaned against the railing, looking back at New York. She could see more and more of it, at first larger and larger, then suddenly smaller as the boat moved forward. It was cold and windy and sunny, and she missed Spangle. She kept watching the skyline. There was a feeling of power in going away from it.

She stared behind her the whole way out, and it was only at the last minute that she looked to her left and saw the Statue of Liberty. She didn't get off. She sat there and looked all around, waiting for the ride back to begin. A few other people also stayed behind: a girl in her early twenties with a man in his fifties who kept pulling her sweater tighter over her chest, his fingers lingering on her small breasts as he adjusted the sweater; a man with a briefcase who tapped his thumb on the lock and never stopped staring at the Statue of Liberty; a young couple with an infant, who spoke in whispers, and a woman in a pink skirt slit halfway up her thigh and a thick, pale-pink sweater, who carried a small dog pressed against her chest. Passing Cynthia, she told the dog, *"Je suis très fatiguée."*

Sailing back to New York, Cynthia began to feel a little guilty. They wouldn't have been able to get a substitute that late in the day, and she couldn't understand why she had taken such a dis-like to so many of the students. She thought that, in part, it might be jealousy. She had always thought that it might be nice to be an ordinary person with an ordinary mind—at best, their minds were ordinary. Spangle always said that that was just wishful thinking: People not worrying about errors in Shakespeare criticism were worried about their wash not coming out clean. And everyone was worried about Skylab.

A little boy sitting in back of Cynthia said quite clearly, "I want to be a car."

The woman sitting next to Cynthia laughed quietly when the child spoke. She shifted a little farther away and put her head

49

on the shoulder of the man next to her. He kissed her forehead. Cynthia pretended to be looking at the horizon. She had liked being alone for a while, but Spangle had been gone too long. She closed her eyes and made a wish: that when she got back to his apartment, there would be a letter from him saying that he was coming back on schedule. It was true that he drove her crazy in New York, making her look up and down and into windows, but he also pointed out cabs coming too fast, people talking to themselves that it was best to cross the street to avoid.

When the boat docked, Cynthia saw the man in the Mouseketeer hat again, but this time he was lying on the grass on his stomach, guitar next to him like one person stretched next to another. She sat on a bench in Battery Park for quite a while, face turned toward the sun. Then she got up and walked toward the World Trade Center. She kept losing sight of it and had almost given up when she saw it ahead of her. She liked to walk through it. She went inside and walked around, looking in bookstore windows, into the flower shop. When she left, she took a cab back to Sixth Avenue and Tenth Street and got her car. She was as tired as she used to get when Spangle was there pointing everything out.

Back in the apartment in New Haven, she got her wish. When she opened the mailbox, the first thing she saw was a post card of Spanish dancers in brightly colored skirts, wide as Ferris wheels. She ran upstairs and opened the door before she read it. She even put on the kitchen fan before she read it. Then she sat on the kitchen counter and turned the card over. The message was not all she had hoped it would be. She read: "Sí, Señorita! The castanets click shut faster than a Southern debutante's cunt. *Olé* and see you soon. Love, Spangle."

Why Spangle? Because there was no one like him, that was part of it. One day in Berkeley he had taken her hand, before they were even out of bed, and asked if he could hold it all day. When they had to go to the bathroom, they had walked back to the apartment so they wouldn't have to let go of each other's hands. They had walked along swinging hands. They had propped their elbows on a tabletop and hand-wrestled. He had kissed her hand, rubbed it. "I'm pretending I can keep you," he had said. "I'm pretending it's as easy as this."

6

JOHN JOEL did not like his grandmother's house. Everything in the house was lumpy: The arms of all the chairs had carvings on them, the bedspreads felt like popcorn, even the dinner plates, with the embossed eagles, made it seem like there was something underneath your food that shouldn't be there. Most of the things, of course, were not to be touched—especially not the vases that were all over the house, centered on black lacquered pedestals. On the first floor, there were heavy brocade drapes that were pulled back in the morning by the housekeeper; underneath them were thin white curtains that stayed drawn so that the sunlight would not fade the colors in the vases. None of the vases were filled with flowers. Outside in his grandmother's garden were clematis, roses, phlox, daisies, violets, coleus, lilacs and marigolds. A gardener came to take care of them, and when he left, he carried away piles of flowers—usually two cardboard boxes full, in the back seat of his car. He tied the stems together loosely with string, misted them, washed his hands under the outside faucet, shook them dry, then got in the car and went away without saying goodbye. He was a good gardener, even though John Joel's grandmother said he was eccentric. He asked his father what "eccentric" meant, and his father said, "Just imagine your grandmother." His mother said that his grandmother dignified her alcoholism by calling it an eccentricity. He noticed that lately his grandmother did not drink.

John Joel did not like his brother. His brother was always pulling and screaming. His brother was baby pretty, with shiny hair and big blue eyes, and his bedroom was as large as the living room at home. There were umbrella stands in Brandt's room filled with his grandfather's canes. They fascinated John Joel. If he could have anything his brother had, it would have been those canes: canes with ivory handles carved in the shape of leaping fish or dancing couples, ebony canes inlaid with mother-of-pearl vines that wound their way up the cane and burst into bouquets near the handle. There was one cane, long and thin, covered with the skin of a rattlesnake. When Brandt wasn't in the room, John Joel loved to go in and spread the canes out like pick-up sticks and carefully lift and touch each one, examining the tiny carvings that were much more interesting than the carvings on his grandmother's chairs, smelling the way the different canes smelled. The rattlesnake cane smelled like soap. You could see the tongue of the lion's head in one of the canes, and he liked to touch the tip of his tongue to the wooden tongue, to hold the cane away from his face and glare at it, to imagine that he was as powerful as the squinting, roaring lion.

He was at his grandmother's house because in the morning, when his father drove into New York, he was going with him. He was going to the orthodontist because his front teeth were starting to stick out. Then his father's friend Nick was taking him to the Whitney to see a sculpture show, and in the afternoon he and his father and Nick were having lunch, and then his father was taking him home. His father had asked him if he would like to sit around his office until five o'clock, and he had said that he would, but apparently his father understood from his tone of voice that he didn't delight in the idea. (John Joel heard his father explaining this to his mother on the phone the night before. "Don't think I don't accommodate myself to the children, too," he had said.) The other time John Joel had sat around his office his father had refused to give him any more money for the candy machine after the first

53

quarter, and he had stayed on his father's sofa reading comics for hours, while his father picked up the telephone, said hello, and tilted back in his chair, looking at the ceiling and sighing, saying hardly anything except "It figures." Nick came in a lot, though, and that was nice. He liked Nick pretty well. Well enough to wish that Nick was his father instead of John. Last year at a Fourth of July party on top of somebody's roof in New York, Nick had followed John Joel into the kitchen to say that he didn't like fireworks either, and sympathized with him: Without a few gin and tonics, he said, he wouldn't have been smiling either. He had shown John Joel where the television was and found him a program he liked. "Even their goddamn sparklers feel like needles shooting into your hand," Nick had said. Nick had stared at his hand. He had been holding a wet glass, full of gin and tonic. He had fished out the lime and given it to John Joel. "It's a jaundiced cherry," he had said, probably knowing that John Joel wasn't fond of limes, but wanting to give him something anyway. At least Nick told jokes and laughed; his father turned all jokes into serious occasions, or into excuses to give lectures. The other nice thing about that Fourth of July was that Mary had gone to spend the night with Angela, and Brandt had had a cold and stayed in Rye. After the party on the roof, his parents and Nick and Nick's girl-friend Laurie had gone to see a James Bond movie. Nick had smuggled a flask into the movie house, and as he got drunker, he got more and more angry about the picture. Later, when Nick and the girl were dropped off at Laurie's apartment, his mother had gotten angry at his father: Interesting, she said, that he knew where her apartment was without being told. Was that what was in vogue now, leaving your wife for a young black woman and then raving about sexism in James Bond movies? His father had de-fended Nick; he had said that Nick was just drunk, that Laurie was a very nice woman, and that he had no apologies to make about knowing where she lived because several times when he had his car in town he had dropped Nick there after work, on his way back to Rye, and he had even stopped in for a drink. "That means a mad orgy," his father had said. Then she had tried to argue with John Joel. She had asked why Nick took him inside and parked him in front of the television. "I was in there already," he had said. "Why?" his mother had asked. So he had echoed Nick, and said that the sparklers were like needles. His mother had turned around and looked at his father. "That's what he thinks the Fourth of July is," she had said. "Needles going into your hand." "He thinks what he thinks," his father had said. "That's right," his mother said. "Everything's cool: screwing black women ten years younger than you, boozing in the movie theater, taking every occasion to get drunk." "You don't see him on every occasion," his father had said. John Joel had curled up in the back seat and stopped listening to them. Listening to them made him tired, and the night was over, and pretty soon they would be back at his grandmother's, where all the lights would be on, even though she and Brandt were asleep, so that when they came in they wouldn't knock over any of the vases. Then, when everyone was finally in bed, he could go downstairs and open the cabinets and eat. He planned to eat the rest of the M&M's, and to skip a few of them across the floor for Henri to chase. When his father put on the car radio, that meant that no one was to talk.

"What are we doing this Fourth of July?" he asked his father on the ride into New York.

"I hadn't thought about it. What do you want to do?" his father said.

"Are we going somewhere?"

His father looked at him. His father was driving fast, and if his mother had been there, she would have made him slow down. "I just asked what *you* wanted to do," his father said.

"Nothing," John Joel said. "I just wondered."

"Did you decide you liked fireworks?"

"I like fireworks," John Joel said.

His father looked at him again but didn't say anything. Then he put on the radio. "Hey. Billie Holiday," his father said. "Listen to this."

They listened to the song.

"Do you know who she was?" his father said.

"Black," John Joel said.

"Black?" his father said. His father looked at the roof of the car, shifting in the seat to lean back, the way he did in his office when he got a phone call. "Yes," his father said. "But I'm not sure that really gets to the heart of Billie Holiday." The news came on and his father changed the station. "Maybe Eldridge

Cleaver would think so," his father said. His father changed lanes. "The old Eldridge Cleaver."

"The last day of school Bobby Pendergast brought snakes to school. Things that are called snakes. You light them and they go *chizzz* and curl up and burn. They look like a black snake when they're burned out."

"You want me to get some of those for the Fourth of July?"

"On the Fourth of July when Mary's curled up asleep, you can light *her*," John Joel said.

His father was changing lanes again. He looked at John Joel and cut the wheel, making the car swerve back to where he had been. When the driver behind him honked his horn, John honked back and flashed his brake lights. "Mary," his father repeated. "A joke, right? I don't really have to pay for a child shrink, too, along with an orthodontist."

"You don't have any sense of humor," John Joel said.

"Don't criticize me. It's ten in the morning and I'm late for work so I can drop you at this orthodontist's, who is the only acceptable orthodontist in the world according to your mother's greal pal Tiffy whatever-her-name-is."

"You don't know the name of her best friend?"

"Well," his father said. "Aren't we finding fault with our old dad left and right today."

"Adamson," John Joel said.

"I don't care what her name is," his father said.

"I was trying to tell you a really good joke the other night in the park, and you didn't care about that, either."

"What joke?"

"You don't even remember."

"I hear a lot of jokes. That's what you do in the workaday world, my friend: You fend off disaster and listen to jokes."

"I don't want to go to the dentist."

"What do you want to do? Lie in the tree?"

"I don't always lie in the tree," John Joel said.

"You're acting like a five-year-old today."

"You're just taking me because she told you to."

"No indeed," John said. "I'm doing my best to insure a happy future for my son, so that when he goes out into the workaday world, people will take him seriously. They don't take short men or men with buck teeth seriously. Read what *Psychology Today* says about what's taken seriously. You with your beautiful straight teeth are going to be taken seriously, and then you can sit around and fend off disaster and listen to jokes. When you laugh, you'll do it with a set of sparkling white teeth."

"If you don't want to take me, don't take me. I don't want to go."

"How did we get into this? I got you an appointment. Seeing this guy is like getting in to see King Tut. He's not going to do anything today. He's just going to look at your teeth. Maybe take an X-ray."

"But then he's going to do something."

"I can't help it that your teeth are getting crooked."

His father brought the car to a stop with a screech of tires that made the garage attendant look up and stare. His father sat there expressionless until the attendant came to the car. The attendant put a piece of paper under the windshield wiper and handed a smaller piece of paper to his father. His father put it in his inside pocket and he and John Joel got out of the car. Walking up the ramp, the attendant called: "How long?"

"Two o'clock," John said. " 'Happy ever after in the market place,' " he sang under his breath.

They walked two blocks crosstown to the orthodontist's office. His father pushed a buzzer and they were buzzed in. The receptionist was pregnant, wearing a T-shirt with "Baby" printed across it, and an arrow pointing down. She gave his father a form to fill out and smiled around him at John Joel. When she stood up to take the piece of paper back, John Joel stared at her huge stomach. She smiled again.

"I'll wait and hear what he has to say," his father said.

John Joel shrugged. "I'm not a baby," he said.

"Can you remember what he said?"

"He hasn't said anything yet," John Joel said. It was useless; his father never knew when somebody was kidding, and there was no point in telling him it was a joke, because it had been such a lame one. "I'll remember," John Joel said.

"And you're going to wait for Nick to pick you up, right? At eleven. He'll be in the waiting room when you get out. Okay?"

"Why wouldn't it be okay?" John Joel said.

What John had taken to be small photographs of teeth were, he realized, photographs of shells. There was also a basket of shells on the table in front of the couch, and there were small plastic stands that supported shells on the tables at either end of the room. An old *Life* magazine with Ike and Mamie smiling their round-faced smiles was on one table, along with the current issue of *Variety*, the *National Enquirer* and *Commentary*. John looked over the magazines, thinking that this orthodontist was going to cost. He was reluctant to leave John Joel. At his son's age, he would have waited for his father to leave and then bolted. The pregnant receptionist wouldn't have had a chance of catching him. He looked at John Joel, slumped in a chair, leafing through a magazine, and decided that his son would do no such thing. Mary was right that John Joel hated to exert himself. He was fat and pale, and the braces were going to make him look even more like the Cheshire cat.

"Okay, I'll take off," he said. "I'll see you and Nick outside of the museum."

"How come Nick's taking me to the museum?"

"Because he wasn't going to be busy today. He said he'd like to." John Joel shrugged.

"Okay," John sighed. "See you at lunchtime."

"So are we going to another Fourth of July party on that guy's roof?"

"What did you say?" John was halfway across the room when he heard his son speaking to him. "You're talking about the party last year?"

"Yeah. Are we going again?"

"Do you want to go again?"

"I just wanted to know."

"Well, I just want to know if you *want* to go again. That's not a complicated question, is it?"

"I liked that roof. I just didn't like the fireworks."

"I don't think he lives there anymore. I think he moved to the East Side a couple of months ago."

"He wasn't a good friend of yours?"

"No. Why?"

"So how come you went to his party?"

"I work with him. He invited me. How come you're so talkative all of a sudden?"

"I just wanted to know."

"I don't think he's having a party this year."

"No big deal," John Joel said.

John sat down again, thinking that John Joel must have started that conversation to get him to stay. Maybe he was afraid of going to see the orthodontist, or maybe he doubted that Nick would show up. John picked up a magazine.

"I thought you were going," John Joel said.

"Do you want me to go?"

"Sure," John Joel said.

John sighed and got up. He tried to open the door, but he had to catch the receptionist's eye to be buzzed out. She looked at him suspiciously. She looked at him the way his mother would look at him if she knew that he was leaving John Joel alone. She always acted like New York was a huge cage that you walked into, with animals about to leap when you made the first sudden move. She was always jumpy in New York. It was the one thing she had in common with Louise. The most innocent things disturbed Louise: water gushing from a fire hydrant, a woman leaning out a window who was obviously only going to water her plants. Every siren made her turn her head; everyone who stared at her in a subway car was going to follow her off. In the beginning, he had only thought about making her happy by moving them to the suburbs. Now she hated him for being able to cope with the city when she couldn't. And she hated the suburbs because there weren't any intelligent people. Tiffy was intelligent. Only Tiffy. The truth was, she liked *normal* intelligent people, and they were hard to find. Even Nick was too strange for her. A cowboy hat and a black date made him, in her mind, no different from an extra in a Fellini movie. Horst, who had had the Fourth of July party the year before, couldn't have been as normal as he seemed if he slept in his sleeping bag, naked. Which part of that is odd? John had asked her. "Both parts," she had said. He had hoped that just the sleeping bag would seem odd.

He went into a coffee shop, feeling guilty for leaving John Joel alone in the doctor's office. But he hated to treat him like a child, the way Louise did. Maybe letting him handle it on his own would give him self-confidence. He drank a black coffee, pouring a little water into the cup to cool it while two men who worked there argued about what song titles ought to be put in the jukebox. A tall fat man sitting on a stool at the counter kept whispering to them, cupping his hand over a piece of paper. " 'Greek selection' is good enough," one said, and the other hit him with a dishtowel, saying, "The songs have names. You think all Greek songs are 'Never on Sunday'?" Finally, both men had towels and were slapping each other's shoulders. Two women waited by the cash register. " 'Oh you can kiss me on a Mon-day, a Mon-day, a Mon-day,' " one man sang, and the tall fat man shrugged in disgust. The other man swatted the man who was dancing and singing. "Can I have a bagel and a coffee to go?" one of the women by the cash register said. " 'Or you can kiss me on a Tues-day, a Tues-day, a Tues-day, a Tues-day's very good,' " the man sang. He was jumping in the air and clicking his heels together, hands cupped over his head. " 'Greek selection,' " the other man said. "Just write it down, and that's that." The tall man put his head in his hands and let it all go on. One of the women walked out, but the one who had asked for the bagel just gave her order again. John left a dollar, without asking for a check, and went out. The coffee had given him a lift. He looked up at the sky: still overcast, but a few breaks of light. He checked his watch and went to the corner and looked for a cab. Cabs came by him so fast that they looked like they had been launched. Finally he saw an empty one and hailed it. "Thirty-ninth and Fifth," he said.

He hardly ever went into Lord and Taylor's because it made him sad that she worked there. But he wanted to see her. He felt as if he had been running and running and had never touched base. It was a kind of anxiety that came on him lately: that he was rushing forward, but leaving something behind. Not that he could grab her over the counter at Lord and Taylor's. And he had no idea what he was going to say when he saw her.

He leaned on the counter and waited while she folded something and handed it to a customer and thanked her. She knew he was there, but didn't acknowledge him.

"You know what Lois Lane wonders when she's flying with

Superman?" Nina said, without showing any surprise at seeing him.

"What?"

"She's thinking: Can you read my mind?"

"I can't. What are you thinking?"

"That I don't like working at Lord and Taylor's, and I'm embarrassed for you to be here."

"Why should you be embarrassed? Your mother is the only one who believes in success for college grads, right?"

"This place is creepy. You don't belong here. I hope I don't belong here."

"Can you read *my* mind?" he said. "I feel like it's been steam-rollered. I feel like a tumbleweed might blow out of my ear when the winds shift in the desert in there."

"God," she said. "Stop it."

"I can't come over tonight," he said. "John Joel's at the orthodontist's, and I've got to take him back to Rye this afternoon."

"Then come back," she said.

"Come back *again*?" he said. He hesitated. "Maybe I should have dinner with them."

"Then do it," she said.

"What are you going to do?"

"I don't know."

"Sit around and get stoned," he said.

She shrugged.

"I'll drive back in," he said. "I'm meeting him for lunch. He and Nick and I are having lunch. Maybe that's good enough."

"Listen," she said. "If you think you should have dinner with them tonight, do it."

"He was telling me . . . Did you ever see those things called snakes? They're about the size of a cigarette, and when you light them they expand and curl like a snake? I hadn't thought about them since I was a kid. Do you know the things I'm talking about?"

"I don't think Lord and Taylor's carries them."

"Come on," he said. "You know the things I mean?"

"Yes," she said.

"You're not just saying that?"

"No. Why would I pretend to know what snakes are? The boy

who lived next door to us used to light snakes. What about them?"

"I don't know. Do you want to get some snakes and sparklers for the Fourth of July?"

"All right," she said. "Why?"

"You sound like my kid."

"Is this another one of your things about how much younger I am than you? Even if I am, I'm more together than you are."

"That's the truth."

"Maybe you ought to go to work," she said. She laid her hand over his.

"I was scared to death of those things," he said. "The truth of it is that I hated caps and cherry bombs and snakes. How did I ever make it through the Army?"

"I don't know," she said. "I was barely born. Remember?"

"I want to get a snake and have you light it, okay? You light it, and this time if I feel like jumping back, I jump back."

He realized for the first time that a woman was waiting politely beside him, holding a package of panty hose.

The *de rigueur* picture on the desk: Nantucket, rented boat, August vacation. The children: not the children as they really were, even then. Mary in her gingerbread-man bathing suit, wet pigtails tied with red ribbons, staring seriously into the camera; John Joel still a baby, sitting on the deck at Louise's feet, Louise's face a little blurred because at the last second she had moved slightly, trying to make him look into the camera. Before he was fat. When he still had his downy, shoulder-length baby hair. Louise tall and tanned, seven months pregnant, wearing a gingerbread-man bathing suit like Mary's, but without the ruffle. And from the left, harsh sunlight, washing out the deck so that it looked as if Louise was poised on the edge of something, a woman not bending forward to direct her little boy's attention to the lens, but moving to protect him from something more serious. At the right was the jagged shadow of the ship's big sail. How strange that years later he would be fascinated not by the people but by the light and shadow, the light washing out one side of the photograph and the dark shadow jabbing toward them from the other side. He could not remember, and the picture did not help him remember, what it was like to take a family vacation in Nantucket. How easy to look back and see that things were ending, going wrong. Even the way shadows fell in a snapshot became symbolic.

When Mary and John Joel were asleep, they had lain in their cabin and she had curled on her side, with her back to him, and he had made love to her that way, holding her stomach in the front. They had been afraid that the children, separated from them by a wall the thickness of cardboard, would wake up, that a wave would toss the ship at the wrong moment, that it was late in the pregnancy and there might be pain.

Not true: Those were easier things to say to each other than what they were really afraid of.

7

MARY WAS watching as Angela dipped the tiny sable brush into the small glass bottle, wiped the brush on the lip of the bottle, then opened her mouth as though she were singing "o" and slowly outlined her top lip with the plum-colored lip gloss.

Downstairs, Angela's father was complaining about his latest case to Angela's mother, who was reading the evening paper and eating an apple. His ranting had driven Angela and Mary upstairs, and then they had started to fool around with Angela's make-up.

"He lost five hundred dollars over the weekend in Saratoga," Angela said. "And Mom says that he thinks he's going to lose this case."

"That looks great," Mary said. "Your mouth is so sensual. It looks like Bianca Jagger's."

"I've got big lips," Angela said. "I read that if you emphasize your worst features people will think they're beautiful because *you* think they are." Angela shrugged. She was sitting on an old piano stool, covered with red velvet, in front of an Art Deco vanity that her grandmother had given her for her birthday. Inside one of the drawers (her grandmother got the vanity at an auction) there had been a card with ten heart-shaped buttons on it, and in another drawer what was probably the veil from a hat, dotted with little white flowers that had curled into balls with age and dirt—and, best of all, scratched in the top drawer, "Richard loves Daniel." Angela had taken the veil and the card of buttons and put them in that drawer. She opened it again to see if the message, surrounded by the big scratched heart, was still there. It was.

"He's really fucked-up," Angela said. "Maybe he lost a thousand dollars. Sometimes he takes a thousand."

"Peter Frampton gets his hair curled, I think," Mary said. "God —I wish I looked like his girlfriend. The one who sued him. She was so incredible."

"Bobby Pendergast took Annie's copy of 'I'm in You' to the park and was playing Frisbee with it. She went down there and she goes, 'What are you doing?' and he goes, 'He's a faggot.' All those Pendergasts are creeps."

"I don't see why we're sitting around waiting to be invited to a party at the last minute," Mary said. "Big deal anyway—the Fourth of July."

"What?" Angela said. "You're liberated or something?" Angela was dotting on lavender eye shadow with a Q-tip. "I told you: Marcy told me that Lloyd was just being cool, and she saw that he was going to ask me to the party. The phone rang twice yesterday, and the person hung up. He's just afraid to ask. So I'm going to sit here and *assume* he will." Angela widened her eyes the way her father did when he punched words. Angela's father was always telling them, "Get some inflection in your voice. When you talk, you'll bore people if you don't *emphasize* anything."

"I don't believe that he had a list drawn up of who he was inviting to this party," Mary said. "That's like what my mother would do. She writes notes to herself: 'Take trash down front.' Jesus."

Angela looked at her watch. It was a silver watch with single diamonds at the top and bottom of the face—another gift from her grandmother. She was waiting exactly half an hour, as she always did after dinner, for the food to settle in her stomach, but not be digested. Then she would turn up the volume on the stereo and go into the bathroom and stick her finger down her throat to vomit so she would stay thin. By the time her father shouted for the music to be turned down she would already have thrown up and flushed the toilet—she gagged a few times before she turned up the volume, then ran into the bathroom to finish the job. The lipstick she had just stroked on wasn't the color she was going to wear to the party anyway, so that didn't matter. And she had gotten used to the routine: She could vomit without her eyes even watering anymore. Mary was the only one she let in on her secret. Mary refused to do it with her, though. Mary hadn't even believed her until she watched. "Models do it," Angela said. "Lots of people do it." "You're a pervert," Mary had said. But Mary thought everybody was a pervert: her brother, because he was fat; Henri, the poodle who had gone to live with Mary's father and grandmother, because he sniffed crotches; Lloyd Bergman. Mary thought that giving hickeys was perverted. Angela had tried to find out, earlier in the day, whether Mary had ever French-kissed somebody. She knew that if she asked, Mary would tell her that she was a pervert for asking, so she had done it subtly, talking about another girl they knew. Mary didn't say "yuck," so Angela decided to assume that she had done it. Then her curiosity overwhelmed her, and she said, "I'm surprised you don't think Frenching is yucky," and Mary had said, "Not really." Of course, that didn't mean that Mary had done it. If she hadn't, Angela wanted her to do it at the party. Everybody did that at Lloyd Bergman's parties.

"We could go see *Moonraker*," Mary said. "I don't want to sit around here all night. Why would you believe his ten-year-old sister anyway?"

Angela looked in the mirror and stuck her index finger down her throat.

"Turn the music up," Angela said. "Be helpful."

"You are so disgusting," Mary said.

"I don't care," Angela said.

"You ought to save it in a bag for Lost in the Forest."

"*That's* gross," Angela said.

"Stop it," Mary said. "You're really gross."

Angela stuck her finger down her throat again, crossing the room to turn the music louder. The record was *Parallel Lines*. The song was "Heart of Glass."

Mary decided to ignore Angela; she sat on the velvet-covered piano stool and looked at the tubes and pots and cakes of eye-shadow. She decided to brush some of the gold-colored shadow over her eyes. Angela was vomiting in the bathroom.

"I can count on having to ask every night for an end to the noise, can't I?" Angela's father shouted from the foot of the stairs. Angela was still retching in the bathroom. Mary put down the gold-flecked brush nervously.

"Angela!" her father hollered. "Turn that *down!*"

Mary got up and turned it down. She was relieved that Angela, in the bathroom, had stopped gagging. Angela came out, looking fine, holding *Vogue* open to a page of a doberman snarling by a model's ankle. "This magazine is really neat," Angela said. "Your eyes look gross. That's the worst color. Put on something nice for the party."

"If we were going to the party, he would have called."

"He'll call," Angela said.

Mary looked at *Vogue.* She envied Angela for having subscriptions to every fashion magazine available. They were so much more interesting than *She Stoops to Conquer* and *Pride and Prejudice.* That was all just a lot of crap, and didn't have anything to do with the way people lived, or how they could look better.

"What do you think my worst feature is?" Mary said.

"Your eyebrows," Angela said. "But they wouldn't be if you'd just pluck them."

"My mother'd kill me."

"She wouldn't care. She'd like it when she saw how much better you looked. You look like Talia Shire. You can pluck them, you know. The thing is right there."

Mary picked up the tweezers. They were old and ornate: They had belonged to Angela's grandmother's mother. Mary knew the history of everything on Angela's dressing table.

"I don't know," Mary said.

"You're hopeless," Angela said.

"You pull out the ones underneath, right?"

"I can't *believe* you've never plucked one hair out of your eyebrows."

"Big deal," Mary said. "You criticize a lot, Angela."

"Because I'm your friend. Nobody has naturally pretty eyebrows. If you'd tweeze them, your eyes would look bigger. Your eyes are your best feature."

"Okay," Mary said.

"It helps if you put an ice cube on them first," Angela said. "Wait a minute."

She had a small refrigerator in her room. She took an ice cube out of the tray, shaking her hands to get the flecks of ice off, putting the tray on the rug.

"Don't drip it in my lipgloss," Angela said, pushing one of the little pots to the back of the vanity. "You don't have to freeze your skin pink, either. Just hold it there about ten seconds. Give it to me," Angela said. Angela took it back to the tray and put the tray in the refrigerator.

"Just do one at a time," she said. "Pluck mostly in the middle."

"Now I'll always have to pluck my eyebrows."

"So?" Angela said. "You want to, anyway."

"Shit," Mary said.

"You didn't freeze it enough," Angela said.

"That ice felt gross. Forget it."

"There it is," Angela said. "I told you."

Angela's mother called up the stairs to Angela. Angela walked across the room and picked up the phone on her night table. "Hi," she said. "Who's this? . . . I don't know. Maybe."

"Blondie," Angela said. "Do you want me to bring it?"

"I'll think about it," Angela said. "If I do come, do you want me to bring Blondie?"

"Maybe," Angela said. "What time are people getting there?"

"Mary might come with me," Angela said. "If we come."

When she hung up, she gave Mary a smug smile. Tears were pouring down Mary's cheeks—mostly the pain of pulling hairs, but also a sudden flash of embarrassment that she was always tagging along with Angela, and Angela was so much prettier; she was the one the boys wanted at their parties. She went on plucking because she thought she should look good for Angela—Angela would stop bringing her along to the parties if she started thinking she was hopeless.

"I bet he was really happy when you said I was coming," Mary said, sorry for herself.

"Listen," Angela said. "You're not going to believe this, but do you know what I read in Cosmopolitan? That one night Marisa Berenson and Diane von Furstenberg, before she was Diane von

Furstenberg, were in Paris and they didn't have dates for New Year's Eve. Can you believe it? They were sitting around feeling sorry for themselves, and then the two of them went off to a party together, and years later Diane von Furstenberg married Egon von Furstenberg, and look at how famous Marisa Berenson is."

"I'm not going to be famous," Mary said.

"So?" Angela said. "You can still marry somebody rich. You have to look good, though. To be honest with you, you've got to tweeze out another whole line of hairs."

"Do you think you're going to be famous?"

"I think so," Angela said. "I don't know as what. My grandmother's getting me singing lessons in the fall. I might join a band."

"I can't believe you'd do that," Mary said.

"Why not?"

"But you can't sing."

"So? I'm taking singing lessons. If you're pretty, you only have to sing halfway good. I mean, if everybody's singing together, it's not like you've got to sound like Judy Collins, Mary."

"I don't like the way she sounds anyway."

"Well, then think of somebody you *do* like, and you don't have to sing as good as *she* does. You ought to think about it. There are all-woman bands, you know. I just read about one that played at the Mudd Club."

"I'm not as pretty as you," Mary said.

"You've got beautiful eyes and beautiful hair. You just don't spend any time working on yourself. You should take some of my duplicate cosmetics and spend more time learning to make up your eyes."

"What time is the party?"

"Eight o'clock. I don't want to get there before eight-thirty, though. And if he's with another girl when we walk in, we walk out. But I'll bet he isn't. I'll bet he's waiting for me."

"How can you be so self-assured?"

"Because I know I look good," Angela said. "I wouldn't go over there without any make-up, in this baggy pair of jeans, you know. Did you see the Chemin de Fer jeans my grandmother bought me? I have to lie down to zip them up. Size seven."

"You showed me. They're really beautiful."

"So?" Angela said. "You should get a pair."

"I wouldn't look the way you do. You walk right. I don't know how to walk like that."

"You think people just know how to walk? You learn to do it."

"How did you learn?"

"You have to have limber legs. See where that picture's hanging over there? I stand beside it and kick as high as the bottom of the frame fifty times every night before I go to bed. You have to have really limber legs to wear those jeans, because they're so tight it's hard to move in them."

"I don't want to go to the party," Mary said.

"Oh. Great. We sit around half the day waiting for the phone to ring, and I say I'm bringing you, and you decide you don't want to go. Pluck your other eyebrow."

"My mother is really going to be mad."

"If she is, then she's trying to hold you back."

"What's so great about Lloyd Bergman? I can't understand why you think it's so cool to get a hickey. He's not that good-looking."

"I like the way he looks. He looks like an intellectual."

"Did you see James Taylor on television?" Mary said. "I don't know how Carly Simon could be married to him. He has his hair cut like a prisoner. He sings okay, but he looks really old now. Carly's cool."

"Should I wear this T-shirt or this one?" Angela said. "The red one's tighter."

"Wear that."

"I guess so."

"Did you see Bobby Pendergast in his Mr. Bill T-shirt? I wonder if he knows Mr. Bill looks like him?"

"He is so nowhere," Angela said. "I can't even believe that Lloyd likes him. I hope he isn't there tonight."

"If he is, I'm not talking to him."

"Well, you shouldn't," Angela said. She was putting on a brassiere. "I love brassieres that hook in the front. I think they're so sexy."

"Rod Stewart gave all the money he's earning from that song to some charity," Mary said.

71

"God," Angela said. "Did you see that picture of him at Ma Maison with Alana Hamilton? She's so beautiful, I can't even believe she was married to George Hamilton. You know what my mother told me? That he used to go out with the President's daughter."

"What President's daughter?"

"Julie Nixon, I think."

"I can't believe that," Mary said.

"There's this picture of Julie Nixon and David Eisenhower when they were little kids, standing together. They knew each other all those years. It's a famous picture. I think Nixon and Eisenhower are both in it." Angela adjusted her brassiere. "I can't even *believe* that people get married without even living with each other. Maybe if you're the President's daughter you have to. Then secret service agents live in your house with you. I'd hate that."

"They do not. They live across the street." Mary had finished the other eyebrow. "How do I look?" she said. "Can I wear the blue T-shirt if you're not?"

"Here," Angela said, draping the T-shirt on the piano stool. "And take a drink of this, too, so that when you show up you *say* something."

"What's that?"

"It's vodka. What does it look like? It doesn't have any smell. I read about this model who uses it like an astringent, after her shower."

"I don't want any."

"Oh. So you're going to go over there and stand around and not say anything. I can't believe you sometimes."

"You're gross. I don't want any."

"Do you want it in some orange juice?"

"I don't want any."

"Then don't stand by me when you're not talking. If you stand there and nobody talks to you, it's not my fault."

"If nobody's going to talk to me, then I'm not going."

"We've got to get going," Angela said, brushing her hair. "Come on. Or do you think I should put this pineapple barrette in my hair?"

"It's dumb. You look better without it."

"These jeans are so cool. My grandmother couldn't even believe it that people lie down in the fitting room to zip them closed."

"You're lucky your grandmother's cool. My grandmother's as bad as Lost in the Forest. She's so senile. I can't even believe that my father can stand living there with her. Her house is like a museum."

"My grandmother's really cool. She used to go to the fights and watch this wrestler called Gorgeous George, who had curled hair. She thought he was so beautiful. And when she was young she lived in Paris for ten years, and sitting in her bathtub she could see the Eiffel Tower. Diane von Furstenberg's *office* is in her bathroom. It's supposed to be really spectacular. I can't believe she has so much style." Angela put the brush down. "My mother was talking to my father about how your father doesn't live at home. She was saying that if he kept losing at Saratoga *he* ought to go live with *his* mother. He never would. She lives in Brooklyn and she won't move, and he says she's going to be killed. My grandmother who lived in Paris is so neat, and the Brooklyn grandmother is really crazy. She sends *Easter* cards and makes a big thing of *Easter*. I don't even believe that she calls up on Easter, like it's Christmas or something. She's not religious, either. She talks about rolling eggs and the Easter bunny and all that stuff. She's totally weirded-out."

"What are you going to talk to Lloyd about?"

"I don't know. I just drink some vodka and see what happens. It doesn't do any good to plan what you're going to say."

Downstairs in the living room, Angela's father was sitting in a chair, writing on a legal pad.

"I finished *Pride and Prejudice*," Angela said. "We're going over to Lloyd Bergman's."

"Bergman and his Mercedes," Angela's father said. "He loses more cases than I do. You tell me what he's doing with a Mercedes. Besides showing off."

"Your reverse discrimination is disgusting," Angela's mother said. "What's this sudden love for the common man?"

"I don't think much of anybody. It's true. There should be a monarchy," he said.

"I want you to be home by midnight," Angela's mother said.

"Okay," Angela said. "See you."

"Bye," Mary said.

"There they go," Angela's father said. "Communicative. Well-educated. Happy. Are you girls happy?"

"Give up," Angela's mother said. "Everybody doesn't have to subject themselves to your cross-examination day and night."

"And such respect for the *law*," Angela's father said. "Such belief in the power of the law. I'm proud to be a lawyer, in spite of the fact that my family would like me to shut up like I'm some stupid store clerk. As it is, you've robbed me blind. If your mother didn't kick in for her couturier fashions, we'd be starving."

"I told you not to tell him what blue jeans cost now," Angela's mother said to her. "Was I right?"

"All this withholding of evidence," Angela's father said.

"Bye," Mary and Angela said again.

"Goodbye," Angela's mother said. "At least you're not going out to gamble."

It was a half-mile walk to the Bergmans' house. Angela had a silver flask with the vodka in it in her purse. It was a tiny purse, on a long strap, and it hung at her waist. The flask made it bulge.

Mary's eyes hurt. She had looked into the mirror too long, staring as she pulled out hairs. She touched her finger to her brow and it felt swollen.

"Do my eyes look okay?" Mary said.

"Sure. That lavender is nice."

"It feels like the skin is swollen underneath my eyebrows."

"So?" Angela said. "It'll go away by the time we get there."

"I should have held an ice cube there after I finished. Before I put the make-up on."

"I thought you didn't like the way it felt."

"But I didn't want to go to the party with swollen eyes."

"You can hardly tell," Angela said.

"If they were swollen, you'd tell me, wouldn't you?"

"You think you're going to die of this or something?"

"I don't mean that. I mean, you wouldn't let me make a fool of myself, would you?"

Angela gave her a disgusted look and shook her head. "Right," Angela said. "Actually this is a pig party, and that's why I'm taking you."

Mary stopped by a wall thick with clumps and swirls of honeysuckle and picked a flower. She sat on the wall, crushing the honeysuckle underneath her. Angela looked at her from the road, sighed and went to where Mary sat. She picked two flowers from the honeysuckle vine and with her free hand pulled her T-shirt out of her jeans so that she could put one flower in each cup of her brassiere.

"I don't even believe that you've got such an insecurity complex," Angela said. "If you'd feel better if you had a drink, say so."

"Go without me," Mary said. "I don't want to go."

"I'm going to be really insulted if you don't come," Angela said. "I'm going to think that you don't think I'm your friend."

Mary twirled the vine through her fingers. She was always in this position: Her father was going to think she wasn't nice if she didn't pretend that John Joel was thin; her mother thought she had flunked English just to rebel against her. Now Angela wasn't going to be her friend if she didn't go with her.

"If you keep being moody when you grow up, you're never going to get somebody to live with you," Angela said. "Maybe if you'd practice smiling, it would help a little."

Mary was already sure that she wasn't going to live with anybody. She didn't want to. She wanted to live alone, and not have to listen to what people expected all the time. She hoped that when she was twenty she didn't have one friend. She hoped that everybody at the party hated her so she could practice not caring, so people's opinions wouldn't matter to her when she was an adult. She would have told Angela what she was thinking, but she couldn't stand the sound of her own voice. Boys wouldn't ever like her, because she would never be able to think like Angela. In a million years, she wouldn't have thought to put honeysuckle in her brassiere. She would never have hidden things working for her, because even things on the surface didn't work for her. She wished she had worn her own T-shirt, because it was stupid to imitate Angela. Angela was as good as gone, anyway: It was just a *matter of time until she was famous, or married to somebody rich. And when she was, Mary wouldn't be speaking to her anyway.*

It was quiet walking along the road—so quiet that she could hear Angela swallowing vodka.

8

JOHN JOEL and Mary had an easy life. It was too easy, and now both of them were slipping and sliding. Mary had been a bright child, almost all A's in elementary school, but when she got to junior high, she stopped trying. He could actually remember Louise's saying that it was a phase. He noticed it in her friends, too—that nearly manic combing of the hair, the chewing gum and talk about music. They disparaged everything, and their talk was full of clichés and code words. He did not envy Mary's summer school teacher. Mary and John Joel wanted only to avoid things. He had tried to find out what she thought of *Vanity Fair*. "I've been reading it," Mary had said, sulkily. "I read the damn books. Don't sweat it." He had tried not to be antagonistic when he asked.

They had gone to the Chinese restaurant, and Louise tried to get them to order sautéed vegetables along with the rest of their food. He tried to care that it was a good idea, but finally he said, to keep peace, that there were a lot of vegetables in the dishes anyway. Louise stopped talking. He watched out of the corner of his eye as John Joel gnawed on one sparerib after another, thinking, all the time, what a pleasure it was to eat with Nina. He tried again:

"Did you feel sorry for Dobbin, did you feel happy that he became a hero?" "I don't know," Mary said. "He's like something out of a soap opera. John Wayne probably would have liked him. If he'd been bloodthirsty on top of being such a goody-goody." So he switched the conversation to John Wayne, wondering if one other family in America could possibly be having such a Saturday night discussion. He said that he didn't forgive John Wayne for his position on the Vietnam war, sure that Mary would agree with that. She shrugged. "He's dead," she said. As they ate in silence, he noticed that the Muzak was playing "Eleanor Rigby," followed by "You're So Vain."

"Do you like Carly Simon?" he asked Mary.

"God," Mary sighed. "I feel like I'm at dinner at Angela's house. Her father is always trying to find out what everybody's thinking, like we're all plotting or something. He says that at dinner you ought to fill your head with ideas the way you fill your stomach with food. He actually said that."

"I just asked if you liked a singer."

"James Taylor looks really wasted," Mary said, picking up a spare-rib. "I don't know."

"If you don't like eating at Angela's, why don't you eat home more often?" Louise said.

"What is this?" Mary said. "You want me to talk, I talked. I said something, and everybody's jumping on me." She turned to John. "How was work this week? You say something."

He hadn't known what to say. Perhaps: I've got to tell you about my lover's dope-dealer friend who's got a tongue as fast as a race car at the Indianapolis 500. That's because he's on speed, of course. The grass she bought was from Cuernavaca. Very good stuff. I got stoned before I drove out to Rye, and what do you think I saw there? Grandma, drunk as a skunk, out on the lounge all wrapped in mosquito netting. So I went into the house and called Nina—that's my lover—and I was half laughing and half crying, and I kept saying to her that she had to help me, but she was stoned and sad that I was gone, and it wasn't a very good call.

"Why do you always have something sarcastic to say about my going to work? Who do you think supports you? It's not that unusual to have a father who goes to work, Mary."

"Angela sleeps with people," John Joel said.

"What did you say?" Louise said.

John Joel lowered his eyes, but he said it again.

"I don't even believe this," Mary said. "Like, she's my best friend, and I'm supposed to sit here and listen to this from the ten-year-old? I don't even believe that he lies the way he does."

"Why did you say that?" John said.

"Because we were talking," John Joel said.

"You and Angela were talking?"

"No. The four of us. She said something about Angela's father, didn't she? So I just said something."

"You are so out of it," Mary said.

"Oh yeah? Parker's cousin works at the garage and he's got a car behind his shed he's restoring, and the door was unlocked, and Angela and Toddie was in there."

"*Were* in there," John said.

"I don't know if she does or she doesn't," Louise said, "but this isn't what I want to discuss at dinner on Saturday night. Please."

"Everybody has to talk about just what you want to talk about," John Joel said.

"You should be nice to us and not speak that way," John said to John Joel. "Your braces are going to set us back two thousand bucks."

"I don't even want them."

"So what," Mary said. "You have to have them." She smirked at John Joel.

Louise turned to John. "Don't speak to him *kiddingly* about showing respect for his parents. He *should* speak to us nicely, damn it, braces or no braces."

"Everything's fucked," he said. "What does it matter the way things *should* be?"

Louise put her napkin on the table. She refolded it in its original triangle shape. He did not know that Louise knew how to make a napkin cone-shaped. She fitted the napkin into her full water glass, got her purse from the floor and walked out of the restaurant.

"Jesus," Mary muttered.

"You started it," John Joel said.

There were little dishes on the table: mustard, duck sauce, *dim sum* dishes with bits of rice cake, an empty dish where the spare-ribs had been. And leftover food: a little pork ball in a dark brown sauce, chopped shrimp on lettuce, and the stuffed duck's foot, which he had ordered out of curiosity. It had indeed been a duck's foot, with a small ball of something in the claw. The industrious, frugal Chinese. No Chinese would ever be having such a dinner. And this had been an attempt to do something right, instead of taking them on a picnic.

"What do you want to talk about now, brilliant?" Mary said to John Joel.

"Pissball," John Joel said.

"Maybe if this is the way things are going I *should* get a polyester leisure suit and be an asshole," John said. "I feel, when I am with my loving family, that everybody is conspiring to beat me down."

Mary sighed. John Joel reached for the last pork ball.

"No one is going to see where Louise went," John said. He was not asking a question, just stating a fact.

"So what could *I* do?" Mary said.

"No one cares," John said.

"So?" Mary said. "What about you?"

"I care," he said, "but I have to pay the bill. I don't work all week—that unusual pastime of mine—for nothing. I am here to pay the bill. One book I remember very well from college has a character in it who behaves well. A novel by Ernest Hemingway, which I'm sure you'll never read. *The Sun Also Rises.* A woman runs away with some other man, but the hero pays the bills. That's what I do: I work, and I pay the bill. I also care about where my wife is. Not as much as I would have cared years ago, but enough so that I will summon the waiter and go out and try futilely to find her. Don't let me interrupt your meal. If I do find her, I can stand outside with her while she screams until you're done."

The Muzak was playing a medley of songs from *Oklahoma.* It was all high-pitched and too fast.

"In French, it's *Le Soleil se lève aussi.* I read it my freshman year at Princeton. That was considered very avant-garde then—to go to the Cape in the summer and take novels written in French. You saw *L'étranger* all over the Cape. You know who was President?

Eisenhower. And all these rich kids were wandering around Provincetown reading *L'étranger*. I was not as rich as my classmates, but still rich enough. The real wealth came when my father died, and his attorney could finally make the investments he wanted to make. I don't think he even embezzles money."

"Like the suntan lotion," John Joel said.

"What?" John said.

"Whatever word you just said."

"*Soleil*," John said. He took a drink of beer, then a sip of tea. His appetite was coming back, and that was inconvenient, because he should be running after Louise. Would be running after her. Any second. "So that's what you have to say about my fine story. That *soleil* is both a suntan lotion and a word in the title of a novel by Ernest Hemingway."

"That's the thing about Angela's father," Mary said. "When you do say something, it's never intelligent enough. If you don't have a graph, or *Newsweek*, right at the table, what you're saying doesn't mean anything."

"Mary," John said. "Mary, Mary. Is this actually a defense of your brother?"

"She's right," Mary said. "You *are* sarcastic."

"What do *you* say?" John said to John Joel. "A defense of your old daddy? Mary defends John Joel, John Joel leaps to Daddy's defense, and like the three bears, they march off to find Mommy."

"Go ahead and put us down," Mary said.

"What?" he said.

"No matter what I say now, you'll just send it back to me. If I open my mouth, you'll say something nasty."

"It's because it's all too much for me. Do you know how much your crack on the phone about Superman hurt? Don't you think I might already realize that my existence is a little silly? Do you think I had visions of working at an ad agency dancing in my head like sugarplums? Everybody I work with, with maybe the exception of Nick, is stoned on Valium all day. I think of preposterous ways to sell preposterous products. And I think back to college all the time, Princeton didn't just come to mind tonight. I thought I was going to be a bright boy. Well . . . I am that. You don't want to go to Princeton. I don't know."

He stopped talking because Mary was staring at him, and as he looked at her looking at him, he thought: What if Angela really sleeps with people? What if *she* does? What if I'm not the only one keeping quiet? At any rate—whether it was the way he looked, or what he had said, she felt sorry for him. She even did a very grown-up thing: She changed the subject. "I haven't finished the book," she said, "but that's what *Vanity Fair* is like. Things just fall into place."

When they left the restaurant, Louise was outside. He was surprised. He imagined that he would have to go on a wild goose chase to find her, that she would be deliberately hiding from him, to frighten him and punish him. There she was, on the hood of the car, reading a magazine. The car was parked in front of a drugstore, and she had gone into the drugstore—who knew what she was thinking?—and she had bought a magazine. There was something sad and childish about Louise, sitting on her old Chevy, locked out because she hadn't brought her keys, her long, tanned, bare legs hanging down, sandals on her feet, legs parted enough that you could see up her skirt. It wasn't even a self-consciously casual pose; she had really gotten involved in the magazine and forgotten to keep her knees together.

"Apologize" was all she said.

He apologized. He was so relieved to see her, so happy that it was not going to be a night of crazy driving around and calling people she might be with, that he simply apologized. John Joel hung back and didn't look at her. Mary looked at her and looked away. He got behind the wheel and unlocked the car on their side. Mary and John Joel got in the back seat. Louise leaned into the car. "Take them home," she said. "When you've done that, come back for me. I'm going into the drugstore for a milkshake. That's what I want—a chocolate milkshake. I'll be outside when you get back."

Driving home, he no longer felt relieved. He put the radio on and heard two people discussing a recipe for bleu cheeseburgers. When the woman gave the direction "add two tablespoons Worcestershire sauce," the announcer said, "Worcestershire sauce." He echoed everything she said, and when he did, the woman said "Uh-huh" and continued. At the end, the man said, "Doesn't that sound good?" and the woman said, "Oh, it is." The man thanked her. She said he was welcome. Another voice broke in, apologized for interrupting, then started again, saying that tomorrow there would be more suggestions for summer barbecues. "You know," the announcer said, "a lot of people out there don't like bleu cheese. I think these can be made just as well with your favorite cheese—cheddar or jack or whatever." A song from *Saturday Night Fever* came on. He had gone to that movie with Nina, and when John Travolta gave away the first-prize trophy he and his date had won to the couple who should have won the dance contest, Nina had leaned over and whispered: "That's you." It was a little irritating that she pretended he had such good impulses, that his guilt was so great. She asked him, when they first met, if he was a Catholic. She kept up the joke, too: Late one night, after he had made love to her, before he went back to Rye, she had come into the bathroom when he was showering, pushed back the shower curtain a few inches and said: "I will hear your confession." Cold air had come into the shower and something about the tone of her voice and the rush of air had actually frightened him; he had never been in a confessional, but he sympathized for the first time with people who had. It was easy to make her stop teasing, though. All he had to do was reach out and touch her fingertips. He took very hot showers—so hot she wouldn't get in with him unless he agreed to let her regulate the water—and that night, one of the first nights he was with her, he could remember the steam escaping, how quickly she became foggy, her smile through the fog, their fingers touching. He had had to stare to see her, and only partly because of the steam. For a second he had thought she was unreal, that she had always been an apparition. He knew that he had to look at her, and keep looking. If he had not reached out to touch her, it might have gone on forever. Nina's smile, through the steam. The smile that was worth suffering a blast of cold for.

"You ran a stop sign," John Joel said.

"Leave him alone," Mary said.

John said nothing. He slowed down. He looked in the rearview mirror and saw John Joel, pressed against one side of the back seat, and Mary, all the way to the other side. He wondered if they might really hate each other, if when they were adults they would live on different coasts and exchange Christmas cards. What

84

was it like, so early in your life, not to love someone you were sup-posed to love?

He thought: I'm not John Travolta. I'm Father Frank Junior, in a disco for the first time, caught up in it and put off by it. At first, he had been uneasy with her friends—all young, a lot of them spacey, one or two more heavily into drugs than he could be com-fortable with. He had accused her of liking him because he was safe and sane, a father-figure. "That's a lot of easy bullshit," she said. "But I like it that you think you're sane."

He pulled into the driveway—imagine her thinking, even for a second, that there would be columns at the base of his driveway—and the car sideswiped bushes weighted down by the rain the day before. Big white flowers brushed against the side of the car. He turned off the ignition and got out and stretched. He looked at the sky. It was still light, but the moon was already out. By the car was John Joel's tree, the tree where the robin had built its nest. He wished that he had something to concentrate on other than what was coming: that he could be holding the delicate piece of egg, blue like no other blue, and that he could feel its lightness and fragility. The blue egg, in the little dish in Nina's apartment.

On the way back to pick up Louise, he stopped at a phone. He asked the operator to charge the call to his home phone. "Is there anyone there to verify?" she said. "No," he said, without any hesitation. A butterfly—late in the day for a butterfly—hovered by the phone for a minute. He looked again at the moon, more visible now that the sky was a little darker. He shook his head at the ab-surdity of what he was doing: standing at a phone on a country road, as though no one was at home, no one was waiting, as though Nina would pick up the phone in her apartment on Columbus Avenue and suddenly his heart would stop pounding and he would feel the breeze that was blowing. The butterfly flew away. The phone rang ten times, and then he hung up and went back to the car. He sat there for a minute before starting it. Then he put the radio on. The same song from *Saturday Night Fever* was playing, as though the last twenty minutes—half hour?—had never hap-pened. *Things just fall into place.* If Mary knew that, from reading the book or from what she knew of life, she could not deserve to flunk any course, let alone English. Of course, if that was what she

85

thought, then there wasn't much point in her trying to organize her life or in any of the things he had believed about getting ahead, the necessity of getting ahead, when he was her age. Maybe a few years older. He got out of the car and got the operator again, and billed another call to his home phone. He called Nick. Nick picked it up on the first ring. "Goddamn Metcalf," Nick said. "Called me *twice* today with the same joke. I keep telling him that I don't like jokes. He tries to joke with me about not liking jokes. Metcalf."

"What was Metcalf's joke?"

"Same old joke," Nick said. "Jesus Christ. What's up with you?"

"I tried to call Nina and couldn't get her. I just wanted to talk to somebody."

"You should have been around today. The whole city left town. I went with Laurie to the Metropolitan and we sprawled in the grass in Central Park. Nice. Going to Hopper's tonight. The bad news is that my wife called to say that Martin has to have his tonsils out. I told her to find a more progressive doctor—they don't yank tonsils the way they used to." Nick sighed. "I went over there early in the morning and talked to Martin. I asked him if he wanted to come along with us, but he didn't. He was going roller-skating. A fever almost a hundred, and she lets him go roller-skating." Nick sighed.

"I'd tell you what I'm in the middle of, but I don't know myself. I'll have a good story for you Monday morning. Want to meet me at the Brasserie early for coffee?"

"Sure. Eight?"

"Eight."

"Nina all right?"

"I guess so. There wasn't any answer."

"I almost didn't answer it. I thought it was Metcalf again. How he stays sober as a judge Monday through Friday, I'll never know."

"Valium. That's not really sober."

"He doesn't take that much. Beats me."

"What was his joke?"

"You know the joke. I'm sure you know it. Stop me, so I don't have to tell the whole thing: What's the difference between a Polish woman and a bowling ball?"

"What?" John said.

"Come on. You've heard it."

"I haven't heard it."

"Why would anybody laugh at a sexist Polish joke anyway?"

"Okay. Forget it. See you Monday morning."

"The other thing Metcalf does—Metcalf doesn't call you on the weekends, does he?"

"No. He doesn't bother me at work, either."

"He's afraid of you. He's not afraid of me, and he calls me. You know how he starts conversations: 'Hey, gork—' Not even hello."

"Gork?"

"I don't know. His twin brother's a neurosurgeon, and he gets these medical acronyms from him. It's something insulting. I think his brother's being a famous neurosurgeon fucked him up royal. I was out at his house in Sneden's Landing last summer when his brother was there, and Metcalf was running around chasing his brother with a bread knife, saying he was going to do a vasectomy."

When they hung up, John tried Nina again. No answer. He got in the car and drove, fast, to the drugstore. Before he got there, he could see that the lights were out. He pulled into one of the empty places in front of the drugstore and looked around, without getting out of the car. It was getting darker. In half an hour, on the ride home, it would be dark. He didn't see her. If she had meant to run off, why wouldn't she have done it when she left the restaurant? He got out of the car and peered into the dark drugstore. He stood with his back to the door, looking to the left and right. A man on a motorcycle pulled into the next space, turned off the ignition and kicked the kickstand down. He had on a helmet, gold and silver flecked, and mirrored sunglasses you could see out of, but not into. "Have change for a quarter?" he asked.

John reached in his pocket. He sorted through a palmful of change, and gave the man two dimes and a nickel.

"Thanks," the man said. "I was going to buy a Hershey bar, but the drugstore's closed. Suck-ass motherfucking town." He walked around the corner.

"Louise!" John hollered. "If you're here, this is your chance for a ride."

The man jerked his head around the corner. "What'd you say?" he said.

"I came to pick up my wife," John said. "You said it about this motherfucking town." He looked at the motorcycle rider, who looked half interested, half put off. "What's the difference between a bowling ball and a Polish woman?" John said to him.

The motorcycle rider didn't miss a beat. "If you were really hungry, you could eat a bowling ball," he said. He smiled. He was missing a bottom tooth. "Good joke," the motorcycle rider said, and walked around the side of the drugstore.

John followed him around the corner. The man came to a stop in back of Louise, who was talking on the phone. The man put his hands in the back pockets of his jeans and bounced on his toes, as Louise talked on the telephone. The phone booth was against the side of the drugstore. Louise had her hand cupped over the receiver. She was standing with her feet crossed at the ankles, talking quietly. She looked up and saw him.

"I guess you didn't hear me," he said, coming up next to her.

"See you tomorrow," Louise said. "The hero has returned." Her eyes were red. Her hair was pushed behind her ears, and she looked about twelve years old. Her face was freckled from the sun. She hung up and walked past John without speaking, on her way to the car.

"What was that, a conference call to Gloria Steinem and Susan Brownmiller?"

"Very funny. Feminists as a class are very funny. We all know that."

"I apologized," he said. "But you had to get the upper hand, didn't you?"

"I don't want to argue," she said. "What I'd like to do is take a drive out to the water. If you don't want to do that, I'll drop you at home."

He thought about it. It would be nice to see the moon over the water, particularly if she didn't want to argue.

"All right."

"In fact, I'd like to drive, unless you would consider that getting the upper hand."

"You want to drive?"

She nodded yes. He thought about it. When they got to the car, he opened the door on the driver's side and closed it when she sat down. As he moved away, the headache hit. When he got to the other side of the car, he was glad to sit down.

"I'm sick," he said. "I've got a headache. Let's just go sit by the water."

"That was where I was going."

The air changed when they went around the next bend. He reached out and turned off the radio; in his pain, he had been conscious of, and not conscious of, the way to stop the quiet rumble of the man's voice. Leaning forward to turn off the radio sent a jab of pain through the top of his head. He rubbed it. He closed his eyes and kept rubbing.

"You know what I'd like?" she said. "Even if you hate me. Hate all of us. I'd like to go to Nantucket before the summer is over."

"I thought you didn't like it there."

"I've been having dreams about it. There were things I did like. I'd like it if we could rent a boat."

"You made me sell the boat," he said.

"You did nothing but complain and worry all summer. And all winter, whenever anybody mentioned the boat, you'd roll your eyes and talk about how many problems it had and how much it cost. Remember on Christmas Eve when you started going through July and August's checks, and adding up the cost of keeping up the boat?"

"Christmas makes me nervous. I was acting funny because it was Christmas Eve."

"That's a lie," she said. "When you don't want to talk straight, you don't talk straight."

"I don't want to talk," he said. He had also just realized that the window on his side was rolled up. He put it down and put his elbow out the window. He tried to rest his head on his arm, but that made his head pound worse.

"I'd sympathize if I thought this had to do with your emotions," she said, "but at the risk of making you mad, I'll say it anyway: You should tell them to hold the MSG. MSG gives you headaches."

The air was almost cold. He waited for her to tell him to put up the window, but she didn't. He opened his eyes and looked at her, finally. Her short hair was lifted by the breeze, but it just fluttered in place; there was no way for it to tangle, no strand long enough to blow forward and obscure her face. She had on lipstick. She had had an argument with him, and eaten, and talked on the phone, and through it all, her lips were not their real color. They were pinker. A color pink he didn't see women wear anymore, but he thought it was preferable to the red-black lipstick women in the office wore. Their nails were always painted the color of a bruise.

"Well," he said, "I don't see any reason why we can't go to Nantucket."

"Agreeable of you," she said. "I'm surprised. Should I press my luck?"

"Why not? Go ahead."

"It's either you or me, and I would rather that you do it. Someone has to speak to Mary's teacher. She won't get credit for the course if she gets a D, and all of her papers but one are D's."

"What's the matter with her?" he said.

"Ask her teacher."

"Okay," he said. "When?"

"Call and make an appointment."

"Okay," he said.

"Remember when she was born and you used to blow on the fuzz on top of her head and she liked it so well she'd close her eyes?"

She stopped on the hill above the marina and got out. He sat there while she climbed on the hood of the car again and looked at the boats bobbing. A man and a woman were dancing on the deck of one, in their bathing suits, to "Heart of Glass" on a portable radio. Down the road, he could see the cluster of cars at the soft ice-cream stand. A big black dog, the sort of dog a boy would run away with, knapsack on his back, in a Norman Rockwell painting, bounded down the middle of the street. No cars came by. He made it to the ice-cream stand, a boy about eight years old trailing behind him with a leash. It was almost dark, and he worried for both the boy and the dog. Louise was watching them, too. Probably she was thinking about her dog that had died. Years ago, before she decided that fishing was cruel, she used to fish at the marina, from the base of the hill, or from the Pendergasts' boat. The dog went with her and sat, quiet and panting, and leaped with joy when she pulled up a fish. Then he would lick it and guard it as it flopped. The dog had immense respect for Louise, and Louise for the dog.

He got out and sat beside her. The people on the boat were summer people. The Pendergasts' boat was there, but they weren't on it. He was glad, because he did not want to have a drink with anybody. He thought that an ice cream would taste good. He asked Louise if she wanted to walk down.

"In a minute," she said.

He watched her watching the boats. Her eyes were still red, and she didn't seem to care what she looked like. She had brushed up against something and gotten dirt on her leg. She ignored him as he looked at her. Finally he looked away, into the water, almost still, inky and still, lit up by the three-quarter moon.

After a while they walked to the ice-cream stand. The big black dog was there, hanging around, begging for ice cream. The boy with the leash was nowhere around. John asked a little boy in line ahead of him if he knew where the dog's owner was. "Nope," the boy said. The dog was staring at John. If the dog was still there when he got to the window, he was going to buy it a dish of ice cream.

The dog was still there. He got it a large dish of vanilla, and he and Louise got vanilla cones. The dog almost dove into the dish. "Hey! Lookit the stupid dog!" one boy said, and John almost exploded. "Leave the dog alone," he managed to say, calmly. He stood there while the boy and his friend backed off. They had been about to grab the dog's dish. John half wished that he had let them, and that the dog had bitten them. The dog slurped and slurped. Melted ice cream ran down John's wrist, because he forgot to keep turning the cone and licking.

As they were walking away, a girl got out of a car giggling. A boy jumped out the other side, and then another boy. It was the two Bergman boys. Andy with his long mane of nearly white hair, cowboy shirt unbuttoned except for one button above his cowboy belt. The buckle was enormous, shaped like Texas, mother-of-pearl, surrounded by a thick silver rim. Andy was the errant son—

the last John had heard, Andy had flunked out of his second college and was doing lights for a band in New York. Lloyd was almost as tall as his brother, but without the mane of hair. He had on yellow aviator glasses, and he had caught up with the laughing girl and was pretending to be about to grab her, lunging and zigzagging from side to side like a basketball player blocking a shot. She had something she wasn't giving him, and John might have found out what it was if Andy Bergman hadn't recognized him and said hello. Then the game stopped. Angela pushed her hair out of her face and said hello very properly. She had on canvas shoes with high heels, shorts, and a tight T-shirt.

"What do you think?" Louise said, walking away, licking her cone. "Is what John Joel said true? Can you really tell by looking at them?"

They walked to the car in the dark. With his tongue cold from the ice cream, his headache felt better. He leaned against the car for a minute before he got in. He would have thought no about Nina, when actually she had been attracted to him and had been waiting for him to ask. So the fact that he thought yes about Angela probably meant no. He got in the car, chewing the last of the cone.

"What you did for the dog was nice," she said. "You didn't really dislike Mr. Blue, did you? Why did you act like you didn't like my dog?"

"It just got to be a standing joke. I don't know why."

"But you liked him."

"Yeah. Of course I liked him."

"I am not going to cry," Louise said. "I am going to drive, and if I did not cry in the restaurant I am not going to cry now."

When they were home, in the bedroom, she lay on her side, leafing through the magazine on the floor. He looked down and saw a picture of a woman standing beside a car with its door open, her hand on the door, her foot raised, resting on the doorsill, a gold buckle on her shoe. The woman was looking off to the left. She wore a scarf, long and white, the sort Isadora Duncan must have had hundreds of. The scarf dangled down the front of a maroon velvet jacket, and beneath the jacket was a long pleated skirt, as silvery as tinsel. Behind the woman was a string of fuzzy lights. A person with cataracts would have seen the lights that way, all aura and haze. The scarf was so white you couldn't see the texture. The woman's fingers held the edge of the scarf, as she stood with one foot in the door, one foot on the pavement, looking away.

"V*ogue*," Louise said. "Care to make a comment?"

"I like the scarf," he said.

He went into the bathroom. Through the wall he could hear, very faintly, the radio playing in Mary's bedroom. She did not seem to be worried about flunking English in summer school. He supposed that it was his obligation to Mary to confront her teacher and say: She told me that *Vanity Fair* was about how things just fall into place. She's fifteen years old and she knows *that*. Why is she failing English? He would imply, of course, that the teacher was not attuned to Mary. Not stimulating her. He tried to imagine Mary stimulated. She was always lethargic, resigned, sarcastic—though she had been right about *his* sarcasm. She had been the one to end that game, at dinner: Mary grew weary of things. He wondered if she might be weary of her weariness. If yes meant no in Angela's case, then no might mean yes in Mary's. He shook the thought away. He took a shower, blasting himself with hot water. He took four Excedrin before he got into the shower. It felt as if they had lodged about six inches down his chest and were there, still and heavy, like pebbles in a pond. He soaped himself briskly. The suds came up fast. Just as fast, he rinsed them off. He cupped his hands and splashed water on his face, then held his breath and turned his face up into the spray. When he took his face out, he thought he heard "Heart of Glass," but when he turned the water off, he realized that what he had been hearing had been a man's voice on the radio. It was not "Heart of Glass" for the second time that day, the millionth time this summer, after all. Nick had told him that once in Boston, years ago, he had been out of money and out of food, and the woman he lived with had left to keep bees with a sixty-year-old ex-professor of Slavic languages, and his eighteen-year-old sister had just put her baby up for adoption, and the girl he had hoped would be his new girl had called to say she had drawn night duty for the rest of the week. He had been sprawled in the hot Boston apartment he shared with four other people, the window in his room jammed so that it would open only a couple of inches, wearing the same clothes he had worn for four days, with a slow, drumming toothache coming on and no money, late at night. The people in the apartment next door had come home and they had been laughing, and he knew that pretty soon he was going to have to listen to them, having more fun on their mattress than he was having on his, and the most he had been able to do was roll to the far side of his mattress. And then two amazing things had happened. A breeze had started, as strong as the low speed of a fan, a breeze after days of nothing but still air; and at the same time, from the apartment next door, a song so beautiful that he had wept but decided to stay alive: Diana Ross singing "Everything's Good About You." Nick credited the breeze and the song with saving his life. Nick was only five years younger than he was, but when Nick told stories like that, it broke his heart, as much as his heart broke when something terrible happened to one of his children. Actually, nothing really terrible had ever happened. A couple of frightening runs to the emergency room with infants whose fevers rose and rose and wouldn't break, but lately—summer school? The crisis was that Mary was not doing well in summer school. He would take care of it.

He got out of the shower and threw his sweaty clothes into the hamper, but not before removing the small package, wrapped in paper napkins, from his shirt pocket. He put it on the back of the sink, and reached in the medicine cabinet for adhesive tape and scissors. He cut off the right-size piece and taped it to the dry edge of the sink, then dried himself well and unfolded the napkins. Inside was the duck foot from the Chinese restaurant, gray and curved. He taped the duck foot securely to his penis, then put on his pajamas and went into the bedroom. If she didn't laugh, it was really all over. It was even more all over than he had thought it could be. He got into bed and she closed the magazine and dropped it on the floor.

"Hot night," he said.

She was lying on her back, with her eyes closed. She had combed her hair, and her lipstick was gone.

He struggled out of his pajama top. Then the bottoms. She didn't look. He pulled the sheet over them and took her hand.

He got up on one elbow and kissed her on the forehead. She had no expression on her face, before or after.

"Hey," he said, moving her hand down his stomach.

"Not on your life," she said.

He kept moving her hand, until her fingers were touching the duck foot. She yanked her hand away, turned toward him, pulled back the sheet. He held his breath, trying to choke back his laughter. She looked into his eyes.

"Is this what you and the New York girls are into?" she said.

The grotesquely funny was obviously much in vogue. Women wore purple pedal pushers and hacked off their hair with a razor. A put-on. To be ugly is to be funny. To be funny is, maybe, to get through. But did he even realize that the horrible duck foot was a joke directed at himself and his own sexuality? He had changed so much. He would do things more childish than what the children did, and although he didn't actually harm himself, there was something self-destructive in his shock tactics. A month before—three weeks before, five weeks, it didn't matter—when there had been so much sun and the blackberry bush bore fruit so early in the summer, he had been picking up sticks in the grass before he mowed it, and she had been planting seeds in the garden. She had looked up to see him clasping his heart in mock-horror, a circular smear of red on his forehead. She had watched him lurch toward her, eyes big, the ugly red smear like a child's finger-painting, then collapse without a word. He had mashed the black-berries and pretended to be wounded. He had been playing a game with her, but she could not imagine what part he had expected her to take. She had almost wanted to rush toward him—not because she was fooled, but just that if she grabbed him, if she got that close, she might find out something. Or break the tension. Or even laugh with him. But what he had done hadn't really been that funny. The strangeness of it, the impetuousness with which he had acted, had convinced her that he really did have another life: not the life in Rye, but another life, a real life, a life she didn't understand anymore. When he finally got up—slowly, like an exhausted person doing a final push-up—he had cocked his head and looked at her, and not wanting to look fazed, she had smiled at him. Just smiled. And then she had gone on sprinkling seeds, evenly, looking to see where they hit the dirt. They were so tiny that of course she couldn't see. She would see when they came up. She would find out what was going on with John when he left her.

But Mary: What she had done, plucking her eyebrows, hadn't been done as a joke at all. That was pathetic because it wasn't an imitation of a joke, like pedal pushers spoofing what had been a genuinely ugly fashion; it was an imitation of what Mary really thought was beauty.

Louise rolled over in bed. She had been so upset because with her eyebrows plucked, Mary's eyes had looked so large. They had looked so innocent. It had been an innocent gesture to pluck her eyebrows, and harmless, really. Yet when Louise saw Mary's eyes, it had made her sadder than she had been in a long time. Sadder than she had been when John went through his crazy charade on the lawn. As much as John wanted to be a child, Mary had wanted to be a grownup, and that was even more pathetic.

9

DID PEOPLE ever walk into a high school, however different it might be from where they had gone to high school, and not feel, by the sight and smell of it, somehow transported through time, back to their own school?

The lockers at Mary's school were gray metal, with built-in locks. The lockers at his school, which he would not have believed he remembered, he could envision in exact detail. They had been green metal, with padlocks, and they had had vents in the top. All that had been trapped in there had been books, yet there had been vents in the doors—a half-gesture at letting something breathe.

He was surprised that he felt nervous, that he didn't feel on top of things, ready to talk as one adult to another. He felt like a child again. A crazy image flashed through his mind of himself, slamming a handball against the wall at the far end of the hall, slamming it and slamming it until he was caught and punished.

He took the small folded piece of paper out of his pocket. The teacher's name was Cynthia Forrest. He had not planned what he was going to say to Cynthia Forrest. He thought that perhaps his stomach felt funny because he was hungry and hadn't eaten, or because he had wanted to talk to Nina on the phone and he couldn't get her. He had called Lord and Taylor's and they had tried to connect him, but no one picked up the phone. He sent her a message, squeezing his eyes shut and making a wish: Me, Nina. Pick it up. Not some lady wanting to order stockings with gold flecks in them. Me. In Connecticut. Answer.

He walked into the classroom. He had passed only three students in the corridors—none of them kids he knew—and he hated empty places. He still hated to be the only person walking up a flight of stairs, the first person in line. Behind him, it seemed as though wind might rush in.

"You're Mary's father," she said, getting up from her desk and putting out her hand. Her hand was light, and shaking it disturbed him. He didn't know why. He smiled at her. His eye was drawn to her desk—the same sort of desk his teachers had had, the color of dry leaves, with nicks and scratches. Were there any desks with nice wood in schoolrooms?

"Please sit down," she said.

He sat on one of the low desks with an inkwell. Used now for gum, of course. To hide notes, as if in the hole of a tree. He wiggled his thumb in the inkwell and felt better when his finger rested on a bump of dried gum. If you knew some of the inevitables, it kept you on top of things. Nick's philosophy: Know as much as you can, because one tiny thing might help you. Nick knew how to tie fifteen kinds of knots.

"What can I tell you?" Cynthia said.

"I'm here because my wife and I are worried about Mary's doing poorly in summer school. It was quite a shock that she failed English to begin with, and my wife says she isn't doing much better now."

Cynthia nodded and didn't say anything.

"Why?" he said.

"Why?" Cynthia said. "One reason?"

She did not say it unkindly, but he was taken aback. He felt as ridiculous, as out of control, as he had thought he would a few minutes ago when he was walking down the hallway, reminding himself that he was one adult who would be talking to another adult.

"I know there isn't any one reason for anything," he said, "but I wondered if you had any ideas."

"What does Mary say?"

He thought: She thinks of you as Lost in the Forest, but obviously you are not.

"Actually," he said, "we were talking this past weekend, and I tried to get her to talk about one of the books you were having them read. *Vanity Fair*. I must say she didn't seem eager to talk about it. I don't think kids are comfortable talking about books when they're her age. I know I wasn't. But that isn't what I started to say."

She was looking at him. She looked tired. She was quite pretty, and he wondered what she was really thinking. Whatever she had been thinking earlier had been erased. He looked at the swirls and streaks of white on the blackboard behind her.

"What were you going to say?"

"Oh," he said, looking back at her. "Sorry. I was going to say that she acted as if *Vanity Fair* was silly. I asked her how she felt about Dobbin and she seemed to think he was ludicrous. But later she said a very perceptive thing. We were talking about something else entirely, and she said, in passing, that *Vanity Fair* seemed to be about how things just fall into place."

He realized that he was leaning quite far forward. He eased himself farther back on the desk. Looked at her, trying not to appear anxious. He was anxious. He was not sure about what. About what Mary had said, in part. He was wondering if that was true. Maybe things just fell quickly because of gravity, and when they stopped, you said they were in place.

That thought disturbed him so much that he stood up.

"You've read *Vanity Fair*," she said.

He nodded yes. He did not tell her that he had just bought it.

"I wonder if you'd like to have lunch," he said. "Have you already eaten? I mean, you might just want to go on with what you were doing, and not spend an hour listening to some student's father—" He broke off.

She got up. "I'll go to lunch with somebody who's read Thackeray. Sure," she said. "Just a minute."

And then he was alone in the room. It seemed strange to be

there alone—almost as if something dangerous might happen. He wondered what might happen, and smiled at the image that flashed through his head of himself, backing up toward the dusty blackboard as though a magnet were drawing him, getting his clothes dirty. He would have to wear this same jacket and this same pair of pants into the city.

Everybody he knew had problems with their children. They all had children who needed braces, or were doing poorly in school, or had run away. Last week, Metcalf's eight-year-old son had fallen and broken his glasses, and Metcalf had brought them into New York to get new lenses made up. That morning he kept calling people into his office to see the glasses. He had put them on the corner of his desk, on a stand with a curved piece of brass that usually held a strange shell. A small pair of glasses, both lenses cracked, tiny cracks like the points of fire shooting away from a sparkler: a small pair of horn-rimmed glasses, useless to see out of, set out for people to look at like an *objet d'art*. "Eight years old, and blind as a bat without them. On my lunch hour I'm taking them to a place that can grind new lenses and put them in by five o'clock, and then I'm driving out to Sneden's Landing with them and giving them to Paul, and he'll put them on and see again. He's a nice kid, and he'll probably even thank me. He was upset about breaking them, and he cried. Eight years old, and blind as a bat. I'm the big-shot today. I give him his sight back for forty smackers. Costs that much only because the frames got screwed up, too. But he's blind. Eight years old, and my kid is blind. When I was eight years old, I was blind, too. My wife has 20–15, my kid and I are blind." Coming out of Metcalf's office, Nick had turned to him and said, "I almost did it that time. I really almost walked over to him and smashed him. He tosses off everything as a joke, constantly. If he came back from the dead, you know what he'd do? Deface his own gravestone." It had seemed irrelevant to tell Nick that years before, when he first came to work for the agency, he had gone out with Metcalf one Friday after work and they had gotten drunk, and Metcalf had gotten maudlin and talked about how he was going to be cremated, no stone, his ashes scattered over Korea, because he had liked Korea. Not the war part, but Korea. He had liked Korea.

"Okay," Cynthia said, coming back into the room. She had combed her hair and did not look quite as tired. He suggested a restaurant a few miles down the road from the school, and she said she'd follow him in her car. At lunch, he was going to have to think of something to say to her, to find some way to get her to pass Mary. He would certainly never think of anything to say to Mary to persuade her that she should try harder. If he were Nick, he could dazzle Cynthia with all the knots he could tie. He smiled. Nick had sworn to him that that really dazzled women. That they would do anything for a man who could tie fifteen different knots.

All right: That was the truth of it. He found her attractive. She had Nina's direct gaze, and she obviously deserved better than to be in that school teaching those kids, the way Nina deserved better than Lord and Taylor's, and when he felt sorry for women a feeling of longing often got mixed up with the pity.

He turned on the radio, kept moving the dial. "And this one, you can be sure, is one of the best," the announcer's voice said. "This is a recording of 'Don't Worry 'Bout Me' which was used as the theme song for a movie I'll bet a lot of you have forgotten called *End of the Road*. Billie Holiday recorded this one in 1957, with the Ray Ellis Orchestra, and the man you'll hear on alto sax is Mr. Gene Quill." The announcer had a surprisingly calm, quiet voice—a late-night announcer's voice.

Billie Holiday was singing. She was singing, and the lyrics, of course, were not to be understood as meaning what they were saying. When she sang "I'll get along" it was painful; the restraint in her voice, the way she absolutely did not mean it, but not self-pitying either. Nina could do that: She could say something about her ability to survive that would shock him with her lack of faith in herself, but she wouldn't give in. She really pretended to be a survivor, to the extent that at times he feared for her life, actually thought she might be dead when the telephone rang in her apartment and she didn't answer. Nina hated him to talk that way. She said that he had been a Boy Scout too long, that she did not care to be helped across the street. But once, early on, surprised at the intensity of her feeling for him, she had gotten drunk at dinner. He had held her arm crossing the street, and she had not objected. She wanted to marry him. Nina.

He pulled into the parking lot outside the restaurant. Cynthia passed his car and parked farther down, on the opposite side. His parking place was closer: He should have left it for her, but he didn't think of it. Or maybe Nina was right about his being too much of a Boy Scout. If they had taught him to tie knots in the Boy Scouts, he didn't remember it.

The restaurant was air conditioned, and the instant he felt cool he wanted a drink. He asked her if she wanted a drink, hoping that she did. When the waiter came, she ordered a glass of white wine, and he ordered a gin and tonic.

"I was thinking, driving here, that I don't envy you," he said.

She smiled. She seemed to know what he meant, and he was glad, because after he said it, he realized that it might have seemed a condescending thing to have said.

"I was wondering why you weren't at work," she said.

"I had to have a conference today with my daughter's English teacher."

"Well," Cynthia said, "I'm glad you took the English teacher to lunch. She was hungry, and she doesn't like sitting around that classroom."

"You write on the blackboard," he said.

"Yes," she said. "Quite a few teachers, I think . . ."

"I just meant that I forgot that information gets communicated that way. I'm used to memos. I guess you couldn't very well send the students memos about Thackeray and have them initial them and send them back."

"What?" She laughed. She picked up her glass of wine and had a drink the minute the waiter put it on the table.

"Footing the bill, too?" she said. "The English teacher is almost broke."

"Sure," he said. "Of course."

"This is odd," she said. "This isn't what I thought I'd be doing today."

"I was hungry," he said. "I was embarrassed, thinking you could hear my stomach growl."

"I didn't."

"You didn't," he repeated. He picked up the menu. He wanted six cheeseburgers. If he only had one drink, he would order a turkey sandwich. If he had two, he would order a cheeseburger.

"In answer to your question," she said, "I know that your

daughter can read the books and understand them, and that she can write about what she knows, if she wants to. I do *not* have that feeling about everyone in the class. I do have the feeling that she doesn't care, that it isn't cool to care, and that neither you nor I can probably make her care."

"I like what you said about there not being one answer for things," he said.

"What do you mean?"

"You said, when I asked why she was doing poorly, that there wasn't any one answer."

"I know," she said. "I mean, what do you think the answers are?"

"I agree with you," he said. "They're fifteen years old now and it isn't cool to care."

"And what else?" she said.

"She thinks Thackeray is irrelevant. It's summer—"

"I don't know if it's important whether it's irrelevant or not. I mean, I don't think it *is* irrelevant, but those aren't even terms I think in."

She took a drink. He took a drink. He was afraid that if he asked her what she did think, she might tell him, and it might surprise him. It was too early in the conversation to ask what she was thinking.

"When I feel like giving up—not showing up to teach—when I'm in a bad mood, I see it their way. I see the absurdity of thinking about any time but our own. I can see wanting books to hit me over the head and tell me what to do about my problems. I don't want to know what the *Odyssey* has to do, indirectly, with my problems: I want Ann Landers."

"But Ann Landers is predictable. You have to distrust those answers because of that."

"Is she?" Cynthia said. "I don't read Ann Landers."

She had almost finished her wine. It was a small glass. He got the waiter's attention and ordered another glass of wine, and before he was tempted, another drink and a turkey sandwich to be brought at the same time. She ordered a salad.

"Why fight it, I guess," Cynthia said. "It was predictable that I'd order a salad and you wouldn't." She fiddled with her napkin.

"You can get caught up in that—thinking that because you can make everything seem ironic, that things genuinely are. You can put an ironic front on anything. I felt sort of the way they must feel—the way I *think* they must feel—when I was younger than they are. In grade school, when we used to go down to the cafeteria and sit on the floor and put our hands over our heads—what we were supposed to do if the bomb dropped, if the bell went off for real and a bomb dropped. Then we'd file upstairs and hear about Washington crossing the Delaware. But everybody's had that experience, or a comparable experience. Constantly. I'm not so sure that these times are as mind-blowing as those kids pretend. I'm not sure that they aren't just lazy, and that it isn't easy to be lazy."

While she talked, he looked at her hands. They were small hands, thin, with long fingers—a young woman's hands. How was it possible that Louise's hands were so much larger? How could hands get bigger as you got older? She was staring at the tabletop.

"What are you thinking?" he said.

"Oh," she said, shaking her head in apology. She shook her head again. "I was thinking about a friend of mine who has nightmares about the bomb. Very specific nightmares. He dreams that it's exploding, and he's not supposed to look at the fireball." She took another drink. "This is an odd conversation to be having. Did I start this odd conversation?"

"I don't remember."

"Did we somehow get to Spangle and the fireball by way of your daughter's problems in summer school?"

"Spangle?"

"That's his name. He's in Madrid, trying to talk his brother into coming back to the States to reenroll in law school. Ann Landers would say he's doing the right thing, right?"

"I imagine," he said. He was tapping the salt and pepper shakers together. "I'm glad you wanted to come to lunch," he said.

That seemed to be the wrong thing to say. For some reason, that seemed to embarrass her, while other things hadn't. She sat up a little straighter and didn't say anything. He looked at some of the other people in the restaurant. It was definitely not a restaurant in New York at one o'clock. The middle-aged women leaned forward or sat close together like conspirators, and the few younger women in the restaurant seemed formal, stiffer, almost alienated from each other. He saw only two other pretty women, neither one as pretty as Cynthia. And he suddenly remembered part of the reason he had dreaded meeting her: that notice she had sent around, with a picture of herself on the top, like an egomaniac's stationery. Perhaps she had done it as an ironic frame.

"On the off chance that I get drunk," he said, "tell me what ideas you have, if any, about how Mary could pass the course."

"Tell her to come see me. I asked her to twice, and she didn't. If she and I could work it out privately—if nobody else has to know that she cares about passing the course but Mary and me—maybe she'll be more willing to try. We can hush it up that she cares."

"All right," he said. He moved his hands above the tabletop, crossing one over the other. "Now you don't see them," he said, when his hands were over the salt and pepper shakers. "Now you do." He moved his hands again. "You don't care, and then you do."

She was staring at him, with her mouth open.

"What?" he said, smiling nervously.

"What you just did," she said. "What a coincidence. I was thinking about a magician, and that was such a strange thing to have happened." She picked up her wine glass and put it down. "There's a man in New Haven, where I'm living, who turned up last night. I met him a little while ago, at a laundromat, and last night when I was going out I bumped into him again, except that I had the spooky feeling that I didn't really bump into him, that he had been out on the street on purpose." She picked up the glass again and took a drink of wine. "Never mind," she said. "I'm sorry. I didn't get much sleep last night because the damned fan doesn't work."

"No," he said. "Go on."

"Oh, he's just a harmless eccentric, I'm sure, but it was so strange seeing him again, and he wanted to have the exact conversation we'd had before, in the laundromat. That didn't make sense, because it was obvious that he recognized me. He stopped and said hello, and I said hello to him, and he turned and started walking in my direction, and he started to tell me all over again how he was visiting his mother in New Haven, that he lived in

California. I was sure he had the same things to do tricks with in his pocket." She shook her head. "This is silly," she said. "Forget it."

"What happened?" he said.

"Nothing, really. He just acted like we were old friends, or something. When I told him I was in a hurry, he just kept pace with me. So I got in a cab and got away. But it was strange, having him walk toward me on the street, and acting so casual, but when I was looking for a cab he seemed almost desperate to tell me things about some Houdini conference that was held every year, and to tell me what was behind Houdini's trick of breaking out of chains when he was under water. I was really getting frightened. I just—I thought he was going to do something to me."

"Christ," he said. "I don't think that's nothing. I think you ought to stop going out alone."

"New Haven's full of nuts. It doesn't mean anything."

"Really," he said. "The way you describe it, it doesn't sound harmless at all."

She stopped running her fork over the top of her salad. She stopped, and ate some lettuce. He wanted to say more, but he didn't want to scare her, and it was obvious that she wanted to change the subject. He picked up his sandwich and bit into it.

"You drive in all the way from New Haven?" he said.

She nodded yes.

"But you don't like living in New Haven."

"It's close to Yale."

"Do you live there alone?" he said.

"No. I live there with a man. The one who has the nightmares." She laughed. "One of my students' parents comes to see me and I say I'm living with a man who's scared of looking at a fireball."

"My heart can take it," he said. "My sense of morality is not outraged." He took another drink. "People should live together before they get married."

"Except in the world of Vanity Fair."

"Of course," he said. "Of course not in the world of Vanity Fair."

When they had finished eating, the waiter came and asked if they wanted anything else. He went away to add up the check.

When he came back, he put the small tray with the piece of paper on it by Cynthia.

"He guessed wrong," Cynthia said.

He reached for the check, took money out of his wallet. "Do you need money?" he said. He realized that even asking would be embarrassing, but if she did, maybe she would take it. Then maybe they would have another lunch sometime and she would pay him back.

"No," she said, embarrassed. "I hope it didn't sound like I was hinting for money."

"Oh no," he said. "I just thought you might need some money."

They were both a little embarrassed, and he was embarrassed, too, in the parking lot when they had to shake hands. He almost always found it awkward to shake hands with a young woman. He also felt strange because her hand was so much like Nina's, and he felt strange because there was a Nina, and strange that he had almost told Cynthia about her, but he had stopped short and only said that people should live together.

He drove into New York at sixty-five, sixty-eight, needle edging onto seventy at times, almost hoping that he would be stopped. He wanted to think, but he didn't have time to stop and think. He was late for work.

He took a paper cup out of the dispenser by the water cooler and thought of two things: the robin's egg (just as the cup seemed too fragile to hold water, the egg seemed too thin to have contained anything living) and the napkin, folded into a triangle in the Chinese restaurant, Louise carefully refolding it, putting it into the glass, walking out. He had another throbbing headache and he would have to work until eight or nine o'clock to get everything done. The headache had come on him like a mosquito bite rising. His temple had suddenly been filled with pain when he opened his car door in the parking garage. He had gotten out, turned when the man gave him the receipt, and leaned back, touching the car, standing there with his hands curled into fists on top of the roof, supporting his head on them. The young black man working in the garage had hit him on the shoulder. "Don't you grieve for it now," he said. "Seven dollars and ninety cents, you can have it back any time." The man had laughed at his own joke. Don't you grieve for it. Certainly everything was not loaded with meaning. Why was he getting stopped by things so often?

That things just fall into place. Because he wouldn't be able to rest until the situation with Nina was settled.

He stood at the water cooler. Two aspirin weren't going to help. He thought about going down to Nick's office, but he didn't know what to say. He took the aspirin and went anyway.

"What's the matter?" Nick said when he saw him.

"I had lunch with her teacher. Mary's summer-school teacher. I held her hand—I mean, I shook her hand—and with my eyes closed, it could have been Nina's hand. I stood there shaking the hand of Mary's summer-school teacher, and I wanted to go to bed with her."

"So?" Nick said. Nick put down the piece of paper he had been studying. It was a graph: stalagmites and stalactites on an eight and a half by eleven sheet of paper. "Why do you look so awful?" he said.

"I've got a headache. And you know what I think about that? You know the old I'm-too-tired, I've-got-a-headache routine?"

Nick opened his top drawer. "If you know so much, Freud, how come you've got cancer of the jaw?"

"Jesus Christ. What if this is all some midlife crisis? If I'm just becoming aware I'm losing my youth, and—"

"You were running down how old you were when I came to work here three years ago. Three years ago. You were thirty-seven."

"You're only thirty-five now. You want to disbelieve Passages?"

"You're drunk?"

"I'm not drunk. My head is pounding."

"You're talking to me about Passages. Passages. I want to not believe Passages. Correct. You're in a midlife crisis: correct or incorrect. Okay. This is the stupidest conversation I've had all day, and that includes nearly an hour-long conference with Metcalf this morning. This teacher was pretty?"

He sat in the chair across from Nick's desk. Behind Nick was a Betty Boop clock. Out of her surprised mouth came two black arrows telling the time. Five of three.

"I love it," Nick said. "In all my youthful innocence, I mean—that you care what the fuck the reason is. You must have gotten along very well with that schoolteacher today."

John tapped Nick's paperweight (a picture of Mary Pickford's house, Pickfair, under glass) against the edge of his desk.

"My head is killing me," he said. He put down the paperweight. "Thirty-five," he said. "Did you ever read L'étranger in college?"

"The Stranger, by Albert Camus. I read it," Nick said. "You can speak English here. You're among friends."

IO

PARKER LIKED to eat as much as John Joel did, but he never had any money, and John Joel got tired of lending him money he knew he'd never see again. He couldn't very well eat in front of Parker, though, so he ended up buying Parker's lunch when they were in the city and not stopping for as many snacks as he would ordinarily. Parker hated the hot weather and was always mopping his brow with one of his assortment of Western bandannas. Today it was a wadded-up yellow bandanna to go with the yellow shirt he wore. He let the shirttail hang out of his slacks so that he could lift it every now and then and fan up some breeze. Parker liked to wear cotton shirts instead of T-shirts, and he thought jeans were too hot in the summer. John Joel felt vaguely as if he were with his father. Nobody else his age dressed like Parker. On Fridays Parker took the train into New York to see his shrink on West Fourth Street. Lately John Joel had been taking the train into town with him. There were no hamburgers in Connecticut to compare with New York burgers.

They were on Madison Avenue, where they had gone to pick up a photograph of some relative that Parker's mother had dropped off to have restored. The man in the store had carefully lifted the tape that sealed the brown package, separated the two pieces of cardboard inside, and revealed to them the enlargement of a picture of a lady in a gray blouse, with buck teeth and a gray-blue flower in her hair—some relative that Parker didn't know. The original, the man said, was in the envelope. The envelope was taped to one of the pieces of cardboard. The man smiled over the counter at them. "Is there a family resemblance?" he said, cocking his head at Parker. "She's ugly and I'm fat," Parker said, fanning his shirt away from his stomach. "What do I owe you?" Parker's mother had given him a blank check, and he filled in the amount. Earlier in the day he had filled in a check at the railroad station, and then again at the shrink's. All the cash he had was eight dollars, and since the bus was too hot, that would all go to splitting the cab fare to and from Grand Central.

"She looks like a spitz," Parker said, the package under his arm.

"A what?"

"That dog. Isn't it called a spitz?"

A thin black woman with her hair in a bun passed them, pushing a white baby in a stroller. Parker showed her his stomach to shock her, but she didn't shock. She just kept walking, looking at the wheels of the stroller.

"So when do you get your braces?" Parker said.

"Next week. I don't know."

"Then you're going to have to brush your teeth all the time," Parker said. "Every time you eat. Otherwise that stuff will get in your braces and putrefy."

"I don't care," John Joel said.

"Putrefy is a good word," Parker said. "Can we get something to eat?"

"I'm supposed to buy, right?" John Joel said. "Right?"

"Where do you get all your money?" Parker said.

"Mostly from my grandmother. She didn't use to give us money, but she feels bad that she doesn't like us. She likes my brother, but he's a baby. She gives Mary and me money. Not all the time, but maybe every other week or so. She gives Mary more than she gives me."

"So why does the kid live with her?" Parker said.

John Joel shrugged. "Where do you want to eat? That place?"

"I get sick of hamburgers."

"That's what I want, though. So that's what I'm going to buy you. What did you want?"

"Éclairs."

"We can get some éclairs. Let's get a hamburger."

"Where can we get éclairs?"

"We can even get them at Grand Central. Let's get a hamburger."

"Okay," Parker said.

They went inside. A fan was aimed at the counter, and square glass ashtrays were on top of the napkins so they wouldn't blow away. There was a sign asking people not to smoke. Parker saw the sign and put his unlighted cigarette back in the pack in his shirt pocket. He smoked Salems. He played with the edge of his napkin, waiting for the man behind the counter to take their orders. He took out a cigarette again and tapped it on the counter but didn't light it.

"You ought to see the stuff across the street, down at the Whitney Museum," John Joel said. "I was in there with a friend of my father's last week. All these plaster people sitting around on subway cars or sprawled in bed. Some of them are naked. Some of them are painted colors."

"Let's go thcre," Parker said.

"I was just there."

"So? It's right down the street."

"It costs money."

"Listen: I tell my mother we went to the Whitney and show her the stubs, she'll give you back the money you paid for both of us to get in, I promise."

"What do you want to go to an art show for?"

"Why'd you go?"

"I told you. My father's friend took me there. We were killing some time between the orthodontist and my father meeting us for lunch. My father gets on this thing that I should be escorted around New York."

"We going or not?" Parker said.

"If your mother's paying me back, we can go. It's no big deal. It's just a pretty weird art show."

"I want to see the naked plaster people," Parker said. "Are they real thin?"

"They're average."

"Are they fucking?"

"They're just lying in bed. They're asleep."

"But they're naked, right?"

"What?" John Joel said. "Didn't you ever see anybody naked in bed?"

"I just think that's a pretty weird art show," Parker said.

"No smoking," the man behind the counter said.

"What?" Parker said. "I'm tapping out a song that's going through my head, that's all. We want a couple of hamburgers."

"What with them?"

"French fries. Two orders," Parker said. "Coke for me."

"Cow juice," John Joel said. There was a sign on the wall that advertised milk as cow juice.

"What song's going through your head?" the counterman said. He turned and began filling a glass with ice.

" 'Stayin' Alive,' " Parker said. "You see *Saturday Night Fever?*"

"That show where they do the gag routines," the counterman said. "Sure I've seen it."

"Uh-uh," Parker said. "The movie with John Travolta in it."

"What am I talking about?" the counterman said.

"You're thinking of *Saturday Night Live.*"

"Yeah," the counterman said. "The blonde's pretty. The one who gives the news. Not any prettier than the one who gives the news for real, though. Some of the stuff's funny."

"You know that song?" Parker said. He took out a book of matches and put it on the counter and flipped open the cover with his thumb.

"Nah," the counterman said. "I don't go to movies with actors in 'em. I go to see actresses."

"There were girls in it." Parker tore out a match.

"What I read," the counterman said, "it was about John Travolta."

"Hey," the other counterman said, turning away from the grill and wiping his forehead on his arm. "You going discoing this weekend, Sal? That what you're talking about?"

"That'll be the day," Sal said.

" 'Disco, Disco duck,' " the other counterman sang, turning hamburgers on the grill.

"*He* goes discoing," Sal said. "Sure. Look at him. Look at him shake. During the day he stands in front of the grill and shakes. Nights, it's his ass. Show the boys," he said, and laughed. His laugh turned into a cough.

"I don't show boys," the other man said.

"*Saturday Night Fever, Saturday Night Live,* who keeps it straight?" Sal said. "Two fries, right?"

"You ought to see that movie," Parker said. "I saw it when it was R-rated. It's changed now, but there wasn't that much good stuff to begin with, so it's pretty much the same." He had lit the match. He watched the flame burn toward his finger, then blew it out.

"Day I pay to see John Travolta dance," Sal said.

"Day you do *anything* you don't do every other day, I'll stand up on this grill and do a slow fry. Flatten myself down on this grill like a hamburger and sputter. You going to a disco. I'd like to see that."

"A priest goes to the disco in the movie," Parker said.

"A real priest?" Sal said.

"Well—he's thinking about not being one anymore."

"He goes back to the church, I bet," Sal said.

"Nope," Parker said.

"So what does he do?"

"He drives off. I don't know what he does. I don't think they say."

"So everybody's still riding off into the sunset. When I went to pictures and I was a kid that's what they did. Still doing it, huh? Priest doesn't know what he's doing. Shit. Quit one thing for another. Day I do that, you *better* get up on that griddle and melt yourself, Robby. You'll know the world is in sorry shape the day I do that."

"He loves to work. Sal loves to work," Robby said.

"Make fun of me," Sal said. "I like to work. I like heat. That's it. I thought this was where I'd end up. Sure. What started this, anyway?" Sal said. "Are you cooking today or not?"

"What does it look like I'm doing? Discoing?"

Robby turned back to the grill. Sal wiped his hands on a towel under the counter.

"Maybe there's something better to do than go across the street," Parker said.

"It was your idea. I don't even want to go."

"Let's go," Parker said. "It's right across the street, I guess." He squirted a blob of ketchup on the side of the plate. The plate was shiny with grease. He ran the French fry through the grease and salt to the ketchup, pushed it around, and picked it up in his fingers.

"My one grandmother doesn't send me money because she's dead," Parker said. "The one that's alive sends me stuff, but not money."

"When did she die?"

"Last summer. Swimming in the Adirondacks. She had a stroke or something."

"I never thought about a grandmother swimming," John Joel said.

"What's yours do?"

"She doesn't do anything. She takes my brother and the dog to the park sometimes, I think. She reads books."

"My grandmother had the Kinsey Report on her bookshelf in the kitchen with her cookbooks. It was boring. Just a lot of crap."

"What'd she keep it there for?"

"Adults don't think they have to hide anything," Parker said. "No. I take it back. My father hides things. But nothing as stupid as the Kinsey Report."

"What does he hide?"

"He's got pictures hidden. He's got a dirty deck of cards. I opened what I thought was his fishing box, and it was full of stuff like that. Maybe it isn't even his. When my grandmother died and my grandfather went into a nursing home he hauled home all kinds of crap. I don't even think the stuff is his, come to think of it."

"What did you think when you found it?"

"You sound like my shrink," Parker said. "Would I have to beg for a milkshake?"

"They're a dollar ten."

"Will it do me any *good* to beg for a milkshake?" Parker had torn two matches out of the book. He pushed them toward each other, head to head.

"Okay. Tell the guy we want two."

"*Garçon*," Parker said to Sal. "Two chocolate milkshakes, please."

"I was in Paris in World War II," Sal said. "Give me a sentence in French and I can answer you. Go ahead."

"I don't know French."

"You sounded like you did there, for a minute. What kind of milkshakes?"

"Chocolate," John Joel said.

"Chocolate malt," Parker said.

"My brother was in the Philippines," the counterman said. "Used to get the monkeys drunk as skunks. Leave beer in the cans. Monkeys would swing around, loaded, fall out of the trees. Monkeys were certifiable alcoholics. He brought one home with him, smuggled it in. Drank with him at night. Staggered around the house. There was a lost soul. My brother, I mean. There's somebody who never figured out what he was going to do and never did it. Spent years drinking with a monkey."

"Here we go," Robby said. "Sal: responsible hero of the family."

Sal put two metal containers under the machine and turned it on. Water ran down the sides of the containers. Parker took out his bandanna and wiped his forehead.

Robby was still standing in front of the grill with his hand over his heart.

"I should disco and get drunk with monkeys. Sure," Sal said.

"Their milkshakes are ready," Robby said, pointing.

Sal put two glasses on the countertop—the kind of glasses Coke used to be served in. He poured each glass half full and set the containers on the counter.

"I never spent so much time talking to kids in ten years," Sal said. "How did we get talking?"

"We're fat and jolly. People can't resist us," Parker said.

"That's the truth. You won't dare weigh too much when you're chasing the ladies, though. Listen to me: I sound like somebody's father. If I'm somebody's father, I don't know about it."

"You're somebody's father, I'll fry a leg on this griddle," Robby said. "I'd like to see what you do besides work."

"All this because I wouldn't close up shop for August. You'd think this was the French Riviera. That he'd do anything worthwhile if I closed for August."

"My sister's got a condo in Ocean City. How many times do I have to tell you?"

"Yeah. And a pool that fell through the ground. A swimming pool brought down by carpenter ants."

"There's the ocean, you know, Sal."

"Yeah. I can see it. Full of seaweed. Stay here where the fan's going."

"I might quit," Robby said.

"You're not going to quit," Sal said.

Parker tapped his cigarette on the counter. He knew that Sal was watching him, that he was making Sal nervous. Earlier in the day he had tapped the cigarette on his psychiatrist's table. In front of the sofa the patients sat on, the psychiatrist had a table with magazines on it, as though the patients might tire of talking and just stop and flip through a magazine. As though they were waiting to see the doctor instead of being in the room with him. Some of the old *Life* magazines Parker thought might be collectors' items, but he didn't want to get into that with the shrink. He would rather have spent the hour eating. He had no interest in talking to the shrink about why he wasn't doing anything all summer.

"Let's get going," John Joel said. "Let's go to the museum and get it over with."

"Leave me a big tip," Sal said. "He quits on me, I'm going to need cheering up. He goes off to Atlantic City, I'm all alone here. Just me and his grill."

"Ocean City," Robby said.

"Probably you're going to march in the beauty parade. Leave here and put on your Easter bonnet, march in the beauty parade."

"You're all screwed up," Robby said. "Don't tip him but five percent."

John Joel left a fifteen-percent tip because he knew he'd go back to the hamburger shop. He looked at his watch and saw that they didn't have much time. Nothing was worse than being caught in New York late on Friday and having to ride the commuter train home. The few times that he had done that with his father, his father had always stood in the bar car instead of sitting down, standing and being shaken around, saying that he knew he couldn't really get out, but standing gave him the illusion of escape. When the voice came over the p.a. system and began announcing where the train was headed, the message always started: "Make sure you're right." John Joel's father always sighed and bent his head back when he heard that, and then shook his head as the announcement went on: Stamford, Noroton Heights, Darien . . .

On the street, they passed a man in jeans, smoking a cigar, standing and staring in a bookstore window. Parker coughed and fanned the air. They went into the Whitney without discussing it again. Parker gave his package to the man behind the desk, and they went to the booth and John Joel bought two tickets. Then they walked into the museum and had to turn back for their stubs—John Joel had almost forgotten that Parker's mother would reimburse him if she saw the stubs. He put them in his pocket, and they waited for the elevators to come.

"Walk," Parker said.

"Are you kidding? It's too hot."

"It's air conditioned."

"Are you kidding?" John Joel said.

Eventually the elevator came and the door opened and they got on. It was a huge elevator, like somebody's room, without furniture. John Joel thought that there should be at least a pole light in one corner, a pillow or two on the floor.

"Walk," John Joel snorted.

They got off at the third floor and started looking around. John Joel could tell that Parker was really interested in the show when he went to look at a group of people who weren't even naked. Parker stood and stared so long that John Joel wandered off and read what was written about the scene Parker was looking at on the wall:

> Though the figures are cast from friends,
> by adding color to them, I touched
> on terror, hallucination, nightmare.

He stood beside Parker and looked. The most interesting figure was the one that was all blue. By a process of elimination—because he was sure that that was Antony and Cleopatra sprawled on the floor, and because he could recognize Catwoman and Superman and Pussy Galore—the one he liked had to be Bottom.

"Come on," he finally said to Parker.

"How much does he get paid for doing this?" Parker said.

"He's a famous artist, so he's got to be rich. I don't know."

They looked at other pieces of sculpture: a woman on a subway car, with something rigged up so that the lights of another subway car seemed to be passing the window. A person behind a counter. Someone seen through a window, watching television. Then they got to the good stuff: a man and a woman sprawled on a brass bed, with an old mattress beneath them, the man's penis half erect, the sheets a mess. Parker stared. He crossed the gallery and looked at the other bed scene, a blue woman sitting on the side of the bed and a man asleep. The beds both looked very uncomfortable. The lighting was odd. He stared for a while longer, then looked for John Joel.

John Joel was looking at the sculpture that Nick had stared at for so long the week before. There was a girl emerging through tile—tile like the tile that was in their shower at home, but she was breaking through it, her left breast showing, her left leg and pubic hair, some monster of the shower, with eyes that you couldn't really look into because they were looking down, just indentations, or because of the way the light was. To the side of the woman breaking through the tiles were four other women, or rather fragments of women's bodies. John Joel was thinking about Mary, and how much he would like to be able to push her from behind so that she would go through a wall like Superman, though hopefully with more pain. The woman breaking through the tile didn't look upset, though. John Joel couldn't imagine why she was doing what she was doing, and thought maybe she couldn't, either.

"Nick says the guy who does these stands around his friends' bedrooms and when they're asleep, he does this." John Joel was pointing to the figures on the bed, and Parker, beside him, was staring at them.

"Creepy," Parker said.

"I bet he gets a hundred thousand for that," John Joel said.

"What does he do? He puts plaster on his friends, like Goldfinger, or something?"

"I don't know. Nick said he watched them."

"Who'd go to sleep with somebody watching them? And if he's such a rich artist, how come he knows people who've got such lousy mattresses? They look like rafts with the air going out of them. You know the way a raft curls up before it flattens out?"

"You're the one who wanted to come."

"Hey. You mentioned it. I didn't even know there was a show."

"You wanted to come, didn't you?"

"I didn't say the stuff was bad. I just said the guy who did it must be a weirdo."

"You want to look at other stuff?"

"Nah. What about an éclair?"

"There's food downstairs, but I don't think they have stuff like éclairs."

"Let's get the train. My feet are starting to hurt. Too bad I didn't see this thing this morning. It might have given me something to talk to my shrink about. I could have said it was something I was doing this summer. The shrink always wants me to do things. Shrink sits around behind his desk all day, and I should be out running around so I can report on it."

"What do you go to a shrink for, anyway?"

"Same reason you're getting braces. My parents made me."

"What did they make you for?"

"Because they've all gone to shrinks. Who knows."

"Maybe you're really sick, Parker."

"Sure. Look at me. I'm sick. I'm hot and hungry, that's all."

"I've only got ten bucks left."

"Ten bucks? I thought you had twenty."

"No. Ten."

"For the train and everything?"

"Yeah."

"We've still got enough for éclairs," Parker said.

They took the elevator downstairs and went to the counter and got the package. "Ugly bug," Parker said, in falsetto, when he took the package, pretending to be staring at the picture of the woman inside through the wrapping. "Ugly, ugly, ugly," he chanted in a high squeak.

They walked up to Park Avenue and got a cab. Parker sat on the jump seat and smoked a cigarette, facing John Joel. "I wonder if it's worth anything. Some of those old pictures are. We could sell it and I'd say I lost it. She's always yelling about something."

"You wouldn't."

"Sure. What am I supposed to do, take this thing home and have to look at it?"

"You don't know where to sell a picture."

Parker thought it over. He didn't.

"I wish I had money," Parker said. "How can I get some money?"

"What do you want it for?"

"I just want it."

"You don't have any relatives?"

"I've got an uncle in Maine who's an alcoholic. He floats those little bottles of vanilla extract in the toilet tank. He's real crazy. He and his wife are poor. They're not going to give me any money."

"That's the only relative you've got?"

"A cousin I never see in Greenwich."

"You don't even have other kids in your family. You're lucky."

"If I had them, I'd get rid of them."

"Sure. Drown them like the kittens."

"My mother stopped me. I would have drowned them."

"You wouldn't have. You were just waiting for her to stop you."

"Old alley cat. Wasn't even ours."

"You liked them," John Joel said. "Did I tell you about how our dog got hit by a car? It was sort of my mother's dog. It ran out into the street and *smoosh*! It was all over the road. She talks about it all the time. 'My dog, my dog, my dog.' "

"I can see liking a dog. Not an old alley cat."

"So why'd you try to kill all the kittens?"

"My mother wanted me to. Then she changed her mind."

"She changed her mind because she was just joking, and you freaked her out."

"Lay off," Parker said. "I'm not a sissy like you. I'll do things. You think I'm the only person that ever thought to get rid of kittens?"

"I'm not a sissy," John Joel said.

"Oh yeah? You let your sister do anything she wants to you."

"Come off it."

"You do." Parker threw the package onto the seat of the cab. "Tear it up."

"For what? What would that prove?"

"That you'd do something. Go ahead and do it. Or did you think she was pretty?"

"Yeah. She was real pretty. She was your type, Parker."

"So get rid of her," Parker said.

"Yeah. Then you'll tell your mother I ripped it up."

"I'm not taking it home. Are you going to rip it, or am I?"

"Lexington Avenue okay?" the cab driver said.

"Okay," John Joel said.

"Go ahead," Parker said.

"Leave it in the cab if you don't want it. I don't want it."

"You're afraid to do it."

"*You're* afraid. So you're trying to put it on me."

John Joel paid the cab driver. They got out and walked into Grand Central.

"What's the matter with you? I bought you hamburgers and French fries and a milkshake, and you want an éclair out of me, and you're not speaking to me."

"Nothing's the matter. You just won't admit that you're a coward."

"Okay. I'm a coward. Now snap out of it."

"Yeah. You're saying that, but you don't believe it."

"Jesus," John Joel sighed.

"I might not have a lot of friends, but you don't either."

"Jesus. What's this, I'm with a five-year-old?"

"What did you talk about the cats for?"

"They never got to be cats. Your mother gave them away. They're gone. Big fucking deal. An alley cat."

"Tear it up. Go on," Parker said, shoving the corner of the package against John Joel's arm.

"You're gonna make me mad, Parker. I'm gonna leave you here and get on the train without you."

"I've got eight bucks."

"Okay. Then pay for your own ticket. And stop hassling me."

Parker got in line for a ticket. John Joel stood in the line opposite him and watched him out of the corner of his eye. Parker was sweating. It was hot in the station, but not that hot. Parker got this way a lot: He'd harp on something that didn't make any sense to begin with, and he wouldn't quit until somebody really sat on him. He was always shoved around in school. In fact, John Joel didn't really pal around with Parker in school. It was easy to avoid Parker, because Parker was twelve, and two classes ahead of him. When Parker wasn't around, he'd laugh with the other kids at things Parker said and did. But during the summer he saw a lot of Parker. Parker was always coming over, and nobody else called him when school was over. He called people a couple of times to see if they were home, but their parents always answered, so he couldn't be sure. He hung up when their parents answered.

Parker got his ticket first and walked away, heading for the gate. John Joel wondered if Parker would wait for him, or if Parker expected him to find him on the train. He decided that if Parker wasn't waiting, he wasn't going to look for him. He didn't care if Parker's mother gave him a ride home from the station or not. He'd call his own mother. She didn't like Parker, and if he told her they'd had a fight, she'd probably be glad.

Parker was waiting, just inside the gate. He was standing and watching a woman arguing with a man. The man was in his early twenties and he had a magazine that he was trying to give the woman, and she was objecting. She tried to involve one of the conductors in the discussion, but he walked past the two of them as if they weren't there. A lot of people began to come through the gate; a few looked at the two people quarreling, but nobody but Parker actually stood and watched. John Joel tried to get his attention so he'd move—they always kept the doors on the damn train closed until you'd walked half the length of it, and John Joel wanted to get on the train, where it might be cool. He sighed and stared at Parker.

In another few seconds the man walked off, and the woman stood there, talking to herself. "It was a wig," she kept saying.

John Joel gestured for Parker to come on. Parker paid no attention, and John Joel decided to give him ten more seconds and then start walking. Parker was crazy if he thought the woman wasn't going to turn on him and start giving him a rough time if he continued to stand there. Parker was always getting involved in situations where he'd put his face in the middle of something. It was happening now; the woman, slowly realizing that Parker was there, was turning toward him, complaining. Parker listened, a silly smirk on his face. Then, after a few sentences, he interrupted the woman, and John Joel was amazed to hear him asking her if she believed in the Kingdom of Heaven. "The *real* Kingdom of Heaven," she said to Parker loudly. "Not some man in a wig. That magazine wasn't really about Heaven." And then John Joel watched as Parker said something he couldn't understand. The woman didn't get it, either; she leaned forward and cocked her head. She stopped talking. Parker was doing all the talking. He was holding out the picture to her, still in its wrapping, telling her that the other man was just testing her, and that she had passed the test. Her reward was a picture of herself in the Afterlife. The woman began swaying as he talked to her. "Who are you?" John Joel heard the woman say. She began to back away from Parker. The crowds were thinning out. They were going to miss the train. He decided to give him five more seconds, and then walk away. Parker was getting into another one of his crazy routines, and what he was doing was sure not to make any sense. He stared, along with the woman, as Parker fanned his shirt away from his body with one hand, then pushed the package toward her. "You might as well see it," Parker said. "This is who you're going to be." The woman reached out for the package just as John Joel turned and began to walk quickly toward the train. There wasn't going to be a seat, just because Parker was so crazy, just because he was always kidding around. He turned to see Parker running behind him and the woman ripping open the package. A man with a beer can in his hand and a briefcase in his armpit rushed past her, past John Joel and Parker, mumbling to himself.

"*Now* what are you going to tell your mother?" John Joel said.

"I gave it away, didn't I?" Parker said. "Didn't I tell you?"

John Joel sat down in the first seat he saw. He didn't care if Parker stood all the way. But when he turned around he saw that Parker had found a seat not far behind him. John Joel had been right about feeling Parker staring at the back of his head. Okay: So Parker had given away the picture, if that meant so much to him. He wondered why he felt guilty himself; he wondered if the right thing to do wasn't to get off the train and run back and try to get the picture, if the crazy woman was still there. The doors closed and the train started to move out of the station.

They hadn't bought éclairs, and he was hungry. He had the nervous feeling in his stomach that meant he ought to eat something soon. He decided he'd get some peanuts from the bar car. Walking down the aisle past Parker, he was surprised to see that Parker had his bandanna out, and was rubbing his eyes. Parker was crying. Sitting on the train, crying. John Joel kept walking, and pretended not to know him.

When they got off the train, John Joel waited on the platform for Parker. He half thought that Parker wouldn't get off, but he did. His eyes weren't red and the bandanna was back in his pocket. Parker had gotten so sweaty that his shirt clung to him in rivulets of wrinkles. Parker shook his head to the side, and if his hair hadn't been so damp, it would have fallen across his forehead the way Parker liked it to. He gave up and smoothed it straight back, and as he walked, he took a cigarette out of the package and put it in his mouth. He did his trick of lighting a match by bending one forward, closing the book, and striking it with his thumb. He held the match to the cigarette and shook the flame out.

"I'm walking," Parker said.

"Walking? All the way home? You'd never be able to walk all the way home."

"She won't do shit to me," Parker said. "She knows I'd tell the shrink. She's gonna be half-crocked by the time I get home anyway."

"Come on, Parker. Call."

"I'm not going to New York with you anymore," Parker said.

John Joel sighed and kept walking. He felt guilty about the picture being gone and didn't know why. It wasn't his fault. Parker was always acting crazy, and it was his mother's fault for asking him to do an errand like that. He tried to imagine what his own mother would do if she had sent him for a picture and he had done what Parker did. She'd probably find some way to start talking about her dog. It would probably remind her of her dog.

"You'll get your money," Parker said. "Give me the stubs and I'll show them to her and you'll get your money."

John Joel reached in his pants pocket. His pants were tight, and he had to worm his finger down hard to bring up the two small ticket stubs. He handed them to Parker, and Parker smiled.

"Now, watch," Parker said. Parker stopped on the sidewalk, away from where everybody was walking. He put one stub on top of the other and squatted. John Joel knew what he was going to do. He was going to light them.

He wanted to fight with Parker. He was afraid of getting hurt, but he was so tired of Parker and his craziness that he wanted to hit him. Instead, before he really thought about it, he tried to push Parker over, but Parker just braced himself with his left arm and didn't fall. His right hand was already holding the burning match to the ticket stubs.

Some man with a briefcase looked over his shoulder at the two of them, and John Joel met the man's eyes. The man gave a little smile and kept walking. John Joel kept watching him, but he went into the bar across from the station without turning around again. John Joel stared at the door of the bar, at the other people walking in. Then he shrugged and sighed and looked down at Parker.

"Big deal. So you burned them," John Joel said. "You don't want to be friends, we don't have to be friends."

He walked away. He hoped that Parker wouldn't follow him, because he thought there was going to be a fight. Only he didn't think that he was going to start it anymore: He thought that Parker was. He kept walking and didn't turn around. He was trying to think where the nearest phone was, so that he could call his mother to come get him. As he walked, he kept thinking of the woman in the picture, and how ugly some women could be. He wondered what Parker's mother was going to do to him, whether Parker might not tell her what he'd really done.

Then she was there: Parker's mother, in the Oldsmobile convertible, a white visor pulled low on her forehead. She played tennis all day and got very tan in the summer. When she pulled over and raised her hand to wave, John Joel saw she had a sweatband on her wrist.

"Where's Parker?" she said.

He shrugged. "Back at the train," he said, guessing.

"Well, why is he there?" Marge Pendergast was sitting next to her, drinking something from a Styrofoam cup. Her hair was all tangled, and she wasn't brushing it out of her eyes. They both had on tennis dresses.

"Get in," Parker's mother said. "I had a feeling you'd get this train."

"Nah," he said. "Thanks. I've got to go somewhere."

"What are you talking about?" Parker's mother said. "I'm giving you a ride home. Where's Parker?"

"At the train," John Joel said again.

"You really don't want a ride?" Parker's mother said.

"No, thanks."

"Go on," Marge Pendergast said. "I'm hot and I want a shower."

"John Joel, while I'm here, why don't you get in the car and we'll find Parker and I can drop you where you're going."

"No," he said, and turned and started to walk away from the car.

He listened for the car to pull away, and in a few seconds it did, with a screech of tires. He wondered if she'd find Parker, and he half hoped that he was gone—that there was no chance that she'd find him and that Parker would try to blame him, somehow, for the lost picture. He wondered if that woman in the picture ever suspected how she'd end up, the trouble her picture would cause. He regretted all the money he'd spent on Parker. He wished that he had another friend, because even if Parker called him, he wasn't ever going to see him again.

A mile up the road, he went into the food store and bought Pepperidge Farm Mint Milanos. He started eating them as he stood in line waiting to buy them, two bites to a cookie. Outside the store, when he finished the first layer, he took the paper cup out and wadded it until he made it into a ball in his fist. Then he threw it, as if he meant to strike somebody out. The ball had no weight and only went a few feet before it hit the ground.

"Why don't you pick that up?" a woman in the parking lot said, opening her car door.

He had only gone a few yards when he felt, for the first time, a painful sting: He had gotten a blister on his little toe in New York.

II

"COME WITH ME," Louise said. "It'll be fun. It'll be more fun than lying around the house all day."

"I don't want to," John Joel said.

"Come on," Louise said. "Tiffy's made lots of picnic food and we'll go berry-picking. I'll make a strawberry pie. But you have to come help me."

"Mary doesn't have to come."

"Mary is at Angela's. Come on. Why do I have to urge my children to *move*? It's not going above eighty today. It's a perfect day to pick berries."

"Why can't I stay here?" John Joel said.

"To tell you the truth, you can. But I wish you'd come with me. I know you're depressed about something, and if you won't tell me, at least let me try to cheer you up."

"I don't like Tiffy," he said.

"How could you not like Tiffy? You'll like her. You hardly know her. Your father badmouths every woman I know. Don't pick up all your father's prejudices."

"I don't even see him," John Joel said.

"You see him on the weekends," Louise said. "Come on. If we

start talking about this, *I'm* going to get depressed, and I'm in a good mood today."

"What am I supposed to say to people who want to know how come he's never around?"

"Is that what's bothering you?" Louise said. She sat on the sofa, across from the chair where he was sitting and reading a *Zap* comic.

He nodded yes. It was a lie, but he wanted to see what she'd say.

"Say we're separated," she said.

"He's here on the weekends," John Joel said. He hadn't wanted her to say that. He hadn't thought she would.

"Ask your father what you should say. As far as I'm concerned, it's an adequate answer to nosy people to say we're separated."

"It's going to be plenty hot getting berries today."

"I think you can stand it. Last time: Are you coming?"

He put down the comic book and got out of the chair. "Mary doesn't have to come," he said again, but he didn't want her to be coming, and he knew that his mother knew that. She didn't say anything. She got up and stretched and went into the kitchen and began taking containers out of the cabinet.

"Wear an old shirt and shorts so it doesn't matter if they get stained," she said.

He went upstairs. It had been three days since he and Parker had been in New York, and Parker hadn't called him to apologize. Even if he had, he wouldn't have seen Parker again, but he wanted to be able to hang up on him. He hoped that Parker had gotten into trouble with his mother.

He tried to put on his madras shorts, but they wouldn't zip up all the way. He put on a pair of cut-off denim shorts that didn't button, but that zipped and that had a reliable zipper. He put on a white shirt with a rip down the back, from snagging himself when he was getting out of the tree. His mother never mended things that were ripped. She'd approve of his choosing this shirt to go berry-picking in.

"Why are you so blue today?" she said when he came downstairs.

"I'm not. Lay off."

133

"I can't even inquire about how my children are feeling without being told to lay off?"

"I thought we were going out," he said.

"As soon as I find a bag to put these containers in."

"What's for lunch?" he said.

"I don't know. Tiffy's bringing a picnic."

"Chicken," he said. "I'll bet you."

"It probably *is* chicken. Will that be all right with you?"

He held the door open for her. She walked out, swinging the bag she was carrying, humming a song. The car was hot inside from sitting in the sun. She opened her door, then went around to his side and unlocked it and opened that door. Heat poured out of the car.

"You never told me what you did in New York," she said, getting in her side, throwing the bag into the back seat. He got in and closed his door. His shorts were tight across his stomach.

"Nothing much," he said.

"Nothing much. New York City. If you want some suggestions, I can offer a few the next time you go in."

"I'm sick of New York," he said. "It's too hot in the summer."

"Take the boat out to the Statue of Liberty. Remember when we all did that last summer? Or the summer before, I guess. I love that ride. It's not too long, and it's so cool. I was telling your father that we ought to go to Nantucket this summer and rent a boat for a week. Would you like that?"

"Sure. I guess."

"Tell him," she said. "If we gang up on him, he'll take us."

"Isn't he taking a vacation?" John Joel said.

"Of course he'll take a vacation. But we're going to have to persuade him to take it in Nantucket."

"Maybe he's going on vacation alone," John Joel said.

His mother was turning on the air conditioning, steering with one hand as she rolled up her window.

"Why do you say that?" she said.

He shrugged. "Maybe he'd go alone."

"Did he say that to you?"

"No, he didn't say it. I just thought that since you're separated he might not take a vacation with us this year."

"Yes he will," his mother said. She didn't sound sure. The air conditioning was already making his knees cold. He drew up his legs.

"Are you going to tell me about the fight you had with Parker?"

"I told you. It wasn't any fight. He's just stupid."

"I'm not too crazy about him myself. Did something happen in New York with Parker—is that why you don't want to go back?"

"I'm going back next week. I've got to get braces, don't I?"

"I mean for fun. And yes, you have to get braces. I know you don't like the idea, but you wouldn't like crooked teeth when you grew up, either."

"I wouldn't care."

"You'd care then."

"I wouldn't care," he said again.

"God," she said, sighing. "Maybe you wouldn't. You're a pretty blasé kid."

"What does that mean?"

"Blasé? It means you let everything roll off your back like water." She smiled. "I didn't realize what an old-fashioned expression that was," she said. "I guess it is."

She always came to a full stop at stop signs. It drove him crazy. A dog was running at the side of the road. He waited for her to say something about her dog. She looked, but didn't say anything.

"I'll tell you one thing Parker did. We went to the museum and he told me his mother would pay me back if I showed her the tickets, and then he—" He broke off, and decided it would be better to hedge on the truth. "Parker tore up the ticket stubs."

"On purpose?"

"Sure, on purpose."

"What was the point of that?" she said.

He shrugged. "He's stupid."

"The other thing that surprises me is that you went to a museum. What did you see?"

"Where'd you think we'd go? Some porn movie?"

"I do have some faith in you, John Joel. I just didn't think the two of you would go to a museum. I think it's wonderful that you did."

"Nick took me the week before," he said.

"Really? And you liked it and went back?"

"I sort of liked it. It was these plaster people."

"Oh," she said. "You saw the Segal show at the Whitney."

He shrugged.

"Well, tell me about it," she said.

"I read what he wrote about one of the things, and he said it was his friends. One of them was all blue, and it had a face like a goat."

"I'd like to see that," she said.

"Some of it was dumb," he said. He decided not to tell her about the people naked in bed, or the women's bodies.

"Do you like Nick?" she asked him.

"Sure. He's okay."

"Just okay?"

"I don't love him or anything."

"Your father does. Your father worships him."

John Joel shrugged. "He's a nice guy," he said.

"Maybe I'm just jealous," she said. She turned down the air conditioner. They were passing the reservoir, with the geyser of white water shooting up.

"Nick's got a pretty girlfriend," he said.

"A lot of them," she said. "Was this one black or foreign? Or white for a change?"

"She had *huge* eyes and she was pretty. She worked at some department store. Nick was surprised to see her, when she showed up outside the museum. Dad was late. He finally showed."

"Nick finds a new one every week," she said.

"Her name was Nina," he said. "I just remembered."

"Nina who works in a department store. Let me guess: Bloomie's?"

"She didn't say."

"Bloomie's. And she was twenty-five, right?"

"You would have liked her," he said.

"Right?" she said.

"About," he said.

"They don't come over twenty-five. That model gets discontinued."

"You sound like you're talking to Dad."

"I'm sorry," she said. "I guess I envy those lunches—flirting with somebody nice, all of it paid for with an expense account."

"You want to flirt with somebody?" he said.

"Oh, you know what I mean. Or maybe you don't."

"You shouldn't dislike Nick," he said. "He's okay."

"So I hear. Constantly."

"You're the one who wanted to talk about him," he said.

They were going up the steep hill that led to Tiffy's house. Another dog, out on a lawn; this time it was a German shepherd, the kind his mother's had been, and he would have bet all the money in his wallet that she'd say something. He would never forget being out on the front lawn with his mother the day Mr. Blue was hit by a car. His own scream had sounded like a woman's, and his mother had opened her mouth but made no sound at all. The paper boy—there had been a new paper boy, and he would throw the paper onto the lawn from the other side of the street . . . his mother's dog had been standing at the side of the house, and it had seen the paper boy raise his arm with the rolled-up paper, and suddenly the dog had gone bounding into the street because he thought the paper boy was playing "get the stick" with him. He had lunged into a car with a heavy thump. Now, John Joel looked at his mother. She was looking in the rear-view mirror and had seen the dog, but wasn't saying anything. She said: "This is pretty in here. It's quiet, too—off the main road."

"Do you wish you worked in New York?" he said.

"Why do you ask that?"

"I thought you might."

"Sometimes," she said. "Sometimes I like it here. I think I'm lucky that we have enough money that I don't have to work and that when the sun is shining and I'm feeling pretty good, I can go meet a friend and have a picnic and pick strawberries. It's a pretty nice life." She came to a full stop at the stop sign, then went slowly forward about twenty feet and stopped again, where she could see. "I don't know what kind of a job I could get anyway," she said.

"Tiffy's got a job."

"Tiffy has a Ph.D. and teaches at NYU and will probably be booted out before she gets tenure, on general principles."

"Couldn't you be a teacher?" he said.

"What's this? You're trying to send your mother off to work?"

"Just if you wanted a job," he said. "You could get a job."

"Thank you," she said. "Seriously. I'm glad you have faith in me."

While he wasn't looking, a little dog ran across a lawn close to the car, and she said, "I wish I had had a job when Mr. Blue died. I don't know why I took it so hard, but to this day it's all I can do to look at a dog that reminds me of Mr. Blue in any way. That one was nothing like him—just the way it was having fun, running across the lawn after something."

"I was talking about the cats to Parker. He said his mother told him to drown them."

"You shouldn't talk about that," his mother said. "He's going to a psychiatrist. Things like that you should probably leave to the two of them to talk about."

"Yeah, but you don't even think he should tell the truth?"

"I think he's embarrassed the story got around. I don't know how it did. I think his mother told some people. I think part of Parker's problem is that his mother is more interested in everybody else than she is in her own son."

"Yeah, but he said it was an alley cat."

Louise laughed. "A two-hundred-dollar chocolate point," she said. "That's crazy, too: his mother paying that kind of money for a cat, and then having it put to sleep. It wasn't the cat's fault that he tried to go after it and the kittens. You'd think at least she would have tried to find a good home for it."

"She's pretty strange, too," John Joel said.

"Everybody is, I guess. Everybody has their little secrets and their little half-truths. All those people at lunch in New York hedging and dodging like football players."

"I know something about her even she doesn't know," John Joel said.

"About Parker's mother?"

"Yeah. I shouldn't tell."

"How could you know something she doesn't know?"

"Promise you won't tell?"

Louise shrugged. "I can't imagine what I'd find out about her that I'd care about. All she does is play tennis, anyway. Does it have to do with her tennis game?"

"No. It's that Parker put a pinhole in her diaphragm."

Louise snapped her head around to look at him. "What did you say?" she said.

He blushed. Parker had had to explain to him what it meant. Now he knew what it meant, and he was suddenly embarrassed to have mentioned it. He should have told her, instead, about the naked plaster people in the museum.

"What?" she said again.

"Parker did it. With a pin."

"Parker *said* he did it. Parker wouldn't *do* that, would he?"

"Sure," he said. "Parker'd do it."

She was still staring at him. "You realize—" she began.

"I know," he said, and shrugged. "Parker thinks it's a real good joke. He says it's her fault if she doesn't check."

"But that's *awful*," she said.

"Parker found it. It was in her top drawer. He thought it was a big compact. He opened it and didn't see any mirror, and then he found out later what it was, and he pricked a hole in it."

"She'll see it, won't she?" Louise said. "Does Parker think that's funny? She'd never *dream* Parker would find her diaphragm and do that."

"She ought to. He'd do anything."

"What do you mean?" Louise said. "Has he done something worse than that?"

"He just does strange stuff. What I told you about the ticket stubs isn't exactly the way it happened. He burned them, on the sidewalk outside the train station. He does stuff there's no point in doing."

"He's very disturbed."

"He's no friend of mine," John Joel said.

"But honey—are you sure about that other thing? Mightn't he just brag that he'd pulled a stunt like that but not really do it?"

"No," John Joel said. "He'd do it. He wouldn't care."

"Imagine Georgia having another little monster like Parker," Louise said. She brushed her hair out of her face. "I didn't know you knew what a diaphragm was," she said.

He blushed again, looked out the window. "I knew," he said.

"But that's just *horrible*," she said. "Parker's a monster."

"He rolls cigarettes like they're joints, but they're not. He carries them in the pack with his Salems and he smokes them going down the street with his hand cupped around them and he drags on them funny, like they're joints. He smokes a pack a day of real cigarettes."

"You don't smoke with him, do you?"

"He's no friend of mine."

"But do you?"

"No," John Joel said. He was embarrassed that he didn't, that he wasn't lying to her. He didn't know why he'd told her so much. He slid forward in the seat and looked out the window, as they pulled into Tiffy's driveway. There were day lilies, very tall, falling forward into the driveway, and there were daisies and tall electric-pink phlox. Tiffy's husband was working in the garden, staking a rosebush. He waved with a pair of pruning shears.

"Hi," Louise said, getting out of the car. "Tiffy inside?"

"She's in the garage," he said. "Hi," he said, pointing the shears at John Joel.

"Hi," John Joel said.

"Hi, Tiffy," Louise called. Tiffy came out of the garage, wiping her forehead on her arm. She had her hair in braids, and for a second that made her look, to John Joel, a little like Nina, in New York. She had on white shorts, and a white halter top, and she was carrying a plant she had just repotted. "I have to take a quick shower and then I'm all ready to go," she said. "Come inside where it's cool."

They followed her into the house. Louise pulled out a chair and sat at the kitchen table. John Joel pulled out a chair for himself and sat down. The shorts were cutting into his thighs. It smelled like chicken in her kitchen, and he looked at the clock to see how close to lunchtime it was. It was noon. If he were home, he could be eating.

"There's wine in the fridge," Tiffy called downstairs. The water went on in the shower.

Louise didn't get up. "Do you want a Coke if she has one?" she said. He shook his head no. He wanted a Coke, but he wanted more to get out of the house. He wanted to pick the berries and have the picnic and have it over with. The magazine on the table wasn't worth looking at: *The New Republic*. All Tiffy's cups were pottery, and Coke tasted funny in cups like that. He thought about the milkshake he had bought Parker and wished he had his money back.

Louise got up and took a blue pottery cup down from the shelf over the sink and went to the refrigerator. She poured wine into her cup from the jug and put the jug back in the refrigerator. Tiffy's refrigerator was always interesting: It was filled with colors instead of with wrapped packages: apples loose on a shelf, peaches, limes and lemons, pale-sea-green bottles of Perrier, orange juice in a glass bottle so that you could see the deep-orange color. Tiffy was hollering something from upstairs, but they couldn't tell what she was saying.

She came down in a few minutes, in green slacks and a black halter, wearing tennis shoes, her hair still braided, but sopping wet.

"Let's go, let's go," she said, picking up the basket on the kitchen table. She said to John Joel: "What are you doing this summer?"

"Nothing much," he said.

"My car," Tiffy said. "I cleaned it inside, and everybody has to praise it."

"It looks wonderful," Louise said.

"I want to sit in the back," John Joel said.

"There's no place to vacuum your car around here," Tiffy said. "I gave up. Last night I wet a sponge and sponged this car clean. It was full of grit and dog hair from my sister's dog. It looked horrible. Does it smell like dog? I can't even tell anymore." Tiffy waved to her husband as she pulled out of the driveway. He had on a straw hat, and he tipped it as the car pulled away.

"Now tell me what you've *really* been doing this summer," Tiffy said, looking in the rear-view mirror. He slid around in the back seat. He couldn't think what to tell her except to tell the story about going to the museum again. So he told her about the show he had seen, or tried to, but she broke in: She'd seen it, too. And Calder's Circus. She started talking about that, how quirky it was, how it always made her smile to see it. How she wanted to shrink and get inside with the circus animals and performers, and tumble around in the case with them at night, because she was sure they did. "I don't know," she said to Louise. "Maybe I'm just getting old, but when I went through the Segal show, I felt so frustrated. I felt like those things were so *still*, and when I stopped to look at Calder's Circus again on the way out, I felt like they had little hearts beating, and that their little eyes blinked and their mouths smiled when they were alone. When Segal's people were alone, I thought they'd be just as still. That they couldn't move, under any conditions."

Tiffy's car was an old Cadillac, a black 1955 Cadillac, and it rode as though the shocks were completely worn-out. He had been in her car once before, and he just remembered that it had made him sick. It was hot in the back seat, too, even though Tiffy was driving fast enough that wind blew through the car and slapped him in the face. He tried to concentrate on not being sick. He kept thinking about the picture of the relative that Parker had given away, of how strange the woman in the picture looked. Pictures of his mother when she was a young girl looked the same way; not that she looked anything like Parker's funny-faced relative, but the pose was the same: The faces looked flat, and they were close to the camera. There was a picture on his father's dresser—what used to be his father's dresser—of his mother when she graduated from high school. It was a hand-colored photograph, his mother had told him, and the pearls she wore around her neck were the same color as her teeth and the whites of her eyes. She had on a pink sweater in the picture, and a barrette in her hair, and he could not imagine his mother looking that way. As mothers went, she was pretty. She wore a little make-up, unlike Tiffy, and she didn't have a horsey face like Parker's mother, and nobody was as ugly as Marge Pendergast. All her children were ugly, too. He wished that he looked more like his mother or father. He wondered if he would be better-looking if he weren't fat. Mary wasn't fat, but she wasn't very good-looking, and he thought that was true objectively —not just because she was his sister and he hated her.

Going back to his grandmother's house in Rye, the day he had had lunch with Nick and his father and the girl whose name he had forgotten again, his father had asked him if he liked any girls. He hated to be asked that, because there weren't any girls he liked. So he had made up a lie about a girl he had liked who had transferred to another school in the middle of the year. He had even described her: bangs, glasses, tall. They had been in the drinking car, standing up. He had been having a ginger ale, and his father had been having a gin and tonic. "What girls do *you* like?" he had asked his father. It had just come out, before he realized what a ridiculous question it was. His father had been taken aback by it. His father had said that he liked Louise. "What did you think of Nick's girlfriend?" his father had asked him after a while. And for some reason he hadn't wanted to let on that he thought she was pretty. He had shrugged. His father had said, "Not your type, huh?" There was another long pause; then, finishing his drink, his father had said: "Well, I think she's quite pretty."

In the front seat, Louise was telling Tiffy about the last picnic the family had gone on.

"There were these two silly girls at the park on Friday night. They were with two boys, and all four of them were drunk, and I actually envied them for having such a mindless good time."

"There's nothing wrong with having a mindless good time once in a while."

"At least I said something that night that I'd wanted to say for a long while. Not that there was any response to it, but I finally said it. It was about my dog. I said that I wished I had the dog back, and that I could be playing 'get the stick' with Mr. Blue. No wonder I liked the dog. It was so dogged. It was just like me. It would've played 'get the stick' until it fell over dead, and I'd go on those stupid picnics and trudge through the snow if he kept saying we should go there." Louise sighed. "I'm sorry," she said. "I talk about the dog too much."

"You don't talk about it very much," Tiffy said.

"She does," John Joel said. "All the time."

Tiffy pulled into a graveled drive, in the shape of a half circle, and parked behind a yellow truck. Tiffy had found out about this place from a friend: It wasn't advertised, but one day a week the farmer let people come and pick berries, and he weighed them on a scale on his back porch. Tiffy always knew about things that no one else knew about: meetings in people's apartments, places to pick strawberries, places to swim without getting caught, books that had been written but not published. Whenever she talked about a book, she'd say: "You have to read it when it comes out," and when she talked about a movie she'd seen, it was always "at a screening." He could understand why his mother was in awe of Tiffy, but she was so unlike his mother in so many ways that he was surprised his mother liked her so much. According to his mother, Tiffy did everything right. His father didn't take Tiffy seriously. His father just thought that Tiffy was pretentious and talked a lot. He hoped that his mother wouldn't tell his father about this day on the weekend, because they were sure to get into a fight about it.

As he followed his mother and Tiffy through the high grass to the strawberry field, he picked up snatches of the conversation. Tiffy was talking about what was wrong, politically, with *The Deer Hunter*. She kept stressing that word—*politically*. His mother nodded and didn't have much to say. It was hot in the field, and he wished he had on looser clothes. Tiffy had left the basket with the food back in the car. They probably wouldn't be eating for another hour. He swatted a yellow butterfly away, and when it fluttered he saw that it was a butterfly and a smaller butterfly, or a moth. They swirled up and flew away. A mosquito buzzed in his ear.

There were about ten people over the crest of the hill, picking strawberries that grew in neat rows. He hated the idea of bending over in the heat to pick berries and wondered why he'd come. There was no way out of it. He took the container his mother held out and went to one of the rows and began groping under the leaves for the berries. Every berry was ripe and large, so it didn't matter what he pulled off. He thought about the pie his mother had said she'd make, and hoped that she'd make two. He hoped that Mary would eat at Angela's.

His mother and Tiffy were talking about his father. He moved to another row, where he wouldn't hear them. He had found out enough. He had found out they were separated. He suddenly felt sorry for himself, and a little dizzy in the heat: What if they had done it when he was a baby, what if they had given him away, even, and he had been an orphan? It would be nice if they had given Mary away and kept him. Brandt was already gone. He envied Parker for being an only child and wondered what made him so messed up when he didn't have anybody he had to share things with or be polite to, except his parents. Nobody would put crap in Parker's bed that he'd roll over on or cut his foot on. If Parker thought it would be fun to have a brother or a sister, he should just spend a day in his house and see how awful Mary was. He had bought Parker two hamburgers and French fries and a Coke and a chocolate milkshake, and Parker had set fire to the ticket stubs. He bent over too far and lost his balance and remembered shoving Parker and not knocking him over. He thought about seeing Parker one more time—maybe waiting until fall and ganging up on him with some of the other kids—and letting him have it. Then Parker would have something to tell his shrink about. Then he could talk about how he was such an asshole that he'd gotten slugged.

"Are you scowling?" his mother said, "or is the sun too much for you?"

"Sun," he said.

"Do you think we have enough?" she said.

He nodded yes. He thought that Tiffy would want to keep picking, though, and he guessed right. He and his mother started back for the farmer's porch before Tiffy did.

"What's the matter?" she said to him.

"Nothing's the matter. Everybody's always asking me what I'm doing and how I'm doing and what girls do I like . . ."

"Who asked you that?" she said.

What had he said that for? He didn't want to go into it. "Parker," he said.

"Normal enough questions, all of them, aren't they?" she said.

"Yeah," he said, kicking a rock. "Everything's normal."

"Well," she said, "I wouldn't say that about Parker."

"He's not my friend anyway, so I don't care."

"I think he *is* your friend," she said. "Why don't you call him and make up?"

"Make up? He's an asshole. Parker's an asshole."

"I think he's disturbed, but everybody can make mistakes. Maybe you ought to overlook what he did the other day, if it's going to bother you so much that he's not your friend anymore."

"It doesn't bother me," he said.

"It bothers me that I don't have many friends. Tiffy's my best friend, and I don't have a world in common with her. Sometimes I just think she feels sorry for me."

"Why would she feel sorry for you?"

145

"What reason would she have for liking me so much? There's the whole faculty of NYU to talk to if she gets lonesome, and she always knows better than I do what's going on. She tells me about things. I never tell *her* about things."

"You tell her about Dad."

"Does that bother you? That I talk to people?"

"I don't care who you talk to," he said.

"You say that you don't care so much that I don't know when you're serious." She ate one of the strawberries. "Good," she said. "I guess it's cheating to start eating them before they're weighed, though."

"Parker'd probably burn them. He'd probably pick them, then try to light them."

"Strawberries flambé?" she said. "Maybe people just take Parker too seriously."

"How come you're on his side all of a sudden?"

"Oh, I'm not really on his side. I just hate to think so badly of him when he's just a twelve-year-old child. I was pretty strange when I was twelve years old."

"How?" he said.

"Well, I guess you'd call it being very straight. I wouldn't let anybody cut my hair. My hair was my proudest possession. And I was very shy and very quiet. I played the piano. Did you know that?"

"What for?" he said.

"What for?"

"Yeah. Did you want to be in an orchestra or something?"

"I never thought about it. I just liked music. My friends all took music lessons. But in those days girls didn't think in terms of a career, the way they do now."

"Huh," he snorted. "Mary with a career."

"Mary's very interested in music, actually."

"Junk music."

"She likes music. That's the important thing."

"I like to think about Mary having a career. She could be a nurse and do mercy killings."

"If you did some nice things for your sister, she might do some nice things for you."

"What? Leave me alone?"

"I don't know what the truth of that is either, John Joel. Do you two really dislike each other that much?"

"I'd just as soon have Parker for a brother as her as a sister." He ate a strawberry. He wished it were a cookie. "She's just as crazy as Parker is."

"You know she isn't."

"You don't know."

"What don't I know?"

"Never mind. I'm not ratting on Mary."

"Why did you say it if you didn't want me to know?"

He didn't answer her, because the farmer was on his way out of the house to greet them. "Going to make a pumpkin pie, are you?" he joked, looking at all the containers filled with strawberries.

Tiffy was running to catch up with them. "There's a little snake in the grass. It's thin, and had stripes, and it was about this long." She held her hands apart.

The farmer pretended to be horrified. He spread his arms as wide as they'd go.

"Is it just harmless?" Tiffy said. "It didn't go away when I was picking, it came toward me, sort of."

"Friendly," the farmer said. "Just a grass snake."

"I was so nervous I left my basket up there."

"John Joel," his mother said, "will you go get it for her?"

He took his time going back with the basket, and he swung it and let some of the strawberries fall out. He was thinking that Nick wouldn't give Tiffy the time of day. He thought Nick was a lot cooler than Tiffy. He wondered, because he liked Nick more than any of his mother's women friends, if he was a queer. When he got back with the basket, Tiffy was talking to his mother.

". . . the role of women in certain fairy tales," Tiffy was saying. "I guess it's obvious to people now that most often it's the women who are monsters or the ones who have to wait for Prince Charming. But I was wondering today what those fairy tales would sound like if even the most evil, stupid women told it from their perspective. Even granting that they were evil. I wonder if a lot of them weren't evil just because they were so worn down. I can imagine the fisherman's wife thinking: If he chooses this as his work, then let him have the long days, the cold and the risk. Let him pull with all his might, and instead of coming up with a fat, golden bass, let him snag a sunken tire. Let it be as round as the world, with a great hole in the center." Tiffy was talking loudly and waving her arms. "If that's what the man wants, then let him have that."

He handed the basket to his mother.

"Thank you," Tiffy said, reaching for it. "That was awfully nice of you."

"How come you're a feminist and you're afraid of snakes?"

"What?" Tiffy said, looking embarrassed. "Being afraid of a snake has to do with politics?"

"John Joel," his mother said.

"What about lunch?" he said. He was tired of waiting for it.

The farmer tipped the berries onto the scale and wrote down how much Tiffy owed on a white pad stained with strawberry juice. He showed her the figure but didn't read it out loud, as if it were confidential. Tiffy reached into her pants pocket and handed him a ten-dollar bill.

"Maybe there's someplace cooler than here to have a picnic," his mother said. "Let's go somewhere near the water, if you feel like it."

"It's fine with me," Tiffy said. "Actually, we could sit under the big tree in my backyard if you'd like to. Isn't that crazy? To put everything in a picnic basket and then end up on the back lawn? Like some funny French film or something."

"Her car makes me sick," John Joel said to his mother, loud enough for Tiffy to hear him.

"What?" his mother said. She also looked hot. He thought that if he hadn't come along, his mother and Tiffy would probably have had a good time. He felt sorry for her, and he wondered why she had insisted—almost insisted—that he come. At least he was better company than Mary. Mary was always looking for a fight, and all he wanted to do was keep quiet. "It makes me carsick," he said.

"Well, sit in the front this time and see if that makes it better," his mother said. "I'll sit in the back."

"That's not going to help," he said. He didn't know if it would or not, but he didn't want his mother in the back seat. He didn't want to ride next to Tiffy, and he didn't want his mother to have to be in the back. "Forget it," he said. "I didn't puke."

"John Joel," she said, "don't be ridiculous. It's nothing to be ashamed of if you felt sick. We'll have Tiffy drive slower, and there won't be as much motion in the front seat, I don't think."

"Come on," he said, kicking a rock. They were in the driveway now, and Tiffy was walking ahead of them. "Forget it, okay?" he said. He knew that if his mother didn't forget it, he was going to cry.

"Just give it a try," his mother said.

"I don't want to," he said. "Come on. Forget it."

"Why?" she said. She put her hand on his shoulder and tried to get him to look at her. "Why does everybody try to fight me on the smallest thing?"

"Get off," he said, shrugging her hand off. Her hand felt light on his shoulder, and warm. It made him realize how sweaty he was all over, once the material was pressed against his skin that way. Suddenly he wanted to be out of his clothes, somewhere cool. He thought about the men and women, the white-plaster men and women, in the museum. He thought that it would be wonderful to be so white and still.

"Tiffy," his mother said, "let John Joel ride up front with you. The motion in the back seat is making him sick."

"You don't mind riding with a feminist?" Tiffy said to him.

"I didn't even want to come," he said, whirling to face his mother.

"What am I supposed to do, just let you lie around the house all summer? You're ten years old. You must be interested in something besides hanging out with your father and Nick and going to lunches with whatever pretty girl there is that week. Last summer you went fishing," she said. "What's gotten into everybody? My son tells his father jokes about feminists, and my daughter has to be forced to leave her shrine to Peter Frampton to endure an evening with the family."

"I'm sorry," Tiffy said. "I was just teasing. Get in the car, both of you."

He tried to get in the back seat, but his mother climbed in before he could. She was faster than he was—faster and thinner, and she just squeezed around him. He glared at her, not appreciating it at all. He got in next to Tiffy and rolled down his window. The strawberries were at his feet, and he had the urge to take his foot and just start mashing them. He *did* have a better time with Nick and his father, and if he wanted to be left alone, he didn't see why he couldn't be left alone. Mary got out of everything by having somewhere to go. She was always at Angela's and he was around the house, so his mother picked on him. Maybe being an orphan wasn't so bad; if you were an orphan, maybe people didn't notice you all the time. He pushed his hair out of his eyes. Tiffy was humming, pretending everything was all right. His mother was in the back seat, not making any effort to talk. And the car was going over ruts in the road, and he hoped again that he wouldn't be sick. He didn't want anything else to happen. He just wanted to go home. He wanted to eat. And he wanted to slam Parker into a wall, break his arm for the way he'd acted. He was acting badly, he knew, but Parker acted even worse, and for that, he wanted to kill him. He was also sure that Parker hadn't called—that if he had stayed there all day, he still wouldn't have had the pleasure of answering the phone and hearing Parker apologize, so he could hang up on him.

His mother began laughing in the back seat. First just a sound he thought might be a hiccough, then a genuine laugh. She put her hand over her mouth and tried to stifle the laugh, but it was no good: She just took her hand away and fell over against the door. Tiffy looked at her in the rear-view mirror. "Dare I ask?" Tiffy said. "Oh," Louise said, "I can't tell you, but I was thinking about a secret John Joel told me on the way over, and it just—" She couldn't get her breath. He found himself smiling, though he didn't mean to. "It just puts everything in perspective. It's such a *dirty* trick that one person pulled on another. I wish I had nerve like that, sometimes. I really do. It's really really horrible, but it's so awful and so funny." She was wiping her eyes. He turned around and saw her wiping her eyes.

"You can't tell," he said.

"Oh," she said, "I wasn't going to tell. It's just all so *ghastly*. It's selling you such a bill of goods to tell you that you should get married and have a family and be *secure*. Jesus! What your own family will do to you."

"This sounds like a real whopper," Tiffy said.

"It is," Louise said. "But don't worry. It's not somebody you like. This is somebody who almost deserves it." She started to laugh again, and he thought he was going to be sick—it was as if her laughter was shaking the car. There was noise in his head he couldn't get rid of, and if he was going to not be sick, he needed to be quiet to fight it down. But it passed. It passed, and his mother stopped laughing and by the time they got to Tiffy's she wasn't even smiling.

They had the picnic in the backyard, and when a bird flying over dropped its white shit on the sheet Tiffy had spread on the grass, Tiffy said it was symbolic. Her laughter wasn't like his mother's, though; it sounded entirely different.

They were riding home from Tiffy's house, and he was thinking about being on the train with his father. One of the bad things about being ten years old was that he wasn't yet six feet tall like his father, and in all kinds of small ways, being short was an embarrassment. If you were fully grown, you could look at something in a museum out of the corner of your eye if you didn't really want to be seen looking at it. You could stand in the drinking car of the train and just put your fingertips out to steady yourself when the train swayed or lurched, instead of having to reach up and hang on like a child. He always got tired standing on the train and wondered why his father didn't. It seemed that since his father was taller, and weighed more than he did—though not by much—that his father's feet would hurt more than his did. "I'm full of illusions about making an escape," his father said. "Some days I think about it so much, in so many different situations, that I'd out-worry a prisoner of war." The trees and buildings sailing by the train. The cold blasts of air conditioning. The heavy door opening and closing again. He had wondered, standing and being shaken by the train, whether part of the reason his father wanted him to be escorted around New York didn't have to do with the fact that his father would envy him for getting lost. His father always arranged things for him to do and places for them to meet, when his father knew perfectly well that he and Parker went into the city on the train alone. Sometimes he envied Brandt for having his father around so much. He couldn't remember how his father had acted toward him when he was a baby Brandt's age, but he had thought, even then, that his father probably liked him better than he liked Mary. Fathers liked sons better. But he knew that what his father had been saying on the train included him; his father had meant escaping from all of them—not just to Rye, and not just by going into the city to work. He understood what his father meant.

On the train, his father had said, "Not your type, huh?" And he had been embarrassed that he was so young, that he didn't have a type, that he didn't think he ever would. If anybody liked him, ever, he would be grateful. The older girls he knew were like Mary, or worse. Angela was worse. He really couldn't imagine the sort of girl he would ever like. When it got time to kiss a girl, he would have braces on, and he'd be embarrassed to do it. Thinking about it made him want to escape, too.

"I guess Tiffy wasn't all that nice to you today," his mother said. "She can be pretty insensitive to people's moods sometimes."

"I'm not in a mood," he said. "I just didn't want to go. I knew it wouldn't be any fun."

"What would your ideal day be?" his mother said.

"Have Mary out of the house," he said. "Have the air conditioner on and read comics. No big deal."

"But wouldn't you like to do something exciting?" his mother said.

"What?" he said. "Run around New York in the heat?"

"You and Tiffy are both depressing," she said. "In your different ways. It's so hard to really talk to either of you. You act like it's a big effort to speak two consecutive sentences to me, and Tiffy just reacts to what interests her. When you told her about the show at the Whitney, she wanted to talk about Calder, and she didn't care what you had to say."

"She's like a teacher," he said. He put his fingers under the band of his shorts and felt the skin wrinkled where the material had cut into his skin. "She is a teacher," he said. "Figures."

"Maybe she's not a very good teacher," his mother said. "I never thought about that. I just think about all the things that she does—I never really thought about how good she was at them."

"You're nicer than she is," he said.

"Well," she said, "since you dislike her, I should hope so."

"Not my type," he said.

His mother laughed. "No," she said. "I could tell that."

"Who's your type?" he asked his mother.

"What an odd question to ask your mother. I'm married to your father, so he must be my type, right?"

"Yeah," he said, "but you're separated."

"I'm not looking for other men, if that's what's got you worried."

"A movie star or anybody," he said. "I just meant do you always like men like Dad?"

"There are movie stars I think are good-looking, but they're not really my type," she said. "Do you mean who do I think is good-looking?"

"Do you think Nick is?" he said.

"Definitely not my type," she said.

"But a lot of girls like him."

"Nick," she said. "That's a funny idea. We really don't like each other."

She had come to a full stop at a stop sign and wasn't starting away. "Donald Sutherland is good-looking," she said. "Donald Sutherland in Klute."

"What are we sitting here for?" he said.

"I was just thinking for a second."

"Come on," he said, "get going."

"It's terrible," she said, pulling away. "I don't even have fantasies anymore."

"What fantasies did you have?"

She started to laugh. "Unbelievable," she said. "I'm talking to my ten-year-old son, driving down a road in suburbia, and he's asking me about what fantasies I used to have. Oh, it kills me. It kills me that a man, even if he's ten years old, can still stump me. How did we start talking about this, John Joel?"

"I don't remember," he said.

"I guess Tiffy has always been a sort of fantasy. I guess I've always wanted to think that she was nearly perfect, and that she had it all together, and that there was a way I could be like her. But I'm not even so sure that's true."

"Donald Sutherland," he said. "Was he in that movie about football?"

The huge white fountain of water was blowing nearly sky-high in the reservoir. She slowed the car to look at it as they came up on it, and speeded up again when they passed the rows of tall trees that blocked their view. "I guess you always wonder," she said, "if you'd be a different person if you lived somewhere else. It's so beautiful here, and we don't notice it very much, and when we do, it doesn't seem to help us be happy." She looked at John Joel. "You must think I'm really silly," she said. "Do you think I make a good adult?"

He wondered what would happen if both his parents made an escape at the same time.

"My God," his mother said. "All it's going to take is one little sperm to wiggle its way through a pinhole, and she'll never know. See that water?" she said. "One microscopic sperm has got as much power as that."

12

JOHN JOEL was in Parker's bedroom. There was a poster of Donna
Summer on the wall above Parker's bed, and another poster of the
Incredible Hulk. Parker had cut Donna Summer's face out of the
poster and put it in the Incredible Hulk's hand. In the space where
Donna Summer's face had been, he had put a picture of his
mother. He had hung it behind the poster, frame and all. You
could really tell that that face did not go with that long black hair.
John Joel looked more closely at Donna Summer's head in the
hand of the Incredible Hulk. Parker had put a wad of gum over
one of Donna Summer's eyes. There was also a picture of Washington crossing the Delaware in the room. On the glass, over
Washington's face, he had put another picture of Donna Summer's
head that he had cut out of a magazine. His mother was always
asking him to straighten up his room.

Parker kept a towel in his room, on a towel rack. Once he had
gotten poison ivy after using the same towel his father had used
when he had raked and burned leaves and showered, and since
Parker had not been outside the house that day, he was sure that
he had contracted poison ivy from his father's towel. He bought

himself five red towels with money he had gotten for his birthday and told his parents never to use them. His mother had said that he was being ridiculous, and that she wouldn't launder the towels—they'd bleed for the first ten washings, probably. So Parker took care of his own towels: He arranged them a certain way on the towel rack, so he could tell if they'd been tampered with, and he washed them in the basement sink, and he had never had poison ivy again. He had never forgiven his father, either. Before he got poison ivy, Parker wouldn't do yard work unless his father paid him, but after he got poison ivy, no amount of money would get him into the yard.

Parker tossed down his comic book. The comic, which he'd bought in New York, was called *Endless Torture*—it was a parody of genuine sadistic magazines—which Parker paid bums fifty cents to buy for him in the city. In the comic, people bleeding to death with their arms cut off were always trying to hail cabs on deserted streets, and people who had had their tongues ripped out were shown one frame later gagged with their own tongues. People spouted blood like fountains; their arms and legs went sailing through the air like Frisbees; their eyes really popped. Parker kept all the magazines and comics neatly laid out between his mattress and box spring. He knew where they all were; he had their positions memorized the way a chess player can close his eyes and envision all the pieces perfectly. He knew whether to lift the mattress near the pillow or at the foot of the bed. He could also close his eyes and flip the book open to a given scene. The book would fall open exactly on, or maybe two or three pages before or after, the picture he had in mind. He also had a few men's magazines: *Playboy* and *Oui* and *Hustler*. He liked the pictures in *Hustler* of what syphilis would do, and he gave thanks that the poison ivy hadn't done anything like that to him. But these magazines weren't his favorites. He thought that the funniest magazine was the one called *Animal Antics*. It told stupid fairy tales about animals, and there were black and white and a few color pictures of animals dressed up. Most of the pictures showed the animals' genitals. Parker always thought the pictures were just as funny, even if he'd just looked at them five minutes before: the monkey in the ballerina's pink crinoline tutu bending over to get a banana, its pink anus pointed at the camera; a cow on its side, udders full, staring blankly at the camera, a big yellow bonnet on its head and blue make-up above its eyes. There were also close-ups of a bunch of red ants feeding on a Hershey's Kiss melting in the sun, swarming around a discarded used prophylactic.

Parker liked to stay in his room. He had a ten-speed Schwinn he had gotten for Christmas mounted on the wall of his room, and he never went out riding. He had skates that he had gotten the same Christmas that he sometimes put on and rolled around the basement on when nobody else was home. He had weights that he didn't lift and a punching bag that he didn't punch. His father gave him the things for presents, thinking that he might lose weight if he weren't so sedentary. Parker wouldn't use them, and when his mother asked him to straighten up his room, he always replied by asking her to have his father load out all the things that he had given him. There was a picture in *Animal Antics* of an ape in tennis shoes and a white sweatband around its head, slugging a punching bag that was painted with big breasts. In this, as in all of the pictures, the animal's face was expressionless.

"So when do you get your wires?" Parker said. He opened his mouth and made his eyes big, imitating Jaws in the James Bond movies. Parker curled his fingers and pretended to be gripping something in midair. He cocked his head and slowly, with his eyes huge, pretended to be biting the thing in half. "See *Moonraker?*" he said. "It's not as sexy as some of them, but it's good. Jaws gets on Bond's side for a while, and in space there's a war and they blow off each other's heads with lasers." Parker twitched like a person being electrocuted. He was jerking his finger at John Joel, pretending it was a gun. "You'll get braces and look like Jaws," Parker said. "But you'd have to wear stilts. I wonder if you're going to grow any taller. You're supposed to start growing about now. I grew a lot in the last year."

"You're still as ugly as a Baby Ruth."

"Listen to who's talking. Brace face."

"A lot of people have got braces."

Parker hooked his big toe under the top of one sock and began to push it down.

"Did you see *Moonraker* or not?" Parker said.

"I didn't see it yet."

"I saw it with my mother, but it's gone from that theater. It's still in New York, though. Do you want to go?"

"Where would you get the money?"

"I've got ten bucks, smart-ass," Parker said.

"How'd you get it?"

"I found it blowing down the street. Okay?"

"You took it from your mother's purse again."

"Boy," Parker said, slipping his sock onto the floor. "You'd better report me to the Boy Scouts. A person like me isn't safe to take old ladies across the street." Parker laughed. The other sock came off and he flipped it to the opposite side of the room. "What'd you come over for if you wanted to act like an asshole?"

"You called *me*, Parker," John Joel said.

"Yeah. I call you and you act like you're my girlfriend or something, and I hurt your feelings or something, and you hang up and then you come over here. I wasn't going to answer the door. I didn't want you standing out there like an asshole, hollering at the window all day, though."

"I ought to get going," John Joel said.

"Yeah. Now you want me to beg you to stay. You're weird, man." Parker raised his hands again and bit down, into air. "Jaws cuts the cable when they're in this glassed-in car, riding down the mountain," Parker said. "You know what my mother says about the movie? She keeps talking about the girls in the movie, like it's Miss America or something. Marge Pendergast was with us, and that creepy kid Stanley of hers, and she kept asking Marge how come the girl with Bond can run all around in those high-heeled shoes. They kept talking about how good the girl's hair looked. They go to movies to see how women can run in high heels."

"What's your mother hanging out with her for all the time? I thought they had a big fight."

"They did. But Marge is always up for playing tennis. My mother hates doubles, and Marge is always up for playing singles with her. I wonder what she looks like with her tits cut off." Parker sucked at a mosquito bite on his wrist. "My father knew a guy that just had one ball. One dropped down and the other one didn't, so they did something to look for the other ball, but it wasn't in there."

"Who does *your* mother hang out with?" Parker said.

"Tiffy."

"Yuck," Parker said. "I saw her during that big snow last winter in these men's work boots and this big parka of I guess her husband's, in the grocery store, and she stopped and looked at *me* like *I* was weird." Parker picked the cuticle of his big toe. "I'll bet she's twice as ugly as Marge Pendergast, even *with* her tits," Parker said. "I wouldn't mind doing something to scare the shit out of her."

"What would you do?"

"Just something. Scare the shit out of her." Parker smiled. "You could bet *she* wouldn't come running out of a burning house in high heels. She'd have on those manure clompers and she'd probably be dressed up like a man and her husband would be dressed up like a woman. My mother says her husband's faggy. She probably takes all his clothes and leaves him hers." Parker smiled again. "I've got an idea," he said. "You want to send her something?"

"What do you mean, send her something?"

"You know that picture of her in the paper? My mother's got it around. That picture of the bunch of them, at the sale? We can take one of these—"

Parker rolled off the bed, and let himself fall to the floor. "Uggggh," he groaned. "They got me." He stood up. "Come here," Parker said. "Come on, I want to show you."

When Parker opened his bedroom door, he always looked both ways down the hallway. He did it even when he knew that nobody else was home. "This way," Parker said, and John Joel followed him. They ended up in Parker's mother's bedroom. By the bed there was a big table, and Parker started to shuffle through folded newspapers and letters she had opened and stuffed back in their envelopes, looking for the picture. "Look," Parker said, when he found it. "Come on." John Joel followed Parker again, back to his room. Parker closed the door. He took tape and scissors out of his desk drawer and sat on the floor. "Watch," he said.

"What happens if your mother looks for that picture?"

"She doesn't find it," Parker said.

"But Parker—what if she notices it's gone and Tiffy tells her she got something funny in the mail?"

"Fat chance. And even if it happened, all I've got to do is deny it. What do you think they're going to do to me?"

Parker was lifting the top corner of his mattress. He held it up and took out the fourth magazine from the top. It was *Animal Antics*, and with his eyes closed, Parker flipped it open to the picture of the monkey bending over to get the banana. The picture had been taken indoors; the banana was on wall-to-wall carpeting. Parker shook his head, then carefully ripped the page out of the magazine. He put the magazine back under the mattress before he did anything else. Then he went back to the spot on the floor where John Joel sat, where the scissors and tape were, and cut Tiffy's head out of the newspaper picture. He positioned it over the monkey's face and taped it down, using little pieces of tape. John Joel had to admit that it was funny. "Let's get an envelope," Parker said. He opened his door and looked both ways again. He went into the hallway and opened a drawer in a table and took an envelope and a stamp out. Then he went back into his bedroom, closed the door, folded the ape picture twice and put it neatly in the envelope. He printed her name, in big letters, across the envelope. Then he went out into the hallway again, to look up her address in the phone book. When it was finished, he said, "Let's go mail it."

"You're gonna get in trouble, Parker," John Joel said.

"Stick around and I'll show you something," Parker said.

Parker was taking another magazine out from under the mattress. It was a GI magazine, and he was tearing off the cover. A Marine, bayonet raised high, was yelling and beckoning troops forward, and behind him a soldier who had stepped on a land mine was being blown sideways, through smoke and flame. John Joel looked at the little soldier. He had a horrible expression on his face, and a blob of blood where his nose should be. John Joel studied the picture, as though the nose might be somewhere else. Then Parker cut out Louise's face and put it over the face of the screaming Marine, her hair partly obscuring the helmet, and began to tear off small pieces of tape to fasten it in place.

"What do you think I'm going to do with that?" he asked Parker.

"It's funny," Parker said, laughing. "Imagine if your mother was a Marine. I should have used this one for Tiffy and the other one for your mother, maybe. This is nice of me, you know. This magazine cost me a buck and a half."

"I thought you told me you lifted it."

"Oh yeah?" Parker said. "If I said so, then I did. I forget which ones I bought and which ones I smuggled out. Stupid old baldie who runs the candy store, you could take money out of his cash register and he wouldn't know it, I bet."

The gray and white newspaper picture fit in with the gray-green helmet and almost looked as if it belonged there. For some reason, it embarrassed him to look at the picture.

"Here," Parker said, pushing it toward him.

"I don't want the thing," he said half-heartedly.

"You don't know what's funny when you see it," Parker said. "To tell you the truth, you probably wouldn't get half of what's going on in *Moonraker*. It's got a big snake in it, and you're even afraid of old garden snakes. You're even afraid of those Fourth of July snakes."

"I am not," John Joel said.

"Maybe when Tiffy's husband sees it, he'll squeal," Parker said. "I'm going out to mail this. Are you coming?"

"Why can't you mail it later?"

"Come on," Parker said. "When we come back, I'll show you something."

"Why can't you show me now?"

Parker looked disgusted. He started picking things off the floor without saying anything. He put the magazine back under the mattress, and put the tape and scissors in his desk drawer. When he turned around, he didn't look as disgusted. "Okay," Parker said. "Are you going to tell everybody in the world I showed you this?"

"What for?" John Joel shrugged.

"Because you couldn't wait to tell your mother that I burned the ticket stubs, and she told *my* mother."

"She did not. You just told me this morning on the phone that *you* told her, and that she didn't believe you, and that she wouldn't give me the three bucks back."

Parker smiled. "I was just testing," he said, "but I'll bet you told her, didn't you?"

"What's it to you? She didn't tell *your* mother. She wouldn't."

"That illustrates what I was telling you before. That illustrates why Tiffy isn't going to tell my mother what she got in the mail, and if she does, my mother's not going to put two and two together. Your mother knows about the diaphragm, doesn't she, she even *knows*, and she's not telling my mother."

"She doesn't like your mother."

"She doesn't like my mother because my mother's a tennis pro, just about, and nobody but Marge Pendergast can keep up with her."

"Talk about who loves their mother."

"I don't love her. I just said that she plays pro tennis."

"You love her," John Joel said.

"Get off," Parker said, brushing something imaginary from his arm. He went to the door, opened it, and looked both ways. "Just keep your mouth shut about this," he said.

"What's this going to be?" John Joel said.

"Scared?" Parker said.

"What would I be scared of?" John Joel said.

Actually, he was a little scared. He thought the way Parker looked both ways before he came out of his room and crept around the empty house was scary—it was the way people moved in the old movies, when somebody really was hiding and was about to jump out at them. The house was like an old-movie house, too: There were big overstuffed chairs, and there was almost nothing modern around. It had been Parker's grandmother's house, and when she died, Parker's family had moved in.

"This is probably going to be nothing," John Joel said.

"Oh no, Mr. Bill, don't go down those steps!" Parker squealed. As they went down, Parker was making sounds of explosions: "Pshew! Whew! Boom!"

The basement smelled like Raid. There was a hum from the sump pump behind the stairs that kept the basement from flooding. It was a creepy basement, full of things that looked like worms but weren't. Nothing was down there but a washer and dryer and Parker's father's workroom. He followed Parker into that room. Above the work table there was a picture of Parker's grandmother and grandfather, standing beside some hollyhocks. Both of them had on straw hats—hers was wide-brimmed, and part of a hollyhock had been tucked in the band—and they were holding hands and smiling into the camera. The picture was probably from long ago; it was probably taken before Parker was born. There was a picture of three men in Army uniforms, with beer mugs raised—a picture all brown and white, with spots here and there on the picture, like little match flames. And there was a picture of Parker as a baby, sitting in his diapers, holding a toy rabbit. Parker wasn't a fat baby. He looked nice when he was a baby.

"One of those guys is the guy who only had one ball," Parker said, pointing to the picture of the three men in uniform. "This one of them married somebody who's a famous dancer, and the one with one ball runs a bar in Santo Domingo, and that one's my father." There was a chain dangling from a fluorescent light above the table. Parker pulled the light on. It blinked a couple of times, and then the table was flooded with bright light. Parker pushed aside a hammer and a jar full of nails and screws and lifted two fishing tackle boxes from below the table onto the tabletop. He opened one and put aside several carefully folded wide ties with geometric patterns on them. Underneath the ties there was a pen that, when tilted, showed a tiny woman becoming naked.

"I've seen those," John Joel said.

"Seen this?" Parker said. He turned the pen slowly, and from the other side a small naked man with his penis sticking out began to come toward the small naked woman, slowly and imprecisely, like someone floating in space when there's no gravity. The penis touched the woman's side. Parker smiled and put the pen back in the box.

"Look at this," Parker said. He held out a little dish, or an ashtray, with a drawing on it of a huge woman, being sculpted out of stone by a man who was carving with his penis.

"This is what I really wanted to show you," Parker said. He put the things back and opened the other box. In that box there were more ties, some letters and a small black gun. Parker took them out, put them aside, and took out a cardboard box. Inside there was a piece of cardboard that unfolded into the shape of a penis, a narrow black scarf with tiny mothholes in it (Parker held it over his eyes for a second), and a folded piece of paper with a picture of a vagina, pink and brown, about three feet high. "Better than pin the tail on the donkey," Parker said. Parker chuckled. He zoomed the cardboard penis against the vagina. "It's not his stuff," Parker said. "It's my grandfather's." Parker began refolding the piece of paper. "He's never going to tell me this stuff is here,

I bet," Parker said. He put the two boxes back under the table and pushed the hammer and the jar of screws back into place. "He goes into the boxes. I wet a hair and put it up against that box," Parker said, pulling the chain to turn the light off. "And the hair was gone."

"How do you know that when your spit dried, the hair didn't fall off?"

"Because I did it three times," Parker said. He turned around and showed his teeth, like Jaws. Walking behind him, John Joel saw Parker's head, in profile, and his hands raised again, holding the imaginary cable that his teeth would snap. Parker's head fell forward and snapped straight. John Joel kept walking.

"Well," John Joel said, "I've got to get home, I guess."

"What for?" Parker said.

"Because my mother's working today and she told me to take the chicken out of the freezer at two o'clock."

"All you've got to do is say you forgot."

"Nah," John Joel said. "I guess I'll go do it. You want to come over?"

"There's nothing to do at your house."

"What are you going to do here?"

"Read my magazines. I got a new one I haven't read yet. It's called *Tons of Fun*. About fatsos."

"You've started laughing at yourself?" John Joel said.

"I laugh at myself," Parker said. "If I didn't want to be fat, I wouldn't be fat. I like to look this way. It drives my father crazy."

"My father, too."

"So?" Parker said. "Then it's worth it."

"I don't have to be fat either," John Joel said. He had never really thought of that before.

"Want to see *Tons of Fun?*"

"Nah. I've got to go."

"Why doesn't your sister take the chicken out?"

"Because she's always over at Angela's."

"So call her and make her go home and do it."

"She wouldn't."

"She's a douchebag," Parker said.

"A what?"

"Get out of here," Parker said. Parker flopped on his bed.

"What's a douchebag?" Parker said. "Get out of here." He started to laugh.

"Are we going into New York later on, or what?"

"Get out of here," Parker laughed. "Throw me that box of graham crackers on the floor where you're standing."

John Joel picked up the box and threw it to Parker, meaning to hit him. The box hit the side of the bed and fell to the floor.

"I could fix your sister," Parker said. "Your sister really needs fixing."

Walking home, John Joel remembered the time when Parker had had poison ivy, the way it had gotten in his ears, the way the swelling had nearly closed his eyes, the sores that were partly inside and partly outside his nostrils; and how he had gone up the stairs, talking to Parker's mother, and how she had opened the door and there was Parker in the bed, painted with some white stuff that almost covered his body, lying there just staring into the room, though there were only slits where his eyes should be. He was holding a glass of lemonade that Parker's mother had given him. Parker had not said hello. He had not tried to cover himself, even though he was naked. John Joel had stood there and wondered if what he was seeing on the bed was some huge swollen mummy of Parker, if Parker hadn't really disappeared, and this was what was left. He had been afraid to get too close to him. He had tried to get Parker to say something, but he wouldn't. The whiteness of Parker, the way he had looked on the bed, was like those plaster people at the museum; and thinking about the museum reminded him that Parker had gotten his way: Parker had seen the show and done him out of being reimbursed. Parker wasn't really his friend, and he had always known that. He had been surprised, himself, that when Parker called he had been happy. He had been even more surprised that he had gone over there, and that he had stayed so long. Sometimes he thought that Parker could read his mind. That was part of the reason he had gone: Because whatever he had said to him, Parker would have known what he was really thinking. He would have known that he was glad to hear from him. He would have known, the way he had known that he had told his mother about Parker burning the ticket stubs.

He was thinking about Parker's poison ivy, and he decided not to risk cutting through the lot that separated Angela's house from his house, even if he was careful to avoid the shiny-leafed vines that wound through the lot. It was better to walk the long way, and be safe.

Parker knew that he was afraid of firecrackers and snakes. Parker knew what everything sexual meant, and Parker had stopped telling him. For a long while, he had been able to ask, and after an eye roll or a shrug, Parker would tell him; but now Parker was learning more and more and he wouldn't say anything. And that day he had gone berry-picking with Tiffy and his mother. He was sure that he was right about the way he felt: that if he hadn't been there, they would have talked during the picnic; that they wouldn't have just sat there awkwardly; that the only laugh wouldn't have been about the bird that crapped on the cloth. His mother and Tiffy were like one person, in a way, and he was an extra. He felt the same way about his father and Nick—that they weren't really talking the way they would talk if he weren't there. When he was alone with his father they talked, but he always said the wrong thing, even about small things, even about Nick's girlfriend. He was thinking about his father saying, "Not your type, huh?" He couldn't imagine being part of his father's and Nick's world, even when he grew up. He couldn't imagine having a good friend when he grew up. He thought that Parker would still be around, and that Parker would always know more than he did, that he would always take risks and not care; and that he would always be in the position he had been in, standing in Parker's bedroom doorway, trying to get Parker to say something and Parker not talking. He had talked, finally. He had made a joke that wasn't really a joke. He had said, "Come over here. I want you to get poison ivy." Then he had laughed, the way his father had laughed on the train when he said, "Not your type, huh?" Both of them were sad laughs: Parker's because for once he couldn't impose his will; his father's because when they talked, no matter what either of them thought about how pretty Nick's girl was, and no matter that the rocking train threw them into each other time and again, they were still worlds apart.

13

NINA WAS almost exhausted, and things were starting to get too crazy. She thought that when Horton left things would calm down, but Jonathan and Spangle had almost been on a rampage since he left. She could hardly imagine Horton being a stabilizing influence on anybody, but he had talked so much that the two of them had been outdone. Of course, when Horton was there a couple of hours ago, nobody was as stoned as they were now. She wished that she had had less to smoke, or at least that she did not have to go to work the next day. She knew she was going to be standing there for hours, with her head hurting and her eyes not functioning right, having flashes of this night. It was hot, even with the window open. The window was really open—he had tried to fix the screen and had pushed it out, onto the sidewalk. Thank God nobody had been walking underneath. All of them knew better than to make an appearance outside, even to do something as simple as retrieve a fallen window screen.

The game now was pin the tail on the donkey, but instead of a tail there was her green bathtowel, and instead of a donkey there was a yelping, stoned person who thought he was playing another game, insisted on it, and was getting very annoyed at being pursued as a donkey. At least, that's what it seemed like. No one was communicating terribly well.

"Charades!" Spangle screamed, and she groaned and rolled over on the rug. She couldn't believe that just a few hours ago—no, probably many hours, more hours than she wanted to count up, because then she would know how late at night it was—the two of them had come in and taken over again, as though it were old times, simply old times, and here they were.

"It can't speak for itself," he said, pointing to the towel on the rug beside Nina, "but it's doing its imitation and it's a book. The fucking towel is a book. And it wasn't easy to spread it out flat on the floor, so everybody had better try to guess. What's that towel on the floor? Name of a book."

Jonathan kicked the towel and almost tripped on his way to the bathroom.

"You're ruining it," he hollered, and Nina said, "Sssh."

"Okay," he said, straightening the towel. "Towel on the floor, name of a book. Okay. What am I?"

"What are *you*, or what's the towel?" she said.

"What's the towel. I know what I'm doing. I'm concentrating," he said, wandering into the kitchen. "Four words. No, five. Five words, a charade of what that towel on the rug is impersonating. Not hard to guess. Running out of Coke."

"Go home," she said. "I've got to work."

"That's six words," he said.

"What?" she said. "Did you close the refrigerator door?"

She hoped so. She didn't hear it creak closed, and she didn't see how she could get up right away to close it.

"I'm completely fine," Spangle said, coming back into the room and collapsing on the sofa. "If I was on an airplane, they wouldn't serve me. They saw me trying to get on a plane like this, they wouldn't let me on. You can't get on an airplane when you're in this kind of shape. They'll leave you on the ground forever."

"Metaphor for your life," Jonathan said, coming out of the bathroom. His jeans were much too big for him, and he'd realized it. When he lost the belt the last time he'd gone to the bathroom, he'd stuffed a washcloth in the waistband. He hadn't put the washcloth in very well. It was wadded up and stuffed in like a lumpy baseball.

"What did you say?" he said.

Jonathan went into a coughing fit. "I said it's too hot in here," he said.

"We've got to leave the country," he said to Nina. "It's too hot."

"That's not the answer," she said. "Hard work and no play," she said. "That's the answer."

"We're in the middle of a game. What do you mean? See that towel on the floor? You know what it reminds me of?"

"What?" Jonathan said.

"The answer is *How Green Was My Valley*." He put his arm over his eyes, as if he'd been struck blind by the sun. "I gave it away," he said. "Fuck me, I gave it away."

"What's he talking about?" Jonathan said. He pulled the white washcloth out of the waist of his jeans and threw it on top of the green towel. "One's short and the other one's tall, but they're the same kind," he said. "They'll get it on. Lots of pale-green hand-towels."

"How come you two are still here?" Nina said.

"What?" he said. "I'm not still here. I got stoned and died. I left the refrigerator door open."

"Can you close it?" she said to Jonathan.

"I can do anything," he said. He went back into the bathroom and closed the door. She smelled it again: grass. He was smoking more grass.

"No," she said. She thought she said. Nobody said anything.

"I never read *How Green Was My Valley*. You read that, huh? You read that at Bard College?"

"We wouldn't read crap like that at Bard."

"Not at Bard," he said, frowning down at her. "Where are we again?"

"Columbus Avenue."

"Columbus didn't discover America," he said. "I'm fucked. I'm fucked. I smoked grass last week and it calmed me down. If I went out it would be all over. Stop telling us to leave."

"I haven't said that for an hour."

"You've come to your senses."

"No. I just know that you won't leave."

"If I tried to get on a plane in this condition, you know what they'd do? They wouldn't let me get on. I would be denied boarding. I couldn't even get a denied boarding pass, because if the plane was there and I was the one who was fucked, it wouldn't even be their fault. They can crash DC-10's, and that's their fault, but if you have one puff too many, they keep you on the ground."

"We missed the plane. Who cares. We missed the plane," Jonathan said. "Then we got another one."

"This idiot would have brought drugs through customs. You know what you get for being busted in Spain? Seven years and seven days. Longer than it took God to create the world."

"Somebody close the refrigerator door," she said.

"Does anybody object if I take a shower?" Jonathan said. "You'll do okay without my company? Can I be enough at home that I can just take a shower?"

He was undressing. He left his T-shirt and jeans by the towel in the living room and walked—stumbled—into the bathroom in his Jockey shorts. He didn't close the door. He relit the joint he'd left in the soap dish and started humming.

"Turn the water on," she said. Thought she said.

"He's taking a shower," Spangle said. "I can close the refrigerator door, I just don't want to. The truth is I *don't fucking want to*."

"Shut up," Jonathan called from the bathroom. "I can hear you in here."

"Bring it out, you grass-hog," he said. "If you come out and don't see your shadow, you can go back in with it."

"How am I going to see my shadow out here?" Jonathan said, stumbling out into the room. "It's all dark in here. You can't see your shadow in the dark. Never mind shadows, there might be *people* all over, and you can't see them in the dark."

"Mind games," he said. "You know who's here."

"I'm going to close the refrigerator," Jonathan said. He got the towel from the floor and headed toward the bathroom. He left the towel there and came back into the room, jumped over Nina leapfrog style and went into the kitchen and closed the refrigerator door.

"Let's send out for a pizza," Jonathan said.

"I don't want to eat," Nina said.

"I don't want to argue about what goes on the pizza," Spangle said.

"Who said we had to argue? Extra cheese and mushrooms," Jonathan said.

"So send out for a pizza. We can hang it on the wall and use it as a dartboard."

"It would drip down the wall," Nina said.

"Like that surrealist clock," he said. "You could have an original work of art on your wall, Nina. Let's fix Nina's wall."

"What does it cost to send out for a pizza?" Jonathan said. He looked over his shoulder. "Excuse me," he said. He went into the bathroom and closed the door. Nina heard the water running.

"Here's a riddle. See if you know this one," he said. "Why did the little moron throw the clock out the window?"

"He tripped. There wasn't any screen in the window. The clock fell on Columbus Avenue."

"Fuck you. Come on, Nina. Why did he?"

"That's such an old joke. I can't believe you're telling me such an old joke. I can't believe you're here. Will you round up Jonathan and please go home?"

"I can't believe *you're* here. New York chic. Christ's thorns."

"It's a dumpy apartment on Columbus Avenue."

"It wasn't a riddle, it was a joke. Different thing. Pardon me. Let me go into the kitchen and see if he closed the refrigerator door."

Spangle got up and felt his way along the wall into the kitchen.

"He closed it," he called. Then everything was silent, except for the water slapping down in the tub. The showerhead was broken and had to be tilted a certain way to make the water spray out instead of pouring out of the spigot. Jonathan didn't know that. She thought about going in and telling him, but she couldn't move.

"Here," he said, holding out a joint to her. It was wrapped in blue paper, and she had no idea where it had come from.

"That's a pencil," she said, taking it.

"I know it. Write down my number so you can call me. It's

173

unlisted. It's not in the phone book, and if you go to call me, you won't be able to. Write this down."

"What am I supposed to write on? The rug?"

"I don't know where there's any paper. We both closed the refrigerator door. *You* could get up and find the paper."

"Call me and tell me your number," she said, dropping the pencil.

"Maybe we should order a pizza," he said. "Is there somebody who delivers?"

"There's a book by the phone. Look under 'pizza' in the book."

"You could write my number in the book, then," he said. He walked over to the phone. She thought, watching, that he looked like a person standing upright and swimming. It was dark in the room, but things had bright edges, because of light from the sign across the street.

"I'm writing in the book," he said. "I'm writing you a poem. What rhymes with Nina?"

She sighed and closed her eyes. New York working girl.

"Piña colada," he said. "Will they bring a pizza with onions and meatballs and a pitcher of piña coladas?"

"The pizza man brings his dog. It's a corgi. It's named Bess."

"Is that the truth?" he said.

"One time he brought it, one time he didn't. I don't like pizza. I never eat pizza."

"New lover's got a lot of money, huh?"

"What did you do with all *your* money?"

"I spent it. If you have money, you can buy things. I bought some things. My possessions all linked arms and disappeared over the hill."

"Be serious."

"I am. I want to order a pizza before he gets out of the shower. There's nothing in the book under 'pizza.'"

"Give it to me," she said.

He got up and gave her the book. He sat down beside her and blew into her hair, to watch it separate.

"What's this?" she said, pointing to the word "pizza."

"Tell him to bring piña coladas, too," he said. "I'm going to have a drink. Do you want a drink?"

There was about an inch of vodka left in the bottle. He swirled the vodka, shook it, stared at it and put the bottle down.

"Does anybody have any money?" she said.

"The plan is," he said, "we call him and order the pizza. When he comes we overpower him and kidnap the corgi, and if he wants it back, we say that he has to leave the pizza and find a pitcher of piña coladas."

"So he leaves and finds the cops."

"So we throw the corgi out the window."

"Were you two drunk before you got here?" she said.

"All day," he said, holding up both hands in surrender. "I swear to you. We have a high tolerance level. That grass is a wipeout. Moves your brain cells around like a tidal wave. Little deuce coupe."

"What?"

"The Beach Boys singing *Saturday Night Fever* music," he said. "Double whew."

"The Bee Gees," she said, closing the book and dropping it on the rug.

"Bee Gees. Sure. What a relief. Thank God," Spangle said. He sprawled on his stomach next to her. "You think somebody who came in here would think I was Tab Hunter and you were Sandra Dee?"

"Let's see if he guesses when he comes out of the bathroom."

"What's he doing? He's taking a shower? I thought he was going to call for a pizza."

"Forget it. I don't want anybody up here."

"You're unsociable. Even avoid all your old friends. New York chic. We can go out for a piña colada."

"Really," she said, "really, it's true, I have to work tomorrow."

"Tell 'em they don't have to buy stockings if they don't have any legs. Tell 'em all they've got to do is head for some subway platform and wait for a loony to push them under and their stocking problems are solved."

"They reattach everything."

"Surgeons? They don't drink. They've got to be sober men. Bite my mouth: Surgeons are women, too, right? Women—what do you call them?"

She could hear him breathing. The water. A sound that might have been Jonathan, breathing louder than the water was falling. She shook her head in confusion. Had he just asked what you called women?

"Microsurgeons!" he said. "I thought of it! It's microsurgeons. Women microsurgeons reattaching legs—they call them limbs, right? Microsurgeon attaching a limb that a train ran over, some loony just stands there and pushes and splat! Lady microsurgeon to the rescue."

She thought he was funny. She couldn't stop laughing, and she was too weak to laugh; she was trying to pay attention to something, but when she was laughing she couldn't think what. "Go in the bathroom," she said. "See what that sound is."

The sound was the hair dryer Jonathan had turned on for some reason as he got into the shower. It was blowing a blast of air into the shower. He had the shower curtain back so he could feel it, and he was smoking a joint with no hands, letting the water pelt his back. The hair dryer lay on its side on top of the toilet.

"That's what it was," she said, when he came back and collapsed beside her again. "I told you I heard something."

"Maybe some street vendor will come by and holler and we can get a pizza. You're right about not having somebody come here when we're so wrecked. We could all take a shower and not dry off, and if we seemed odd, we could tell the guy with the corgi that a tidal wave hit us. The Beach Boys. The fucking Brian Wilson Beach Boys."

"Don't you have to work tomorrow?" she said.

"No," he said.

"What about Jonathan?"

"No. Nobody has to work tomorrow. *You* don't have to work tomorrow. Call and tell them the work went away—you tried to catch it, but it got away."

"When I was a little girl, I wanted to be a dancer," she said.

"That's totally off the subject," he said. He blew gently into her hair and watched a strand lift up and fall back in the same place. "I couldn't get it up to save my life," he said.

Jonathan came into the room, dripping wet and naked, strutting around singing "Yes, We Have No Bananas." Jonathan shook his head, went back into the bathroom and closed the door. She heard the roar of the hair dryer again.

Spangle picked up the phone and, without dialing, cupped his hand and said, "Yes, that's right: large pizza with anchovies and lasagna on top and a pitcher of piñas to travel. Thank you."

"He's fucked," Jonathan said, coming out of the bathroom with his too-big jeans falling down his hips, one toe cut—no, wait: big joke—one toe with polish on the nail. It wasn't dry, and when he stumbled, it smeared on the wood floor. "What's he doing?" Jonathan said.

"I have to work tomorrow," she said.

"You can't," Jonathan said. "Don't be ridiculous."

"You left the hair dryer on," she said.

"Refrigerator door, dryer, next you'll nag me to make my bed. I don't have a bed. I don't even live here. I've got to shove off. Is he okay?"

"I don't think *I'm* okay," she said. "I can't drink and smoke. Why did I drink vodka if I was going to smoke?"

"Call that guy at the radio station. Have him figure the situation out and send you a free T-shirt."

"I'm not calling anybody," she said.

"I think somebody is playing Smokey Robinson and the Miracles," Jonathan said. "God damn. I've been thinking about them for a week."

"Make Smokey sing 'Special Occasion,'" he hollered out the window, yelling in Jonathan's ear. Jonathan grabbed him and pulled him back in. "And make him dance when he sings it! No fudging on the high notes!" he screamed. His voice cracked. He started coughing, and when Jonathan hit him on the back he fell over. Jonathan started laughing then, which made him start coughing too.

"Hans Castorp, go up to the mountain," he said, coming out of the coughing fit first. Jonathan stood, helping himself up by pulling on the window ledge. He looked down at the street, swaying. The man with the radio had gone away. A man and a woman were standing there, looking up at the window.

"Somebody has tuberculosis," Jonathan said to the two people on the sidewalk. He didn't want to yell, but he spoke too quietly.

He was just leaning forward, water running off his hair, whispering to the couple on Columbus Avenue.

"I've got to go. I've got a date," Jonathan said.

"You're lying. You don't have a date."

"I've got to get out of here," Jonathan said. "If I come back, I'll bring a pizza. Green pepper and pepperoni."

"Go ahead," he said. "If you're going, go ahead. You've got to dry off, though. You'll get tuberculosis going out there like that."

"Oh Christ—how am I going to go to school tomorrow?" Nina said. She got up on one elbow, and tried to blink the room straight. Blinking made it tilt left and right. She said: "Why did I say that? School instead of work?"

"She's got TB and she's hallucinating," Spangle said. "Do you think she needs the shower cure?"

"There isn't any more shower."

"What are you talking about?"

"I turned it off," Jonathan said, and bent forward, sliding his hands down his thighs to his knees, laughing. "Fooled you good," he said.

"Oh fuck," Nina said. "I'm really going to be mad if I throw up."

"Lie still," Jonathan said. "I'll get you a washcloth."

"I don't want a washcloth," she said.

In a couple of minutes he brought her a washcloth, with very little water squeezed out of it. She moved it from her mouth, where he had put it, up to her forehead. Then she was both cold and dizzy.

"I've got to go," Jonathan said. "Don't anybody say anything funny, so I can get it together to go."

He put out his hand and took Nina's. She didn't shake it. She just rested her hand in his. "No offense taken," he said. "We are *wrecked*."

He put on the rest of his clothes, talking to himself, telling himself to button buttons, roll up sleeves.

"Admit you don't have a date," Spangle said to Jonathan.

"I don't have a date," Jonathan said. "I've got to go."

Nobody stopped him. When he left, Nina said, "Can you shut the door?"

"That door?" Spangle said, looking out into the hallway.

"That door," she said.

"I can shut that door. Sure," he said. He walked to the door and slammed it, then put his back against it and looked at her. He squinted and moved closer, to see where she was cut. Not blood on the floor by her ear. Good. Something else.

"Hey, Nina," he said, "I haven't seen you for so long. How are you? I mean, how were you before you got wrecked?"

"I don't remember," she said.

"You *do* remember. Come on."

"I don't know," she said. "Am I going to lose my job?"

"You're not going to lose your job. There's always another job."

"What does that mean? That I'm going to lose it?"

"Only if you show up," he said. He stretched out beside her. "I think I overdid this," he said. "I overdid this."

"Where did he go?" she said, looking at the closed door.

"He probably had a date. He has dates at funny hours. I don't know anybody besides him who'd begin a date at eleven o'clock."

"He said he didn't."

"You can't tell with him," he said.

"Well, what time is it?"

"What time is it? It is . . . this time?"

He held his wrist toward her, but she couldn't see the numerals on the watch. She saw one hand, sweeping, and a lot of little circles and designs.

"Tell me what time it is," she said.

He told her that it was ten of three in the morning.

"I have to go to sleep," she said. "I'll lose my job."

"I'd tell you a bedtime story, but I'm too wrecked. I can tell you a poem. Wynken and Blynken and Nod fell asleep and turned into a pod."

"Don't," she said. "I'll have nightmares. That horrible movie. Somebody was just saying something about that that gave me nightmares."

"In the morning," he said, "tell me how you are. Were."

"Why did I ever do this?" she said.

"It's our fault. Wicked stuff. I hope he took it with him. Wait a minute: If he's *responsible*, I hope he took it with him. How was he when he left?"

"He looks so much younger with his hair cut," she said.

"He's such a ladykiller," he said. "He probably did have a date.

179

I'm too old to have dates. I just look up old friends." He patted her hand.

"You live with somebody," she said.

She fell asleep and woke up when he began talking to himself in his sleep. She put her hand on his stomach, and he stopped talking.

When she woke up the next time, she could see his watch. There was a horrible ache over her left eye, and her mouth was dry, but with one eye closed she could see the watch, and she could stand up and go into the bathroom. She wanted to splash water on her face, but she was afraid that touching her face that way might spread the pain. She tilted two aspirin out of the bottle in the medicine cabinet and swallowed them, washing them down with a handful of water. She took off her clothes, put them over the towel rack, and got into the shower. She adjusted the showerhead and ran the water, stepped into it when it was the right temperature. She was sore all over from sleeping on the floor. She had no idea how she had bruised her thigh so badly. She took a quick shower, decided at the last minute to bob her head under the water, and when she saw that she could take that, squirted a little shampoo into her hand and massaged the top of her head. She closed her eyes and let the water beat on her head until she thought the soap was all washed away. Then she got out, stepped onto the floor full of puddles, and stood in water, rather than on the sopping wet bathrug. She dried off, patting her body instead of rubbing it.

The phone rang, but she decided just to let it ring. That, or he could answer it. She turned on the hair dryer, but something was wrong with it: It hardly put out any heat. She patted her hair and wrapped a towel around herself and walked out of the bathroom. He was still asleep. He hadn't even heard the phone. No: He was smiling at her; awake, but still wiped out. "Good morning," she said, on her way into the bedroom. She dropped the towel on the bed and got a robe out of the closet. It was John's robe, that he left at her apartment: a present from her, found in an antique clothing store in the Village, a satin robe with a lunging lion on the back and a rising sun above the pocket on the front, the name Neil P. stitched in script above the blood-red sun.

"I feel like I'm going to live," she said, holding the robe closed and going out to the living room and standing over him. She tied the sash and rubbed her face and sat down beside him. "Last night was an exception, right?" she said. "You're really not into dope that way anymore, right?"

"Never," he said.

"Do you want an aspirin?" she said.

"I'm okay," he said. "What time is it?"

She picked up his wrist and looked, and told him it was five of seven. He groaned.

"Don't tell me you're going to work," he said.

"Stay here and sleep," she said. "If you feel better later, pick up a little."

"Whew," he said. "In Nina's apartment on Columbus Avenue."

"You were putting me down good last night," she said. "Calling me the New York working girl."

"I hope you didn't pay attention to me."

"I didn't."

"I wonder where Jonathan is," he said. He got up, slowly, and went to the window. "Leave your window open *here* and no bugs get in," he said, shaking his head. "That's amazing."

She went back into the bathroom, to brush her teeth. She closed the door and bent over the sink, and realized that the aspirin had already started to work; the blinding pain was disappearing from above her eye. Her eyes were bloodshot. She was going to have to wear dark glasses.

"Nobody came in through the window," he said, outside the bathroom door. "Want me to tempt fate for real and answer the door?"

"There's somebody at my door?" she said, opening the bathroom door.

She came out of the bathroom, and went to the door. She forgot to ask who it was. The chain wasn't on, because neither of them had remembered to put it on when Jonathan left. In fact, she opened the door certain that it would be Jonathan.

John was standing there, and even before he realized that a man was standing beside her, he looked terrible. It was the first time he had ever come to the apartment in the morning. He walked in without saying anything, and then just stood there, looking from Nina to Peter Spangle.

He walked up the stairs, trying to remember that he was in love. There was a fact, and an important one: He was in love. He was there because she said more in a glance than anyone else said in a touch, and a touch from her meant more than an embrace from anyone else. When you were in love, it was logical to go be with the person you loved. Only, he didn't know where to begin. What he had to talk about seemed to have nothing to do with the world of love and everything to do with the world of hate, and that world had never been real when he was with Nina. If she was getting away, it was because he was letting her get away. She was inside the apartment. He knew that she would not have left for work yet. She would be having her little-girl breakfast of cereal and fruit, and brushing her hair, listening to the news on the radio, tidying up the room. She wasn't mean in the morning. You could talk to her and she'd answer. The two times they had gone away together, he had been amazed at how cheerful she was in the morning. He tried to remember that it was morning now, that if he put his mind to it, he could stop his legs from shaking enough to climb the stairs, that at the top was Nina, that he could reach out and touch her and she would be there. He felt as crazy and foolish as an old drunk who finds his way home but can't remember to climb the stairs, so he's found in the morning and catches hell anyway. God—if he was really comical. If she meant that, really, and didn't just say it to tease, because she was fond of him. If it was all explained in Passages: a simple answer. Nothing was simple. Not even loving Nina was simple. This was the only place he could imagine being, and already he felt that the place wasn't there, that he wasn't going to make it to the top of the stairs, and that if he did, he wouldn't know where to begin. He would have to invent some logical explanation for what he was going to tell her, or maybe it was just because he was in a panic that he thought that. He realized that he was in a panic, and that gave him enough energy, returned enough breath to him, that he was able to continue walking up the stairs. He couldn't believe what he had left behind, what he had just walked out on. He had thought at the time that he was doing the logical thing, that he was doing something out of self-preservation. There had been so much chaos: He had been afraid that he was losing his senses, going deaf. And only the summer before, the six of them, his mother, Brandt, John Joel, Louise, Mary and he, had been at the carnival. Brandt—as usual—hanging on to his arm and trying to bring him to the ground, dangling and swaying. They had been a family at a carnival. He had been awake all night, and he couldn't think straight. He knew that he would have to get to the point and not edge up toward it; that he couldn't talk to her about the summer before, the things they had done as a family; that there was no point in trying to explain to her that they were typical; that maybe even his love for her figured in a pattern; that they were typical and then suddenly they weren't. He was going to say to her: I want you to help me. He didn't know what help he needed. He had no memory of how he had gotten from Connecticut to New York. He did remember being in the city, and taking the car to the garage he usually went to, the keys left behind, the cab to Nina's. The cab driver had talked to him about the weather they were supposed to have over the weekend, and he had remembered, only then, what day it was. He had just stuffed wadded bills into the cab driver's hand because he couldn't think—he might as well *have been a man in a foreign country where he didn't understand the currency. Better just to overpay and run, to be embarrassed that way rather than the other. He tried to breathe more softly. He wanted to at least be breathing normally when she saw him. More than anything he wanted to see her standing there. He wanted no harm to have come to her, at least. At the top of the stairs he made a fist and knocked. The reverberation that began in his hand shot through his arm and ended in his heart. And then she opened the door.*

14

SPANGLE'S MOTHER was wondering if she should have her old mouton coat updated, as she put it, for Cynthia to wear in the winter. Cynthia listened, keeping the phone clamped against her ear with her raised shoulder, carefully stroking clear nail lacquer on her fingernails as she talked. The smell was powerful so close to her nose, and she wished that she could put the brush down and sit comfortably in a chair and do her nails and not have to talk to Spangle's mother. It was wrong to blame Spangle for his mother. It was even wrong to blame Spangle's mother for trying to be nice, but it had been a long day of teaching, and their stupid faces still bobbed before her in the empty apartment, and she did not think that she could be tactful much longer.

"I suppose you don't want it, even if I have the bottom part narrowed," Spangle's mother said.

"I think the coat I have is fine. I appreciate your offering, but I don't really think I'd be comfortable in a fur coat."

"Don't think I'm dense. Don't think I don't know what you mean," Spangle's mother said, "but in terms of mental as opposed to physical comfort, think about how you would feel with some perfume squirted on and a strand of pearls and a thick, warm mouton. You could update the look yourself by dyeing your hair red and chopping it into one of those crew cuts and wearing neon pants and a cowboy shirt. Don't think I don't read fashion magazines anymore. I do. I read them, and I know that women want to look like whores at a party, and that work is considered a party. Stiletto heels at work. Silver skirts. *Really.*"

"I appreciate the offer," Cynthia said.

"It's wicked to keep it hanging there in its little purple garment bag. I can't wear it because it reminds me of happier times. I wish I could just put that coat back on, and squirt on some Toujours Moi and fasten my pearl necklace and feel good, the way I did in the old days. My husband's dead. Two sons, both in Madrid, and a biopsy that fortunately came out benign. *Two* sons crazy as loons. I put them in their little sleeper suits and read them bedtime stories, and they grew up handsome and smart and ended up with psychiatrists and amphetamine problems and they ran away, both of them, on *my* money, to Madrid." She sighed. "Their father's money. Whatever."

"I don't want to take the coat because I'm not sure that I should take something when I don't know if I'm going to be around or not," Cynthia said. "This isn't my idea of living together this summer, that he disappears to Madrid and sends me one one-sentence post card."

"You're mad," Spangle's mother said. "I'm mad, too. It's my money and your time. That gives us a common bond. The mouton would give us another one: I'd give a fine present, and you'd be indebted. If the next lump is malignant, I could count on a visit from you."

"That's a horrible thing to say. You know I'd come to see you."

"I think that when called upon, most people fish out a travel brochure."

"*You* insisted that he go to Madrid."

"Oh no. You're mistaken there. I insisted that he track down his flesh-and-blood brother to bring him back to this country. He has a responsibility to his brother. His brother has followed his example for years. If Peter told him to sniff nutmeg, he sniffed nutmeg. I'm not exaggerating. All of a sudden the Hardy Boys books had a dusting of nutmeg over them."

"Then grass and drugs," Cynthia said, finishing the sentence for her.

"Sports cars, grass and drugs. My God: I used to measure out little spoonfuls of medicine and wobble forward to their little-baby mouths with them, and I cut aspirin in *quarters*, and they grew up and jumped into a sports car and threw away their money on houses they never wanted and women they hardly knew and drugs—they'd try anything. My God: He told me he wanted to go to Bard College because it was a small place—it was so pretty there, and he wouldn't just disappear in the system. *Bard College*."

"I'm sorry," Cynthia said, "but I'm very tired. I want to hang up and do some things before I have to go to bed."

"Oh, I know. I'm from another world. What must you think about a woman who grew up getting another pearl for her neck-lace every Christmas and birthday? I was so embarrassed that the chain filled up so slowly with pearls. I don't know where I put that thing."

Cynthia hung up, being careful not to touch the phone with her nails. She was becoming less and less sure that if he came back from Madrid she would even want to see him. Might as well give up on him and do something else. Screw Mary Knapp's father, who acted at lunch as though he wanted to screw her.

But she was starting to dislike men. She was starting to get very tired of all the hassles they caused, the way they just put themselves in front of you, and suddenly you had a barrier to run around. They *were* stronger; they *did* have a different kind of energy. Spangle didn't have any money, and he'd managed a trip to Spain, while she was teaching five days a week in a hot classroom —teaching boys who thought everything was either funny or point-less. When they were vocal, it was always the boys. And the god-damn magician, that completely crazy, boring, stupid magician who hounded her. If the police weren't men, she would call the police and try to get them to keep him away from her. She went to the window and looked out. A fat woman was walking a cat on a leash. A man was walking a few paces in front of her, smoking a cigar. She tried to figure out if they were together. A teenage boy in a light-blue leisure suit ran down the street, and the man with the cigar turned to look. Cynthia saw that what she had taken for a man was really a woman—a tall, heavy woman smoking a cigar.

The woman with the cigar waited. The woman with the cat caught up with her. They walked down the street together. The magician was nowhere to be seen, but if she went out he would be there. He knew that she was sick of talk about magic, and a couple of nights ago he had switched the topic to health insurance: Everyone should demand national health insurance. He had asked her to have a donut and coffee with him, and she had refused. She had even told him to leave her alone, that she was going to tell her husband that he was bothering her. That didn't stop him, because obviously her husband wasn't there. She went into the kitchen and turned on the useless fan. The idea of Spangle as a husband amused her. Once, she had wanted that: Spangle, off stoned in Madrid, who probably thought that he was going to come back and worm his way into her heart again. On the shelf above the sink was a bottle of tequila with a worm in the bottom. She thought that it would be nice to pickle her students: to have rows of canning jars, with little shrunken students inside. She wondered if the magician could help her with that plan. Because he was out there. She was sure that he was out there. If she stepped out he would be there—it would be as simple as holding out a sugar cube to a horse, a pole to a sinking person. If she went out, the magician would come for her.

She drank some Kahlua and felt sorry for herself. She put an ice cube in the glass and drank some more, tilting the glass and knocking the ice cube against the side.

She curled up in a chair in the living room and wrote her sister a letter, an ugly letter that accused her of selling out for money. She asked her sister if she would like a newly tailored mouton coat. There was no danger in writing her sister such a letter, because unless a carrier pigeon came for it, there would be no way to get it to her. There would be no way, because the mailbox was on the street and so was the magician. If she really thought that it would be as simple as her going out and his snapping to her side like a piece of iron to a magnet, she would call the police and let it all happen. But she realized that if she called them, either they would come and the magician would see them and not approach her, or else, inexplicably, he would not be there. Then she, herself, would be perceived as yet another New Haven nut. She reread the letter. It was coherent and true, and if she had the nerve, she would mail it. She had to agree with Spangle's mother that it was awful to see people throwing their lives away, and her sister was being very one-minded about dedicating herself to a rich, eccentric old man. Cynthia went into the kitchen and poured the last of the Kahlua into the glass. The first drink was all right, but the second and third were candy-sweet. She thought about calling Mary Knapp's father and asking him to come over with a bottle of gin and a bottle of tonic. He would. She thought he would. She thought that Spangle had no right to have stayed with her so long—*he* had stayed with *her*, not the other way around—only to take off, stay away. He could be anywhere, doing anything. And she had to get calls about mouton coats. If she picked up the phone—which was ringing—and it was Tess Spangle again, she was just going to hang up.

It was someone named Bobby, whom she didn't know, who said he was an old friend of Spangle's from the Cambridge and Vermont days and wanted to know if Spangle wanted to come to a party at a waterfall in New Hampshire. She told him that Spangle was in Madrid. He told her that he was going to be going to Africa in September. After they had finished talking, he said: "I haven't called the wrong number, have I? I really wanted to get in touch with Spangle. I haven't seen him since 1972. Last week I called a wrong number—a restaurant, to make a reservation—and they took my name and number and *everything*, and I'd never reached the goddamn place. I went to the restaurant and we couldn't eat dinner. My girlfriend was with me," he said. "We're going to Africa together."

She hung up and sat in the chair. From the apartment next door, she could hear music. It was a group of people singing "I'm a Yankee Doodle Dandy." The people next door had come over once, the first week she stayed in the apartment, early in the morning, to see if she had any goat's milk she could spare. "Oh man, I really didn't think so, but the things you least expect can happen sometimes," the man had said. The woman with him had just said, "Thank you anyway." She never talked much, Cynthia found out —in fact, the first time she knocked on the door, wanting Cynthia to play Go with her, she had just smiled and held out the box. They apparently had a record of "I'm a Yankee Doodle Dandy," and were singing along with it. There seemed to be lots of people singing. There was a noise that sounded like a chair crashing. The record played on, but the people stopped singing. After quite a while, during which Cynthia thought black thoughts about Spangle and her students, someone started singing "Tammy." The woman who sang it had a clear, high voice that would have been very pleasurable to listen to, if she had been singing something other than "Tammy."

Cynthia thought that she would like to have enough money to have a house in the country—Spangle had once had that—and to be able to sit in it and not hear a sound. There would be no phone in the house, and there would be no colorful locals, and if there were, they wouldn't be magicians. They would be traditionally crazy, maybe—religious fanatics, conservatives. It would be nice if there was a garden, and a deer or two; and if the deer grazed in the garden, she would not shoot them. It would be nice to worry, every summer, about what to do with so much zucchini. Zucchini bread. Zucchini bisque. Zucchini biscuits. Zucchini soufflé. Zucchini balls. Zucchini-lentil casserole. Zucchini with zucchini sauce. How had she gotten bombed on three Kahluas?

It was unbelievable. Pendergast's mother had come in, and why had she wanted her son to pass the course, in spite of his having failed every assignment? Because she did not think that she could cope with one more thing after her double mastectomy. She had said this wearing a thin cotton blouse that was as flat as a piece of paper against her chest. "All I want to do is play tennis and enjoy my summer and hope that I live," Pendergast's mother had said to her. The woman had smelled of alcohol. Scotch, probably. Drunk or not, the woman had no breasts. The thought of it made Cynthia jump out of the chair. She went to the window again, and looked out. The street was empty. Finally a little girl and her mother came by. She watched them until they were out of sight. Of course she couldn't flunk Pendergast. She wondered if she could flunk Mary Knapp. She wondered if she would ever have a better job than the one she had this summer.

There was a fight going on in the hall. A woman was crying. She thought about putting the chain on and peeking out, but decided not to. The woman who was crying—no, a different woman, because the crying kept on—was saying: "You recorded me singing 'Tammy,' you son-of-a-bitch. You give me that goddamn cassette." Another noise that sounded like a chair breaking. People running down the stairs. She went to the window and looked out. A girl about twenty, in a long, wraparound Indian cotton skirt, red running shoes, and a silver halter top was running to the left, and a man was chasing a woman, running to the right. The man caught the woman, picked her up and carried her back toward the building. They passed the building, though, and laughing, continued down the street. Why couldn't the magician be interested in them? Another woman, with a sailor's cap and white pants and a black shirt, came down the steps. She didn't seem to be drunk. She turned around to wave, and Cynthia jerked her head back from the window. She peeked again, to see if the magician was out there. He was, but she couldn't see him. He really did manage to come out of nowhere. She tried to imagine where he could be hiding that he would have a view of the street in front of the building, but she never saw him.

Pendergast's mother had asked her if she played tennis.

Bobby called again, this time to give her a message for Spangle. The message was that he was saving an article for Spangle from the *New York Times* about umbrella bamboo, which flowers once every hundred years, then dies. All the world's umbrella bamboo was about to flower and die. "It's not as depressing as it sounds, if you read the article," Bobby said. "When Spangle gets back, ask him to call me. Here's my number. Have you got a pencil?"

She found enough Grand Marnier, left over from a soufflé they had made a long time ago, to have a shot-glassful. She drank it, thinking that it was probably possible to combine zucchini and Grand Marnier. *The Desperation Cookbook*, she would call it. At the end of every recipe it could say, "If desperate, substitute any ingredients." My God—imagine not having your breasts. What awful things happened to women.

She went into the bedroom and undressed. She took her cotton nightgown from the foot of the bed and put it on, thinking that she would shower later. There was nothing in the apartment to eat, and undressing removed the temptation to go out and find food. There was a *New York Times* on the bedroom floor. She got into bed, put Spangle's pillow behind her pillow, and stretched out. Flipping through the paper, she found some answers to a quiz she hadn't seen:

2. Mr. Niehouse, an American businessman, was rescued and returned to the United States after having been held captive by leftist guerrillas in Venezuela since his kidnapping in February 1976.
3. The number of passenger cars has remained about the same.

She looked through the rest of the paper. Mayor Koch, she found out, had refused to control the pigeon problem by shooting them. His reason was: "When you go after a pigeon, all the people who love pigeons will hate you." She read about police officer Ignatius Gentile, who jumped in front of a subway car in Brooklyn. She learned that Bloomingdale's had quickly sold out of its Skylab Protective Helmet. She spent most of the time studying the crossword puzzle, wondering about 49 down: "——Across the Table," 1934 song. Five letters. The Grand Marnier was gone. Spangle was in Madrid. Pendergast's mother's breasts were gone. Only the magician was sure to be out there, all revved up, full of tricks, eager to talk. If she thought he was dangerous, she would have been terrified, but she was more frightened of that crazy what's-his-name in her class, with his motorcycle and his painted-on smile, than she was of the magician. Maybe she could agree to have coffee and donuts with him in exchange for his coming to her class and doing magic tricks. He could have the students jump through a burning hoop, and if they missed, what the hell.

The phone rang, and she almost didn't answer it, but at the last minute, the eighth ring, she thought that it might be Spangle. She went to the phone. It was her sister. Cynthia told her that she had written her a letter, but that she didn't have to worry—it wouldn't get mailed. In the morning she would be sober, and in the morning, when she dared to go out, the temptation to send it would be gone.

"How nasty was it?" her sister said.

"I said you'd sold out for money and security."

"*That's* certainly true. What was the nasty part?"

Cynthia sighed. "I'm glad I didn't bother to go mail it."

"What did you mean before, when you said that in the morning you'd dare to go out?"

"Oh, I wasn't really serious. There's some creepy guy around here who's from the West Coast—I guess that part is true, at least—and he's got a crush on me. Guess what he is."

"A midget?"

"No. A serious guess."

"A Rolfer."

"No. You're getting close. Sort of close."

"Don't let a Rolfer touch you. It's just sadism."

"Come on, guess."

"Where on the West Coast?"

"Los Angeles."

"Not much help. Is he a shrink of any kind?"

"No."

"Movies."

"Nope. Not movies."

"If he's not a midget Rolfer who's writing a screenplay, I can't guess."

"A magician. A pull-the-rabbit-out-of-the-hat type magician."

"Jesus. I'd watch out for him."

"I guess I wouldn't talk about him so much if he didn't sort of give me the creeps. I've only seen him three times actually, but he just *appears*. He's odd. He talks like we're old friends."

"You're right. Don't go out. You can insult me on the phone. It's Bill's money, too. Fifteen cents for a stamp."

"Is he richer and richer?" Cynthia said.

"God, yes. Of course. He wants to have a baby."

"Don't do it."

"Honey, I wouldn't. Things are just calming down with us. I overate strawberries, and you remember how fruit used to make me break out? I went to a dermatologist and told him I sprayed myself with cologne all over, and he said it was the cologne, of course, and that I had to stop using it. I made him put it in writing. At first Bill wanted me to try new scents, but I told him that the dermatologist had said no: nothing on my skin but Castile soap. So for the first time in years I don't smell like a florist's. If he hints around about trying a new cologne, I just buy a pint of strawberries and eat them on the sly. But the baby thing—my God. He read that Leboyer book, which he got from some guy flying first-class with him from Atlanta to New York, and by the time he hit LaGuardia, he could hardly wait to get the limo home to tell me that he thought something of ours should be born to the Moonlight Sonata. *God*. The idiots you meet in first class."

"You're not going to marry him, are you?"

"Well, I might. I just wouldn't have a baby. I know it's corny, but I really do love the Moonlight Sonata, and once I'd gritted my teeth through it, it would be ruined forever."

"What are you eating?" Cynthia said.

"A vegetable burrito. Leftovers from last night's dinner. The same man who gave him the Leboyer book gave him a recipe for vegetable burritos, and he went out and bought all the ingredients and made them. *God*." She stopped chewing. "But the reason I called is to say that we're going to have a house on the Vineyard next month, and we want you to come see us. He has a rich friend who isn't too old. Fortyish. He'd love to meet you. Spangle doesn't deserve you. If he wanted to get home he could haul ass, you know."

"I'm pretty disgusted with him. With his mother, too. She calls almost every damn night, and she means to be nice, but I just can't stand to talk to her. She's crazier than Spangle, in her way."

"I never thought Spangle was particularly crazy. I just don't think he has enough money. We'll have a convertible on the Vineyard."

"He'll get you pregnant. Then what will you do?"

"Honey, I am *not* helpless."

"He's going to trick you, somehow."

"*You're* the one *I'm* worried about. It would be just like Spangle to come back to New Haven and propose to you, and I think you might even do it."

"No. I feel differently from the way I felt when he left. It's hot in this apartment and I work all the time, and I feel like I've been abandoned. I'm not in the mood to tie a bandanna around my head and be a happy housewife."

"Come to the Vineyard. We'll have the house full-time, after this weekend. It's going to be a Mustang convertible."

"Thanks for the invitation. I'll probably come."

"Spangle's welcome, you know. I say awful things about him, but I like him. I even downplayed how crazy he was a minute ago. That was a nice thing to do for him, wasn't it?"

"It would take a lot more than a casual remark from you to convince me at this point. I keep having the feeling that he's not in Madrid, but I guess he is. I mean, where would he be? He wasn't mad at me when he left. He was kidding around, like always."

"Anybody could be anywhere. I'd say listen to your hunches."

"I feel like he's around. I feel that way about the magician, too, so maybe it's just paranoia."

"I thought you told me this magician kept appearing."

"He does. But not every time. Never in the morning."

"Stay in until morning," she said. "Jesus." She was chewing again. "I got lonesome for you tonight. I liked it when we saw each other more. Why don't you come live near us in Philadelphia?"

"Why don't you find me a job?"

"I *found* you a man. Good-looking, too. Forty-nine, to be honest with you, but a very nice body. He doesn't even wear glasses. And there are no children. One Irish wolfhound only. He talks about getting another one, but I doubt it. You can see him running down the beach every morning with the dog from all the windows across the front of the house we're going to be renting. Sometimes it just kills me that Bill has so much money. Like Dylan says: 'I can't help it if I'm lucky.' "

"Where does Dylan say that?"

"The song about how somebody gets shot and he runs away with the man's wife, and she's got all her husband's money. Bill's wife just dropped dead at fifty-four. I never even met her. I have nothing to feel guilty about. You've got a job and I don't, though. Not that I ever wanted one, but maybe that was because I worked such shit jobs. Remember the telephone company? That awful dress shop where everything stank of incense?" She laughed. "God, there's a whole bank of white hyacinths in the courtyard outside this window. The spotlight is on them, and there are moths flying above them, a storm of moths. You promise to come to the Vineyard?"

"I promise," Cynthia said.

When she hung up, she went to the window again. A police car drove down the block very fast and turned the corner with its light flashing. A tall, thin girl that she recognized walked into the building. It seemed to be a normal night of street life. She was probably silly for staying in, for letting some pathetic, odd man get to her so much that she wouldn't go out for food. She wouldn't. She went back into the bedroom, set the alarm for early and went to bed.

It was strange not to have Spangle in the bed. She had gotten used to the way he tore the covers up from the bottom and turned and thrashed all night, flapping his arms like some big, heavy bird. She was even used to him screaming, his arms covering his head, his body tensed for the fireball that he imagined rolling toward him like a bowling ball rolling down the lane—the lane was the bed he slept in. It was so quiet in bed when Spangle wasn't there. She bounced on the mattress a couple of times, to hear it make a noise. Then it was quiet again. When Spangle was there, he fell asleep so deeply so soon that she spent the first hour in bed awakening him, consoling him, carefully pulling covers out of his fist, across herself. When she was alone, she thought. She thought about what had become of her sister, and about Mrs. Pendergast's breasts, and about what she had said—that she only wanted to play tennis. There were a lot of things for which graduate school did not prepare you. That was the virtue of it, Spangle said—that you could spend years learning, and in the end, almost nothing you learned would apply. But Cynthia thought it would be helpful if something prepared you for a talk with Mrs. Pendergast. When she had to think quickly, she could never think of anything to say. Her advice to Spangle was easy—she had it down to four words now: "There is no fireball." She had not even thought of that many words to say when Mrs. Pendergast had started crying. It seemed wrong just to say no when she was asked if she played tennis. But that was the one word she had said. She suddenly remembered which Dylan song it was: the one that began, "Someone's got it in for me."

He had intended to play it cool, but for days he had been thinking about seeing her, and it was a hot night and he couldn't sleep, and finally it started to make sense to him that he should dress and go out. He wouldn't see her, but he would see where she lived. Maybe his walking by would generate some good energy and he could send it to her, and she would feel it. She would probably be asleep. It was almost one in the morning. He would think thoughts of love and close his eyes and try to send the thoughts like little darts into her dreams.

He put on his white painter's pants with the loops on the sides. Keys on key rings dangled from each side of his pants. Keys to the crazy millionaire Tucker's house in Beverly Hills: Tucker gave away keys because he thought that it would assure him of not being killed in some bizarre Manson-type murder. His astrologer had told him so, and he kept a brandy snifter full of Andes mints, matches from The Palm, and house keys on the hall table by the door. Keys to his friend Roy's beachhouse in Malibu: three locks on the front door, and Roy wouldn't see an astrologer on a bet. The keys to his mother's apartment here in New Haven. A key that he had had for years, found in Golden Gate Park, a heavy, old-fashioned key with a tiny piece of tape across the top with J. Brown lettered on it. He liked to think that it would fit the lock in Governor Jerry Brown's apartment. That would be a lot more status than having one of the many keys to Tucker's.

He wished that he had her key. He would put it in the lock, thinking good thoughts: that she shouldn't be afraid, that he only wanted to talk to her, that he was willing to talk about things other than magic. To tell the truth, he got tired of thinking and talking about magic all the time; he had been reading the newspaper at his mother's and getting mad about all the injustices in the world, and about how little the country did for its citizens. He had read, in the New York Times, that the mayor was not in favor of shooting pigeons, although the mayor did agree with somebody else who had said that they were like rodents with wings. If the mayor and all his staff and all the working people in New York got together and thought, it might be possible to send messages to the pigeons to get them to go away and roost somewhere else. He was glad that the mayor was not going to give his okay to pigeon-killing, even though he said he didn't like the pigeons. People gave the okay to things too much, and that ruined the world for magic. When so many things of all sorts were happening, people's minds got overloaded, and they stopped caring whether a woman was sawed in half or levitated from a table. They didn't care that one rabbit could burst into twenty. It would be hard to care about magic if you read the paper every night, because there were so many explanations: why pigeons thrived in New York, how we could be sure that there wasn't gasoline hidden in tanks in New Jersey, what you could do if you were followed by someone you thought meant you harm, how to plant zucchini. When people did calm down and got ready to watch magic, all they cared about was what was behind it. Or else they wanted something from it: They wanted you to wave a wand and send the pigeons out of New York; they wanted to believe that you could make their zucchini multiply overnight, instead of waiting for the seeds to germinate. But he was thinking about magic again, and he'd sworn to himself that this would be a real vacation, and he wouldn't think about magic all the time. He tried to think about national health insurance, but his mind bogged down and he got images of dogs leaping through hoops and disappearing. A green plant on a table, then the plant covered by a cloth, and when the cloth was pulled back, an orchid was blooming on the plant. He wondered if it would make an impression if he took her an orchid. He did not think that there was anywhere to buy an orchid in New Haven at one in the morning (he thought he knew where he could do it in Malibu), and even if he had it, of course, she would be asleep. His mother's Vogue *had suggested that the caring hostess might put a fresh orchid on her guest's pillow.*

His mother heard the keys jingling and said, "Where are you going?"

"I'm going to take a walk," he said.

"When are you going back to California?" she said.

He wished she would stop asking that. He wondered if even an orchid would shut her up, and decided that it wouldn't. He didn't answer her. He picked up his false nose, on impulse, and put it in the pants pocket and went out the door. He turned around and pulled the knob three times, to make sure that it was really closed and not just stuck. She always got up after him to check the door —it was a funny door—and if he did manage to have a nice night somehow, he wouldn't want to ruin it by coming back to the apartment and having to listen to one of her tirades.

He walked until he came to her block, and then to her building. He was nervous. He had given up cigarettes six months ago, so he fished his false nose out of his pants pocket and tapped it onto his nose, took it off again, put it in place again. Then he put it back in his pocket. The one rabbit that became twenty was in the pocket, too. She had liked that. Maybe he had just shown her too much too quickly. He could have shown her the tricks over a period of time.

He was not sure which window was hers. One was dark—the one he thought was hers—and in several other apartments there was faint bluish light. As he watched, someone began to move around one of the apartments. The person opened the window. It wasn't her. Maybe it was her husband, if she really had a husband. The way she had said it, he had doubted it, and he was usually good at picking up those vibrations. He crossed the street and looked at the building, sending good thoughts into the windows. In response, music started playing. The thoughts had gotten in to the people! They were joyful; there was music! He crossed the street again, and close to the building he heard that it was a sad song he had listened to when he was a child; but it didn't sound like Debbie Reynolds singing. "Wish I knew that he knew what I'm thinkin' of . . ." It was always so hard to get through to people, even if you tried to speak to them directly sometimes; by sending thoughts, you could do better than speaking to them. He reached in his pocket and took out a handkerchief and tossed it toward the windows on the third floor. As it rose, the handkerchief opened and unfolded into something close to the shape of a dove. He kissed the tips of his fingers and waved his hand in the direction of the handkerchief-bird. Then, when it fell, he retrieved it and shook it flat and put it in his pocket. Of course, at almost two A.M., she would not be awake. But somehow—psychically—hadn't his loving thoughts come home to roost?

15

"THIS IS a friend of mine from college," Nina said. "I can tell from the expression on your face what you're thinking. A great number of people act very strangely, but my strangeness is that I'm so predictable. I didn't sleep with him."

The man, whoever he was, laughed. He got up from the sofa, where he was sprawled in his underwear, and came forward, with his hand out. "It's true," he said. "How do you do? I'm Peter Spangle."

He shook the man's hand. Nina went into the kitchen, and he could see her, bowl of cereal on the counter at her side, peeling an orange.

"I have to talk to you," John said, going into the kitchen. He rubbed his hand across her shoulder blades, low, where the yellow tiger was lunging. "My robe," he said. "Nina?" he said.

"I've got to go to work. I don't have a rich husband like you to support me. If I don't go to work, I get fired. It's nobody's fault but mine that I got wrecked last night, but I am trying—" She nicked her thumb cutting the orange. She put the knife down and went to the cold water and turned it on. She put her cut finger under the water, and started to cry.

Jesus Christ, he thought: *blood*.

"You two want to talk. I guess I ought to get going anyway," Spangle said. He pulled his T-shirt over his head. "What she said was the truth," he said, brushing his hair out of his face.

"I'm sure it *is* the truth."

"I'm sure it doesn't much *matter* to anybody," Nina said. "We never really discussed it, but since you think I'm so perfect, that must be something you're liberal-minded about, right?"

John leaned over, bracing himself with his elbows on the kitchen counter. "Why are you doing this?" he said. "Nina?"

"What are you doing here at seven o'clock in the morning? I might like a little privacy. People show up whenever they want, spend the night—you *don't* show up and spend the night, you do that when you feel inclined and you don't when you don't, and you show up in the morning as though I'd owe you some apology."

"I'm going to call you," Spangle said. "Take care."

"Wait," Nina said. "Just wait."

She followed Spangle out of the apartment, closing the door behind her. "I embarrassed you," she said, at the foot of the stairs.

"You didn't embarrass me. You're his girl, right? You didn't sleep with me. We both agree. How can I be embarrassed?"

"Please don't go," she said. "Wait a minute. I'm not even clear on what you two were doing here."

"We flew back from Madrid and I didn't feel like going back to New Haven, and he certainly didn't want to check in with my mother, and my esteemed brother scored some hash in the toilet at Kennedy and we looked you up in the phone book, and the rest of it—Horton what's-his-name—is all your fault." Spangle looked down, shook his head, laughed. "My motives weren't pure," he said. "Maybe if we hadn't gotten wrecked, you wouldn't have been telling him the truth this morning."

"I would have told him the truth whatever it was."

"Then I'm glad we didn't. After a night like that, the last thing I need is to have my head knocked all the way off."

"*I'm* embarrassed now," Nina said.

"Then we're even," he said. "You were right. I *was* embarrassed. You ought to go back up."

She shook her head. "I don't know," she said. "I still can't believe that I'm standing in this hallway talking to you. The two of you were in Spain all these years?"

"I was just over there a couple of weeks. He was shacked up with some señorita who was trying to get him to pay for a lot of expensive dental work she needed done, it turns out. I went over to get him."

"I wish I had a sister or a brother," she said.

"You've got good friends. Reliable friends," he said. "They might go a few years without seeing you, but eventually they show up."

"It makes me nervous that everything just happens," she said. "I mean, I can sort of count on people, sometimes, but other times . . . for some reason, I just didn't appreciate his coming over here this morning unannounced."

"You'd better go back," Spangle said. "Jonathan's going to be staying with friends in the West Village. I'll be coming in to see him. Can we see you? Straight?"

"What about the girl you live with? Isn't she coming?"

"I've been trying to think about that, and all I know is that right now I can't think about that. I don't think I'm going back to New Haven right away. She blames me for living. She's got a lousy job this summer, and she takes it out on me. I guess she's got a right to. I'm just not up for it today."

"Where are you going?"

"I don't know."

"Do you want me to leave you the key? You could come back here when I'm at work. You could use some sleep."

"The offer's just for the key and sleep?"

She sighed, shook her head no, but said, "I don't know. Do you want it?"

"I'd be a real shit to louse things up for you," he said. "No. But let's have dinner, you and me and Jonathan."

"Okay," she said. "Thanks."

He turned to go.

"It was so strange seeing you again. I shouldn't have gotten that stuff from Horton. It was my fault."

"I don't know how to deal with anything either," he said. He took his comb out of his pocket, ran it through his hair a few times.

He could only comb the top part; his hair was long, and it had gotten hopelessly matted from the ears to the shoulder. He looked the way he had at Bard. If she remembered correctly what he had looked like when he first walked in, he had even looked healthy. No living on Drake's Ring Dings and reds; the sunshine of—where was it?

"Where were you in Spain?" she said.

"Madrid." He shook his head. "I know," he said. "Fucked, fucked, fucked. Call you later in the week."

"Call me," she said.

"I'll call you," he said.

"Call me," she said.

He laughed and she smiled. She went upstairs smiling. She had not recovered as well from the night before as she had thought; she realized it when she went to open the door: Her finger was still bleeding, and blood stained the sleeve of the robe. She took it off the minute she got in the door, disgusted, and took it to the bathroom, holding the sleeve under cold water in the sink.

"What's the matter?" he said, standing in the doorway to the bedroom. He wanted her to say: *Nothing. What's the matter with you?* She didn't answer him.

He watched her washing the sleeve of the robe. She had on a pair of white underpants, and nothing else. Her hair wasn't combed.

"I cut up the orange for you," he said. He walked away, went to the sofa and lifted books and papers off it and sat down.

She went from the bathroom into the kitchen without saying anything.

"I think what I blurted out was the truth: that I hardly ever see you, and if I work all the time, I should get to have fun, too. Why don't you give your wife your money and me your time?"

"Jesus," he said. "You really don't know what you're saying."

"Why don't I know what I'm saying?" She started to sit next to him, decided to sit on the floor instead. When she sat down, everything started to slow up: She couldn't say the sentences she had thought to say; lifting the spoon from the bowl to her mouth was an effort. Her finger throbbed, and she looked down at the toilet paper she had wrapped around her finger, to see if it was red.

It was white. She spooned another piece of orange off the top of the cereal and put it in her mouth and chewed.

"Why don't I know what I'm saying?"

"Can we talk?" he said. "Are you going to rush out of here?"

He was crying. She looked up and saw that tears were rolling down his cheeks. She got up and walked to the sofa, sat down beside him. "What is going on?" she said.

"You're right," he said. "I don't do *this* well, and I certainly didn't do *that* well."

"Wait a minute," she said, lifting his hand off his leg, grabbing it hard. "What is going *on?*"

"I don't know how to say this," he said. "I'm just starting to realize that it's odd that I'm here. Will you call Nick? Can you see if he's going to be around?"

"Call Nick at home?" she said.

"It's early in the morning, isn't it? I forgot that. I can call Nick later," he said.

"In the meantime, why don't you tell me what's going on?"

"Jesus Christ," he said. "What if you had slept with him? What if I walked in on that?"

"You could call before you come over."

"But I never even thought about that. I think of this as home."

"It's *my* home. Your home is in Connecticut. Or Rye. Wherever you want to say it is."

"It's here," he said, balling up a pillow. "It's here, whatever you say." He threw the pillow, hard. It tipped over an empty bottle—a ginger-ale bottle with cigarette butts in it. He stared at the chaos of the room.

"Nina," he said, "I was coming up those stairs, and you don't know what I was going through, trying to get to the top. It would have been such a goddamn *soap opera* if you had been here with somebody else."

"Maybe it's a soap opera anyway. A quick dinner and an off-camera fuck. Sometimes I think trying to keep you is hopeless, like trying to keep a hat from blowing away in the wind, when you can't even put your hand up to hold it. I feel that powerless—that I can't even grab on to the edge of something. If we hadn't gotten stoned, I don't know what things would have been like when you appeared here this morning. I just know that I'm tired of trying to keep things together. I feel like I don't have any control. I'm sick of it. I might as well sit here and smoke the rest of that grass and lose my job, and not fucking *care*. You can support me, like a *real* mistress. Make this a *real* soap opera." She got up, because her words were coming out funny, and she thought she was going to cry. She picked up the bowl of cereal and sat down again. She realized that the bowl was not a crystal ball, but she stared into it.

"You can't go to work," he said. "You aren't going to work, are you?"

"You'd better tell me what's going on. I've given all the explanation you deserve, and more, about what was going on here. Now you tell me why you showed up here at seven-thirty in the morning, and why I can't go to work."

"It's not a quick dinner and a quick fuck. I've spent eight hours here a lot of nights. I've gotten back to Rye at three in the morning, and had to work the next day."

"You want it to be over. Is that it?"

"That is the last thing I want."

"Shall we play twenty questions?"

"Can we go lie down? *Just* lie down?"

He wouldn't talk when they went into the bedroom. After a long while he rolled from his back to his stomach. He was too still, and too quiet, to be asleep. She decided to say nothing and wait. She even felt sorry enough for him, after a while, to put her hand on his back. She got up on one arm and put her hand on his back, stroked it down his spine, up again, lightly massaged his neck. She stared at the clock. Five minutes passed. She called Lord and Taylor's and said that she was sick. Crying helped. She went back to bed and saw that he had rolled over on his back again, and that his eyes were very red—from being against the pillow, or because he had cried, she couldn't tell. She stroked her hand down his chest. She unbuttoned his shirt and stroked the bare skin.

"Okay," she said. "What?"

"What I was feeling coming up those stairs," he said. "It was like coming to you was happening in slow motion. There were so many feelings, and they kept getting heavier and heavier. They were stopping me from moving."

"It's good you didn't get stoned with us. If you think that when you're straight, you wouldn't have been a good influence last night."

"Last night," he said. "My God. Last night."

"Look," she said, "tell me you're all right, and we can sleep, or you can have me play twenty questions, or if you just want to talk, I'll listen to you. All right?"

Her finger was tracing the line of his breastbone. He could close his eyes, and feel a small path being traced on his body. Her finger inched along, traveling little distances. He had driven, on no sleep, from Connecticut to New York, gone to the garage, gotten a cab to her apartment, and now he was feeling more than he had felt in all the time he had been awake, traveling, going crazily from one place to the next. He was here, and still. Her finger was moving, curving around his body.

"*I'm* all right," he said. "Mary isn't. John Joel shot her."

*He was walking up the stairs. It was a simple accomplishment—
the sort of thing they teach brain-damaged people to do. Later,
when they master the mechanics of climbing, they teach them not
to frown or squint. The trick is not to show that you're concentrating. There was a school for brain-damaged people—teenage
children, mostly—somewhere near where he worked, and several
times during his lunch hour he had seen them parading down the
street. They had things to do: trash to throw away. Well—maybe
that was the only thing. They had trash to throw away. He and
Nick had been coming back from lunch the first time, and Nick
had called his attention to them. As months went by he and Nick
had watched their progress. It was horribly slow progress, and it
might never have occurred to them to think of it as progress at
all if Nick hadn't noticed the way they had stopped holding hands.
At first, they held hands like small schoolchildren. Then they
walked close together, almost shoulder to shoulder. Then, by the
time spring came, when everybody else in the city was walking
close together—men steering women along, their hands on their
bare shoulders, people hip to hip on the grass in Central Park—the*

brain-damaged people had let go of each other and walked farther apart. Either they had been taught not to frown and look frightened or the spring had touched them in some way. One time, as they watched, a man carrying a blaring cassette player got into the middle of them, and they started to scatter like frightened ducks; then the two men at the front came and tried to round them up. Eventually they did, and the parade huddled together again and turned the corner. Nick claimed he watched because it reminded him that there were worse problems than having to deal with Metcalf. He claimed he watched because Nick had gotten him hooked. He was not used to seeing slow, regular movement in the city. He had gotten used to watching people slap down change for the newspaper without missing a beat, to arms suddenly stretched out for cabs, to people walking down a street so that you couldn't tell whether or not they were together. Even when they spoke to each other, that didn't mean for sure that they were together.

Walking up the steps to Nina's apartment, he had thought for a second that something was missing—a leader was missing. And no one was behind him. He was there alone, doing this simple thing; and he thought that he was never going to be able to make it to the top, and that if he did, it was too much to expect that he would have a pleasant expression on his face when he got there. He would just have to get there and be there, and then—and then what? The stairs were buckling and shifting under him; they were delivering him to a room that would tilt crazily. He rubbed his face. He hadn't had any sleep, and he was exhausted, and the faint stinging-itch across his neck, below his ears, had started: the signal that he was about to have a pounding headache. He must have been on the stairs for a long time. He kept looking over his shoulder, as though there were better air below him, and if he turned his head he might be able to breathe. He kept turning his head, and the building was quiet—no one behind him. But every time he moved forward, there were just as many stairs, it seemed. His legs felt heavy. His head. Finally he had dashed up the stairs and gotten to the top, panting, feeling as crazy as one of the brain-damaged people would feel if he were capable of seeing himself in perspective. If the piece of paper drops on the sidewalk instead of into the trash container, so what? So what? he was saying out loud. So what? he whispered. No one heard the whisper, and he did not hear any noise: no breakfast dishes clattering, no radio music, no alarms going off. He put his hands over his ears and took them away, to see if there was more sound when he removed his hands. His hearing was fading. What if Nina opened the door and said something, said some important thing, and he didn't know what she was saying? His eyes hurt too much to concentrate on reading her lips. Her lips. Nina. He knocked on the door, and he smiled. He heard something. From inside, he heard water running. And then he knocked again, and then she was there: he could see her breasts almost down to the nipples. She had on the robe she had given him, and when she spoke, he heard what she said. He saw the man, standing to the side. For an awkward second, nobody said anything. He looked behind him and saw the stairs. When he blinked, they stopped slowly swaying.

16

ALTHOUGH HE HAD promised Brandt he would take him to see the Little League game that night, he had gone to the house in Connecticut, instead of going back to Rye. Louise had called him and said that she wanted to talk. "Can you give me a hint?" he said, hoping that he was keeping his voice even. It had to be that she wanted a divorce. All that hanging out with Tiffy Adamson had paid off in the long run; Louise had not called him at the office for a year, except about the most trivial things. Certainly her calling him in New York and asking him to call the house in Connecticut because she was too busy, and Mary had to put hamburger meat out to defrost, was a little dig at him, a reminder that there was a world there he wasn't a part of. It also let him know how banal she thought that world was, but that she was doing the proper thing, coping with it, while he was not. She had called and asked *him* to ask Mary to put hamburger meat out. He laughed, telling Nina later, and Nina had said that she thought it was sad. "Which part of it?" he said, and she said, "All of it." So Tiffy had gotten through to Louise. She had convinced her to ask for a divorce.

"No hints," she said. "Will you be here for dinner, or later?"

"I'll come for dinner," he said. He was suddenly feeling generous. The end of summer was coming, and she was making it easy for him—she was asking him to go instead of making him ask her. She was going to tell him that she wanted a divorce.

After a little while, he felt almost melancholy about it. He told Nick, when he came in with iced coffee for the two of them, that his sadness wasn't really much about what he was losing: Visiting rights would give him as much time with Mary and John Joel as he spent with them now; and if he gave Louise what she wanted and she was halfway reasonable, they might even be friends in the way they hadn't been friends for years. His sorrow was that he felt that he was losing so little. Or maybe he had lost a lot, fast, years ago; he had lost it and the loss had never caught up with him, and now he didn't feel much emotion about saying that it was gone.

"It would serve you right if she demanded a mink coat. If that's what the call was about," Nick said. "My wife used to call when we were fighting it out in court. She would be in the courtroom the day before and wouldn't even look at me, let alone speak, and then as though nothing had happened, she'd call and tell me about an August fur sale at Bendel's."

Nick was talking, but John was only half listening to him. He was looking at the picture of his family, minus Brandt, on Nantucket, and thinking how sad it must be to have old pictures, happy pictures, and suddenly see something ironic in them years later. Or for those pictures to give you a sense that something meaningful had been lost. He looked at the picture, and felt the same way he had felt when the roll of film came back from the camera store, the same way he had felt when he picked out the one he wanted to have enlarged to five by seven—that this was the expected picture. It was a picture he had known would exist one day before he ever met and married Louise. He stared at Mary's bathing suit, at the rows of gingerbread men, arms outstretched, touching hands. A band of gingerbread men, and then another, and then another, as evenly spaced, as regular, as the gray bands on his mother's television screen, but not rolling—no movement. Just the line of them, brown and expressionless. The gingerbread men looked like Mr. Bill. The man in the camera store had said that it would cost more, but that they could fix the print; they could burn in the deck, for instance. "Burn it?" John had said.

The man at the camera store was young—probably some starving young photographer, probably some genius of a photographer, sick to death of looking at pictures like this day after day. "When you develop a picture—if it's there in the negative—you can give some parts of the picture more exposure time than the rest, and that will darken it, bring in detail." He had been so interested in the things the man described that he had bought a book about developing and printing pictures that he found for a dollar at a tag sale that summer. But he had not had the picture improved. He had just wanted it enlarged, and then he had framed it. No burning or dodging. Holding back, putting more in—it was a joke, how sexual everything was. He looked at Louise, her stomach big with Brandt, forcing her rows of gingerbread men to curve.

He had a picture of Nina that he loved—the only picture he had ever seen of her as a child, a picture her mother had sent to her when she was cleaning out the house. It had been taken, Nina thought, at a table in a seafood restaurant they went to in Atlantic City. Nina was sitting in an inside chair, next to her mother, a too-large white sailor's hat perched on her head like Jughead's crown, and her hands were neatly folded on the table—it could have been a Bible, instead of a food-stained tablecloth—and Nina looked beatific. He had had trouble explaining to her why he used that word. The glass of ginger ale—it had one of those silly paper umbrellas resting on the rim of the glass, and a cherry sunk halfway down—might have been a chalice. Her face was clear and pretty, and she looked like the Nina he knew now did when she was sleeping; but her big child's eyes were open in the picture, and she was smiling a little more than she ever did in her sleep. Her father sat across from her. He had her wide-set eyes, her widow's peak, her mouth. Her uncle—her mother's brother—sat next to her father. There was a beer bottle in front of her uncle's place, a Coke bottle beside a glass where her mother sat, and her father had a glass on a stem, a martini glass. Nina could remember her father telling the woman who came to the table to photograph them that he would take one big picture and a set of matchbooks. What had become of a dozen matchbooks with Nina's family on them?

"When they start to harden, they want fur," Nick was saying. "Ever notice that? When their hair gets dry and they go to exercise class and get all toned up, they start thinking about fur." Nick puffed on his cigarettte, not inhaling. "When they start to get old, and they're afraid of getting cold. They think about being hard and cold and in the ground, and the answer is a mink coat."

"What the hell are you talking about?"

"Metcalf just passed on one of his accounts to me. I've got to think of some way to convince the twenty-five-and-under crowd that they want to wear mink and not worry about dead animals. I've got to convince people twenty-five and under that it doesn't matter that some animal is trapped and killed." Nick got up and looked out the window. "I don't want to," Nick said. "Days like today, I'd like to just lie in the grass naked. Maybe I could do something along the lines of the avocado ads, where the woman grows the plant from the pit. I could offer the twenty-five-and-under crowd a free bag of mink bones with their coat. Tell them their wishes would all come true if they wished on a mink bone. Poor minks. Poor fuckers."

Nick wandered out of the office. In the corridor he turned and said: "I wish you luck. I really do. I hope she wants a divorce and doesn't take you for everything you've got. But I guess it doesn't matter much to you. I guess you're serious about liking that tiny apartment on Columbus Avenue."

He called Nina at Lord and Taylor's to tell her that Louise had called, and that he thought she was going to ask for a divorce. He changed his mind about telling her, though, and he was half glad when he was connected with the wrong person. He knew that Nina thought he was a coward. "A wise coward," she said, qualifying it. "I don't know that I'd walk out on a family." She had had dreams, when they first met, that she was bobbing in the water along with Louise and John Joel and Brandt and Mary, and that he was in a boat only large enough to take one of them on board. Sometimes he would reach for her, sometimes Louise, sometimes one of the children. She would tread water for what seemed like hours. And then she would dream the rest of it: No matter who he reached for, everything got blurry, and then she was somewhere looking down, puzzled because what was in the boat was a starfish, or a sea nettle, a sea anemone, a water lily, a conch shell. Some small, beautiful sea creature would be in the boat with him. She had told him the dream in early May, the second time they had gone away together, to Nick's sister's house in Provincetown. High up on one of the dunes, a bright day with still an edge of winter, she had suddenly remembered, looking out at the water, her peculiar dreams about the drifting boat, the outstretched arm. They had sat on top of one of the dunes, the beach deserted, and she had told him about it, shaking her head in embarrassment, because the dream obviously meant that she thought he could save her. He had made light of it. The truth was that he did not think of her as someone who needed saving. He thought that she could save *him*, that her light grip on his arm, as they sat on top of the dune, was anchoring his body to the earth. Who *would* he really save if they were all in the water? He thought that he would try to haul all of them into the boat, too ashamed to claim the one he really wanted. She was right: He was a coward. He kicked a little sand down the slope and watched it gather more with it and go like a trickle of water until it stopped. Now the shape of the dune was different, though no one else would notice. He looked at it. He couldn't look at her. He didn't know what to say when she was so honest. He didn't know how to say, simply, okay, if you think that having me will save you, you can have me. If he could really have believed that he would be leaving Louise and the children to save *her*, then he probably would have done it instantly, but he was sure that he was leaving to save himself. She thought she couldn't cope very well with things, but she could. She was more complicated than she knew. She dreamed questions while he dreamed answers: In the morning her questions were still good, but his answers were simple, facile. They didn't apply. Later that day he and Nina had gone back to the house, sure that everyone would know that they had made love, and Nick had been in the kitchen with Laurie, who was his girl then, scrubbing clean a bucket of mussels. They had had a stew made of mussels and shrimp, and they had all gotten a little drunk on ale. Nick's sister had a movie projector, and they had watched *Dial M for Murder* after dinner, and then gone for a walk along the beach. Nick's straw hat had blown off, and Laurie had chased it into the cold, black water. When she retrieved it, she shook it and put it on, holding the hat with one hand, and Nick's hand with her other. Back at the house, Nick had talked about living with people who mattered to you: having some huge, grand house somewhere by the sea, and all your good friends living in the house. There couldn't be any cats, because he hated cats; but there could be dogs, hundreds of collies, poking their long snouts into everything, miracle collies that would go to the beach to sniff out mussels and come up with truffles instead. Truffles would roll around the huge house like billiard balls. They would play indoor miniature golf with truffles. Nick's sister had sighed. She was just back from France, and had made the mistake of telling him about the white truffle she had brought back with her. The next afternoon they had eaten it, grated over pasta. When they left on Sunday night, they were high on nothing but the good time they had had. He and Nick had bought a present for Nick's sister at a greenhouse they walked to early Sunday morning: a plant with pink and silver leaves. He remembered driving a nail into the top of her window frame, and Nick standing below him, handing up the plant. Those wide, tall windows, the view of grapevines and poison ivy just starting to leaf out, clots of tangled green pouring over rocks and onto the sand behind the house. And then the way that scene had looked later, when it was almost dark: the way the vines turned and tangled had reminded him of some nightmare creature crawling toward him, all legs and arms and lumpy greenness. He had jumped when Nina touched him from behind. He hadn't known she was there. She had complained—jokingly, but she had also been serious—that he never let her out of his sight. That was Nina: She thought he was her salvation, and she didn't want him around all the time. What Nick had said earlier about a group of friends living together had really touched him; he talked to Nina about it, standing at the darkening window. It was so nice to see plants outside, instead of a parade of retards; it was so nice to be able to breathe clean air. "You'd never make it living this way," she had said. "You'd be like Thoreau, going home to get his wash done."

Now, in the office, he was thinking again about Provincetown in the off-season: that it would be nice to stride down a sand dune, feel the sand shifting, see it moving into new patterns. Instead, he would be going to the parking garage: walking down the concrete ramp to the cashier, waiting for the black man to bring his car and turn it over to him, then up the ramp, into the traffic, the long drive from New York to his house in Connecticut. And then he would have dinner with them, watching John Joel taking seconds and thirds, and Mary sullen and bored, and Louise—how would she act? He remembered the night in the Chinese restaurant, and how he had tried to get a conversation going with Mary and failed. He wondered what he would try to talk to them about at dinner. It would be a real challenge to be polite and calm. She would never make a public announcement. He would have to wait until John Joel and Mary weren't in the room, and then let her speak. Then she could say that he should go, and he could admit that he wanted to go. Then she would either be ugly or not be ugly. Either way, he knew that he would not spend the night, but go back to Rye; and in the morning, before she went to work, he would call Nina and tell her.

Metcalf came into his office, knocking as he walked through the open door.

"Why does Nick hate me?" he said.

"What gave you that idea?"

"He subscribes me to magazines and checks the block where it says they'll bill you later. He's one of the best idea men we've got, so I pay a hundred bucks a year, probably more, for magazines that come to my house."

"Why don't you cancel the subscriptions?"

"You admit it?" Metcalf said.

"No. I just think that if it's true, you should cancel the subscriptions."

"I thought that *Country Journal* was one of his jokes. I just found out that my son was having it sent to me for my birthday."

John nodded.

"You're supposed to ask when my birthday is."

"When's your birthday?"

"Monday. Bring me a present. A gag present. Just bring something. I'm sick of birthdays without cake and ice cream and presents." Metcalf picked up a pen from the desk and tossed it in the air. "Look at that. A pen that's not even the company pen. You work better with your own pen. I like that. Are you happy?"

"I might be going to be happy."

"Ask me if I'm happy."

"Are you happy, Metcalf?"

"No. I'm going to be fifty years old." Metcalf put the pen back on the desk. "I know I'm obnoxious," he said. "I like to be asked about myself, and nobody ever asks me." He turned to leave. "You're my *second*-best idea man. Does that make you jealous of Nick?"

"No," he said.

"Trying to create a little friction so I'd have a friend of my own," Metcalf said. "I haven't invited either of you to the house this summer. You notice?"

"I noticed."

"Ask me why."

"Why?'" John said.

"I don't know," Metcalf said. "I just don't feel like having one of my usual summer parties and spending a lot of money on food and liquor just so I can get soused and put everybody on the spot. I'd rather just do it on a smaller basis—walk into your office and toss off an insult or two. You might be going to be happy. Is that what you said?"

"Yes."

"That makes me jealous. I'm not going to be anything but fifty," Metcalf said. "Take me seriously about the present."

When Metcalf left, he closed his eyes and silently prayed that Metcalf would not continue on to Nick's office and talk the same way. It would take a week to calm Nick down if that happened.

"When will you find out if you're going to be happy?" Metcalf said, putting his head back in the door.

"Tonight."

"What do you know," Metcalf said. "Notice how I don't ask you what will determine whether you'll be happy?"

"I noticed."

"Ask me why."

"Why didn't you ask me?" John said.

"Because I've got *some* manners. Not many, but a few," Metcalf said. He smiled and went away. John watched the doorway for a long time before he picked up the phone, certain that Metcalf was gone. He called his mother, to say that he wouldn't be home until late. The new housekeeper, Ms. Amoy, answered the phone. She said that his mother was sunbathing, and she would have to get her. A long time passed, and then his mother's sleepy voice came on the phone.

"I'm going to have dinner with Louise tonight," he said. "I won't be home until late."

"In the city?" his mother said.

"No. In Connecticut."

"You're always in the city. You *live* in the city. Why didn't you have her come in and have dinner there?"

"I didn't think of it, to tell you the truth. Something she said made me think she wanted to see me there."

"It's your life," she said.

"What do you mean?"

"You run around too much. You can afford an air conditioner in your car, and you don't have one."

"How's Brandt?" he said.

"Ms. Amoy, as she prefers to be called, is not so cold-blooded when it comes to Brandt. She and Brandt picked berries today, and she let him drop them into the bread mix. He dumped them all in in a pile, after she told him to sprinkle them, and she didn't criticize him. He's taken to calling her 'A,' whether because she told him to or not, I don't know."

"How are *you?*" he said.

"I'm all right. I went to the store today, in my air-conditioned car. I haven't done much else."

"I'll see you late tonight," he said.

"I certainly hope so," she said. "I like to think of you sleeping. That pleases me as much now as it did when you were a troublesome little child, and I wanted you silent and out of my sight. Now I like to think of you sleeping because I worry that you'll get sick, leading such a hectic life."

"Thank you for worrying about me."

"Worry leads to alcoholism," she said. "If all the ice has melted in my gin and tonic while I've been inside talking to you, I'm just going to dump it out. If the ice is still there, then it's a signal that God meant me to go on drinking it."

He hung up, flipped through an artist's portfolio and wondered whether or not it was deliberate that one long black hair was stretched across two sample layouts on top of the plastic. He lifted the hair off carefully and dropped it to the floor. The person had probably figured that he wouldn't look through the whole portfolio. He had an idea. He went down the hall, to Amy's office. Amy had long blond hair she wore in a ponytail. He asked for one of her hairs. She paused a moment, then took the rubber band off and pulled out a hair. She held it out to him.

"Thank you," he said, taking it carefully. She pushed her hair behind her ears and put the rubber band around it again.

"You're not going to ask why I wanted it?" he said.

"Jesus," she said, "what is this? Are you going around in back of Metcalf like his shadow and imitating him?"

"Oh," he said. "Metcalf was by?"

"*I will not answer one more question,*" she said, and turned back to her typewriter.

He went back to his office and put the hair where the other one had been, then looked through the rest of the portfolio. He wrote himself a note about the artist's work, put the portfolio to the side of his desk with a note to the secretary to return it. At five o'clock, before anyone else, he left the office. The wise-cracking attendant wasn't in the garage. Someone else got his car. He got in and wished that he had air conditioning. Out on the street traffic was bumper-to-bumper because of a truck double-parked, and because it was five o'clock. He sat and waited. While traffic slowly filtered through the narrow lane between truck and parked cars, he listened to music on the car radio. He switched the station to the one that gave traffic reports. No bad congestion, it seemed. He went back to the music station, and caught the end of "Blue Bayou." He turned it off when a message for hemorrhoid sufferers came on.

It had to be that she was leaving him, or asking him to leave her, because why else would she call him at the office and say with that grave tone of voice—that was it, she had sounded *grave* —that she wanted to see him right away? That night. Tonight. He had been so anxious to face it that he hadn't even called Nina, as he did every night. He would stop on the way, at a phone. He would just not tell her that it was happening, not until it was all over. He hoped that he and Louise could discuss it tonight, and then the rest of it would be legal technicalities: It would actually be over. The closer he got to the house in Connecticut, the more he doubted it. If she did not want a divorce, though, what could she want on a Tuesday night? What could she want that she couldn't talk about on the phone?

He smiled to himself, remembering telling Nina that there were pillars at the base of his driveway. There were no pillars, but at the foot of his driveway was a police car parked sideways, blocking the way. He had been about to turn into the driveway without even thinking, and it had taken a few seconds to register that he couldn't, and another few seconds to register that the black car was a police car. He got out of his car, but he could only stand and stare. He left the engine running, and reached back in through the window to set his hazard light blinking. If it was anything horrible, she would have told him on the phone. She was calm on the phone. But there was no way that a police car blocking his driveway could mean anything good. He walked around it. Two men with walkie-talkies were in his backyard: men in dark suits, standing back by the tree. They looked at him and didn't say anything. He said nothing to them. The back door was open. If it was something really awful, and if she had not let on, if she had made him walk into it this way deliberately, he was going to kill her. Then he thought, suddenly: Is she dead?

A man with a camera was sitting behind his kitchen table. The camera was beside him on the table and the man, with a can of Coke in front of him, was sitting there with his elbows on the table and his hands cupped one on top of the other, and his chin on his hands. "Who are you?" he said, when John walked in.

"Where's Louise?" he said. The house was so quiet. So cool, without any air conditioning. He saw a raw chicken, in a roasting pan, on the stove. Plates and glasses and silverware had been pushed aside so the man could lean on the table and drink his Coke. From outside, a buzz from the walkie-talkies droned on, what sounded like a doorbell with a short in it, a doorbell that kept ringing on its one note, maddeningly.

A policeman came into the room, followed by Tiffy Adamson.

"Is she dead?" he said to Tiffy. He knew that he had spoken, but he couldn't hear his words. The man sitting at the table got up, picked up his Coke can, held it.

"No," Tiffy said. She sank into a chair across the table from him. He sat in the chair the man had been sitting in, and they faced each other across the table. You sat like this when you visited someone in prison. When you took a seminar in college. When you were at a real estate agent's buying a house. The policeman stood in back of Tiffy and kept looking over his shoulder.

"There was a shooting," the policeman said to John. "She isn't dead. She's been taken to the hospital."

"Louise?" he said. "I just talked to Louise. Louise shot herself?"

"No," Tiffy said. "Louise is all right. Mary was shot." Tiffy started to cry. "I'm sorry," she said.

"Mary?" he said stupidly.

"Put your face between your knees," the policeman said.

"Do what?" he said.

"You're going to faint. Put your head down. Put it down."

He put it down. He felt his cheeks prickling. Surely Louise wouldn't calmly call him when Mary had been shot? That simply wasn't possible. They were tricking him.

"Where's Louise?" he said. It was hard to talk with his head down between his knees. He felt his Adam's apple pulsing.

"At the hospital," Tiffy said. "Do you want me to call them for you? She's not going to die. They had to operate to remove the bullet."

"What bullet?" he said.

"Put your head down," the policeman said.

"John Joel shot her," Tiffy said. She bit her lip, stared at him. He put his head down. She was the last thing he saw. He saw her face, and it shimmered, and then it slowly started to darken as his face got hotter and hotter. He tried to look at his own hands, holding the edge of the table, knowing that if he could blink, if he could break his stare, that he could also breathe, and if he could breathe he wouldn't pass out. He thought he heard someone talking to him, faintly, and decided that he was talking to himself. The weight he felt was Tiffy's hands, one on each shoulder, pushing him down into the chair so hard that he thought he would fall through it to the floor. He was still staring, but at nothing—at the refrigerator, the refrigerator in back of where Tiffy had been sitting. So that the refrigerator was actually the last thing he saw, and then when he opened his eyes the first thing he saw again was Tiffy. He saw a glass of water in front of him, with ice in it.

He heard the policeman saying that it could have been worse, and he was confused: Had Tiffy called the hospital, and had he talked to Louise? Had Louise really called him and said only that she wanted him to come home? She hadn't even insisted that he come.

He said to Tiffy: "She called me this afternoon. I just talked to her."

"She must have called you before it happened," Tiffy said. Tiffy looked at her watch. "It just happened," she said. "It didn't even happen three hours ago."

"Did you call the hospital?" he said.

"No," she said. "Is that what you want me to do?"

"What are you doing here?" he said.

"It's crazy," she said, "but I was driving by—I'd made strawberry muffins with the berries we picked the other day and I was bringing them. I walked into the kitchen, and we started to talk, and then we heard it."

"No," he said.

"Yes," Tiffy said. "Really."

"Drink the water," the policeman said. "Drink it so we can ask you some questions. Are you all right?"

"No," he said again.

"Put your head down," the policeman said.

"I'm so sorry," Tiffy said. "What happened?"

Tiffy was asking him what happened. One of the men with the walkie-talkies came into the kitchen and opened the refrigerator and took an ice cube out of the bin inside the freezer compartment. "You left your car running," he said to John. "I turned it off." He ran the ice cube over his face and neck, dropped it in the sink.

"The gawkers are starting to show," he said.

"No," he said. He heard a buzz on the walkie-talkie, and then everything went still, and silent. He heard himself breathing.

"Jesus God," the man in the suit sighed. "Do I get tired of gawkers."

"Get out there and chase them off," the policeman said. He had a notebook open. He was sitting where Tiffy had sat, and he had opened a notebook. Before him was a perfectly blank page.

Tiffy was still there when he and Louise got back from the hospital after midnight. They had given Louise a shot of something, and made her take a pill, and given him more pills to give her later, and he had been horrified that they were going to overmedicate her and that she would die right there in the hospital. The doctors asked if he was all right. The police offered to drive them home. He said that they were fine. He agreed to talk to the police more the next day. Mary was in bed, a bullet removed from her side, and John Joel was there too, on a different floor of the hospital. He had thought that his wife was going to ask for a divorce. Nick had thought that she was going to ask for a fur coat. What had happened was that while his wife was talking to Tiffy Adamson and stuffing chicken to put in the oven, his son had shot his daughter—with a gun he had gotten from Parker, apparently. A gun he had fired a shot with, then dropped on the ground. Then John Joel and Parker had climbed down from the tree and were standing there, looking no more amazed than children caught stealing cookies from a jar. Louise had opened the back door, and there they had stood, and Mary was on the ground.

"She was a bitch," John Joel had said, when John went into his hospital room. He was in bed, and he looked tired. Fat and pale and tired, the way any ten-year-old would look at midnight. "He doesn't know what he's talking about," John had said to the nurse who stood in the room. He had not been able to say it to John Joel. He had turned and said it to the nurse. The nurse had acted as if he hadn't spoken. She might as well have been a paper cutout of a nurse. She just stood and looked blank-faced. She was all in white, and his son was all in white. He could think of nothing but Mary's blouse, the blouse that Louise was holding outside the operating room when he got to the hospital, the blouse that they were trying to pry away from her, saying, "She's alive. She'll be fine." They wanted the blouse, and Louise wasn't giving it to them. "We need that," they said, and another person tugged. Louise held on to it.

In the room, he had hugged John Joel. He had heard his son's breathing, and his own breathing, and he realized that his breath was coming fast and hard, and his son's breathing was the calm breathing of near-sleep, that he was squeezing and not getting squeezed in return.

He had been going to take Brandt to a Little League game.

His mother had told him to get an air conditioner for his car. He had wished for an air conditioner for his car. That was something he had thought about, a few hours before—being cool in his car.

He had said that he could drive home with no problem, and he had been lying. He wanted to tell them that he couldn't, but he had found himself saying that he had driven there, and of course he could drive back. The young cop offered two times to drive him. "You could get your car in the morning," the young cop had said, and his partner had said, "He knows that," as he tried to nudge the young cop along. "I didn't know that," John had said. What he meant was that he hadn't thought about it. "You what?" the cop said. The young cop looked back at him. "Ride?" the young cop said. He had raised his hand, then had no idea why he had done it. He had waved to the cops. "Nothing," he had said. He and Louise had ridden to the lobby with the cops, and then the cops had turned and gone one way, and he and Louise had gone another. He was trying to think of the fastest route home, and he couldn't visualize any of it; he couldn't even remember one way to get home. But when he got out on the road—he drove by sight, not by road signs, anyway—he would remember instantly. He wanted to remember instantly. He wanted to be home, but he was not sure if he could drive there. For a second, the older cop's face had blurred and he had thought that it wasn't a face at all, but a scarab. Then the lines had hardened into features again.

Tiffy and her husband were in the house. When they came in, Tiffy's husband rose to greet them, as if they were visitors. Tiffy just sat and stared. Her husband asked if he wanted them to go. He wanted them to go. "No," he said. "Sit down," Tiffy's husband said. They sat down. Tiffy got up and put her arm around Louise's shoulder. "You were right," Louise said to Tiffy. "It was a shot." "Everything's all right," Tiffy said. "I called the hospital. They said you were coming home. We didn't know if we should go or stay. Do you want us to sleep in the living room? Just so we can answer the phone or something?" Louise looked at John. "That's very nice of you," he said. He was thinking: I was at work today. I worked, and I drove back to Connecticut, and Mary and John Joel are in the hospital, and he did it because she was a bitch. He said she was a bitch. It was true that someone could dress very conventionally and still be evil: Nixon with his jacket and tie walking on the beach, for example. But Mary—Gingerbread Mary—a bitch? He wondered what his son had meant by that.

Tiffy and Louise had gone upstairs. He had heard Louise crying, and Tiffy talking. He hardly knew Tiffy's husband, and didn't know what to say to him. They sat there awkwardly for a while, and then Tiffy's husband said that he thought he would take a walk—did he want to come? He said no. He thought that if he went out to walk, he would start running. He was afraid that he would run until he died. He had been so frightened, watching them swabbing Louise's arm. He had thought: It's not to calm her—they're tricking us. "Is this what you want?" he had said to Louise, but the needle was already in her arm. The doctor turned and glared at him. Then the piece of cotton in place, the nurse clamping her finger over it and pushing Louise down into a chair. She sat very still in the chair, and didn't seem to care that she was being stared at. She didn't really seem to notice that he was there, either. She noticed when he walked in, but then she didn't seem to notice him. In the car, she sat with her knees drawn up, hands clasped around them. He had tried to take her hand, but she wouldn't let go. He had put his hand over her hands, steered with one hand. He had found the way home, and now he did not want to go out walking. He thought about calling his mother, Nick, Nina. He couldn't imagine what he would say. And then he had fallen asleep. He woke up and saw that an hour had passed. He heard Tiffy, still upstairs, still talking. Her husband had not come back. He began to pace the house. He went out to the kitchen and opened the back door. Insects were chirping. Moths came from nowhere and flapped past him, into the bright room. He looked at the tree, at the back of the yard, remembered lifting the robin's egg, gently, from the grass: the fragile egg, safe in a dish in Nina's apartment. John Joel had shot Mary from up in that tree, the same tree where the robins had built their nest, the same tree he had voluntarily vacated until the birds were gone. The tree he watched, and kept the neighbor's fat orange cat away from. He closed the door and went to the kitchen table and sat down. Dishes were pushed to one side, and the day's mail, full of bills and advertisements, was on the table, too, and as he flipped through, he found it. He found it and knew instantly why she had called him. It was a travel brochure on Nantucket, and there was a petition— "Petition for Nantucket Vacation" was written across the top of a piece of paper—signed by Louise and John Joel and Mary. They were asking to be taken to Nantucket. That was what it was all about. The idea of packing bathing suits and going to Nantucket seemed more grotesque to him than setting off with snowshoes for Alaska. He put the brochure down, as shocked as if he had found a letter to Louise from a lover. That was what she had called him about.

Then he drove. He meant to drive for a while and go back to the house, but he got lost, and then he found the Merritt Parkway, and it seemed more logical to go than to stay. He was speeding, watching the needle climb. And when he looked at the road again he realized where he was, how close to New York he was getting, and he pushed hard on the accelerator. There was too much wind at such a high speed, so he put his window halfway up. He was going to keep driving for a while, and then go back. He knew he wasn't. He looked at his watch and wondered where so many hours had gone. He must have looked at the clock in the house wrong, or maybe his watch was wrong. A van with a plastic flower on the aerial passed him. A Honda Civic passed him. He was amazed that he was driving so slowly. He looked at the needle and saw that he was going thirty. He pushed hard, watched the needle climb to forty, fifty, sixty. He held it at sixty, watching the sky gradually lighten.

And then he was in New York, and the light was even, and he didn't know what to do but start the usual routine. He took the car to the garage, he walked up the cement ramp to the street, and walked for miles before he thought to hail a cab. "Some son of a bitch threw up after I picked him up at Studio 54," the driver said. "I hope it doesn't still stink back there."

"Have you been driving all night?" he asked the cabbie.

"Yeah. I been working eleven to eleven. Beat the heat."

He pushed a wad of money into the man's hand and got out, in front of Nina's building. He felt light-headed. He stood there and tried not to look like a crazy man or a drunk still stumbling from the night before. A woman with a baby in a stroller walked by and didn't look at him, and a teenage girl dropped her eyes and quickened her pace. A garbage truck was out. It was going to be a hot, hazy day. Nina was right that he was a coward. How could he even admit to her what he had done? He would have to call Louise with some excuse. He had an appointment to talk with the police. But he was not even in Connecticut. He was in New York, in front of Nina's, and the trick was to get into the building and up the stairs.

Child's play: one foot in front of the other. Child's play: bend your finger, pull the trigger. His son had shot his daughter.

17

HE WAS TRICKED. Parker set him up for it. After refusing to go into the city with John Joel, Parker called, suspecting, no doubt, that John Joel wouldn't go alone. They talked for a while on the phone about trying to get a ride to the movies to see *Moonraker*. Parker told him he wouldn't understand half the movie, but if he didn't talk during it, he'd explain what he didn't get afterward. John Joel's mother was doing an errand for one of the hospital patients, though, so she couldn't take them, and Parker's mother had laryngitis. Parker had him hold the phone while he asked his mother if she was in bed because she was sick with something in addition to laryngitis, or whether she could get up and take them to the movies. Parker's mother had written: "You don't have a sympathetic bone in your body." Parker suggested calling Frankie Wu. Wu's mother didn't work, and when they got to the theater, they could ditch Wu and meet him outside when it was over. John Joel said that wasn't a good idea. Parker said, "Ah, you pansy." When they hung up, John Joel went into the living room, sprawled in the chair, and got a comic to read. It was one he had borrowed from Parker, called *Pig Fig*, and it showed pigs being fed into a giant machine that ground them into pulp, and pig-faced bakers molding the pulp into the nearly round shape of a fig.

"So are you going to flunk summer school?" he said to Mary as she walked into the room to get her purse.

She had her tablet and her book in her hand. She picked up her purse, pretending not to hear him.

"Think I'll go to New York today and have some fun," he said.

Mary was doing something in the kitchen. She was humming a Linda Ronstadt song, getting something out of the refrigerator.

"Wanna make me another breakfast?" he said, following her into the kitchen.

"You need it," she said. "You *look* like a breakfast. You know which part? The sausage part." She jabbed her finger into the roll of fat above his Bermuda shorts. A pain shot through his stomach.

"I'm not ignorant, though," he said. "Fuzz Scuzz."

Parker had taught him that insult. Somebody that made you itch to look at them was a Fuzz Scuzz. He said it to her again, curling his fingers and making a face.

"How old are you?" she said. "Ten?"

"Daddy and Nick and I had lunch in New York," he said. "You've never had lunch with Daddy in New York, have you?"

"If Daddy really wanted to see you, he'd live here," Mary said. She got a Tab out of the refrigerator. "You're probably why he doesn't," she said. "He can't stand you."

"I hear you've got a crush on Lloyd Bergman," he said. "Some-body whose brother was at that party you and Angela went to told me. Want to know who?"

"No," she said. She opened the Tab, took a sip.

"Frankie Wu's brother. How come you don't get a crush on him?" John Joel pulled the skin at the corner of his eyes, making them into slits.

"You don't look as ugly that way," she said.

"Are you the homeliest girl in summer school?" he said.

"Beat your meat," she said. She slung her purse over her shoulder and picked up the can of Tab, clutched her books under her arm. She was carrying a lot of stuff, and he watched her, hoping she'd drop something going out the door. She walked very close to the door and opened it with a stiff flick of her wrist. She went out, and he heard the slow hiss as the door closed behind her. As usual, she had topped him with an insult he didn't understand. It reminded him that he was hungry and hadn't eaten for two hours, since his mother fixed him breakfast. He opened the refrigerator, saw that there was hamburger meat, and took out the package, ripped off a handful and made it round. He put a lump of butter in a pan and turned on the stove. When the butter sputtered into liquid, he pressed the hamburger into the pan. It was ten o'clock. She was late for school, and he was surprised that she was going. His mother had stalked out of the house, after calling Mary three times and getting no response. Mary's breakfast was still on the table. The eggs had congealed. The toast was all buttery shine. The bacon looked fine. He picked up a piece and ate it. As the hamburger cooked, he ate the other two pieces.

He was finishing the hamburger when Parker called again.

"What do *you* want?" he said to Parker.

"I want you to come over. I want to show you something."

"What have you got that I haven't seen?"

"What are your big plans for the day?" Parker said. "I've got about a dozen comics you haven't seen, for one thing. My mother made an orange cake before she got sick. She's going out, anyway. Somebody just called her, and she's getting dressed."

"I thought she was sick."

"Listen," Parker said, "I'm not going to beg you." He hung up.

John Joel took his last bite of hamburger and put the plate in the sink. He went outside and ran across the lawn, after a bird that was pecking in the grass. The bird flew away, and he watched it go, higher and higher, until it landed in the peach tree. The peaches got about half the size of peaches in the store, then turned gray and dropped from the tree. Mary had put one in his bed, and when he showed his mother, she had yanked Mary by one arm into the room and made her pick up the peach, which had burst, and throw it away. Then she had made Mary strip the bed and wash the sheet in the laundry tub. It was the first time he had seen Mary cry in a long time. It was also the first time he had seen his mother and Mary crying together. While they were downstairs, he had taken his mother's little manicuring scissors and carefully cut the threads for about two inches along the seam of Mary's jeans, in the crotch. He tugged, to make sure the seam had come apart. When he tugged, a couple of tiny threads he had missed burst. Parker had taught him that trick. He did it to his mother's tennis shorts. "You can do too much or too little," Parker said. "Cutting this much is about right. Don't tug at the seam, and it'll open gradually. It'll open while she's playing tennis." Parker had his own scissors. He had scissors in about six sizes, that his grandmother had given him because he told her he was interested in paper cutting. Parker had cut a butterfly shape out of a piece of paper and sent it to his grandmother with a thank you note written on one wing. His grandmother had sent a small knife that had belonged to his grandfather that seemed never to go dull. Parker used that knife for fraying upholstery.

John Joel climbed up in the tree, saying "shit" when he scraped his leg. He weighed more than he had at the beginning of summer, and it was hard to bend his leg as sharply as he needed to to haul himself up on one of the branches. When he got to the limb he usually sat on, or stretched out on, he settled himself and examined the scrape on his leg. It wasn't bad. It wasn't bleeding. He clamped his hand over it and hoped the pressure would stop the stinging.

There was nothing to do. He stared at the big bumblebees hovering around the abelia, and wished that there were some way to blindfold Mary and lead her into the bush. He looked at the lot between their house and Angela's. Some butterflies flew up from the brush. It was a sticky, hot day. His stomach felt heavy, but he was also hungry. He swung his legs back and forth, too lazy, after just having climbed into the tree, to work his way down and go back to the kitchen for more food. He thought about Parker's mother's orange cake. He had eaten a piece of that cake before. There were thin rounds of orange on the top, around the edge, like little wheels on their sides. When Parker's mother was making bread, or a soufflé, Parker would go into the kitchen, if she was on the second floor, and jump hard outside the oven. He didn't do anything to ruin her orange cakes. His mother had stopped making bread. Most of her energy now went into making orange cakes that were perfectly shaped, tall, beautiful. John Joel watched a bird hopping around on the grass. The bird didn't know he was up in the tree. "Meow," he said, drawing the word out, speaking in as high a pitch as possible. The bird jumped along. John Joel did it again. The bird flew a few feet forward, continued to hop along the grass. Only when John Joel started to climb down from the tree did it fly away.

He hated to have nothing to do but hang out with his mother or go to Parker's. For a while he put it off, flipping through comics he had already looked at three or four times, and *Pig Fig* was really the only funny one. He flipped through that one again, then picked up the comics and decided to return them to Parker and have a piece of orange cake. He remembered to lock the door when he went out, and to leave the key under a big shell that was in among his mother's iris. He would have liked for Mary to have forgotten her key and be locked out, but she'd probably go to Angela's until dinner anyway, and if his mother came home and saw that he'd left the back door open, he'd catch hell.

Parker did his usual routine of not answering the door. John Joel rang the bell, and knocked on the door and yelled Parker's name. Finally, he heard Parker, in no special hurry, coming to answer the door.

"What?" Parker said, opening the door.

"I brought your comics back."

"Yeah," Parker said. "You came for cake."

Parker stood aside, and he walked in.

"I lied about the cake," Parker said.

"I don't want any cake," John Joel said. "I just wanted to return your comics."

"You want it," Parker said. "There is one, too. Come in the kitchen."

He followed Parker into the kitchen. The wallpaper in the kitchen was blue, with a pattern of white chickens, columns of half-inch-high chickens. There was a long plate-rail across one wall, where Parker's mother kept her collection of old plates with animals and farm scenes. There was a blue tablecloth on the table, and salt and pepper shakers shaped like chickens. Parker lifted up the salt shaker and took it to the sink. He put his finger under the water, and let a single drop of water hit the circle of tiny holes in the chicken's head. Then he dried it off and put it back on the table. He got a knife out of a drawer, and two plates. He cut two pieces of cake: a large one for himself, and a medium one for John Joel. He got two Cokes out of the refrigerator, and shook John Joel's can lightly, three or four times, before he grinned and handed it to him. John Joel let it sit there. He only cared about the cake, anyway. And when his piece was gone, he was going to cut another one. He'd like to see what Parker would do to stop him. They ate in silence. Parker thumbed through *Pig Fig* and laughed as he ate. John Joel finished first and picked up the cake knife, but he didn't cut another piece. He wiped the icing onto his finger and licked it.

"Come on upstairs," Parker said. "I want to show you something."

He had already seen what Parker had to show: the two green fishing tackle boxes, with his grandfather's things in them.

"Why'd you bring them upstairs?" John Joel said.

"Just felt like it," Parker said. "He's away on a trip. He's not going to know. If she finds them, serves her right for snooping in my room. Let her find them. I'd like to see her face."

Parker took out the pen with the little lady that did the striptease.

"Hey, Parker," he said. "I *saw* that."

"It's neat," Parker said, handing him the pen. "It got screwed up and he doesn't hit her right. You think there's somebody who repairs pens like this?" Parker tilted it, smiling. "Look," he said. "Stupid man's aim is off."

Parker put the two boxes on his bed. He lifted the ties out again, and put them in a pile. He had something small in his hand that John Joel couldn't see.

"Reach out," Parker said.

"For what?"

"Because I said to. You scared I'm going to blow you up or something?"

"What have you got?"

"Jesus, are you an infant," Parker said. "Go to shake hands with me. Come on."

John Joel put his hand out. It was sticky from the cake.

Parker's hand came forward, and John Joel saw a thin ring of metal around Parker's middle finger, and then something hard pressed into the palm of his hand. It was a palm buzzer. Parker took it off and showed John Joel the small circle of metal with a bulge in the middle that made a loud buzzing sound when pressure was put on it.

Parker put the ties and the palm buzzer back into the box and pulled some comics out from under his bed. He flopped onto his stomach and started to read one. John Joel went to the bathroom. He undid the button at the top of his shorts, and pulled his shirt out, to be more comfortable. He ran the cold water and wiped his wet hand over his face, patted his face dry on somebody's towel. He felt even stickier. He went back to Parker's room, thinking about asking for more cake.

He and Parker read comics. Parker got up from the bed and touched his toes. "Bet *you* can't," he said to John Joel. John Joel was pretty sure he couldn't. He ignored Parker. He ran his tongue over his teeth and thought how much he didn't want braces. Parker had a magazine about dentists—a picture book, on cheap paper that almost fell apart when you touched it, so Parker turned the pages carefully, like the pages of a rare book. The magazine showed dentist's instruments, larger than life, and there were pictures of women with their eyes like pinwheels and their legs spread, dentists pressed against their crotches, bending over and probing into their mouths. The writing in the magazine was all in some foreign language, but the people in the pictures looked like Americans.

"You should have seen *Marathon Man*," Parker said. "Ask your orthodontist if he saw that."

After a while, when John Joel said he was going home, Parker got up and offered him another piece of cake. They went to the kitchen and Parker cut two slices, this time even more unequal in size, and flopped them onto the same plates they had eaten off before. The morning paper was on the table, and there was a picture of Rosalynn Carter standing with some foreign woman. "Dumb hag scumbag," Parker said, examining the paper. He turned the picture of Rosalynn Carter face down on the table and picked up his piece of cake and ate it out of his fingers.

Parker trailed him home. He kept walking behind him, and

when John Joel turned around Parker would puff out his cheeks and waddle.

"You're so thin yourself," John Joel said.

"Let's see you touch your toes," Parker said.

Parker picked up a rock and threw it at a squirrel. When a car came down the road, he zigged and zagged, so that the car didn't know if he was going to run out in front of it or not. John Joel didn't know how Parker could do things like that: What if the person in the car knew him, or his parents? Parker picked up another rock and threw it at a tree. It hit the tree and rebounded, and John Joel ducked. Parker laughed.

"You're a real asshole," John Joel said.

He saw his mother's car in the driveway and was secretly glad that he could get rid of Parker. Parker wouldn't hang around if his mother was there.

"I want to show you something," Parker said.

"I'm going inside," John Joel said.

Parker pulled the small black gun out of his pants pocket.

"Get that out of here," John Joel said. "If my mother sees that, both of us are going to catch hell."

"What," Parker said, "there's a law against it?"

"There *is*," John Joel said. "There's a law."

"What's it called: the Scaredy Baby's Law? Come on. I want to show you something."

He couldn't go in the house with Parker carrying the gun, and Parker wouldn't put it away.

"Come on," Parker said, walking to the back of the lawn.

Parker climbed the tree. John Joel climbed behind him. He wished that his mother knew he was home, that she would call him. He hoped she might look out the kitchen door and see him. She had put on the sprinkler, and it was turning in a circle, jetting water out over her iris, wetting the abelia bush. The bees hovered anyway, jerking back from the spray, a few flying forward, into the soaking bush. Some bees hung to the wet bright-green branches, clustered almost like Japanese beetles, even though the water kept raining into the bush.

"What do you want now?" John Joel said.

"Ambush," Parker said.

On cue—exactly on cue—John Joel saw Angela and Mary, walking into the field.

"Pshew! Pshew!" Parker said, aiming the gun at a bird hopping by the tree. "Wait'll you see *Moonraker*, when all those guys floating in space get zapped by lasers."

"Put that away," John Joel said. "You'll scare her. If she sees you with that, it's going to get me in trouble with my mother." John Joel stared at Parker. "I *mean* it," he said. "I'm *telling* you."

"Don't talk to me like that," Parker said. He seemed more dismayed than angry. He seemed unreasonable. Parker had the gun in his right hand, and John Joel, on his left, couldn't think how to get it away from him.

"You are really stupid," Parker said. "You think I'd carry a gun around that had a bullet in it? That would make a lot of sense, wouldn't it? If you're so scared, you can hold on to it, so I don't blow your sister away," Parker said, handing him the gun. "You love your sister? You fall in love with your sister?"

"I hate her," John Joel said.

Angela waved and turned back toward her house. Mary walked forward, jumping over something, zigzagging because she knew the path to take to avoid poison ivy. If his mother saw her in the field, Mary would catch hell. He hoped that his mother would come out into the backyard and see her.

Mary didn't see them in the tree, or if she did, she was doing a better-than-average job of ignoring them. A bird flew away as she was almost out of the field. She turned and flicked something off the back of her jeans. Something small fell back into the field, a burr or a bug.

He called her name, and pulled the trigger, because he thought that Parker had been telling the truth. He didn't even have the gun aimed, and still he hit her.

Tiffy lifted the slice of lemon out of her glass of iced tea and let tea drip into the glass. She sucked the lemon, put it on the table next to the glass.

"I never thought about it until last night—it never struck me as strange in any way, because I'm so conditioned. I'm so slow to come around to understanding some things. Think about it: The fairy godmother changes a pumpkin into a coach, mice into horses, a rat into a coachman, lizards into footmen, and work clothes into a silver and gold dress, and what does she say when she sends her off to the ball? To be back at midnight. If she had the power to do all those other things, did she really lack the power to make them last past midnight? It's just another story about virginity. You've got to read My Mother, My Self. Nancy Friday can't be wrong." Tiffy sucked on the lemon. "Interesting, too, that she doesn't transform anything into glass slippers—that she touches her magic ring to Cinderella's work clothes to turn them into fine threads, but the glass slippers are just brought forward, as if they always existed. Do you know what Freud says about shoes?"

Then they heard the shot. They both knew it was a shot, but

Louise said to Tiffy, "What was that?" and Tiffy said what it was. They got up from the table together, and Louise heard another sound, the sound of Tiffy's glass turning over. She looked back at the table and saw Tiffy reaching for the toppled glass, but too late: a pale-brown puddle was washing over Perrault's Fairy Tales. *Louise stared stupidly. She was afraid to look, because she knew what it was. She knew that something horrible had happened, because there had been no sound before the shot, and no sound after it was fired: It just existed in itself, strange and loud, and then there was nothing but whatever it was she was going to see when she got to the door. The door was closed—Tiffy had suggested that, saying that the kitchen would be cooler with the fan going and the door closed, that the screen door let in more hot air than . . .*

While she was thinking, Tiffy passed her and threw open the door.

18

CYNTHIA HAD talked to Bobby on the phone, and now she was talking to him in person. Spangle's old friend had become a writer, and he was on his way to New York to talk to agents. That didn't delight him, but as he talked he found more and more reasons to like the idea of going to New York. Bagels—he could get bagels there. Bookstores—he might be able to find a copy of Thomas Wolfe's book about writing a novel at a bookstore he'd heard about off Broadway at 95th. He had heard that a copy was there, and the stupid friend who'd told him—his friend Honig was so stupid he couldn't believe it—he'd told Honig to look for the book, and Honig hadn't realized that he had meant he should also buy it. Used-clothing stores—they might have a cowboy shirt similar to one he had lost, with a satin skull that looked as if it had been drawn by Georgia O'Keeffe sewn over the pocket.

"How did you lose a shirt?" she said.

"I was at the laundromat and I think somebody saw it going into the washing machine and pulled it out when I left to buy a newspaper. That's all I can think. I've lost shoes, because I've forgotten I was wearing them. You know—at a lake or something, you just walk back to the car not thinking about shoes—but I can't think myself how else I could have lost the cowboy shirt. Actually, maybe cowboy shirts aren't really my thing. Maybe it was just that one I liked. I hate cowboy *boots*. These are what I like."

Bobby held up his foot. He had a huge foot, and he was wearing bright-orange running shoes with a white stripe curving around the side. "Can't wear these to teach in," Bobby said. "Got to get shoes. What else is there to buy besides cowboy boots for shoes? Some goddamn old man's shoes that lace up? Jesus, do I hate to think about teaching."

"When does the semester—" she said.

"Hey!" Bobby said, before she finished her sentence. "Excuse me for breaking in, but when I think of something, if I don't say it, I lose it." He took off his glasses, blew on them, wiped them on the tail of his shirt. "I forgot what I was going to say," he said.

"Were you going to say something about teaching?"

"Oh," he said. "Right. Right. I was going to ask you about Yale. You said you're at Yale."

"I don't even want to think about it. I just want a vacation. All I want is a rest, and for this heat wave to break."

"Where did I say that bookstore was?" Bobby said.

"Broadway and 95th."

"God!" Bobby said. "If you hadn't remembered, I would have lost it just like that."

He snapped his fingers. They didn't make any sound, because his hands were wet. He was drinking beer, and the can was sweating. Bobby kept wiping his hand on his denim shorts. "What are they going to do, come into my classroom and carry me out? What am I buying shoes for, and wearing slacks with a crease down the front? *These* are my shoes, you know?"

Bobby held up his big puffy orange foot. "Do you have a piece of paper?" he said. "If I don't write down that address, I'll get there and I'll never remember it."

She watched him print: B'way 95th
                         cowboy shirt
                         bagels

When Bobby wrote, he bent his head and put his eye down close to the page, the way a young child writes, having to concentrate both on the idea and on the handwriting. Bobby's handwriting was just about illegible. Three typists who had been given his novel had quit. When he wanted to be sure to understand his writing himself, he printed. He explained all this to her as he continued the message to himself: "Kathryn and Daphne?"

"Just had an idea," Bobby said. He put the top back on the pen. He put the pen in his pocket, realized it was hers, took it out and put it on the table. A little blue card fell out with the pen. The blue card said: *"Zut alors!"* Bobby looked embarrassed. He turned the card over; it was a foreign language flash card. She read, in English, "My goodness!"

"My pockets," Bobby sighed, pulling a wad of papers out of his shirt pocket. He spread the things out over the table. There was a fake twenty-dollar bill that he said his nephew had given him, a folded piece of yellow paper that turned out to be a receipt from the dry cleaner's ("The shirt!" Bobby said, pointing to a line of writing. "I've found my shirt!"), a thin pocket calculator, a gum wrapper, several index cards with notes for poems on them, a photo-booth picture, one of three, that he kept meaning to send his sister for her locket (not his idea, she wanted the thing), and a dried leaf that he wanted to try to find out about. She didn't know what it was. "What do you think?" he said. "Is this a common leaf?"

"What did you do with the other pictures?" she said.

"I gave them to women," he said. "They were profile shots. I look better in profile." He examined his running shoes. "Don't want to go running, do you?" he said.

"It's too hot."

"Maybe later," he said.

"Maybe," she said.

"You really wouldn't mind if I slept on the sofa tonight? I don't like to drive into New York at night. I would like a bagel, though. Maybe later we can go out and find a bagel." He finished his beer and bent the can in half. He took it to the kitchen and threw it away, opened the refrigerator and took out another one. It was Coors beer. He had brought a six-pack with him.

"Tell me about your job," he said. "How does that work?"

"How does it work?" she said, amused that he had put it that way. "Well—I get up in the morning and drive to the high school and go into the classroom, where eager, bright students await me: eager to go home and blast any ideas out of their heads with rock music. Some of them try to appear even more ignorant than they are, though, so maybe they're brighter than they seem." She took a sip of his beer. "Anyway," she said, "they don't know anything, and they won't when the summer is over, either. The administration's idea of education is a real kick: You have them read parts of books and plays, and you show them movies and play them records, and you have them enact little scenes. I'd like to give them *The Story of O* and let them enact some scenes."

"*The Story of O*," Bobby said. "That used to be one of Spangle's favorite books."

"You're kidding," she said. "When?"

"Up at his old house in Vermont. I went up there last summer with a lady love. I was nostalgic for the place. Some Indian was living there, growing corn. I'm not kidding: some guy in a serapé —my lady love said it was a beach towel; she swore it was—with his hair in a braid, dark-skinned guy, a hippie, I guess a hippie dressed up like an Indian, and he was out there picking corn when we pulled up. I was going to say I used to live there and ask if we could walk around, but the guy looked pretty flipped out, and he had a doberman tied to one of the poles that held up the clothesline, and it looked like it was just tied up with twine. The stuff you wrap packages with. Nothing more than that. He'd painted the shutters red, too, and I was sure the place was going to look lousy inside, so I put it in reverse and took off. What is it about Vermont, do you think? What's the story on that?"

"Isn't it the same in New Hampshire?"

"No," he said. He took one of the blue index cards out of his pocket, bent his head and wrote a few words down. He put the index card back in his pocket.

"I don't know. I've never thought about it."

"You should get him to take you there and show you the place. Maybe it would depress him, though. He did a lot of work inside that house."

"Did you know his girlfriend?"

"The one that had part of her stomach removed, or the other one?"

"The other one, I guess. At least, he never told me that she was operated on."

"Yeah. I knew that one. I didn't know the one who lost her stomach."

Bobby was rolling a joint. He rolled it, looked at it, put it on the table. "You want a report on his flyaway ladybug," he said. "I don't know. We only overlapped by a week—she came, I went. Pretty. Scrawny. Smart. Left, finally, to go to New York. We went to see her there one night after our dealer got shot in a parking lot in Brattleboro, because Spangle knew she knew somebody in New York. I think she was going to school in New York, and I think Spangle had given her a little bread when she split. Anyway, this guy Horton came over. Somebody she and Spangle had known at Bard. That's right—she wasn't going to school in New York, she'd been at Bard with Spangle. I don't know *what* she was doing in New York. She lived on Columbus Avenue. Now I'm starting to remember. She hadn't been there long, and she was painting the walls white the night we went over, and Horton was fucking around, writing stuff on the wall in white paint before she painted it, stuff about . . . Jesus—this comes back to me: He kept telling what he called Italian-Mormon jokes, about the Angel Tortoni. He was scribbling away on the wall, and it was hard as hell to get his attention. All we wanted was grass." Bobby smiled. "It's funny now. It wasn't funny then. I thought anybody that bizarro had to be a narc." He lit the joint, inhaled, handed it to her. She waved it away. He stubbed it out. He sat silently, waited, exhaled slowly. "She still had her high school yearbook. Under their pictures they all had their favorite saying, and then it predicted what would become of them. I don't remember what the prediction was for her. I just remember the first line of Blake's sunflower poem under her name. *Odd.*" Bobby examined the extinguished cigarette. "I was a lifeguard," he said. "Splash splash."

"I wonder how come women always want to know about other women, and men never want to know about other men?"

"Other way around," he said. "I can't stand it if I don't find out who happened before me, or is happening along with me. I try to find out the first time I see a woman."

"I think that's atypical. Men never ask me about other men I've seen."

"Who do you see besides Spangle?"

She laughed. "That's funny," she said, "because the answer is nobody. I met somebody nice last week, but it was business."

"I find the finest ladies on business. Returning a book, interviewing job candidates. Agents, hopefully. I'm only talking to women agents."

"You seem pretty crazy about the ladies."

"Oh, I am. I've proposed twice this year alone. I know I'm going to do it again. I always propose more in the summer. If I lived in California, I'd be married."

"Why?" she said.

"The weather. Hot weather makes me propose. Ladies in bathing suits and halter tops and shorts, going skinny-dipping and hiking, walking in back of them when we're hiking through the woods . . ."

"You're putting me on."

"I'm not. I'm glad summer isn't any longer than it is."

"What would you do if one accepted?"

"Marry her. I never propose unless I'm serious."

He bent another beer can in half and set it carefully on the table, on top of *American Photographer*. He had taken the magazine out of his suitcase, and looking at the cover—a woman with long hair, in high heels squatting—she thought that maybe it was because of the cover that he was carrying it around. He didn't have a camera, and there was nothing to indicate that he cared anything about photography. He had also brought a green book bag and an antique straw suitcase full of clothes and cassette tapes. He said that he was learning Spanish as well as French, and that he was listening to cassette recordings of some recent novels, including *The Thorn Birds*. "What do you think?" he said. "Books on Tape is a wonderful idea. Much better than listening to junk on the car radio, but what do you think? Are they going to break into my car when they see the cassette deck in New York? If I park in a garage, am I better off?" He was rummaging in the suitcase for a handkerchief. He found it and wiped his face. "It's hot," he said. "It's not just me? You don't look very hot."

"I'm hot," she said. "Do you want to go out somewhere and sit for a while, and get cool?"

He took a shower first, digging into the book bag for the necessary things. "We have towels," she said, and he said, "I always carry my own. Feel this towel. Isn't that great? The most wonderful lady gave me that. Four summers ago we were stretched out on the beach at Ogunquit on this towel." He took out a soap dish with a piece of ribbon tied around it. He went into the bathroom, saying, "I thought I'd put Horton out of my head. I'm surprised I remembered so much about him. What do you think? I didn't do the wrong thing telling you a few things about his old ladybug, did I?"

He didn't wait for an answer. He closed the bathroom door, and when she heard the water running she shivered, realizing how hot she was.

She thought about Spangle in Madrid, and wondered if he was staying there because life here was uninteresting. She had put in so many years with Spangle—a lot of them because he wanted it a lot more than she ever had—so that by staying away, he was withholding more than himself from her. With him gone, part of her past was gone, and that was hard to deal with because the present wasn't any too happy. Soon it would be September, and she would be back in school. She smiled, thinking about the way Spangle got her out of bed, if he got up before she did: He put on the record of the Yardbirds singing "Good Morning, Little Schoolgirl." A lot of things had gone wrong between them the past year, but she couldn't believe that he'd stay in Madrid and not even contact her. She was tempted to want him to stay, just because it would upset his mother, but she had also started to worry. The good thing about being her students' age, she remembered, was being in love with somebody who was around. Some of her girlfriends tortured themselves by loving boys at private schools or military schools, but most of them had a day-by-day boyfriend. Her boyfriend from high school had become a Marine and later acted in an underground porn film about Vietnam that she never got to see. Someone who had seen the film told her that he was in drag in the film—a peasant woman who got raped. The person who had seen it and told her that was pretty unreliable, though. He himself was a failed actor, and it would be like him to be jealous of her old boyfriend and to make up a lie like that. When she turned twenty-one, her old boyfriend had had a birthday cake that said "OM" made for her at Carvel. That was after the Marines, and before the porn film. During the break, there had been an ice-cream cake.

Bobby came out of the bathroom wearing the same denim shorts and a new T-shirt, with a picture of a chocolate-chip cookie on it that seemed as big as a pizza. Famous Amos. He had rolled up the short sleeves punk-style. "You thought of a place to get bagels that's air conditioned?" he said.

She knew a place, but they'd have to drive to it. That was okay with Bobby. He got his car keys and said he'd take them.

The car was parked in the No Parking zone outside the building. A ticket was clamped under one wiper-blade, and he got in and started the car without removing it. After a couple of blocks he turned on the windshield wiper. "Damn," he said, for the first time, when the wipers kept going back and forth, the ticket underneath the blade. He stopped the car, got out and ripped up the ticket and threw it in the street, got back in. He pushed a cassette into the tape deck and listened for a couple of minutes to a man reading with a slight accent, not exactly a British accent but close, in a somber, quiet voice: ". . . George Washington. Famous portrait of Washington left unfinished because artist took on more than he could handle. Very ambitious artist. Washington who chases his slaves or Jefferson?"

Bobby hit the button, and the cassette popped out. "I don't think I'm in the mood for that," he said.

The seats of his Mazda were covered with terrycloth. There was a rainbow painted on the floor. The floor was all vinyl, no rug: It was a beautifully painted rainbow that she didn't feel right about putting her feet on. Hanging from the rear-view mirror was a pencil sharpener, and on the dashboard was a souvenir of New York City: the Statue of Liberty and the Empire State Building, about an inch apart, on a bronze base. A woman's ring was hung around the Statue of Liberty's arm. Around the Empire State Building there were tabs from soft-drink cans. In the back seat was an engine from a toy train. An unopened pack of Camels was on the floor, and several other parking tickets. The bumper sticker, she noticed before she got in, said "I Brake for People Who Brake." He had noticed her looking at it. One of his students ("beautiful girl—it is

absolutely necessary to keep your hands off of first-year students")
had given it to him. She had also sent him a hand-knit red turtle-
neck sweater at Christmas. Next year, he said, he was going to look
her up and invite her for dinner and see how serious she was.

In the restaurant she had a Swiss cheese sandwich with mushrooms on pita bread, and he ate three onion bagels, two with
cream cheese and the last one with butter.

As they ate, she found out things about Spangle she hadn't
known: that he used to cook seven different kinds of spaghetti
sauce; that he read and liked Norman O. Brown; that while he was
fixing up his house, he watched soap operas on TV; that he had
been so terrified of a grass snake he saw slither under his raspberry
bushes that he wore thigh-high fishing boots whenever he picked
berries. It sounded like a calm and funny existence, and she wondered what had driven him out of the woods. He had been
afraid to go on with that life, and she had no idea why. Even
Bobby admitted that Spangle was probably not the same person he
had known: For one thing, Spangle hadn't told her about *him*,
and in the old days, all of Spangle's friends knew all his other
friends. Whenever it rained in Vermont, Bobby said, he and Spangle used to joke about the house as Noah's Ark. The couples
moved around a little, but they didn't move out, except for one or
two times when things got too ugly. The first spring in the house,
there were four couples living there when Bobby went there alone,
and the backyard was a mud pond, and the people with rubber
boots carried the people who didn't have them on their shoulders
when they went out for food, or to the movies. Spangle had an
answering service so that his mother couldn't get through. Spangle's brother Jonathan would come up sometimes on the weekends
with stolen turkeys from the supermarket where he worked, and
they had regular Thanksgiving feasts all through April and May.
The girl who had a lot of her stomach removed had been involved
with Jonathan for a while.

They went back to the apartment and she watched his going-to-
bed routine: pushups, another shower and two spins of "Forever
Young." He said he would rather sleep on the floor than on the
sofa. "God," Bobby said. "I hope the first agent I see tomorrow is
beautiful and single. Did I ruin your night? Did I keep you from
doing your work?"

Her work was *The Old Man and the Sea*, and she had reread it twice recently. She told him honestly that he hadn't, and went into the bedroom. She closed the door to undress, but opened it again when she was ready to sleep because so little air stirred in the apartment. When she went out to get a glass of ice water to put by the bed, she saw Bobby, earphones on his head, stretched on the floor like Christ crucified. He also reminded her of a pilot shot down. He still had on his denim shorts, and his feet in the orange running shoes were crossed at the ankle, and the music must have been loud, because his eyes stayed closed, and he never heard her come through the room. She tiptoed past him.

He was up before she was in the morning. When she went into the living room, she saw a white bag with donuts open on the table. On a blue index card was written: "Dame Daphne's Revenge?" He had made coffee. He was in the bathroom, shaving. He had also gotten the paper. She took a donut out of the bag and bit into it, even though eating in the morning would make her sluggish. She was thinking about what she was going to do: She was going to talk about irony to students who, ironically, were too stupid to perceive irony. They were not going to care that Santiago got his great fish. They were just going to read it, and like the stupid tourists looking down at the skeleton and the boat, hardly even wonder about it. The book was perfect to close the course with, because it was a perfect comment on the course. Actually, it was the only novel they had read all the way through, and that was because it was short, and because she had argued with the assistant principal that they would have the wrong idea about literature if they just read bits and pieces. Not too long ago, she had cared enough to argue. Well, it was perfect: She was Santiago, and her students were the tourists. And the shark? What was out there that her students would have to grapple with? Nothing. They were unintelligent because they had easy lives. They were not stalked by anything. Their grappling with complexity was having a debate about what musician was playing on a guitar break. She had heard two of them arguing about that in the hallway the week before. It was probably the first argument she had heard all summer. They capitulated so easily. They all thought alike, so there was no tension. They looked alike. They were attractive, and you could tell that their families had money, but they were no more substantial than the white carcass slung beside Santiago's boat.

She realized that she was getting carried away with making analogies and bit into the donut. A few crumbs rolled down the front of her white nightgown.

"I've never talked to an agent before," Bobby said. "I wonder what you're supposed to do when you walk in. I've always wondered what people did when they walked into a shrink's office for the first time." He had slicked back his hair—he was bald on top, but the hair was long and curly and frizzy on the sides, and now it hung in tiny wet curls. He had on jeans and a white shirt with "Don B." sewn in red thread above the pocket, and he was wearing the sort of sunglasses people who work in factories wear, with clear plastic cups at the sides so that nothing can get in their eyes.

"Should I cut this name off?" Bobby said. "Do you think it matters? I've got a sports jacket in the trunk of the car that I think will cover it."

"I'd leave it. Writers are supposed to be eccentric anyway."

"Writers are so *reasonable*," he said. "Thomas Wolfe was such a reasonable man. That little book of his Scribner's put out—I hope I can find it. Where did I put that piece of paper? I put it in my suitcase, didn't I? No—I put it in my shirt pocket, and I just stuffed my shirt in the green bag. Okay, take it easy, Bobby." He wiped some drops of water off his shoulders. His hair was so wet it was dripping. "New York makes me nervous. It's going to be a hot day, too. I hope I don't sweat. You really saved my life letting me stay here last night. I'll call you from New York after I'm done, and if you're not doing anything, I'll take you to dinner on my way home."

He sat on the floor, reached up into the bag, and took out a donut. She was flipping through the paper.

"Anything I can bring you from New York?" Bobby said.

"Wait a minute," she said. "This is impossible."

"What's impossible?"

"This," she said.

Her eye had been caught by the name Knapp. It was a short article in the regional news—a girl named Mary Knapp had been shot by her brother. She had just seen Mary the day before, and asked her to stay after school to explain why she was late for class. She had just talked to Mary's father. He had bought her lunch.

"This is one of my students," she said, holding the paper out to Bobby. "What am I going to say in class? This is impossible. She was in class yesterday and today she's shot?"

"Who shot her?" Bobby said. He chewed loudly, excited by the article. "Her brother! What do you know?"

"I can't believe it," she said.

"I know a man in Lyme who ran over his son backing into his driveway. The kid was a hemophiliac. A two-year-old in Lyme, New Hampshire, with the curse of kings—turned into a blood puddle in front of his father's eyes. You just can't believe what happens. I see that guy every time I go jogging. What do you think? His life is ruined. He just runs all day."

She had put her hand over her mouth and was shaking her head.

"What do you think?" Bobby said. "How does a thing like this happen?" He picked up the white towel from the top of his suitcase and rubbed his hair, then draped the towel over his head. "She's never going to be the same," he said. "Just a few seconds determine everything. It's like what would happen if I draped this towel over my head and just like that I turned into a sheik."

"What?" she said.

"I'd be like the rest of them, probably. I'd get every cent I could for oil. Move into Beverly Hills and have statues of naked ladies on the front lawn. New York's not Beverly Hills, at least. Thank God I'm not going to Beverly Hills."

Bobby was walking her to her car and trying to cheer her up. He asked if she wanted him to come to school with her, and she said no, he was supposed to be in New York. Her hand shook a little when she reached into her purse for her car key.

There were flowers strewn on the sidewalk: daisies and small pink flowers she didn't recognize, a rose or two. It looked as if somebody had picked a bunch of flowers from a yard and run, abandoned them, thrown them away—as if they had been taken spitefully, and not because someone wanted them for a bouquet. She didn't notice them until Bobby pointed out a scattering of rose petals beside her car. Then the two of them looked back and saw that there was a crooked trail of flowers from the apartment to her car.

From behind a parked car on the next block the magician was watching it all through binoculars. Damn: She was telling the truth about being married. Her husband was worse-looking than he was, though; and when she got in the car, she didn't kiss him goodbye. He watched her drive away, then turned the glasses to Bobby. Bobby went back into the building, where he had left the straw suitcase and the book bag in the lobby. The magician had

252

put his binoculars down when he saw Bobby come out again, so he raised them again. He saw Bobby go to his car, and he smiled when he saw the New Hampshire license plates. "I Brake for People Who Brake." Nice. Her husband had a sense of humor. Then she liked people with a sense of humor. It had been wrong to talk about national health care instead of telling her jokes. So she and her husband were living apart. That made it even easier. When he found out her name, he would send flowers to her apartment. For now, picking his mother's flowers and tossing them down to make a path had seemed good enough. Romantic, even. She inspired in him a spirit of romance. He even wondered if, by some coincidence, a favorite song of his might also be one she knew. It was the song he had heard the night before on WYBC that had given him the idea to make the path of flowers: John Sebastian, singing "She's a Lady": "Oh lady, lady of ladies, I remember days that felt like it was raining daisies." A shower of daisies. If only such a beautiful miracle were possible. The magician put his binoculars away and went to get breakfast.

19

NINA HAD once said that he was a coward, and in a way he was
relieved that she had said it. It was not a surprise to her now
that he was acting this way. Her dismay was all about the situation
and did not have much to do with the fact that he wasn't behaving
heroically.

He had reached Louise at the hospital, and he had not been
able to lie to her. He told her that he had flipped, and before he
could say anything else, she had said, "I can imagine where you
flipped to. You flipped. I like that." She hung up.

He walked a straight line from the telephone to the bedroom.
Someone on the street was carrying a radio that was playing "Heart
of Glass." Nina was lying the way he had left her, one leg on the
bed, one leg hanging off. He was not crying and she was not crying. He was staring at her and she was staring at him.

"Why didn't you say something when I opened the door?" she
said. "Are you in shock?"

She reached up and felt his forehead when he sat down, and he
smiled. Was that how you found out if someone was in shock?

"I should have said something," he said, sitting beside her on the bed. He remembered the spot of blood on the kitchen counter. Peeling the orange. "I told you, didn't I?"

"You just got in the car and came here? You came here from the hospital?"

He nodded yes.

"That's scary. That you'd do that. What were you going to do if I wasn't here?"

"I knew you'd be here."

"What if I hadn't been here last night?"

"What are you trying to tell me?" he said. "You *were* here last night. I haven't heard from you that you're sleeping anywhere else. You're going to tell me you are?"

"No," she said. "But it would have been so awful if you had come all this way and I wasn't even here. And I hate to think that you think I'm so reliable. I keep telling you not to keep thinking I'm perfectly rational and stable."

"More rational and stable than some people, apparently. He's ten years old. *Ten years old.*"

"And that was all he'd say to you? That she was a bitch?"

He shook his head no, and lay down on the bed, on his back. He lay there with his eyes closed and began to re-create Nina's apartment from memory. You walk in the front door, and you're in the living room. High ceiling, white walls. A circle of peeling paint on the ceiling, above the radiator. A piece of stained glass, found at a dump in Vermont, repaired, now hung in one of the three windows across the front of the living room: one butterfly wing, blue and gold, one half of the body and head, one antenna, leaded around the edges. A blue sofa. A chair covered in striped blue material, bulging like a hunchback, but so wide that you can sit sideways in it, comfortably. A worn Oriental rug, patched with colorless material that looks like tightly woven burlap; zigzags like lightning, yellow and blue, with a gold, blue and white border of geometrically shaped flowers; and in the middle, parallelograms with designs inside that look like four arrows pointing to the same space—the shape of a cross. A painting of two yellow birds, one facing left, one right, that she liked and he paid too much for, in a junk shop on Third Avenue. Her high school graduation picture, cut out of her yearbook and framed. A watercolor of an eggplant superimposed on an American flag. Those three pictures, all in a row, on the left-hand wall. The right-hand wall, bare, opening into the kitchen. The kitchen. The shelf over the sink, with mugs and bowls from the Mad Monk pottery store. A bowling trophy of her father's, 1956, the year his team won a tournament, on the counter next to the sink. Stains in the sink that nothing would remove. Out of the kitchen, back in the living room. On either side of the sofa, stereo speakers raised up on cinderblocks covered with black velvet. A closet door next to the bathroom door. The bathroom. Swedish ivy growing in a pot on the toilet tank, hanging down so you have to know where to reach between the leaves to flush. Black and white tiles. No rug. White shower curtain, white towels, white washcloths. A yellowed swan decal on the mirror. The tiny window above the tub that opens out. Out of the bathroom, back in the living room. The bookshelf, loaded with books and soapstone bookends, almost a dozen pairs of them. In the middle of one shelf, bookends push the books to the left and to the right, and in the space between, little things she has had for years. A hand-painted chocolate cup with a raised gold flower. A small picture, in a frame, of her godchild, Abbie, whom she hasn't seen for five years. A glass candlestick, too high to hold a candle and still fit in the bookcase. A wooden toy with a weight on the bottom, so that when you lift it and swing the ball, a bear plays a drum. A small metal skunk with a slot under its tail to hold a penny. A post card, framed, of skaters in Central Park at the turn of the century. A lipstick tube, mother-of-pearl, with a pearly rose on top. A tiny red glass vase. Two metal toy soldiers, their faces almost peeled away, standing side by side. A black rubber tarantula. Out of the living room into the bedroom. There are two brown rugs, one on each side of the bed. The rugs look and feel like velvet. There is one window above the radiator, with a bamboo shade and old lace curtain. The other window, in back of the bed, has a shade with thicker bamboo and no curtain. The bed is a mattress on a platform a foot off the floor, and it is covered with an antique quilt with a design that looks like a pinwheel in the center. Two narrow closets, one to the left of the door, one to the right. A brass coatrack heaped with clothes that won't fit in the closets, brass visible only at the bottom. At night it looks like a tall monster coming to get you: You see sleeves without hands, a coat with no body, a hat tossed on the top tilts forward, but there's no bowed head inside. Books are piled on the floor, in piles that often topple, next to the coatrack. A big wooden box, almost a foot high, with someone's initials on it and a broken lock is next to the bed. She keeps tissues inside, a pen, a pad. There is one silver iced-tea spoon in the box. There is a porcelain doll's arm. A scarf with tiny black flowers. A plastic bag full of grass. Rolling papers. Matches. Miniatures of Drambuie.

He couldn't imagine, when he first came to the apartment, how she could live in such a small place, how in spite of some pretty or funny objects, she really owned so little. The mugs above the sink, all lined up, were her only glasses. Six small bowls. Two large bowls. A pile of old plates, all different. "What are you doing?" she had said to him. "You're looking at my *plates?* Aren't you supposed to sneak off and look in the medicine cabinet?" He had been a little drunk. A few minutes later, in the bathroom, he had opened the medicine cabinet, or tried to—it was old, built into the wall, and the door was stuck. It had creaked when he pulled, and he had heard her laugh in the other room. He had put a record on her stereo and his hand was shaking and he scratched it. He had kept moving around, expecting something to happen, expecting to find something. It had all looked so unfamiliar. They didn't have the same books. They didn't have the same records. They didn't even take the same patent medicine. In the bathroom, he had gotten the hiccoughs, and he had said that he was going out for a second—he'd be right back. He could remember going into an all-night donut shop and ordering coffee at the counter, so it wouldn't look suspicious, his opening a pack of sugar. The coffee had come, and while it steamed, he had opened the packet of sugar, poured it out into the spoon, swallowed. He held his breath. No more hiccoughs. The one thing he knew he could count on was that particular cure for hiccoughs. When he took a sip of the hot coffee, he burned his tongue. Swallowing, he had realized that he was more drunk than he'd thought. He had gone to a pay phone at the back of the shop and called Nina. "I'm still welcome back, right?" he had said. "John," she had said, "where are you? What was that about? Did I do something wrong?" "Don't make me laugh," he had said. "I'll get the hiccoughs." Standing in a donut shop, staring at two homosexuals piling hand on top of hand on the counter, all four hands in a pile, the bottom hand out, back on top, pulling out, piling up. "You don't think I'm crazy?" he had said to her. "Crazy?" she had said. "Where are you? I don't understand. I thought you'd just suddenly decided to leave." He laughed. No hiccoughs. "What is going on?" she had said.

He hated to talk to her on the telephone and always had. That night he had made a fool of himself by blurting out: "Listen—do you want any donuts?" When he called her at work she could never reply to what he said, and what he said was never what he meant to say. Someone was always standing behind him waiting for the phone; or he'd call from the office and he'd hear her voice and realize how bleak his surroundings were, and overwhelmed by that, would be unable to talk. Or at phones along the highway: He'd know the road was out there and he could never put it out of his mind. There were always dark spaces, highways, impatient people—something to make what he was saying, or trying to say, not make sense. He would call and tell her he loved her as someone pushed change into a vending machine. Something they wanted would be falling through the machine—a soft drink or a candy bar—and his eye would wander, and it would seem that everything was so mundane, that his words couldn't carry any conviction. He woke her up more than he should. He would get obsessed with calling her. At night, in New York, he would tear himself away from her, and then he would stop to call three times before he got back to Rye and then call again from the dark hallway, whispering like a criminal who had broken into the house. He would talk to her about love, standing in the dark of his mother's house, feeling like a child who couldn't possibly know what he was saying. Then, sometimes, he would explain to her, when she was sleepy and perturbed, why he knew he wasn't getting through to her: Suddenly he would be telling her something that wasn't about the two of them at all, but about his mother and father, some memory, or he would describe the place he was calling from, his hand nervously touching the phone, putting his finger into the dial, touching inside the 1, the 2, the 3, his finger probing the phone as if one circle might be the right one, and somehow he would really connect with her. Again and again, standing in the same place, late at night, in the dark, Henri the poodle staring and panting as he whispered, he would hear her voice and his finger would start to move, as though the phone were a Ouija board. Or sometimes he would know that he had awakened her and say nothing about love, say only that he was sorry for having made her get up to answer the phone. Once he had called her from a phone outside the parking garage—he had left her apartment, so upset about leaving that he had walked for half an hour instead of taking a cab—and there was something wrong with the phone. He had had to put four dimes in before he made the connection, and when she answered, he had only been able to tell her that he had walked, that there was a phone out of order in New York. Then he had stared at a couple walking by; he had held the phone tightly in one hand, his claim check for his car in the other, and he remembered thinking that if he let the phone go, he was going to disappear. He had dropped endless nickels into the phone and kept her talking for an hour. She didn't understand about him and the phone. He tried to explain it to her in person, but even then he never really got through. At first when he would leave and call her half an hour later, an hour later, she got angry and accused him of being paranoid and checking on her. She had first said that to him on the phone, and he couldn't deal with criticism on the phone: He would just lose his words, and be silent, and then she would think that he had gone, and he would panic, thinking: Please don't hang up. Think I'm not here, but please don't hang up. It was only in the movies that you could jiggle the cradle of a telephone up and down saying three or four times "Hello? Hello?" and still be connected. He couldn't stand it, either, if she joked on the phone. Once, five minutes after he had left her, he had called and told her he loved her and she had said, sounding genuinely confused, "Who is this?" He would seek out phones because they connected him to her, knowing all the time that that was an illusion: a piece of black plastic, his hand on a piece of black plastic miles away from her hand. How could he think he was touching her? He would call her and imagine her standing there, holding the telephone. She was used to all of it by now. She said "That's okay" reflexively when he said he was sorry for waking her; she would tell him without protest whether she was sitting or standing, wearing clothes or pajamas: whatever he wanted to know. She had said to him, early on, that maybe it would be better if they didn't talk on the telephone, and he had been amazed that she hadn't understood: It was like admitting that they were defeated. They were already separated too much, and the phone was a false link, but still a link. "You wouldn't not answer your phone, would you?" he had said. "Maybe if you didn't look around you when you called," she said, "you could concentrate on what you wanted to say." So he had closed his eyes, holding the phone against his ear, everything black. She had given him a toy telephone for Christmas, her face glued in the center, smiling a big smile. When you dialed the phone, a childish voice would say: "I am five, how old are you?" Dial again, and the voice would say: "Will you be my friend?" He knew that it was funny, but it also wasn't funny: It was his nightmare telephone, the telephone on which you couldn't say what you wanted, on which words were just words and went nowhere. He had given the toy telephone to Nick to give his son. He would have given it to Brandt, but he didn't even want it around. The little circular picture was in his desk drawer. It reminded him of the telephone, and it was the one picture of Nina he didn't really like to look at. But he kept it. It was there. Until Nina had shown him, he had never thought about his favorite sleeping position: on his side, with one arm along his body, the other arm raised, fingers curled, just below the ear. In bed one night, she had faced him, imitating his position, and said, "Hello, John? Everything all right?"

He opened his eyes and saw that she was on the bed facing him now, and he wanted to rouse himself to console her. But his body felt heavy—the sudden heaviness you feel when you've been treading water and are about to sink, a signal from your body that it isn't worth it to fight anymore. He was lying on his back, hot and heavy on the mattress, and she was on her side, supporting herself on one arm, her free hand resting on the sheet. If she were to put her hand on him, that little bit of added weight would push him under. He looked at her hand, and not at her face. It was such a small hand, the fingers long and thin—he had forgotten if he had ever held such a hand when he was young, when his own hand was smaller.

She had once said that he was a coward. Cowardly to leave his family and not totally cut the tie. Cowardly to go, and cowardly to return, and all the time he was in Connecticut feeling heavy—his heart heavy. He felt old, and more tired than he felt when he was physically tired, driving home late to his mother's house in Rye. The truth was that he didn't have much grace. He could have eased Louise into discussions, but he hadn't. Louise could still take him by surprise, and he was afraid of that. The only thing that had taken him by surprise that had been a good surprise, a surprise he could deal with, had been Nina. When she had opened the door and he had seen the man standing there, he had misunderstood, in a flash, what kind of scene he had walked in on; and he had only been able to stand there, as stunned as he was when somebody pulled a trick on him on the telephone, unable to think about what was happening but staring at her breast, the robe fallen away so that he saw the curve of her breast almost to the nipple. He had no idea what he would have done or said if she had not spoken. He could imagine standing there still.

At the hospital, it had seemed that he was watching the action from a great distance, as if he were standing outside a dance hall where strobe lights were flashing. The hospital had seemed garishly bright, and he had closed his eyes often, needing to rest them. When he opened them, he would get a flash of something new, something he would only see quickly: the blood-covered shirt, the notebook that was open and then closed, a needle going into Louise's arm. When he blinked the needle had been pulled out; Louise had been standing and then she was sitting. He saw people but not groups of people; a nurse's hand, but not the nurse's body. His son, in a white bed: For a second he had seen all of him, a little boy in a bed, but then he had seen only his eyes. John Joel had said that Mary was a bitch. His mouth had moved, but nothing else, and he had wanted to move toward him, but the nurse had stepped in. He blinked, and then the nurse was between him and his son, and he was staring at her hand, turning. The corridor stretched before him, long and narrow and bright; and from there, somehow, to the inside of the car, with Louise on the seat beside him. Then he managed to focus on the important things, one by one: key in ignition, hand on wheel, foot on accelerator. He had gotten to New York the same way. He had not seen the whole backyard, but only the tree under which it had happened; and then he had seen his car, gotten into the car, and from there to New York it was a series of simple, mechanical movements. They tell you when you are learning to drive not to stare straight ahead, but to take in what is happening around you. Next to him was an empty seat. He looked at his hands on the wheel, then through the windshield, and then at the speedometer: He watched the needle climb and climb until he was going the right speed. He knew that he was falling asleep, and that he shouldn't sleep. Her hand was on his chest, but he had been wrong—it was inadequate to hold him down. He wasn't heavy, as he had thought, but light, speeding.

"What's the matter?" she said, when he sprang up from the bed.

He stood in the room, shaking sleep out of his head. He had to go back, but he was afraid to move out of the room, afraid to move from the spot he stood in. Nina was standing beside him, pulling his arm the way Brandt did, but she had more power. She could lead him back to the bed. He blinked, and he was sitting on the bed, Nina's arm around his shoulder, Nina pressing up against him. She was crying. He talked to her, said words, said something, but she kept on crying. Talking to her was as futile as trying to get to the top of the stairs. Time had stopped. He was telling her that they were stopped, and she was shaking her head no. She didn't believe him? He decided to trust her. He smiled and pulled her down on the bed with him. If time hadn't stopped, then it was safe to sleep, and when he woke up things would go on. It was possible that things could go on. If he slept, it did not mean that he would sleep forever.

"What are you going to do?" she said.

He thought that she knew him so well that she had read his mind. He thought she was asking him whether or not he was going to stay awake.

On his side, next to her in the bright room, he slept.

He dreamed that Nina was on a train. It was a train in a foreign country, a train somewhere in Europe, and it was winter, a bright day, bare trees and bright sun as the train took a curve and straightened again. She had on a winter coat, black, and she was sitting in a compartment alone, on a long wooden bench that faced another wooden bench. She was looking at the haze of passing scenery out the window. And then a couple came into the compartment, a man and a wife. They had a newspaper with them, the New York Times, *and when they put a section aside she asked to see it. They were surprised that she was also an American. Just the three of them, two facing one, Nina in her black coat. She had taken the paper, unfolded it, turned the page, and there was his picture. Sitting on the train and opening a newspaper she had found his obituary, and that was how she learned that he was dead.*

20

"I'M STILL looking around the farm, and I'm able to count all the chickens. Seems like there hasn't been one chicken dinner, if you know what I mean. Chickens still going every which way, you keep hearing about how they get their heads chopped off and their bodies go running forward, but when I look around, I don't even see any feathers. More and more chickens, nicer and nicer farm. Pastoral. People would say I was an evil character for dealing a few drugs, but look who gets blown away. Not my chickens. Way I look at it, we're all still struttin' around Maggie's Farm. Bunch of chickens struttin' their stuff in the sunshine. You pick up a newspaper and read about what happened at Three Mile Island, you try to tell me that my chickens are causing any trouble like that. Might be a little stoned, but they're just struttin' their stuff in the sunshine, and nobody's catching them for nothing. Too many bad things pinned on drugs. No way that ten-year-old was high, according to you, and there he was, up in a tree, shooting down. No way drugs explain why this is a bad world. Chickens got all upset a while back there, thinking the sky was falling. Acid didn't do that. The United States space program did that. Chickens ought to squawk. They fucking ought to claw the *dirt* about that one. Not that there's any good it would do them. United States government doesn't have to pay attention to a little bit of scratching in the dirt."

Horton was stoned. He was trying to get a Morton's chicken pot pie out of its foil baking dish and onto one of Nina's plates. He liked to remove the top piece intact, but it was already in three pieces, and he hadn't even tilted the pie onto the plate yet. He worked the fork around the edge again, tilted the pie. "Good a thing to eat as any other," he said. "Cheap, too. Hey, I made a joke. Talking about chicken, and I said *cheap*."

"I feel responsible," she said. "I've talked to John about this every day for a week, and I still feel responsible."

"Homewrecker? You feel like a bad lady homewrecker? People don't want their house disturbed, they don't go out looking to disturb it. He just wanted the lights burning all night in the chicken coop. Wanted more production. Willing to risk a tasteless egg or two to take on more."

"Will you please stop talking about chickens?" Spangle said.

He was cutting his steak. No place Nina suggested for dinner had pleased them, and finally they had smoked up again and gone to the food store, and this was what they had come back with. One steak, one Morton's chicken pie, and eight bags of Doritos.

"You told me these were great," Spangle said, biting a Dorito. "Same old taco chips. I don't see any difference."

"This is really getting to me," Nina said. "There's a real crisis in my life, and I end up entertaining the Marx Brothers."

"No way we're the Marx Brothers," Horton said. "Take a look. I'm black, he's white. We might be half-brothers, if Mama was fooling around with the wrong rooster, but there is no way you can take in the two of us and say we're brothers. Shit. We're not even soul brothers. You know who's a soul man now? Not Huey, not Eldridge. Fatso, on *Saturday Night Live*." Horton bit into another Dorito. "You think brother Huey traded in his wicker throne for modular furniture? What do you bet me?"

"Come on," Spangle said. "We go to Vermont and get some sort of jobs. We get out of all this. We can take Horton with us, and he can raise chickens. You like that plan, Horton?"

"The Grand Concourse is as close as I care to come to the country. Spent enough time in the country in my Bard College days. Makes me nervous just to look up above me and see greenery in people's windows. Makes me nervous to see any plants but the necessary five-leaf kind. Unhealthy life in the country."

"Spangle," she said, "would you be saying this if I hadn't told you about what happened in John's family? You came here the other night with the intention of asking me to come back to you and move to Vermont?"

"I came back because I felt myself coming back. I haven't gone back to New Haven because I can't see myself walking into that apartment in New Haven again. The other night when I was sprawled out on your floor I got to thinking that cities make people crazy."

"United States space program makes people crazy," Horton said. "These chicken pies have really stood the test of time. Same chicken pies I remember from my childhood."

"I can't say yes or no right now. I'm all mixed up. I hadn't even thought about you for so long, and now you're back here and you want it to be like you never left. It didn't work out the other time we tried it, remember? You were more eager for me to leave than I was."

"But I was here a week later, wasn't I?"

"Your dealer got shot. You came here to connect with Horton."

"I'm reliable," Horton said. "Never been shot. Never care to be."

"But you're going to think about it," Spangle said.

"You've been with Cynthia for so many years. You're just going to push that out of your mind?"

"I didn't have any plans to be lobotomized. I just had an idea that the two of us could try again."

"I want to be by myself," Nina said.

"What I like," Horton said, "is just the opposite. I like people around that I can talk to. I like to be able to have a thought and spill it out. You can't tell what a thought will be till it's spilled out, like dice. I'm not so crazy yet that I sit around and rap with myself."

"Have you ever in your life been at a loss for something to say, Horton?" Spangle said.

Horton thought. "I don't believe so. I believe the good Lord gave me a tongue to talk. Pointless to have a tongue if you don't talk. Like an anteater showing no interest in ants."

"I think you'd like Vermont, Horton," Spangle said. "I think it would inspire you."

"I've got a bicycle chained to a tree if I get in the country mood. Go get my bicycle any day. Just waiting for me, chained to a tree."

"Jesus," Nina said. "I keep feeling like it's my fault."

"Don't," Spangle said. "If it hadn't been you, it would have been somebody else."

"*That's* flattering," she said. "Thank you."

"I was trying to tear *him* down, not you. I want you, not him."

"I don't care," she said. "That was an awful thing to say."

"*You* just told *me* that it was random. That he happened to meet you when you were with some girlfriend, visiting her boyfriend, and in walked John, so you ended up having dinner that night."

"That wasn't what you meant. You meant that I was just somebody he happened to pick up."

"Don't fight," Horton said. "It ruins my digestion."

"Don't keep joking," she said to Horton. "This is my life."

"I just joke to keep talking. Don't think anything of it. Don't have a serious thought in my head some days. Today seems to be one of those days. I feel like I'm in the barrel going over the waterfall—reach a certain point, and it's just inevitable that you're going to get going faster and faster. Did either of you hear anything about a danger at Niagara Falls? Something a while back that I missed, apparently."

"Whatever it was, the news didn't get to Madrid," Spangle said.

"And what kind of a job would I get?" she said. "What is there to do in Vermont but be a waitress in some diner? All winter it's horrible—cold and snowy."

"At least there aren't gutters to get clogged," he said.

"Put yourself in a barrel," Horton said. "Roll through the snow. Have him push you along with a stick."

"I think you ought to come with us, Horton. In case we get snowed in and get bored."

"Oh no," Horton said. "Put my ideas into practice, and half of them would kill you." He wiped his mouth on the back of his hand. "I believe I have some business to transact in a half-hour. Think I'll just go into the bathroom and tidy myself up." Horton shook his head. "You know I dated a lady for a spell who used to say that? It meant she was putting in her diaphragm." He carried his plate to the kitchen. "Tidying herself up. Yes indeed," Horton said, walking through the living room to the bathroom.

"Hey, Horton," Spangle said. "What about the music? When's your buddy getting out of the hospital?"

"That's the rest of the story. The lady ran off with my friend. He's already *out* of the hospital, and she's off with him some-where, and both of them embarrassed to face me. I joke all the time because I have such a sad life. She's probably tidying herself up about now. Here I stand, all alone, combing my hair." He closed the bathroom door.

Soon after Horton left she asked Spangle to leave too, but he told her that he wanted to stay, and she didn't press him to go. He had been staying with his brother, in some painter's apartment in the West Village. His brother had a date that night, and had asked him to get lost. The painter was out of town for a week, gambling in Atlantic City. Jonathan had been sleeping in the painter's bed, and he had been sleeping in a hammock in the kitchen. Instead of wallpaper in the kitchen, the painter had tacked up stills from old movies, and when Spangle couldn't sleep, his eye would wander over the walls to pictures of Debbie Reyn-olds behind the microphone in "Singin' in the Rain," Sandra Dee in a modest bathing suit, Annette Funicello in her Mouse-keteer costume, Kate Smith singing, Sissy Spacek at the dance in *Carrie*, Esther Williams on the edge of a diving board, Joan Crawford behind a desk working for Pepsi, Mae West, Britt Ek-land, Jayne Mansfield, Kim Novak, glossy picture after glossy pic-ture, pinned to the wall with yellow push-pins. None of the paint-er's work had been put up in the apartment. It was all at his studio in SoHo. Jonathan had been there, and he had said it was filled with mannequins and pinball machines, pictures stacked every-where, racing forms on the floor, a one-armed bandit on the tank of a broken toilet, a geranium growing out of the toilet bowl. The painter hated to paint in the summer, and would go to the studio just to play with the machines and water the plant. He had recently met a woman who admired his work and had a condominium in Atlantic City, and he had started going there and gambling when her husband wasn't around. Gambling was a new kick. Before that, it had been weight-lifting. Before that, snuff films. James Wright's poetry. Homosexuality.

Spangle had not thought for a long time about the bomb exploding. Looking at Esther Williams or Mae West before he fell asleep seemed the perfect antidote. You could not look at Mae West and close your eyes and worry about a bomb exploding. Other things, but not that.

Lying in limbo in the hammock, he had thought a lot about Nina, and about how he would like to try again with her. (He had realized the appropriateness of the hammock right away, and had told Jonathan to put his quarter away: no need to flip for the bed.) Not that Cynthia had done anything wrong, but they were beginning to seem like an old married couple. She was even getting tolerant of his nightmares, soothing him perfunctorily. She had stopped complaining to him, and he had stopped complaining to her. The realization that he did not have a private, separate existence from her began to bother him. He liked Madrid because she had not seen it. He was nostalgic for Vermont for the same reason. They had been to Vermont together a couple of times in the summer, but she had never seen the Vermont of frozen winters and deer hunters and bare trees by the river. She had never known what it felt like to have a house full of lights and music and people, a house full of constant activity, while outside snow fell silently, mounds of wet, silent snow, covering bushes and piling on roofs, rising as high on top of the hanging bird-feeder as the feeder itself. If he had it to do over again, there would not be quite so many people. There would be just as big a house, though, even if part of it had to be closed off. He had torn down walls and sanded floors and glazed windows, and as fast as he had worked, Bobby had written poems about it all. Coming back to the States, on the plane, he had read one of Bobby's poems in a magazine. Crazy Bobby—everything had been an inspiration to him. It was a standing joke with his friends that he could turn anything into a poem: Once he had put the light on in the car and taken an index card out of the glove compartment as they waited on a flooded road in Boston for AAA to come tow them out. The runs they used to make from Vermont to Boston, when it was absolutely necessary to see *Night of the Living Dead* or eat kosher food. Impossible to believe that he had lost touch with so many of those people. Maybe Cynthia would just let him go. The hammock could metamorphose into a huge basket, and he could be set among the bulrushes, and free of her, he would be saved by someone or something else. But it was hard to imagine finding a new person to love when he was still attached to so many people from the past. In Madrid, he had thought of Cynthia, not of going back to the States to try to find a new girl. It amazed him when that sort of thing happened. It amazed him that Nina's lover, John, could just go over to his friend Nick's apartment, and that Nick's girlfriend would have brought her friend along, and that friend would be Nina. That they would joke and talk. That he would end up taking her to dinner that night, and the next night, too; and that then they would go to her apartment. She said that he was so curious that he had even gone through the medicine cabinet. Just like that, you could walk into somebody's life? He was nowhere near John's age, and he was the one who felt old: He was the one who couldn't believe such a thing was possible.

Nina had gone into the bathroom and turned on the shower. He went into the kitchen and decided to make coffee and try to get his head straight. If she was letting him stay, he should at least try to take her problems seriously. He wondered if he had really offended her by saying that if it hadn't been her it would have been somebody else. Because he couldn't imagine her with some middle-aged man, a man with money, who worked at a fancy job and had a fancy house in the suburbs. Lemon lilies on the front lawn. Sprinklers on the putting green at the country club. Was Nina getting old? Was that why that life had started to attract her? He had asked her that, and that had been the wrong thing to say, too: Even if she found it attractive, she said, she wasn't going to get it. And if she had ever had a chance, it was gone now. He was guilt-stricken and he had admitted that he was a coward, and he was right back there now, wasn't he? She had been red in the face, about to cry, and then she had sighed and stomped off to the bathroom. She took showers the way other people got drunk or smoked until they were stoned. She would be reincarnated as a water nymph. He could be adrift in the bulrushes and she could be bathing there, and swim after him. Where would the myth go from there? Bobby would have been able to guess, in one of his poems. He always used to imagine beautiful situations that worked out perfectly. Or at least that was the way he had read Bobby's poems, and it had taken a long time to figure out that Bobby wasn't smiling because he was flattered, but because of the way he, Spangle, almost always misunderstood them. Spangle had had no ear for irony. Cynthia said that, too. She said that she couldn't imagine how he had ever passed freshman English. "How can anybody be smart about life when they don't understand literature?" she had asked him. "What happens to characters happens to characters, and what happens to you and me happens to you and me," he had said. She had asked him, then, if he was speaking ironically. Maybe not ironically, but humorously? He dodged the question. Probably she was smarter than he was. Probably that was the truth.

He was drinking coffee and listening to News Radio Eighty-Eight. Someone was discussing cottage cheese. He listened as long as he could stand it, then changed the station. Someone was saying something about Joe Cocker, and he felt a tingling in his fingers, on the dial, because he thought that what was being said was that Joe Cocker was dead. But it wasn't that. The announcer was saying that Joe Cocker hadn't been heard from for a long time, but he wasn't saying that he would never be heard from again. There'd been enough of that. Enough of everybody dying. Enough of his not getting his own life together. John wasn't the only coward. He was settling for biding time, swinging in a hammock, quite literally, over neutral territory. Here was an irony he understood: He was in Nina's kitchen, wanting her back, and Joe Cocker was singing a song called "Do I Still Figure in Your Life?" He finished the cup of coffee. "Nina?" he hollered. "Want coffee?"

Another irony: While he was sobering up to have a serious talk with her, she had disappeared. He had not heard her go. She had put on her clothes and gone out, without even saying goodbye. Not even the falsely polite goodbye of years ago, when she

271

left Vermont for New York—just a shower, clothes pulled on, purse picked up, gone. He looked for her purse, and when he didn't see it, he was sure that she had done more than just duck out for a minute.

He finished all the coffee in the pot, waiting for her. The coffee made him edgy. The situation made him edgy. He didn't have any right in her apartment after all this time, and he was sure that she had left because she didn't think he would get straight, or care about her problem. She thought he was Groucho or Harpo, just showing up to clown around.

He put *Bitches Brew* on the stereo and waited. He waited a long time, and blamed himself silently for what had happened. He called the painter's apartment, looking for advice, he supposed, from his brother, but the phone rang and rang. No brother. If he had any idea where Nina would go, he would go look for her. If he knew who any of her friends were, he would call them, act casual, try to find out if she was there. She must have been very disgusted to just walk out of her apartment and leave it to him. He must have really done and said the wrong things. He resisted the temptation to roll a joint and smoke it. When an argument started on the street he got up and went into the bedroom to watch. One man was shoving another. A woman in spike heels was holding one of the men's hats, standing there and looking casual. It took him a second to see that a child was standing behind her. He never got a clear look at the child, but while the men yelled and threatened each other, the woman lost interest and started tossing the hat in the air and catching it. She finally put it on her head, took the child by the hand and walked off down the street, and that was what broke up the fight—the tall man wanted his hat. He ran after her, arm outstretched, calling her name. The woman disappeared around the corner and the man behind her followed. Only the short man in the lavender shirt unbuttoned to his waist was left standing on the sidewalk, wiping his forehead. For the first time, Spangle realized that the man's forehead had been cut. He saw a knife on the ground. He had watched the whole thing, and he hadn't known what he was looking at. It had just been a series of jerky movements and curses in the half-dark. Even the woman had stood there as though nothing important was happening. The man took off his shirt and pressed it to his head. He walked away, holding the shirt in a wadded-up ball against one side of his head, ignoring the people on the street as they ignored him. Spangle sat on the bed. She was out there. Somewhere, Nina was out there, and if anything happened to her, it would be his fault.

He paced the apartment, turned off *Bitches Brew* and put on a Mozart string quartet to make himself calm. He called his brother again, but no Jonathan, no answer. How unlike her, just to walk out. How insensitive he had been, not to realize how disturbed she was. She was entitled to her apartment, but he had managed to chase her out of it. The least he could do was be gone when she came home. He deserved to have to worry about her, calling every ten minutes, until he heard her voice and knew that she was back, and safe. He was writing a note to her, apologizing, leaving her the painter's number and asking her please not to hate him so much that she wouldn't just call and say that she was all right, when there was a knock on the door. He got up, thinking: She forgot her key. That was what she had liked about the house in Vermont—no locks. But before he pulled the door open, he asked who was there, to make sure. What he had just seen outside had reminded him where he was.

"John," the voice said.

"What are you doing here?" Spangle said, opening the door.

"What are *you* doing here?"

"Making a nuisance of myself. She was upset, and I upset her more." He stood aside and let John in.

"Where is she?" he said.

"She went out. I pissed her off, and she went out. I was just leaving myself. I guess I'll go ahead and leave. She'll be happier to see you here than me."

"I don't know about that. I called her at work today, and she wouldn't come to the phone. She was there, wasn't she?"

"Yeah," Spangle said. "As far as I know, she worked all day."

"And you don't know where she went?"

"No. She was taking a shower, and I was getting myself together drinking coffee in the kitchen. The radio was on pretty loud, and I was daydreaming, I guess, and when she got out of the shower she dressed and went out without saying anything. I deserved it. She didn't have any way of knowing that I'd get it together."

John sat in the humpback chair, ran his hand over his face. What she had told him had come true: He would come to the apartment knowing she would be there, and she would be gone. At least she was not gone with Spangle. Yet.

"What did you say that disturbed her?"

"It was just some stoned-out discussion." Spangle was afraid John could read his mind, and knew he had said that if John hadn't fallen in love with Nina, he would have fallen in love with someone else.

"Do you want me to make you some coffee?" Spangle said.

"Would you?" John said. As Spangle got up to walk into the kitchen, John said, "Did you tell me you were going?"

"I'll go when she comes back. I think as long as I'm here so late, I'll just sit around for another minute. I'm sure she'll be back pretty soon. She was tired when she went out." Spangle ran the water, filled the pan to put on the stove. "I'm a shit," he said. "I'll bet you could murder me for fucking with her head so she disappeared. You two had a good thing going, and suddenly I show up. I'm a shit," Spangle said. "What she told you was the truth: I didn't sleep with her."

"I believed her," John said.

"But I'm such a shit that I was going to suggest it."

"I believe that, too."

"Smart," Spangle said. "That why she likes you so much?"

"No," John said. "She's seen what a good job I've done making a life for myself, and she probably thinks she can learn from me. Give her an idea about how to be loyal to the person you marry, how to raise children—things like that."

"She doesn't think you're a shit," Spangle said.

"I don't either, really. I'm mad at everyone around me. I got to talk to some shrink that wasn't much older than my daughter— of course, Nina's not much older than my daughter—about my *anger*. See, I was there when my son pulled the trigger."

"You were?" Spangle said.

"Not in fact, but to all intents and purposes I was there. That's what she told me, and then when I got angry, she told me that I was angry at my family. She was suggesting to me that I was to blame for my son shooting my daughter. She had even met Parker —his friend, Parker; that's a long story—and she still thought that what I needed to understand about the situation was that I shared the blame." John shook his head. "Smart," he said. "Right-out-of-graduate-school smart."

"Black or with milk?" Spangle said, getting up.

"Black," John said.

"Jesus Christ," Spangle said. "I'm glad I don't have your life. The only thing I envy you for is Nina."

"It's the only thing I'm to be envied for."

"Is she all right, your daughter?" Spangle said. "Nina said she called the hospital, but they don't tell you anything over the phone except that the patient hasn't died. Not that she thought she'd died. She just wanted to call. Maybe I should just shut up."

"Everybody's fine. They're shot, or they're mentally ill—everybody's all doped up so that we can forget that it happened, or be calm enough to explore the reasons why it happened. They don't like it if you refuse to get doped up. That's part of your *anger*. It's part of my anger that I won't discuss Nantucket with my wife, too. I should get doped up and explore with her the reasons she wants to go to Nantucket. I'm to blame for not celebrating the Fourth of July. I'm to blame for walking out."

"For walking out of what?"

"A family conference. My daughter couldn't be there, because she was shot, and my son couldn't be there, because he's doped up to sleep all the time, and my other son, who lives with my mother, knows nothing about it and was at a Little League game in Rye. But my mother was there, and she was telling the girl who was right out of graduate school that I was running myself ragged leading such a hectic life, and that she had had a problem with alcoholism until she found something that mattered to her. That her life didn't really shape up until Brandt came to live with her, and the girl is writing it all down, glaring at me, not even making a pretense of not hating me for whatever off-the-wall thing any of them said. And there's Louise, wiping her eyes, talking about the beach at Nantucket, and her friend Tiffy—she's inseparable from this feminist, who thinks all the trouble in the world is the result of sexist fairy tales read to us when we were children. So Louise is talking about sailboats and sunsets, and my mother keeps patting my hand and saying that I never sleep, that she wakes up and hears me at four in the morning, talking on the phone. Damn right, she does—to Nina, in New York. Louise just stared at me when my mother said that. I think she said it on purpose. Obviously I'm not talking to the garage at four A.M."

"Everything changes," Spangle said. "It doesn't make any sense how much everything changes. When I first knew Nina, I would have thought that we'd both be in the country forever, and here she is on Columbus Avenue, and I'm in New Haven—I'm not in New Haven, but one of these days I've got to get back there and try to make some sort of order out of that."

"When they were babies I never thought they'd be children, and when they were children I kept thinking of when they'd be grown. I didn't think that somewhere in the middle there'd be a gunshot."

"It's just crazy," Spangle said. "Anything can happen. You do something you really believe in, and the next day it doesn't mean anything to you. The woman I live with in New Haven used to date a Marine, and he came home from Vietnam and acted in a porn film about the war, in drag. I met the guy once, and he told me about pigeons landing outside his window in the morning, how the beating of their wings reminded him of the sound the helicopters made, setting down in the fields. He was living in Harlem. Didn't care what happened."

"What happened?"

"Lost track of him."

John was sipping the hot coffee, coming awake a little. "What do you do?" he said to Spangle.

"I'm a good-for-nothing. I'm on the last few thousand of an inheritance, and then I've got to go to work. I just went to Madrid and got my kid brother to come back and go to law school. Hoping he'll support me someday. Let me sponge off of him."

"Will he?" John said.

"Maybe. For a while. Or the woman I live with in New Haven. Lived with."

"You want Nina," John said.

"I do," Spangle said. "The thing about Nina is that I can never get used to her. It used to bother me, but she's lying, man, when she says she's predictable. She doesn't know what other women are like if she thinks she's predictable. I mean, I don't know how you can live with somebody unless there's a part of them you can't fathom. She was so nice to me the other night, and tonight she just walked out, not even a goodbye." Spangle put down his empty coffee cup. He had now drunk way too much coffee. Bells were ringing in his body.

By the time Nina got back to the apartment, they were no longer talking. John had fallen asleep in the bedroom, in his clothes, on top of the quilt, light on, and Spangle, still wide awake from all the coffee, had been left alone in the living room. John had told him, when he was talking about his day with the psychiatrist, that he had found out guilt was only anger directed inward. But what did you know when you knew that? That he would be guilty if he took Nina from John? He was already angry at himself—what did a little more anger matter?

Nina wasn't happy to see him. "I asked you to leave," she said. She said it even before she realized that John was in the bedroom.

Sitting alone, drinking coffee, looking around the delicatessen and seeing other people, she thought: My God—there are actually other people, like me, sitting here alone. Spangle was so animated that it was like being with several people. That overflow of energy made her nervous. Having people around all the time made her nervous. She thought, sometimes, that if she lived in a tent, people would come and crawl into the tent. Some days she wanted to say to the landlady downstairs: "You're right—this life I'm leading is crazy. Do something to help me. Get them out of here." They were men, always. Not women. Not that there were that many men, but John, and Horton, and Jonathan and Spangle, all in such a short time period. It was too much. She had bought the paper and was enjoying sitting alone, no longer feeling guilty for having walked out. She was imitating John's behavior, and liking it. If they did not mind barging in, she should not mind sneaking out. The other thing to think was that she was already a bad person, damned forever, for causing trouble in John's marriage. His son had shot his daughter. The little boy she had had lunch with not long ago had pulled the trigger of a gun and his sister was in the hospital, and there were lawyers involved, psychiatrists. That poor fat child had shot his sister. She stirred her coffee and wondered, if she and John had children, whether they would be pretty or whether they would look like John Joel. She had never seen his daughter. She was ten years older than his daughter. He kept saying that, as though she and his daughter had something in common. Her cut finger still hurt, and she hated pain. She could not imagine what it would be like to be shot. She lived in New York City, and she could not imagine any of the possibilities: rape, muggings, murder. That was something she read about in the paper. John Joel's shooting Mary was something she read about in the paper. She thought that what Horton said about being comfortable in the city made sense. In the city she just did not have time to think all the time and to be frightened: You either adjusted or you went crazy. In the country, every branch rattling against the house became frightening. She had hated the night noises in the country.

She paid her bill at the cash register at the front of the delicatessen. There was an index card Scotch-taped to the side of the register, with a smiling face on it that said: SMILE. I HAVEN'T HAD A VACATION IN FOUR YEARS. The FOUR had been crossed out and 4½ was written above it.

She went back and just what she thought would happen happened: She walked in and Spangle was there. She told him what she thought about that and, exhausted, went into the bedroom.

It could have been anything in the bed—a lump, in the dark. It was what she thought it was, though. It was John. He moved in the bed. He opened his eyes and looked at her as she was undressing.

"I'd ask what you're doing here, but I have the feeling that I'd sound illogical and you could give a perfectly logical answer," she said.

"I'm hiding," he said.

"You're hiding," she said. "It must be wonderful."

"He wants you," John said. "He told me so tonight. He's after you, Nina."

"You make him sound like a bloodhound," she said. "And me some piece of meat."

279

She got into bed. "You've got a great deal of nerve, both of you."

"You're mad at me?"

"I'm going to sleep," she said.

"You can't go to sleep mad."

He took her hand and squeezed it. He squeezed her cut finger. The stab of pain made her eyes well up with tears. She was going to go to hell for this. He was going to go to hell. They would all meet in hell. It would be small, and swamped with men she knew. All their paths would keep crossing. Spangle was snoring in the other room. She moved against John, to get warm.

21

"I THINK I've spent a lot of time talking to most everybody but to you. How do you feel?"

"Like hell," Mary said.

He nodded. It was going to form a scar—puffy and ugly, the doctor had told him the day before—but there could be a second operation, later, to graft skin over the scar. The doctor thought that a fifteen-year-old girl shouldn't have such a reminder of what had happened. He told Mary that when the plastic surgery was done, she could wear a two-piece bathing suit and no one would know. They would take skin from another part of her body—the inside of her thigh—and graft it. Mary nodded. She closed her eyes often, even when the doctors were there talking, and imagined other diseases, other things gone wrong, that might have put her in the hospital. It could have been mono. Appendicitis. Something simple. Two psychiatrists came to visit her every day, to tell her that this was not simple. It *had* been simple, though. She remembered saying goodbye to Angela. She thought Angela was going to trail her home, insisting that she go to another party at Lloyd Bergman's, but Angela had given up on her. "If you don't want to, you don't want to," Angela had said. Then she had walked through the field, being careful to avoid the poison ivy. Once Angela gave up, the idea of the party seemed more interesting. Walking through the field, she thought about changing her mind. She was still wondering whether she should go to the party or not—the last one hadn't been as bad as she thought—when she knew that something was wrong. It was just a peculiar feeling she had, that something was going to happen. She looked back, suspecting that Angela was following. She saw a bug alight on her jeans and flicked it off. Before she had turned fully around again, and before she thought to look up in the tree, she felt a terrible explosion in her side, and that was all she remembered. One psychiatrist wanted to know what she had thought when she heard the sound, and she told him there was no sound—just pain that knocked her over, and then she didn't remember anything. The psychiatrist told her that there was no such thing as a totally silent firing of a gun, even with a silencer. He asked her to try to remember the sound. She smiled at him. She couldn't. After only three meetings with him, she had figured out that anything she couldn't remember or didn't want to talk about could be taken care of with a smile. When she smiled, he smiled. It also worked with the woman. Then, if she didn't speak, after a while they went on and talked about something else.

She was amazed that John Joel had shot her, of course, but she was also amazed that now she hated him less. In fact, she didn't hate him at all. She was embarrassed to have been shot. She told the psychiatrist that, and he asked whether she was saying that she somehow deserved to be shot, whether she felt it was something she had asked for. "But this was a real gun. It was shot with the intent to kill you."

She realized that it was real. That didn't matter. It mattered that she hurt, but she couldn't believe that she might have died. Now her father was in the room, and he was smiling at her. She did what the psychiatrist did when she smiled: smiled back and didn't say anything. Finally he was the one who spoke. He whispered, "Do you hate me?"

She shook her head no.

"That was a selfish question, I guess. Coming to stand by your bed and be absolved of guilt."

"What did *you* do?" she said.

"I went to live in Rye," he said. "Among other things that I've done."

"Rye seems like a pretty nice place to me," she said. It was a joke. Only in this context did it seem reasonable. It wasn't reasonable. John Joel knew that, and she thought that it was part of the reason why he had shot her. Although their mother liked John Joel better than she liked her. Rye. If he wanted to live in Rye, let him live in Rye. She did not think it reflected on her. But she thought it explained why her brother had done it, in part. The psychiatrists wanted her to think about all the reasons why her brother had shot her, and then they wanted to hear what she thought about those reasons: why she did or didn't think she deserved to be shot. One of them gave her a legal pad. She made criss-crosses on the page, doodled flowers and moths and birds, wrote her name and inked over it and over it until the letters were tall and wide. She would just tell the psychiatrist again why he had done it. That it was because they didn't like each other. That she taunted him. That her brother wasn't happy. That he probably wasn't thinking about what he was doing, for some reason. No—she didn't think John Joel was sick. She thought that he had shot her maybe without even deciding to do it, and that now it was over. Things were going to change. The psychiatrist asked her how.

She tested her father: "Are things going to be different?"

"You're going to get well," he said. He looked huge, standing by the window. Everything in the room was low: the tray that came over the bed so she could eat, the little night table. He was playing with the cord to the Venetian blinds.

"Be different," he sighed. "Yes. Things certainly seem to have changed, don't they?" His little joke. She had made a little joke that it would be better to be in Rye with her grandmother than to be in Connecticut with her family, where she had been shot; he had made a little joke that being shot was a change.

Mary had been shot, and John was standing in her hospital room, playing with the cord to the blinds. The private nurse usually went out when someone came into the room, but he noticed that when he was there alone, she stayed. She feigned interest in the book she was reading, but from time to time she would look up. She disapproved of his fiddling with the cord.

"How would you like things to change?" he said.

"Am I going to flunk summer school? Or will she feel sorry enough for me to pass me? If she passes me, I never want to read another book as long as I live."

"Summer school," he said. "Summer school. She'll pass you, I'm sure. If you have to make up work, you can make up work."

"But I don't have to go back?"

"It's almost over. You won't be out of the hospital, I don't think."

"I mean ever."

"To school?"

"Yeah. To school."

He looked uncomfortable. He didn't answer. He had made a knot in the cord that was too tight. It was going to be a problem to untie it. He ran his thumb over the knot. He thought about it—how to untangle the knot. Then he realized that it was there before he had started fooling with it. The other cord also had a knot. They were made that way. He hadn't done it. He smiled, holding the cord.

"I'd be embarrassed to go back," she said.

"What do you mean?" he said. "It wasn't anything *you* did."

"Yes it was."

"No it wasn't. What do you mean?"

The private nurse turned the page. She was reading a copy of *Life*. *Life* was back. Gone, then back. He wondered how *Life* was doing.

She would have shrugged, but it hurt to move her body that way. She looked at her hands. Angela had painted her nails before it happened. They were an orangey-red, a color she didn't much like. She had already picked the polish off two of the fingers. It felt like a match had just been lit in her side.

"What can I do for you?" he said. "What would you like? Is there something I can bring you here, or something I can promise you?"

"I don't want anything," she said.

"But you want things to change. You want things to change—how? By my being in Connecticut?"

"Be where you want to be," she said.

"I don't blame you for taking it out on me."

"I'm not," she said. "Be where you want to be."

The night before, Louise had said to him: "Maybe you flatter yourself. Maybe all of this doesn't have much to do with you."

The private nurse coughed. "If they keep making movies like this, the world is going to go to hell in a handbasket," she said. She looked at John. "Please excuse me while I get a drink of water," she said. She looked at Mary. "Is there anything I can get for you?" she said. "A Coke?"

"No, thank you," Mary said.

It was the same private nurse his mother had had when she had a tonsillectomy five years ago. Then, he remembered, the nurse had been reading Robert Frost. Now she was reading *Life*. She had also dyed her hair the color of a tangerine, and she wore necklaces that you could hang ornaments on. There were several chains around her neck, but whatever dangled from them was hidden under her white uniform. She wore white clogs and white stockings and a white uniform with a pleated top and a wide skirt. He had no idea whether Mary liked her. Her name was Mrs. Patterson. He had no idea what her first name was. His mother paid the nurse. His mother had arranged for the nurse, and she was picking up the bill. Louise and his mother had worked it out and he didn't know anything about her being there until he walked into the hospital room and she was there. Louise said that she had more things on her mind than to tell him about the nurse—did he *mind* that there was a nurse? Did he suddenly want to be consulted about decisions made in the family?

Mrs. Patterson came back. "They had a perfectly fine movie, a good movie, and they had to do it: They had to show Sally Field's breasts. Norma Rae couldn't just be a winner—she had to be a sexy winner. It disgusts me that a good movie like that existed, and they had to stoop to a—pardon me—a boobies shot." She coughed into her hand. "Pardon me," she said again.

"I thought we might go to Nantucket," he said. "Your grandmother said she'd look after John Joel for a while. He's seeing a doctor. You knew that?"

She nodded yes. He had sniped her, from up in a tree, when she didn't know he was there. It was the first time he had ever gotten the best of her. It was hard to hate him for winning just once. She decided not to tell anyone that she didn't hate him anymore, though. If she ever started to hate him again, she did not want to have to explain it.

"Mary?" John said.

"What?"

"What do you think about the idea of going to Nantucket?"

"If you want to," she said.

"When you get out," he said.

"If you want to," she said. She began to chip the polish off another nail. It was sour on her tongue.

"Your mother and I would like to do something *you'd* like to do. Is there somewhere you'd like to go?"

"The beach is fine."

"You don't want to go," he said.

"It's okay. We can go."

"I don't know what to do," he said. "I'm just guessing about what you might like. What can I do, send for Peter Frampton?"

"He wouldn't come."

"I was just kidding," he said. "But is there anything I could do? Is there anything you'd like to talk about?"

"You know what she probably wants," Mary said. "You could get her another German shepherd."

"Your mother?"

"Yeah. That's what she'd like. Another dog. I'll bet you."

"I think she just liked that particular dog. If she wanted another one, I think she would have gotten it."

"Maybe not," Mary said. "Maybe she just never got around to it."

"Would you like to have a dog around the house?"

"She would. She talks to Tiffy all the time about the dog."

"She talks to Tiffy all the time about you, too, you know."

"She liked the dog better. You know she did. Face it."

"Of course she didn't like the dog better than she likes you."

Mrs. Patterson looked up from the magazine, pretending to be shaking a curl that had fallen on her forehead out of the way. She pushed the curl back in place and bent over the magazine again.

"Mary," he said, "I don't want to upset you, but I can't let you say something like that. You don't believe that."

"I was just kidding."

"No you weren't. Do you believe that?"

"No," she said.

"Good," he said. He thought that she was lying to him and that she had meant it. He was trying to think of what to say next, when a man carrying a lunch tray came in. He took the top off the tray, clattered it onto the shelf underneath his pushcart and said, "There you go," setting the tray on the tray table. Mrs. Patterson jumped up. There were carrots on the plate. Mashed potatoes. Gray meat.

"Doesn't *this* look delicious," Mrs. Patterson said.

He went to the waiting room while she ate. He said that he had to make a phone call and would be right back, but it was a lie. He couldn't stand to see her eat that food. He couldn't stand to think that his daughter thought Louise had liked her German shepherd more than she liked her. There was some truth in it, of course. The dog wasn't distant. It wasn't self-absorbed. But didn't adolescents always draw away from their parents? Didn't they all have a period when they felt superior, when they were critical or distant, just wanting to block their parents out? Mary had blocked them out. They had also blocked her out. His son had shot his daughter. He was not entirely sure who his daughter was. John Joel was much more understandable, even though he still couldn't believe that he had fired a gun, that he had shot not caring if he killed Mary. He was understandable because . . . He got up and went into the phone booth. His son wasn't understandable, and his daughter wasn't understandable, except now, when she was hurting and punishing her parents for what had happened. Louise was understandable, up to a point. He had thought that he had understood her a while back, when he had been standing at the bedroom window watching shooting stars dart and fade in the sky, and something they had been talking about, whatever it was— somehow she had told him, point-blank, that she didn't want to know everything. That meant that she knew, and didn't want confirmation. Didn't want details. Yet if she knew, and if she didn't have much feeling for him or even care if he was there, why would she plan a vacation to Nantucket? And if she did, why wouldn't Tiffy have talked her out of it? Louise had told him that Tiffy said her greatest problem was that she had to develop a sense of pride. He could tell by the way Tiffy looked at him that she hated him.

He called Nick. It was Saturday, and Nick would be home. He dialed his apartment, and a woman answered.

"He went out for groceries," the woman said. "Who's this?"

"It's John. It's not important. Tell him I'll call back."

"Want me to have him call you?"

"I'm not home. I'm at a phone booth. I'll call him tonight."

"You don't sound good," the woman said.

"What?" he said. "Who's this?"

"Carolyn Ross," she said.

He had never heard of Carolyn Ross.

"I'm okay," he said. "Fine. I'll call back later."

"Sure," she said. "He should be back in an hour."

It wasn't until he put the phone back that he realized that he was seeing yellow shimmering around the edges of things. But he never fainted. He couldn't be about to faint after doing nothing but standing in his daughter's room and going out into the corridor to make a phone call. He looked at his hands, and they looked as though small yellow sparks were coming off them. He got out of the phone booth and went to a sofa and sat down. The yellow paled, shimmered, gradually disappeared. He sat there, trying to breathe normally. What would he do with them in Nantucket? Go to the beach. Sail. Watch clouds change shape. Buy fudge. Post cards.

He couldn't. He could do it for a week, two weeks, but he couldn't do it for the rest of his life. He thought of Metcalf, and how he took his lover with him for the family's annual East Hampton vacation. He told his wife she was there to help with the children, and the woman came along. Year after year she came along. He paid her on Fridays, and she took the checks. She lived on Park Avenue, in an apartment Metcalf rented for her. It galled Metcalf that she actually cashed the checks, when he gave her almost twenty thousand dollars a year, plus an apartment on Park Avenue. They did it for five summers, and then Metcalf's wife informed him at the last minute that her sister was taking the children for July, and that the vacation could be for just the two of them. Proud of thinking quickly, Metcalf had said that he felt duty-bound to have the *au pair* anyway, because she had been counting on the money, and that she could come and take care of the house. When he told Jenny, his mistress, what he had worked out, she just stared at him silently. He had no idea, Metcalf said, that asking her to clean house had been the straw that broke the camel's back. When he left, Jenny called his wife and told her what was going on. Bad enough that she had to put up with two bratty kids every summer—she was not going to clean somebody's house, she told Metcalf's wife. Metcalf showed up in the office the first of August, when everybody thought he would be gone, because his wife and Jenny were in the East Hampton house, and they wanted two weeks to work it out and become pals before he went there. Metcalf kept threatening to get in his car and put a stop to it, but he never did. He spent the last two weeks of August there and said that although he'd lost respect for Jenny, he had still never been kissed the way she kissed him, and he was going to go on supporting her. "For a kiss," Metcalf said. "Not a lay, a kiss. The way she kisses." Metcalf had come back and slammed tennis balls against the wall in the corridor outside his office, letting his phone ring, getting violently angry if anyone objected to the noise or asked him a question. "A *kiss*," Metcalf kept saying over and over. "A good *kiss* should be everybody's birthright."

A young man in his early twenties, at the other end of the sofa, was watching John out of the corner of his eye. John was trying to look normal, to convince his body that it could function normally. It would be humiliating to fall over in the waiting room. He tried to breathe normally. To blink. It was difficult not to blink hard and often when you thought about blinking. It was hopeless the way it was hopeless to be aware of your tongue and not have it feel too big for your mouth. The man was holding something out to him, with a little corona of light around it. The light faded as John stared at the pack of gum with one piece slid out, finally realizing what it was. "No thanks," he said. He tried to remember the last time he had chewed gum. With Brandt, about a year ago, to show him how to chew without making faces. Pilar, his mother's cook, had introduced him to chewing gum. She also let him eat raw cookie dough, which was bad for him. However, as his mother always said when she finished a list of grievances against Pilar, she never skimped on lime in the gin and tonics, and never once had they run out of ice. Her stews were very good, although she would make them all summer long unless she was stopped. His mother had recently given Pilar some cookbooks with recipes for cold summer meals. Diced cucumber and cold salmon loaf. Argentine eggs with pasta. He had just been offered a stick of Juicy Fruit chewing gum, and his mouth was watering as much as it would if he had taken the stick and chewed it. He could smell the gum. He looked at the young man. The man was looking at him.

"It's a bitch," the man said.

He nodded. "You know somebody who's a patient here?"

"My wife. She was cutting the lawn, and she fell over. I thought she was dead. What a bitch. Mower kept going and crashed into the house. I wouldn't have known. Had the television on. What a bitch." He snapped his gum three times. "How about you?" he said.

"You probably read it in the papers," John said. "My son shot my daughter."

"I haven't seen a paper in two weeks. My wife and I were in Ashland, Oregon. Come home and unpack, and the next day, whammo! She's on her back in the yard. I thought she was kidding. They think it's her heart, but nothing shows." He had stopped chewing. "I don't know what to say about what you said. I heard you, but I don't know what to say. They young kids, fooling around, or what?"

"Ten and fifteen. My son is ten."

"Holy shit," the man said. "An accident, huh? How'd he get a gun?"

"Apparently it was around his friend's house, in a box. The kid's father didn't have any idea his son knew the gun was there. How the gun got out of the box and into my son's hands is still up in the air."

"Holy shit," the man said. "Ten and fifteen. She all right?"

"Yes. She's going to be all right."

"Holy holy," the man said. "Lucky she wasn't blown away. If you can say anybody's lucky who's been shot. I didn't read about it in the papers. What's it like, having a story about you in the paper? Never mind. That isn't any of my business. You don't chew gum? There's a Coke machine hidden behind that door."

The man pointed. He had a turquoise and silver ring on his index finger. His nails were a little long, and dirty.

"Thanks. I might get one later."

"I wonder how many people are sitting around here, or lying in bed here, wondering what they did wrong? I left the room because the lady my wife shares it with was being examined. Not examined, butchered. A bone marrow extract. My God. One day in Ashland, the next day here." The man lit a cigarette, offering one to John. John shook his head no. "Not exactly the next day. I barrel-assed back from Ashland, but it still took five days, you know? Not the next day really, but so to speak. Holy shit. I can't believe I'm sitting here. Her sister's coming, and it's just as well if I can have a word with her before she goes in to see my wife. Her sister's a nun, and my wife is an agnostic, and I want to try to get her to keep religion out of it. Just seeing her sister in her penguin get-up sets her off as it is. Some orders wear normal clothes now, but not her sister's order. They voted no. Imagine. Jesus."

"I thought I was going to faint a few minutes ago," John said.

"You looked like it," the man said. "I was all set to slide down the sofa and push your head between your knees. That works, you know."

"I should go back to her room now," John said. "They were having lunch."

"My wife blew lunch yesterday," the man said. "Cottage cheese and custard. Maybe not exactly cottage cheese, but something like it. I wonder how many people are sitting around this hospital right at this minute, trying to figure things out. This place is probably sending out more vibes than the Rand Corporation."

He tried Nick again. This time nobody answered the phone. He let it ring six times, then hung up and took his dime back. He wondered if Metcalf could be right: Would Nick really be so childish as to subscribe Metcalf to magazines? It was absurd the way Nick always got riled up about Metcalf: He had a picture of Metcalf (taken at a picnic several years ago) enlarged to eight by ten, and hung it on the bathroom wall, in his apartment, to decondition himself. Nick thought that if he could look at Metcalf's face without going wild, he could handle him better in person. But the picture just drove him crazy. One night when he was drunk, he got spooked about going into the bathroom, even though he knew where the picture was and wouldn't have to look in that direction; he went into the kitchen instead and peed into an empty wine bottle. That absurdity, and the absurdity of Metcalf's scheme to keep his lover around. The absurdity of being out of your mind, showing up at six in the morning, seven in the morning, whatever it was, at your lover's apartment and finding a man there, even if nothing was going on. The craziness of going there. The craziness of finding happiness when you couldn't have it; or of planning to have it, only to have *this* happen. It had happened. And Mary was in the room, waiting for him. He walked down the corridor and into her room. Her face was white, and her hospital gown and the sheets; and the sun had shifted so that the blinds looked bright white, strongly illuminated from behind. The nurse was taking Mary's temperature. When he was a child, his mother had gone around in the evening with a thermometer in her mouth, because she had read somewhere that it would firm up the jawline. For a while his mother had cared about wrinkles. He could remember his father suggesting a straw instead, because a thermometer was depressing. His mother said that a straw would not be the same. You had to know the mercury was in there. You had to be steady and careful. You could not bite down. The thermometer they had at the hospital stood in a white plastic stand when it was not in use.

"Your mother's in with John Joel," he said. "Did I tell you that? She told me that she's coming to see you at two or three. And Angela called this morning, and I told her it would be all right to visit. Was that all right to tell her?"

"She's going to think I look gross," Mary said.

"We're all glad you're all right. That's all," John said.

"That's not all Angela thinks. I talked to her on the phone yesterday, and all she wanted to hear about was how big a bandage it was. She thinks it's better that this happened than that I lost my tits like Marge Pendergast, or something. She wanted to know if they bathed me in bed every day. She thinks it's a resort. She's pretty stupid sometimes."

"Should I have told her not to come?"

"Sure," Mary said. "She's only my best friend."

"Your temperature's normal. I'm not supposed to give any of that information, but it is, and why should I hold out on you about good news?" the nurse said.

"She doesn't have circles under her eyes today," John said.

"When she did, nobody said anything, and that was the right thing to do," the nurse said. "It's discouraging to patients to be told they look bad. I've been in rooms where people walked in and clamped their hands over their mouths."

He pulled the small chair up to her bed. "Was lunch good?" he said.

"Suck-o," Mary said.

"I was down in the sitting room, and I thought over what you said. Do you think it would be nice for all of us if there was a dog? We could get a dog when we come back from the vacation."

"You're moving back?"

"I don't know what I'm doing," he said. Her eyes glazed when he said it, like a sick person's. "In any case, we're taking a vacation, and I think that you're right—your mother might like a dog, and you might like it, too. What do you say?"

"You forgot *him*," Mary said. "He's coming back too, isn't he?"

"Yes. Sure. After a little while. He's talking to some doctors now, and he's going to be staying with Grandma for a while."

"She must think the sky is falling."

"I imagine she does. She doesn't cover up very well. When she's upset she cries and raves. She knocked over one of her vases. You would have liked to have seen it. Pilar ran into the room and dealt with it. Pilar can deal with anything. I once saw Pilar swatting a fly with one hand while she was using a whisk to beat an egg with the other, and she never missed a beat."

"Unhygienic," the nurse said. "This is your mother's cook? I like your mother, though. She's a fine lady. I'm sure this cook is the right person for the job if your mother thinks so."

He took Mary's hand. It was small and tender. He moved his hand over hers, stroking, wondering how her hand could be so warm in such a cool room if she had no fever. He remembered Nina's hand on his head, and the way she had asked, "Are you in shock?" In fact, he had been—or out of his mind, at least.

To prove that he was sane, he had tried to re-create for Nina his trip into New York, but he had gotten bogged down trying to remember whether he said goodbye to Louise or not. He thought he had been in the house and then left, but maybe he had been in the house only when Tiffy was there, before he knew what had happened, when he came home and saw the police car blocking his driveway. He had once joked to Nina that there were pillars, and she had believed it. He could imagine pillars, rising up, 2001 music playing as they went higher and higher. He could not imagine living in that house again, and he wondered if Mary could, either. He was holding her hand, and it was still as warm, as clammy. He bent over and kissed her hand, and she drew it away. There was a Band-Aid in the crook of her arm, from the intravenous. A bruise spread out beneath the Band-Aid. The nurse had put it there, because, she said, looking at needle marks and bruises was upsetting. "Everyone isn't like me. Other people aren't accustomed to things that are physically ugly, and it's easy to forget that. I always try to remember that the patient is the patient, and I am me."

Mary in her gingerbread-man bathing suit. Mary in her white bag of a hospital gown. Mary herself. He had been so surprised to have a baby, and then two, and then three. Different-sized children. Mary the first of them. It made him sentimental in a way he couldn't remember being sentimental before. If she could be born again, it would be in low light, with music playing, and he would be there, humming along with the music. That would certainly make him pass out, if just being in the hospital made him queasy. Mary's birth. The time before Mary. The time before Louise. If you could only go backward, however awkwardly, like running backward without looking, depending on memory so that you didn't crash into something, hoping some sixth sense would protect you. Going backward that way as an adult would be like a small child's going forward—your footing unsure, trusting a hand to be outstretched at the crucial moment, for a table to be sturdy and not light. To be able to walk, to balance, to progress. He remembered Mary toddling, Louise luring her with some toy, shaking an elephant or a lion, calling to her, "Come on, Mary. That's right." Mary hanging back, gripping his thumb, wanting to go but afraid of all that space between hands, the gap between what was behind her and the lion. Then she had half-run forward, awkwardly, and grabbed the prize. Someone had told him (Tiffy? One of the policemen? Somebody, anyway) that she had just fallen, and there had been no scream that Louise or Tiffy had heard. (That's right, Tiffy had told him.) They had just gone out into the backyard and there they all were, four of them standing and one on the ground, as silent as actors about to begin a pantomime. But then Louise had started screaming. Her scream-ing had made Parker cry, and John Joel. And then Parker ran across the field, shouting back that the gun wasn't his, that John Joel had done it, and John Joel had waited in the house, upstairs in his room. He had been sent to his room, like a bad boy, until the ambulance got there. Louise kept trying to move Mary, to shake her, tug at her. Tiffy had had a hard time convincing her to let her be still. His daughter, lying still on the ground. Still in a hos-pital bed. Her stillness had made him move erratically, frantically. Suddenly he was not at the hospital, not at the house in Con-necticut, but in New York, in the familiar garage, talking to a taxi driver, getting out at Columbus Avenue, opening the door and going up the stairs. It hadn't been until then that the tiredness had hit him—the tiredness and the shock. It was like trying to wish yourself awake from a bad dream, steps and more steps, like layers upon layers, and he couldn't make a sound. There had been a little noise on the street, but inside the building, nothing. It was quiet, like the floor of the ocean, and he was trying to reach the top. He could feel the sweat running down his face, and from somewhere far-off—not from any place he could identify—he was watching himself move forward, step after step, moving in slow motion to reach the landing. Moving deliberately in slow motion, perhaps, because what could he say? And if he said it, what could she do? What did he want her to do? What had John Joel wanted from Mary? He had wanted to be rid of her. He had wondered if telling Nina would frighten her, make her go. He didn't want that. He wanted her, he wanted not to be swimming, to bound up the stairs, minus bouquet and top hat but still charming, ready for . . . She did not open the door, of course, in a long gown, and he did not take her in his arms for a dance. There was no graceful movement at all. He was exhausted from the climb, and the man—he had stood and gaped at the man as surprised as if the man were naked. And then Nina had said the man's name, and that she had not slept with him, no matter what he was thinking. He was thinking: I'm alive. Even Mary is alive. My son shot my daughter. But it was impossible to talk about it. Everything went on, in slow motion. His following her into the kitchen, his legs so heavy that he could not believe that they were not ballooning. She had been cutting fruit. Simply fixing breakfast, cutting fruit. He had walked into ordinary life, and the little accidents of ordinary life—Nina's cut finger. While she was gone he had continued to peel and chop the orange. The juice ran down his hands and wrists. He was holding the peeled orange, baseball-sized but soft, soft and juicy, it must have been like something the doctors had seen inside Mary's body. Didn't medical students practice cutting oranges because oranges were like certain tissues in the body? Oranges punctured with needles, as they learned to give injections? He held the peeled orange and stared at it. Then he put it on the chopping board and chopped it, sprinkled the wet pieces over her bowl of cereal. He waited for her to come back. He went to the bathroom door and saw her, washing her sleeve, bandaging the finger. He had wanted to tell her all of it, in detail, but he hadn't been there, he would have to make the details up. He could describe the field, the day, but the blood—he hadn't been there to see the blood, or Tiffy in the field, then Louise, Parker streaking past them, screaming that he had not done it. And what happened from there? How did John Joel go to his bedroom? How had *he* driven into New York? He was in Nina's apartment and she was right—he loved it, small as a womb. He was comfortable with the small movements he could make. And how had he gotten from the bathroom door into Nina's bedroom? In time. Floating. The dead-man's float. Lying face down on her mattress, arms outstretched. He had wanted to tell her, before any more time passed, before she left the bathroom; but she had pushed past him, and he had said nothing, only that he had peeled the orange. Chopped the orange. He wanted to say: Am I crazy? But she would have thought he was talking about his peeling the orange when he knew she was angry with him. When he realized that it was right not to have spoken, he also realized that then he wasn't crazy. If he wasn't crazy, then he would just be a normal person, telling a story about a crazy person. The crazy person was his son. Born of his genes. Seeds of the orange.

Mary's eyes were closed. Mrs. Patterson, seeing that they were, allowed herself to look directly at John. She moved her head, telling him silently that he should go away from the bed. He moved back, cocked his head. She was lying there, suddenly asleep. People got heavier when they were unconscious. He remembered carrying her, when she was a child, taking her along with them when they had dinner with friends, putting her down to rest in the friend's bed, then picking her up again and taking her home, dead weight pressed against him. The awkwardness of it, the way all her weight seemed to be concentrated in the middle of her body: Her arms and legs were so light they dangled and flapped. Inadvertently she would kick. As she got larger, her foot hit against him, kicking him in the balls. He knew she would not kick in her sleep, but still he would hunch forward, warding off the pain, and as he hunched she would slip down farther and farther. He had been awkward in a lot of ways. He had been awkward about leaving, coming back the way a drunken guest returns, apologizing, for a sweater, and then for a wallet, everyone knowing the person is drunk, the person wanting to appear only forgetful. He had wanted to appear sensible, and they had all known that what he was doing did not make sense. There had been the excuse of his mother's illness, but when that passed it was so awkward that he did not go back. He could not go back, because for a long time, for years, he had felt like a guest, like someone who could only go so far, and then have to stop: feet on the footstool, but not tucked under you on the chair; a long soak in the bathtub, but then you had to scrub the ring away; a plant to be admired, but how could you know how much water it needed? Everything was being taken care of. He was visiting. He even had the manners to bring flowers, occasionally. A bottle of wine. He knew the things they liked, and they knew what he liked. It could have gone on. If it had, things might even have changed. It could have gone on like a reel of movie film spinning, but he started to get dizzy, to lose his breath. He started to edge away, delicately, as

297

delicately as he could. Like shaving with a safety razor—you could only do it so delicately. You could know the strokes, the feel of the blade on the skin, just how much lather to put on; but still the skin would pull an unexpected way, a microscopic imperfection of the blade would result in a nick. He had told Louise, shaving, that the move was going to be permanent for a while. That was the way he had said it—awkwardly, like some bumbling child. An adolescent, cutting himself shaving. Lies: because he couldn't stand the commute; because his mother needed him, even if she wasn't dying. A trickle of blood had come up through the lather—a little cut he hadn't even felt. "Do you want me to feel sorry for you?" she had said. She had not moved off the side of the tub, where she sat. She had watched him continue shaving, watched him hold the styptic stick to his cheek, cursing that it wasn't working and he was in a hurry. He suddenly remembered what she had said to him: She had come up behind him, put her arms around him, and said, with her head buried in his back, "You hate blood, don't you?" She was right. She knew him very well. And she was clever, too. Because she had not been talking about blood.

He had not rinsed the washcloth well enough. The razor wasn't put carefully on the back of the sink, but dropped on the small table among her make-up. He was a bad guest. The guest who brings flowers, then gets drunk and chews off the heads. When he left, and didn't come back for two weeks, he had been such a coward that he had sent tulips. Then guilt caught up, and he began the weekend visits. Then his son shot his daughter. In between, there was life with his mother and Brandt, life with Nina, working with Nick, dealing with Metcalf. And then his son had shot his daughter.

Leaving Mary's room, he went to the phone booth. He was about to call Nick, when he realized that he couldn't remember what he wanted to talk to him about. He was standing there, dime in hand, trying to think, when Mrs. Patterson came toward him, carrying his raincoat.

"Thanks," he said. "I knew I'd forgotten something."

When she turned to go back to Mary's room, he continued to stand by the phone, holding the raincoat. The weather. People called other people and talked about the weather. He would call Nick and talk about the weather, the thunder outside the hospital, and it would come to him why he had tried to reach him before.

Nick answered.

"It's raining like hell here," he said. He waited. He tried to think. He thought: I would have walked out into the rain and never remembered bringing my raincoat. Maybe I would have remembered. Gone back. He had tested himself a lot of times, and as little as he thought he could stand it, he was always able to walk into Mary's room. Over and over.

"Do people die from guilt?" he said to Nick.

"No," Nick said. "They die from being interrupted when they're screwing, because some nut calls to talk about the weather. Call me back in half an hour."

From his car in the parking lot, he looked back at the hospital. The thunder had stopped, and it was raining lightly. He counted fourteen windows up, and looked across to the window he thought might be Mary's. It was just a dark square, high up.

Metcalf had heard about what happened somehow, and he had come into his office and sat down without saying anything, picked up the Nantucket picture from the desktop and studied it.

"What can I say?" Metcalf had said. "The truth is, everything shocks me. I couldn't believe what happened between my wife and Jenny last summer. This summer, I can't believe what's happened to you. A man in the elevator this morning that I didn't even know told me a joke about an eggman delivering eggs to a convent that shocked the hell out of me. What if I had been a Catholic? There are still Catholics, aren't there?"

"What was the joke?" he said.

"Never mind what the joke was. It was filthy. You wouldn't laugh at it. You probably need a laugh, though. I was going to come in and tell you some other joke, but I don't have a joke in my head today." He put the picture back in place. "I came in to offer to do anything, if there's anything I can do. How's your daughter?"

"She's going to be all right."

"Good." Metcalf pushed himself up straight in the chair. "Anything I can do?"

"No. Thank you, though."

"What could I do, huh? I could do something, but it wouldn't have much to do with your daughter or her being—" Metcalf bent over, pulled up his pants leg, tugged his black sock higher. "Her being shot," he said. He pulled down his pants leg. "I'm giving you a raise," he said.

"You are? What kind of a raise?"

"Whatever raise you want," Metcalf said, and got up and went out. "Be reasonable about it," Metcalf called back, going down the hallway. He said something else that John didn't catch.

Nina had made that crack about his not supporting her, about having to go to work because she didn't have somebody to take care of her. What would she think, now, about the way he had taken care of Louise and his family? Did she still think that he would be a good father?

Louise had parked her car far down in the lot, and didn't see him. He watched as Louise and Tiffy walked through the lot and across the one-lane road that separated the parking lot from the hospital. Tiffy was always with her, never even an arm's-length away. They walked at the same pace, step for step. He watched their backs disappear through the tall glass doors, into the lobby of the hospital.

Driving away, he wondered what he would do with it if he were granted just one wish. He thought that the wish should be a selfish one, not a wish to change things for other people, but a wish for self-salvation, a wish that dared whatever force governed wishes to come through: that his family all disappear in a puff of smoke, and that he could start over again with Nina. That was two wishes, not one. Either the disappearance, or the starting over with Nina. As he drove, though, it came to him that he was now thinking about wish number three. What had numbers one and number two been? One and two and then a million more: for enough money not to have to work, for a perfect kiss, for rain to change to sun,

sun to change to rain, a bee sting to stop itching, a photograph not to show the lines on his forehead, a ball to fly into his glove, to tag the runner in time, to find pesto in a New York restaurant in the winter, for his headache to go away, for the shell of the robin's egg never to break. He had used up his wishes. So if it happened, it would just have to happen. There was no way he could wish for it.

He wished for it. And that the car radio wouldn't be full of static so he could hear music instead of his thoughts. And that the police not catch him for speeding. That he miss the frog hopping across the road. He looked in the rear-view mirror and saw the frog, still hopping. Mary was alive. He was alive. The doctor was wrong: It wasn't John Joel he identified with, but Mary. He was the victim, not the one who pulled the trigger. He certainly did not think that he had charge of his own life. As the doctor would have put it, he had the sense of reacting instead of acting.

"Would you like to go out for a drink and forget all this bull-shit?" he had asked the woman doctor.

"If I thought this was bullshit," the doctor said, "I wouldn't be doing it. The question that interests me is why you kept going, if you felt you had no control."

"Cruise control," he said.

"Do you have cruise control on your car?" she said, writing.

"No," he said. "And no pillars at the end of my driveway, either."

"What is the connection?" she said.

"No connection. A non sequitur."

"No it wasn't," she said. "Let me in on the joke."

"The joke is that my lover overestimates how rich I am. I told her I had pillars at the end of my driveway, and she believed me."

She said, writing, "You have a lover?"

302

22

THIS IS HOW she found out that Spangle was back in the States: Bobby, in New York, had given his friend Victor the rough draft of chapters one and two of the novel he was writing; and Victor, who thought his apartment might burn and knowing that Bobby never made photocopies, had walked to the photocopying shop on Third Avenue around the corner from his apartment. There he found an old acquaintance, a woman he had dated years ago, manning the counter. From Marielle Dekker, Victor had found out that Jonathan Spangle was in town. She had just run into him at Kenny's Castaways. She said that she had been surprised to find out that he had a brother, because she had thought she remembered a discussion in the far-distant past, when he had attributed his selfishness to being an only child. But there the brother had sat, drinking beer. Victor told Bobby that he had run into Marielle Dekker, and that she had just run into Jonathan and Peter Spangle at Kenny's Castaways. Bobby had said that he had just tried to look up Spangle, and had been told he was in Madrid: What was he doing at Kenny's Castaways? Secretly he was delighted. He found Cynthia very attractive, and fair was fair—if Spangle was back, and not interested, *he* was interested. Bobby had made Victor call Marielle Dekker to ask if there had been a woman with Peter Spangle. No. Peter Spangle had been there alone. Well—fair was fair: If he was back from Madrid and not interested, the road to Cynthia was clear.

After his appointments in New York, and a couple of nights at Victor's apartment (a big Buddha in the corner, wearing a rubber Nixon mask, very realistic), he started back to New Haven.

Cynthia was still freaked out by the shooting, and she wondered what was the correct thing to do. What kind of a note do you write to the father of a student who has been shot? Say that she was sorry—just that, perhaps. Thank him for lunch. Mention subtly that Mary would pass the course. Hope that she would recover from her injuries so she would be able to read the first chapters of a lot of novels. A gift, perhaps: pages torn out of the Great Books. Quote Elvis Costello? " 'Accidents will happen . . .' "

She was thinking about it, pen in hand, when the phone rang. It was Bobby, who had been gone for more than two weeks, calling as if he had just left, from a phone on the highway, asking her not to eat. He was on his way to New Haven, and if she'd wait for him, and they could go out to dinner. She agreed. There was a pause. Then he said, "Have I got news for *you*."

"What is it?" she said.

"First of all," he said, "I would like to talk to you at dinner about the possibility of your coming to live with me."

"What's the joke?"

"No joke. The joke's on you, apparently. Victor saw Marielle, and Marielle just saw Spangle and Jonathan having a night on the town. New York town."

"What?" she said. "Who's Muriel?"

"She's an actress. Works at a Xerox place on Third Avenue, around the corner from Victor's apartment."

"Who's Victor?" she said.

She was stalling. Had he just asked her to come live with him? After spending one night on her floor? She tried to remember what color eyes Bobby had. Instead, she got a picture of Spangle. Could it really be true that Spangle was back, but he hadn't come back to her? Not even a call, a letter?

"Victor runs the lights in a place that does sex shows. He flashes blue lights on people butt-fucking. He was studying to be a bartender, but now he's on welfare. They don't know about the part-time work at the sex show. He paid to have the two chapters of my book Xeroxed, and he's hardly got money to eat. That's Victor."

"So Victor knows Muriel and Muriel knows Spangle?"

Stalling.

"Marielle," he said. "Cynthia, I can't get you out of my head. I had no intention of saying all of this on the phone."

She couldn't think of what to say.

"I bought a dozen bagels," he said. "Assorted. We can just eat bagels if you want."

"I think I'd rather have a meal."

"I don't have any money, though. Except for gas to get back to New Hampshire. I gave Victor what I had. He's sold half of his record collection."

"I have money," she said.

"The disadvantage of teaching is that you don't get paid in the summer," he said.

"You do if you teach summer school."

"I couldn't," he said. "It's the only way I keep my sanity, getting out of there."

"Doesn't matter," she said. "I have money."

"I've upset you."

"You've surprised me. I wonder if somebody made a mistake? Is that woman sure that it was Spangle with Jonathan?"

"There's no mistake," he said. "Oh—I'm so upset. I'm so upset because Victor doesn't realize what he's *doing*, selling off his records. *I* would have gotten money together for him, he wouldn't have had to do it. He'll never be able to find those records again. He told me that one night he was working the lights and he kept thinking there was something familiar about one of the men on the stage, and finally he stopped the strobes and flooded the stage with bright-yellow light, and he saw it was his father's accountant. His father's accountant was belly-down with a Chinaman in a motorcycle helmet, butt fucking him. Jesus. Victor has got to get out of there. I think I can find him a job tending bar in New Hampshire. I know a girl who knows the owner of a restaurant."

"I don't even know Victor," she said.

"You'll like Victor. He doesn't have any interest in what he's doing. He just fell into doing it, answering an ad in the *SoHo News*. He thought they were looking for somebody to drive an ice-cream truck."

She laughed. The first laugh all day.

"I know it," he said. "Poor Victor. Victor had such an amazing record collection, and he just put them in boxes and carried the boxes out to the street and started *selling* them. I can't believe it. He *has* to move to New Hampshire."

The operator broke in: "It is now three minutes. Signal when through."

Bobby seemed not to have heard. "He thought the ad was worded so vaguely because it was a job driving an ice-cream truck, and he thought it would be fun to drive an ice-cream truck. He didn't mind. He tried to find the ad to show me, but he'd thrown it away. I wrote a poem about it. He's very upset. I have to get Victor out of New York." She heard trucks roaring by. "He had 'Please Crawl Out Your Window,'" he said. "He had these records of Sherpas playing wind whistles. At least he got some money for 'Please Crawl Out Your Window.' He's very upset because there was an item in *Rolling Stone* about the new Dylan record being religious. That upsets Victor very much. Oh—it's not that, it's the place he's working. You won't believe what an injustice has been done, when you meet Victor."

"I don't want to meet Victor," she said.

"I've told you the story all wrong. I did everything that I intended not to do. I spilled the beans about Spangle and I told you that I wanted you to live with me and I didn't give you a balanced picture of Victor. Believe me, you'd like Victor."

"Why don't you hang up, and we can talk about this when I see you?"

More traffic, Bobby shouting something into the phone about bagels.

"That's nice," she said, guessing at what he was saying. "But if you want me to live with you, you can hardly object that I'm taking you to dinner."

"Will you?" Bobby said.

"Live with you? Of course not. I'm going back to Yale in the fall."

"We can commute," Bobby said. "The Mazda is totally reliable. In the snow we can take the train. This is the wrong time to ask you. It must have been terrible, going into the classroom and thinking of what to say to them about that girl that got shot."

"They seemed more human," she said.

"People talk about people having hearts on their sleeves. I think that people always have their emotions outside of them—pieces of their soul in a sneeze, even. They have eyes like a deer that's been shot. Nobody can cover up. You should have known Victor before, and then see Victor now. And he's a *genius*. He can point to the one wrong word in a thousand. It's like perfect pitch, but he has it with *words*."

"Why don't you come back to New Haven, if you're coming," she said.

"Because I can't hang up this way. I have to know that you'll let me have another chance. That if I can calm down, you'll let me try to talk to you about all this again."

"I really don't want to hear any more about Victor," she said.

"What have I done?" Bobby said. "I've distorted everything. You think Victor is just another crazy. If you knew him, you'd see that he's absolutely innocent, that he falls into these things because of some honest misunderstanding. He *would* enjoy driving an ice-cream truck. That's really the truth. If something really bad hadn't happened to his head, he never would have boxed up his records and gone out to sell them. He told me he was having nightmares of flying saucers, and he figured out that it was the records—his lost records. Do you think you could meet Victor and forget what I've told you and just *see* if you like him or not?"

"Bobby," she said.

A truck went by. A blur of noise. Bobby shouting over the truck, all of it indistinguishable.

"Will you be there?" he shouted.

"Why not?" she said.

"How does something like this happen?" he said. "What do you think?"

"How does *what* happen?"

"What I've been saying to you. My stopping there by chance, and just when I was deciding that I had to have you, Victor sees Marielle, and she says that Spangle's in New York."

"I'm not a piece of pie," she said.

"I *know* you're not pie. I'm expressing myself all wrong. Will you be there, so we can talk about this calmly?"

"We *have* to talk calmly," she said. "I've had about all I can take today."

"Be there," Bobby said. "I promise—totally calm. Any way you want it."

"Jesus. I just want to forget this summer and go back to school in the fall."

"You don't mean that. At least come to the waterfall party and think about it. You have to give things a chance. I'm already writing something about the waterfall party. Did you know that Crane wrote *The Red Badge of Courage* without having been to war?"

"Please," she said. "Can you tell literary anecdotes later? It's very hard to hear you. Could you just hang up?"

A truck went by. She was sure that he hadn't heard the last part of what she'd said. "Please?" she said.

". . . *fact*," he said. "A fact, not an anecdote."

She hung up and started to cry. She cried the way she had been tempted to cry when she walked into the classroom and the air was different, the faces were different, the game wasn't the same. She walked in as a teacher, and they wanted answers. They didn't know how to ask for them, but by the way they looked at her, she could tell they wanted to know what had happened. And she had wanted to cry: not to analyze, not to begin to plow through some explanation, just to join them, and cry. Instead, she had begun to talk about *The Old Man and the Sea*, and they had stared at her like the young boy staring at Santiago. They were too old for her to get them busy making get-well cards. Finally she had told them that things just happen. She had just said it, tried it on like some article of clothing that wasn't hers. But for a while she could parade around in cynicism.

Actually she fell into things because she wasn't cynical enough. Spangle had tricked her when he had offered to drive her back East, from Berkeley, years ago. What he wanted was for her to be in Berkeley with him, not in school. He really had no respect for what she was doing, but he liked her, or needed her, or whatever it was, and he pretended to be doing something nice for her, but actually he had done it as a ploy: In return for being so nice about escorting her back, he was expecting her not to stay. When he stopped holding her hand, she knew what it meant, but she paid no attention to it: like paying no attention to a shadow on the wall at night because the lock is secure. Paying no attention, really, out of absolute fear. She had been terrified of losing him, because so much of her life was tied up with him. They weren't just *her* experiences, they were *theirs*; and if he went off with a piece of them, it would be like a lock without a key, a ring without a stone. He had wanted them to get married, and when she said no, he had never asked again. He had stopped almost everything, except teasing her in a way that was more cruel than affectionate. Embarrassing her by drawing her face on the ditto master, tickling her until she screamed, making sex into a joke, sending her post cards to shock her, like a dirty little boy, instead of the letter she wanted. Even a lying letter would have sufficed. And if he wasn't coming back, a note, a brief call, at least, about that too. She had been so willing to believe him. She cried, because she had been so willing to believe him. She had even thought that his not understanding irony in literature proved what an honest, trusting person he was: If it was printed on the page, it was to be taken straight. If he was what he said he was, not what he appeared to be, then you had to believe him, didn't you? No. You didn't have to do anything. Not even stay with him because he had said, once, that what he wanted was always to have you. She remembered that she had given him a kite, and after flying it once he had pinned it to the wall, for fear of damaging it. She had thought that she understood him perfectly, and obviously she had not. The kite might stay safely on the wall, but he would fly off himself, fly off and be gone, no word. He would protect an inanimate thing, and hurt her. Hold hands with her all day, because inside he was free, floating, nothing was restricting him.

The phone rang again. She let it ring six times before picking it up. It was the operator, asking if she would pay the overtime charges on Bobby's call.

She went into the kitchen, and looked at the picture she had taken of him in Provincetown: his look of surprise, thinking himself alone. She had felt bad about interrupting him, spoiling even a moment of his fun as he flew the kite, absorbed in what he was doing. She had captured the moment in time, and yet she hadn't, because *she* wasn't in the picture. He liked the picture, but wished that it had never been taken. He wanted both things: He wanted to be private, and he wanted to be accessible. The kite, high up, had looked like some prehistoric bird, and when he began to bring it down, when the air currents changed, it had swooped and dipped, crashing on its nose. It had tried to destroy itself. It had not. She was anthropomorphizing the kite. She had a tendency to see inanimate things as living, and he had a tendency to see living things as inanimate. He thought the tickling would not really hurt, that she could stand to be exhausted, that he could go on and on with it.

She wiped her eyes on a handkerchief Bobby had left behind. If all the men she met were crazy, then she must be looking for crazy men, right? Wrong. They came to *her*. She had never even heard of Bobby until his phone call, and then he had showed up, gone away, then called and said that he wanted her to live with him. What she wanted—and this time she was going to get her way —was to have somebody to go to dinner with, because she had had a bad day and needed company, and she needed protection from the crazy magician who would probably be hanging around outside.

She talked to Spangle's picture. She asked him how he could have done it. She accused him of being a coward. He looked astonished.

She pulled her hair back in a rubber band and took off her clothes and got into the shower. She put her face under the water, and felt the difference between the wetness of water and the wetness of her tears, as the shower spray washed them away. Her cheeks felt puffy, and her eyes felt hot. She had just lost, and someone she hardly knew had had to tell her that. She had suspected, but she hadn't known. She smiled, remembering a game of cards she had played with Spangle years before in a motel room, the two of them on a trip to see his grandmother in Idaho. She had won the first game, and then in the middle of the second, she

had had to ask, "What are the rules again?" A blind person crossing the street, then climbing onto the sidewalk and forgetting
what a sidewalk was. One night she had helped a blind woman
across Chapel Street, and when they were safely on the sidewalk,
the woman had stood there, looking more baffled than she had
standing on the curb at the opposite side, hesitating about crossing.
Cynthia had gone back to her. "You know where you are now?"
she had said, and the woman, sounding baffled, had reeled off the
names of streets to the left and streets to the right. She knew where
she was. Cynthia looked back at her once, and she was still standing there. Why should it be odd that a blind person was baffled?
Because you assume that when they can find their way, they are
all right. What if they can find their way but don't want to, or
are just tired of it? She turned her face into the stream of water
from the showerhead again. She had the feeling that the blind
woman might still be standing where she had left her. And the
feeling, at the same time, that she might be misjudging Spangle.
It just didn't make sense. At least he would want his clothes. All
his sweaters were full of holes—maybe he meant to take the
holes and leave the sweaters. He did not like donuts, and sometimes when he went with her to the all-night donut shop he
would have just a glass of milk, telling the waitress to bring him
three donut holes. That joke went bad the night the store started
baking what they called "donut holes"—round pieces of dough
cut from the inside of the donut.

She tried to hate him, to convince herself that what was behind
all his kidding was a lack of respect for other people. Some days
he could hardly do anything without turning it into a joke. He
would joke at the dry cleaner's (handing over his sports jacket,
saying, "No starch"), he would pull pranks on tired waitresses,
demand a free glass at a gas station that wasn't giving anything
away. He told Johnny Carson better jokes, talking to the television, than Johnny was telling late-night America. She put a big
towel around herself and stood there, in the tub, thinking. These
were not good things to hate him for. At the very least, they showed
that he was alive, that he didn't just go through life like a
zombie, intimidated at the dry cleaner's, oblivious to waitresses.
He didn't mind letting people in gas stations know, subtly, that he

realized they were getting the best of him, that the days of free glasses were over.

He talked a lot, and she was a quiet person. That had always been a problem. She liked to be quiet, and he got edgy when there wasn't noise. Standing in the kitchen, he would idly tap with a fork on the top of the stove as he waited for something to come to a boil; he would shave in the morning with the bathroom door open, so he could talk to her. She had actually managed, after a long time, to understand what he was saying while he was shaving: He spoke in fragments and words that didn't come out right, because of the way he was twisting his face. And he had gotten a pair of earphones so that if he woke up at night and couldn't sleep, he could listen to music without disturbing her.

She was getting sentimental. She was not succeeding in hating him. She stepped out of the tub, dried off, and took her clothes from the hook on the back of the door. She went into the bedroom, where it would be less damp, to dress. When she dressed, she looked at herself in the mirror. It was a mirror that had once been on a carousel, with a scalloped top and curved bottom and a heavy gilded border with raised cherubs and flowers, from which the gilt paint was falling away. He had bought it for a hundred dollars and brought it back to the apartment and put it on the bedroom wall. The silver had started to deteriorate, too, so that great areas of the glass were scratchy and cloudy, nothing to be seen in them. You could still see very well in the right-hand side of the mirror, though. She stood in front of it and looked at herself: prettier than average, but hardly the type a man would ask to come live with him after one meeting. Was it her mind? She always ended up with men who talked faster than she did, even if they didn't think faster. What, then? She had asked Spangle, and he had admitted that it was something he had a hard time explaining. It was that she had self-confidence, he said. She pointed out that she was shy about meeting people. It was that she was smart. A lot of people were smart. It was that he had hung the huge carousel mirror in the bedroom and he had done it knowing it was right, that she would like it, that he wouldn't have to consult her about it. It made her nervous, she said. It was just too big—the way it mirrored the room made the room look like something in a fun house. He admitted then that he couldn't put his finger on it, but he tried again anyway: not exactly self-confidence, but the impression she gave of being at peace—no nightmares about fireballs. Maybe she was too oblivious, she said. It was hardly flattering to be praised for something she did or didn't do in her sleep.

When he was a child, he told her, he had been a sleepwalker. They used to find him curled up by the kitchen stove, like a cat. Now all he did was thrash in his sleep, dream occasionally. She wondered what would happen if she didn't awaken him—if the fireball would get him, if then there would be silence. She never had the heart. She jumped on him like a crazed mugger, a mugger wanting to bring him down and quiet him. He had scared her to death the first time he had done it. He had thrashed as though he were having a seizure, hand thrown over his face, his back arching up off the bed. "I have nightmares," he had explained. Sometimes he was funnier when he stated facts than when he concocted elaborate stories. He would tell her that he really liked hamburgers, as he was eating a fourth hamburger. She liked it that he said the obvious and didn't realize that he was doing it, or that there was anything funny about doing it. She supposed that she could tie that in with his underestimating people's intelligence, but that wouldn't really be true—he did it more out of innocence than anything else. He often said things after the fact. So maybe he was going to call, still. If he called, she wondered if he would concoct a story, or simply tell her that he was back. He had no way of knowing that she would meet Bobby, who would go to visit Victor, who would run into . . . His world—his world full of his crazy friends—no wonder he thought that she was calm and self-assured. She had never run into such a collection of people. They expressed doubt so easily. They didn't hesitate to reveal personal things, self-doubts, failings, any longer than a person with hot toast will wait before buttering it.

She was hungry. She wanted Bobby to come.

What a surprise it would be for Spangle if he did call, or did come back, and she was with Bobby. He would never expect it of her.

Of course he would call, or come back. One or the other.

She brushed her hair and tucked it in back of her ears. She went into the living room, to wait.

He got there not long after she had started flipping through the copy of *American Photographer* he had left behind. He knocked on the door, holding a bouquet of daisies, snapdragons and marigolds.

"How are you this evening?" he said.

"Come off it," she said, sighing. "I'm hungry. Let's just go out and eat, all right? How did it go in New York, with the agents?"

"*Beautiful* agent. Simply beautiful. Everything is all set. Wonderful lunch. Wonderful wine. I love it. I just love it. New York has advantages. Waterfalls don't gush free wine."

"Did you propose to her?"

She was putting the flowers in a jar. She put her nose in the bouquet to check and realized that the marigolds did smell like cat pee.

"I bit my tongue. She had on a wedding band that must have been an inch wide, studded with diamonds. Spike-heel shoes. Oh, I love them. The most beautiful women in the world are in New York. Imagine what hell it would be to live in New York in the summer. I love her. She's going to be a wonderful agent. We had Vouvray."

"You're serious, aren't you?"

"Jesus. They wear shorts on Park Avenue. All those shapely behinds, those perfectly tanned legs, those painted fingernails and toenails, sandals with ankle straps. I just can't stand it. I found at least ten women today that I would have been perfectly happy to live with for the rest of my life."

"Where did you get the flowers?" she said.

"They were thrown outside the door."

"What?" she said.

"My guess is that a cat got into them. There was some pink yarn that had been tied around them, lying a little ways away. They were still piled in a bunch."

"Do you think Spangle's back? That he's doing this?"

"Spangle? I don't think it's his style."

She put the flowers on top of *American Photographer*. The squatting model, with red eyes, looked up at them.

"Any place you want," Bobby said. "You're paying."

"You make me nervous. I can't tell when you're kidding."

"I'm not kidding about any of it. Did I insult you by saying that I saw ten women I wanted? I didn't go up to any of them. I kept thinking about *you*. The minute that I heard Spangle was back, and that you didn't know it, I knew it was bad news for you, but it was such good news for me—I just had to call you and tell you. But I'm going to play it cool now. I'm not going to say anything more about your coming to live with me. You wouldn't have to go to any of the horrible faculty parties. You could cross-country ski—that's wonderful—you could, we could move into a house. I'm not going to talk about it. Do you want a bagel?" He produced a white paper bag. "Victor doesn't even have to visit," he said. "I can go to New York, sometimes, to see Victor. I just feel so *sorry* for Victor. If you knew what a good person he was, you'd feel the same way. I'm not going to talk about Victor," Bobby said. He sprawled on the sofa. "What if we had never met?" Bobby said. "I can't imagine it—what if you were always in New Haven, and I was in New Hampshire and we never ran into each other?"

"Let's go to dinner," she said.

"I'm obsessed, I know it," Bobby said. "I know it, but it's not just me. It's our whole culture, isn't it? What do you think? I was reading an article about the Shah, and do you know what the Shah's son does all day? He sits in his room listening to Rod Stewart singing "Do Ya Think I'm Sexy." Bobby bit into a bagel. "I'm so hungry. Don't worry—this won't spoil my appetite. I'm blowing it, I know I'm blowing it. I guess it would be unfair to you to pretend I'm not an excitable person. I was hyperactive when I was a kid. I think that's why I lost my hair." He swallowed, smiled at her. "Let me start over," he said. "I'll stand outside the door and knock, and you open it. Okay?"

"No. Look—I like you, Bobby, but I'm not really as amused by all this as I might seem. While you were hyperactive, I was in finishing school. I like you, and I think you're interesting, but if you're serious about my coming to live with you, it's out of the question."

"It's my mother's fault that I lost my hair," he said, running his hand through the ropes of curls that hung at the sides of his head. "I can remember demanding candy and more candy, all day long, and she'd give it to me. Worst thing you can do for a hyperactive kid. Well—God rest her soul. I don't want to start complaining

315

about my mother. She was bicycling in Maine and a car wiped her out from behind. Victor came to the funeral. He hitched all the way from New York to Maine, and he made it with half an hour to spare. He and my mother always liked each other. He was crying so hard out on the highway that he couldn't get rides. He wanted to be there hours before the funeral so he could take a shower."

"Bobby," she said, "would you like it if I went out and brought something back for dinner?"

He took out a blue index card and jotted down a few words, holding her off with the first finger of his left hand raised. "Okay," he said, shoving the card in his pocket. "Ready to go. All ready. This is very nice of you. I can't remember the last time I had two meals out in one day, let alone meals I didn't have to pay for. This is very nice of you. I love you."

"Stop," she said.

"Anything," he said, hands up in surrender. "Anything. I don't mean to be disagreeable. I'm just wound up. I'm fine."

She picked up her keys, got her purse, stopped and considered what to do about the ringing phone.

"You answer it," she said to Bobby. "Say I'm not here, if it's for me. Unless it's Spangle."

"If it's him, I'd hang up on him."

"No you wouldn't. Answer the phone."

"I would. I have to be honest with you."

She sighed and headed for the phone.

"All right, okay, I'll get it," he said. He picked it up the second before her hand reached it.

"Garden of the Fallen Lotus," he said, in a surprisingly good imitation of a Chinese.

"Oh Christ," Tess Spangle said. "I dialed wrong. The last thing I need is some fried won-ton." She hung up.

"A woman," he said. "She said, 'Oh Christ. I dialed wrong. The last thing I need is some fried won-ton.' "

"His mother," she said.

"Let's go," Bobby said. The phone was ringing again.

Love was one thing, survival another. The magician was going to have to leave the East Coast, very soon, to do another private party in Ojai. Amazing how even living rent-free, your money just dribbled away. Movies were expensive, food cost a lot, sixty cents to wash your clothes. His money was almost gone, and he hadn't made any good contacts around New Haven. He'd pulled a couple of rabbits out of hats at children's birthday parties, but God— the cost of rabbit food. And living with his mother was impossible. He had to buy things for her. She wouldn't pay for anything when he was around: All she wanted was to criticize and to get a free ride. She talked about how high her rent was, as though she paid any less when he wasn't there. She was allergic to the rabbits, and he had to put them in cages out on the fire escape, and he couldn't put them out there until that part of the building was in shade, so all morning and half the afternoon he was stuck sitting in the park with the rabbits.

It was unrequited love. Again. There was romance, and then there was the real world. He did not mean the real real world, but the world that he had to work in in order to survive. He knew that the real real world was the Pentagon, not a mansion in Ojai, and he was at least thankful that he was not involved in the real real world. Trying to talk himself out of her, trying to make going away seem bearable, he had been saying to himself that she was in the real world. She worked. Was married. Separated. He had a collection of pick-up sticks; she probably had stock. And there was something about her face, however beautiful, that was not spiritual.

At the very least, he had to say goodbye. Perhaps some energy would be exchanged, perhaps some cloud of romance would hover over her until she knew that she would have to go to him. Perhaps there would be some sudden epiphany, and her heart would flutter as fast as the wings of a hummingbird, and in time that movement would carry her to him. He would let her know his friend's number in Ojai, because he didn't have a phone himself, and the friend's live-in maid was always around and would know how to get in touch with him. He would like to give her something miraculous: a hummingbird wing, beating; an opal, hot with real fire. He could think of nothing but flowers. Flowers scattered in a path to her car, the essence of beauty tempering her movement into the real world. He wished that the flowers in his mother's yard were more aromatic. Marigolds smelled sour, like some liquor. They did not feel good against your face. He would like to stroke her face with a white iris. To stroke her with flowers, different flowers for different parts of the body, the way his friend in Ojai stroked women lying naked beside his pool. A rose petal on the forehead. Tickling the bottom of her feet, gently, with a camellia. Watching through his binoculars, he had seen some goddamn fat alley cat sniff the flowers and scratch the yarn away, tugging until he had it, dragging it off only to pounce at it once and then forget it.

Time was short, and he wanted, at least, to say his goodbye. He had gotten there late, because he had had a fight with his mother, and he had not seen if she had gone into the building. But perhaps she was inside, because he had seen her husband pick up the flowers and skip up the steps with them. At least she would have his flowers.

Watching from a distance was stupid. He would go and sit on the step, and when she came home, or if she came out, he would

318

tell her that this was goodbye, and that he adored her and wished only good things for her. He would do a trick, if she wanted him to.

He sat and waited, and finally it happened. He was sitting on the bottom step when the door opened, and she was there. She was there with her husband; and seeing him, she suddenly reached out to grab her husband's elbow, sucking in her breath.

"Freeze," he said, trying to be casual, to joke, to save what was meaningful for a later moment.

The gun he pointed was a red water pistol. What he shot out of it was a plastic rose.

23

IT WAS NOT the vacation he thought they would be having. They were in a borrowed house on the bay in Nantucket. Mary was not with them. She was at Angela's. John Joel was still at his grandmother's, and three times a week she and Brandt and the cook went with him into New York and waited while he talked to a psychiatrist. Louise, sitting in a chair beside the pool in the backyard, wrote them letters every day. Not post cards—letters. Post cards to Brandt. When she wrote the letters and post cards, she cupped her left hand over what she was writing, so he wouldn't see.

She liked the pool better than the ocean. There was a chair that floated in the pool, and early in the morning when he got up, he would go to the bedroom window and peer out through the shelves of gloxinias, the purple and pink bells of flowers, and Louise would be below, with orange juice, floating in the pool. He would go downstairs and sit on the rim of the pool, his legs in the water halfway to his knees. When the sun got stronger, after an hour or so, he would push himself forward and sink down, go all the way under, exhaling, and then pop up again. Then swim. Then try to get her to go to the beach. When she wouldn't, he would open the gate at the back of the pool and go down the fifteen steps to the sandy path, and follow it until it widened onto the beach.

Everyone had forgotten about John Joel's braces.

Tiffy called every morning, and every evening Louise called Tiffy. Tiffy had left her husband and found an apartment on Central Park West. A famous painter whose name he had forgotten lived in the building, and Tiffy was going to take painting lessons. Tiffy this, Tiffy that. Tiffy said that Parker's mother was in bed, trying not to have a miscarriage. Parker's grandmother was there, taking care of things. When John had dropped Mary off at Angela's, Angela's father had had a lot to say about Parker's mother. Very stupid, he said. Knew nothing about law. Parker's father was out of town on business. The police had gone to the house several times to question Parker. Angela's father reported that Parker's mother had told him, with pride, what Parker said to the police: "If I told you to jump off a bridge, would you do it?"

He waded out into the water. A woman in a bikini kept throwing a plastic baseball bat into the water for a big golden retriever. He stood there, far enough away so as not to distract them, and watched the bat sail out into the water, time and again. The woman threw like a man, not like a woman. In other ways, she was obviously a woman. The bikini was cut right to the edge of her nipples, but tight, so that no matter how she moved, you couldn't see anything.

"Isn't he great?" the woman said, as he passed by.

"Yes. Has he always loved the water?"

"Oh yes. When he was eight weeks old, my husband waded out into a pond with him and released him, and he stayed there, perfectly still, and then he started paddling. He made it to shore and barked at my husband and threw himself in the dirt and rolled in it, but then he got tired of being mad and inched back in. We can hardly drive past water without him leaping out of the car. He'll jump off bridges. He's been off a diving board. He loves it." The woman was shaking her head, beaming. The dog crouched, eyes wide, waiting for the bat. She turned and threw it. The dog was running before it had left her hand.

Parker had told his son to jump off a bridge, and he had done it.

"Isn't that dangerous?" he said. "Can he judge what's deep enough water to dive into?"

The woman's expression changed. "I never thought about that," she said. "I don't know if he has a sense of that or not."

He walked on, feeling like a cloud that had darkened the beach.

Every little thing that happened was getting blown out of proportion in his head. The night before, they had made shish-kebabs and cooked them on the hibachi by the pool, and he had burned his tongue, biting into a chunk of beef too soon. He had wanted to cry, to spit out the hot meat and cry. He had sucked air into his mouth instead, said nothing; but after dinner he had taken it out on her, undressing and diving into the pool, not speaking. She carried the plates into the house and didn't come out again. From the water, he watched the coals, still glowing. Shivering in the water, he looked back at the house and saw the light on in the bedroom. The light went off. She had gone to bed at nine-thirty.

It was Friday, and Nick and Laurie, who were going to be on Martha's Vineyard to visit friends, were going to stop at the house that night. He had asked Louise if that was all right, or if she would prefer to be alone. She had not said that she preferred to be alone, and after a few seconds she had said that it was all right. He had the feeling that she thought it was an odd request, but nothing harmful—like someone asking if he can brush his teeth in front of you. He hated it that even on vacation she had brought the little plastic key, and was rolling the toothpaste up, from the bottom. He had removed the key, flushed it down the toilet, and squeezed the tube hard, in the middle. She had not said anything about it. He had been embarrassed after he had done it. He had been embarrassed after he questioned the woman in the bikini. Embarrassed, the night before, when he had thrown off his clothes and a breeze had come up and she had seen him shiver before he jumped. Embarrassed that she had picked up the plates and washed them. Embarrassed that she had gone to bed. To cheer himself up, he kept thinking about what Nick told him— that not all of it was his fault. His mother said so, too. Only Louise did not say so. The female psychiatrist, whom he seemed always to talk to, had granted that it was true, but seemed to think that it was unimportant to notice in what ways he *wasn't* responsible. He wanted to think that it was over, but actually

322

very little of it was over. Nobody knew yet what damage had really been done to all of them. In the evening, he liked to walk on the beach and watch the sun go down. It was so simple to see that the day was over, that the blackness would spread out, intensify. When he was alone, he lost all sense of time: He might sit for an hour, two hours, three. He sat alone in the den downstairs, while upstairs Louise slept. He went over and over it in his mind, gaining no ground. All the facts were so simple: that it wasn't a good marriage, that he loved Nina, that his son had shot his daughter. Louise would not watch the sunset with him because the sun was huge and deep-pink above the water, and when she looked at it, all she could think of was blood. The blood swirling in Nina's sink: a little cut, a small tragedy. The blood on the ground: the cops had blasted it away with the garden hose. They had cleaned up as though someone had made a faux pas. They had taken pictures of the bloody ground, and then they had washed the area with a hose: the polite host, passing no comment, silently mopping up spilled wine.

Nina felt responsible. "You talk as though you were a magnet," he said to her, "as though I had to be pulled along. You're not being fair to either of us. You aren't acknowledging that this is still the right place for me to be. That you want me here." She had kept crying. "Look," he had said, "isn't this where I belong?"

"I *was* a magnet," Nina had said. "I had advantages she didn't have. I *did* pull you along."

"What advantages?"

"Because I'm young, and she's not. Because I have this small, quiet place for you to be, and at home it's the way you always tell me it is when you have a barbecue or something awful like that. You like it here because you're left alone."

"I could be in a cave and be left alone."

"It *is* a cave," she had shouted. "It's *cramped*, it's not cozy. I hate it that you love it so much, that you have so much and you want so little."

"What do I have?" he had said, and she had been completely exasperated. "Pillars at the end of my driveway," he had smiled. "What else?"

"Acres of land. Children. A big house. Try to *realize* what you have."

"You're what I want."

"Do you know what I did?" she had said. "I got a friend of mine to drive me to your house. Do you believe that I did that? Do you know why I did it? Because if there were pillars, I was never going to speak to you again. Because you pretend your house is *nothing*, that *all* of it is nothing, and I know it isn't true. That house is *beautiful*. I looked up the driveway and saw a huge tree. I can't understand what you want with this—with this tiny apartment, with me. Because I'm pretty? Why do you like me? I can't remember."

"It's not as though I want to burrow into this apartment and never leave," he said.

"You're not answering the question."

"God almighty. I *show* you how I love you, don't I? I've *told* you why I love you. Because we have good times together, because there's no such thing as time when I'm with you."

"You always look at your watch and leave," she had said.

Slow time. Slow motion. It had been a hard climb to get to her, in more senses than one. It had been hard to face his feelings for her, when he thought he had all his feelings arranged, under control. It was as if somebody had stood up in the middle of a familiar song and played a brilliant solo: Was it worth being amazed, when things got disturbed so that they would always seem odd if you put them back together the way they were? He had debated. He had not slept with her. And then he had slept with her and pretended it did not matter. It was so difficult, and he was so slow in coming around to what he had to do. She was right that he hid in her apartment. He was hiding from himself, or at best playing peek-a-boo, pretending it was a safe game and that there were only little surprises: the infant seeing that it's still a friend behind the fingers. Rules of the game: The peek-a-boo is always gentle, never shouted. You disappear, but can still be seen. The house in Rye. The house in Connecticut. The apartment on Columbus Avenue. She had joked that he would come back reincarnated as confetti. His son had shot his daughter, and little blood vessels, little pieces of tissue, had torn apart, frayed.

Nina was away in the Berkshires, and he couldn't call her for two more nights. She had taken a week off and gone away to think.

For two of those days, at least, Peter Spangle, on his way to see an old friend in New Hampshire, would be with her. He could really see how you killed somebody over love, but he could not see how you shot someone out of hatred. Maybe that was what it appeared to be, too—that John Joel hated Mary. For the millionth time, the billionth time, he thought: My son shot my daughter.

It was late afternoon. He headed back toward the house. He could feel the heat rising from his collarbones and his shoulders, and he knew that he had gotten too much sun, that his shoulders were going to hurt. He touched the skin with his fingertips and he could feel the soreness, like pressing on a bruise. When John Joel and Mary were little children and they had splinters, bug bites, cuts, he used to examine them before he rubbed medicine on the area or carefully pinched up the skin to draw out a splinter. He hated it when they cringed from him. He was being so gentle. He could remember, one time, yelling at Mary, "You're not being fair. I put my finger an *inch* away from the cut to steady your arm so I could see if you got glass in it. I couldn't *possibly* be hurting you. You're just afraid because I've got big hands." Louise had thought that that was hilarious. She had started laughing, and that had started Mary crying, and he had been so angry that he had stalked off, his hands at his sides feeling like they were encased in catcher's mitts. As Nick said, it was not all his fault.

He watched a child playing in the wet sand at the water's edge, pressing what looked like a gigantic cookie cutter into the sand, standing back and looking approvingly at what she was creating: a chain of big ducks, beaks to tails, stretching and stretching until a wave washed over them, and the child began again, a little farther back.

The woman with the dog was gone. About where she had stood was a woman in a white sailor's hat, sitting in a lawn chair pulled a little way into the water, her big legs stretched in front of her. "Hawaii is better," she said as he passed.

He went back to the path and climbed the steps, feeling how smooth the sand had worn the soles of his feet.

Louise had brought a radio outside. It was playing softly, sitting on the metal top of a table that had a hole, but no umbrella they could find.

"They're putting the former manager of the Beatles in jail for tax evasion," she said. She did not look up. She was reading a paperback.

"Did you plan to go to the store for food, or shall we just go out for dinner when Nick and his friend come?" she said.

"Laurie," he said.

"Laurie," she said. "Which?"

"You're mad that I asked them," he said. "They were coming here anyway. I couldn't very well not invite them to stop by."

"Nick and Laurie," she said. She moved her leg, and the chair swirled a little in the pool. She was almost facing him, but still she hadn't looked up.

"We'll go out to eat," he said. "We'll go to that restaurant you like."

"So that you can keep Nick posted," she said, "you can tell him that I've asked for a divorce."

"What?" he said. "Who have you asked for a divorce?"

She looked up. "You," she said. There was a report on the radio about which traveler's checks to buy. A reporter had bought traveler's checks and left them home on purpose. American Express had come through for her. The people at the Holiday Inn where she had gone to fill out a form and get new checks had been very polite.

"If that's what you want," he said. He thought to himself: coward.

"Nick and Laurie," she said, and moved her leg again. The chair twirled.

"You don't want to see Nick and Laurie," he said.

"I'll see Nick and Laurie," she said. "I'll stay the rest of the week, too. You can go, if you want to."

"Do you want to take a walk?" he said.

"To see if the woman in the bikini is still throwing sticks for her dog? That made me so nostalgic. My poor goddamn dog. Goddamn me, too, for not being able to get the dog out of my head."

He wondered if it was orange juice in her cup. Seagulls were squawking.

"You saw me talking to her?" he said. "You came down to the beach?"

"I started to, but I saw you in the distance, talking to her. Do you realize that you're only embarrassing yourself? I saw her at the drugstore, at the counter, in a tight white skirt, and the man sitting on the stool next to her wasn't more than eighteen years old. Not her son, either. That woman must be forty-five."

"So what makes you think that I was interested in her?"

"You're interested in dogs?"

"I like dogs," he said. "I didn't worship Mr. Blue the way you did, but it was your dog."

"Mary told me that she talked to you about getting a dog, and that you didn't seem too keen on the idea."

"Should I have? Is that what you want?"

"As you said to Mary, if I wanted a dog, I'd just go out and get a dog. I'm not like you, actually. If I decide I want something, I just act on that impulse."

"Why not be specific with your insults?" he said.

"I'm not insulting you. Maybe by implication I am. Saying that you're like me. To be fair to myself, what I said was that *I* was like *you*." She kicked the water, turned. She was sunburned, too. Her face was shiny, her hair wet. She had been swimming. Drinking. It was not orange juice in the cup.

"*Here's* something you haven't thought about," she said. "What if I told you to take care of the children? What if I moved with Tiffy to New York?"

It was something he hadn't thought about. He was silent, trying to figure out if she was bluffing.

"Scare you?" she said. "Your mother wouldn't take two more, would she?"

"They're my children," he said. "Do you think that I wouldn't take them?"

"I don't think they'd go," she said. She spun again. "That's just a guess," she said. "You know when Brandt had the measles? He got them again—German measles. Your mother had never had German measles." She laughed. "She called today. She's peppered."

"What are you drinking?" he said.

"If you stay," she said, "I want to rent a boat."

"I want you to take a walk with me on the beach and sober up."

"I want it to stay summer," she said. "I hate Connecticut in the winter. You know what I *particularly* hate? The birds still hopping around in the cold, the little seed bells you have to hang in the trees for them. Those brown and white seeds all over the leaves. Then the snow."

"Where would you rather be?" he said.

She said, smiling, "Where would *you?*"

She made it come back to him: the rooms, the apartment on Columbus Avenue, the place he had been trying all day not to think about, staring at the ocean, the beach. Seagulls instead of pigeons. Salt air instead of the subway smell. His feet sinking into the sand. His feet so heavy he could hardly lift them, the slight creaking of the stairs. "Be quiet," Nina had whispered, putting her finger to her lips. "The landlady!" He had turned to see a heavy woman in a black dress, her hair in pigtails, coming out the front door of Nina's building, a big white patent-leather purse gleaming under the streetlight. It was the night they had come back to the apartment and Horton had been there, slumped like a Mexican taking a siesta. In front of the landlady, Horton had put his arms around Nina's hips. The woman looked shocked and hurried past them down the steps. "She hates me," Nina laughed. "She sticks her head out the door to see if I've brought anybody home with me. She has a daughter who's the same way."

He had said to John Joel, on the train, "Not your type, huh?" Condescending. He had been condescending to somebody who would pick up a gun and shoot somebody else. That was not something a child would do. His child had done it. If he had under-estimated John Joel that much, maybe John Joel had known all along that Nina was his girl, not Nick's. Maybe John Joel knew that while he was kidding him, saying that she wasn't his type.

"I'm going to drive to the fish market," he said. "You don't want to go out to dinner."

"I'll be sober."

"What makes you think so?"

"Because you'll watch over me." She smiled. Turned the page of her book.

He sighed, and sat on the edge of the pool, swinging his legs over the side. He did watch her. He watched her and tried to think of good things about her, because he was so inclined to dislike her. If she hadn't wanted to come, she should have said so. If she hadn't wanted to see Nick, or let *him* see Nick, she should have said that, too. Good things, he reminded himself. That she had gotten drunk, but didn't seem to intend to get drunker; that she had been about to take a walk with him on the beach before, until she had misunderstood his exchanging a few pleasantries with a woman for flirtation. She had once drawn a hopscotch game on the kitchen floor, amazed that he didn't know how to do it, and they had used as a stone a kumquat from a fruit basket her aunt had sent them for Christmas. Hopping through the kitchen. Christmas, when she always gave him presents he would like. Jumping into the pile of leaves he had raked in the backyard. Winter memories: Most of them were winter memories.

At five o'clock, when Nick and Laurie showed up, she was sitting on a lounge chair beside the pool, wearing a blue T-shirt and white cotton pants. A towel that had been on her wet hair was around her neck. She was polite.

"We're just staying for a little while," Nick said. "We got a late start. We've got to get to our friends' house pretty soon." He said it before he even sat down.

Laurie kicked off her shoes and sat on the rim of the pool. She had on the kind of mirrored sunglasses that you can't see into: He looked and saw the red clouds reflected, and a large shadow that must have been him. You could only tell by her mouth that she was happy.

Nick had brought a horseshoe game. "I've wanted to play all summer," he said. "Does anybody else want to play?"

He went down to the beach with Nick. Nick ground the stake into the sand, then handed him a horseshoe. "My grandmother had one of these over her back door," he said. "For luck."

"Did she have good luck?" John said.

"Not particularly. About average. She also pitched horseshoes. Come to think of it, she was very good at that."

"Shit, what are you doing with a horseshoe game?"

"How's it going?" Nick said to him. Nick threw a horseshoe. Missed. "What I'm doing with it is that it makes me nervous to be around the two of you and I thought it would give us something to do."

329

"We could drink."

"Okay," Nick said.

"I was kidding. Louise is just sobering up."

"How's it going?" Nick said.

"All right," he said. For some reason, he thought that it would be betraying Louise to say that she had asked for a divorce.

"If it's going okay, then I'm supposed to tell you that Nina's back, and she wants you to call her."

The horseshoe went thump in the sand. Neither of them had hit the stake.

"When did you hear from her?" he said.

"She called me yesterday. I don't know anything. I told it to you just the way she told it to me."

"She wants me to be in a good mood if she's giving me bad news," he said. "That's what it is."

"You don't know till you call," Nick said.

"How did she sound?"

"She didn't sound any way. All right. She sounded all right."

"I'm going to go call her."

"Don't do that to me," Nick said. "What if Louise walks in the house when you're on the phone? I don't want to be here if there's going to be some fight. I just got done fighting with Laurie's brother about how she's black and I'm white."

"Then we'll go back to the house, and you ask for some liquor we don't have, and I'll go get it. There's a phone at the liquor store."

"Oh Christ. What if you get depressed and don't come back? Then what?"

"I'm not that out of control."

The horseshoe spun around the stake. "Proof," John said.

"Dumb luck," Nick said. "I'm not even saying it's going to be bad news, but if it is, you'd better come back."

They walked toward the horseshoe stake.

"What liquor don't you have?" Nick said.

"We have just about everything. Ask for something weird."

They went back to the house. Louise was sitting on the rim of the pool, dangling her legs alongside Laurie's. They were sipping drinks.

330

"What have you got there?" Nick said.

"Gin and tonic," Laurie said.

"You know what I've been wanting to try?" Nick said. "Have you seen those ads for that liqueur made from melons?"

"I've never seen you drink anything but Scotch or beer," Laurie said.

"That sounds disgusting," Louise said.

"It's green," Nick said. "I can't think of the name of the stuff."

"Go get yourself a bottle," John said. "The liquor store is two minutes away."

"Nah," Nick said.

"Go ahead," John said.

"You come with me," Nick said. "I don't know where it is."

"Are you serious?" Laurie said. "*Melon* liqueur?"

"*I'll* get it," John said. "If they have it."

"He'd do anything for you," Louise said. She sipped her drink. "Melon liqueur is a *favor?*" Laurie said.

Louise shrugged. Nick sat beside them, kicked off his sandals.

"Be right back," John said. "Anybody want anything else?"

They didn't. He went into the house, picked up the car keys and his wallet, went out the front door and jumped in his car. At the liquor store, he bought a bottle of Midori, surprised at how expensive it was. Then he waited while an old man shouted into the phone about what the doctor had said was causing his high blood pressure. "I will *too* buy beer," the old man said. "I call to give you good news, and you start nagging. I *told* you it was all heredity." He had on a California Angels baseball cap, a white Lacoste shirt, madras bermudas and white knee socks. He wore red running shoes. He hung up and stood staring at the phone, fuming, his face nearly as red as the shoes, while John stood politely in back of him, waiting for him to move away. Finally he did. As John talked to the operator, the old man began to lift six-packs of beer out of the cooler and pile them on the counter.

"I knew you'd call," she said. "Hi. I came home."

He could tell that it wasn't going to be bad. It wasn't going to be something horrible. It was going to be all right.

"We're getting divorced," he said.

"You and me?" she said.

"Never," he said.

"I came home."

"Don't hang up," he said.

"Why would I hang up?"

"Don't say something I don't want to hear."

"There's nothing to say that you wouldn't want to hear. I went to Stockbridge. I rode up that far with Spangle, and it would have been so easy to keep driving, to just keep going. We got stoned and smooched. That was all."

"Take it back," he said.

"Take what back?"

"That you smooched."

"We did. In bed. In a motel in Stockbridge. With our clothes on. Maybe it was for old times' sake. Maybe the other would have been, too."

"Don't tell me any more," he said.

"There's nothing more to tell."

"I'm red in the face because of *heredity*," the old man shouted at the clerk behind the counter. "Give me some bags of those salted peanuts."

"Don't hang up," he said.

"I won't. I wanted to tell you something. I thought you might be amused. It's not funny, really. It's just so strange."

"Tell me," he said.

"I miss you," she said.

"You're not going to say something I don't want to hear?"

"I can't imagine that it would bother you. It's just so strange. I guess the truth is that it bothers *me*, but I don't understand it." She was smoking grass. He could hear her drawing in, waiting. Nina, in the apartment on Columbus Avenue. He could really understand how someone would shoot because of love.

"You remember your dream?" she said. "That depressing dream that didn't make any sense? Well, I dreamed an answer to it in Stockbridge. The air conditioning was blowing on high and we couldn't turn it down, and it was too hot without it and too cold with it, so we were huddled in bed together, but I was still freezing, and that night I had a dream that picked up where your dream left off."

She laughed. He was listening to Nina laugh on the phone. They would invite the landlady to the wedding. Mary had told him to be where he wanted to be, and he was going to take her at her word. The psychiatrist was in the business of fixing people up, and he could fix John Joel. Louise did not love him. She was paranoid about things that were not happening and she didn't care about things that were. The night he had stood looking at the shooting star, she had said to him that she didn't know everything, and she didn't want to.

Nina's dream: She was on a trip—she didn't know where. She got cold, and went into a store to buy a coat. She bought it—a long black coat with a collar she turned up against the wind. She had not been upset that she was in a strange country, but when she left the store she was suddenly confused: Everything looked strange, and people came by talking in an unfamiliar language. The coincidence of having a dream, she said, that overlapped his dream: It was like walking down a street, thinking of a song, and suddenly the person you pass starts to whistle it. She had dreamed this: That standing on the sidewalk outside the store she had reached into the pocket of the coat, and she had been surprised to discover that there were mittens inside.

24

THE MAGICIAN'S name was George.

When Bobby saw him sitting on the steps of Cynthia's building, he figured it out immediately: the path of flowers to the car; the bunch of flowers near the steps. As fast as she grabbed his arm, frightened, he understood and began to smile.

Harmless. It would figure that Bobby would think the magician was harmless. On the off-chance that he was harmless, she still did not want to stand and converse with him.

"I have a crush on you," the magician said.

"I don't even know this man's name," she said to Bobby.

"George," the magician said. "I have to go back to California. I wanted to talk to you one more time."

"We're going out to eat," she said.

Wrong thing to have said.

"Why don't you come along?" Bobby said. He looked at Cynthia; he had just remembered that she was paying. Even Bobby was smart enough to figure out that this man wouldn't be rolling in money.

They both looked at her: the boy who had found a puppy, and the puppy that thought it had found a home.

335

"I've had about all I can take," she said.

"This is such a New York thing," Bobby said. "Let me see that water pistol. Where'd you get that?"

"Hollywood," the magician said. "The magic store I go to in Hollywood."

"A magic store? Really? Are you a magician?" Bobby didn't wait for an answer. "How did you two meet?" he said to Cynthia.

"In a laundromat," she said. She wouldn't look at the magician.

"You were so nice to talk to," the magician said. He said to Bobby, "She was so nice to talk to."

"Where do you want to eat?" Cynthia said to Bobby. She was walking fast. She could kill him. She could take one of his blue index cards and make it into an airplane with a sharply pointed nose and sail it into his eye. It was Spangle's fault. Spangle's friend. Spangle who had moved in with her years ago, when she didn't really want him. And now he'd moved out, without even telling her, leaving her with a crazy friend—woods queer, she guessed—and a magician who followed her around and hounded her. At least he had said that he was going back to California.

"I can't believe it," Bobby said, shaking his head. "You were *courting* her. That's so wonderful. She *is* special."

"You're her husband?" the magician said.

"Can we leave my life out of it?" she said. She stared at the magician.

Bobby said, "We just met."

"*I'm* not coming to New Hampshire with you," she said. "Why don't you see if *George* wants to come?"

He nudged her. "Don't hurt his feelings," he said.

The magician was staring at the sidewalk.

"I did a magic trick with my class the first day of the semester," Bobby said. "You know that old trick of folding a piece of paper into eight squares so that four of the pieces have two smooth edges? I had the students write down four writers they wanted to study, and I wrote down four writers I wanted to teach, and then I borrowed a scarf from one of my students—beautiful girl—and let her shuffle the pieces of paper on my desk. Then I picked four: three of them mine, one of them theirs. We read Proust, Mann, Flaubert and Richard Brautigan."

"They like Brautigan, huh?" the magician said. "I like him too. I have all his books."

"They didn't put down Brautigan—I did. Flaubert was one of their choices."

"I love it," the magician said.

"She was kidding," Bobby said. "I'm heterosexual. Not that I wouldn't be happy to entertain you in New Hampshire."

"What did I say?" Cynthia said. "Only that he should go to New Hampshire. You think everything is sexual."

"Only in the summer, or when I'm teaching."

"I'd like to see New Hampshire," the magician said.

"The real place to see is Vermont. I used to live with her"—he hesitated—"friend in Vermont. Some Indian's living there now, raising corn. That's all right, I guess, but the house looked shabby. We did a lot of work on the house. There always was a problem with porcupines living underneath it, though. You'd hear them running and scratching all night. Find quills in the yard. A friend's dog that was visiting attacked one of them and got a snout full of quills. Had to take it to the vet. I said, 'I was trying acupuncture.' Vet took me seriously. What a good time we used to have. Vermont was really the scene in those days. Still is, I guess. New Hampshire's beautiful in its own way."

They went to Mamoun's, and sat at a table in the middle of the room.

"You know Blake's poem about the lamb?" Bobby said, reading the menu. "Great poem. I can't believe that pretty soon I'll be standing in front of a classroom, smelling chalk. I'm very anxious to see if a certain young lady enrolls in my class again this fall, though." He took Cynthia's hand. "She can't compare," he said. "Idle interest."

"What will you be doing in the fall?" the magician asked.

"I'm a graduate student," she said. She stared at the menu. She felt young and stupid, like a teenager dragged along by her parents to meet some friend's very nice son. Bobby could not possibly have thought that she would want to have dinner with some West Coast crazy who had been bothering her all summer.

"I hate New Haven," the magician said. "I'm just staying at my mother's place for a while. I didn't grow up here, though. She

337

moved here from Providence when my father died. Not much of a city, that I can tell." He smiled at Cynthia. "Remember?" he said. "You asked me if I could change the color of your clothes."

She said to Bobby: "I had put a red shirt in with the wash by mistake. That's what he means."

"The laundromats in California are nice," the magician said. "California is nicer than the East."

"What exactly do you do out there?" Bobby said. "Magic tricks? How does that work?"

"Oh," the magician said, "I've got a rep out there. I do parties sometimes. Private parties. I do quite a few parties for a guy who lives out in Ojai."

"How long have you been doing it?" Bobby said.

"Since I got out of college. During college, a little. I met a guy at the Santa Monica pier who got me interested in it. We used to set up on the pier and do some tricks. Now people are afraid to come around, because they think you're going to ask for money. Or they're too busy roller-skating."

"So you do private parties," Bobby said.

"Yeah. One of my best tricks is with a brown paper bag—the kind you get groceries in. I show them the bag inside and out, and I put it over my head, and when one of them lifts it off, my nose is a penis. Of course you can see that it's a store-bought rubber penis. But they don't know where it came from."

"Would you like to order?" the waitress said.

They ordered. Cynthia looked around the restaurant. Two women, each reading her own paperback copy of Going Too Far, waiting for their food. A man at a table, alone. At the front of the restaurant, where they had come in, was a counter, and a man behind it, cooking. There were giant jars of honey on the counter. In the pastry case was halvah, baklava, some kind of pudding.

"Rickie Lee Jones is invited to this wrap party in Ojai I'm going back to do," the magician said. "I think I saw her a couple of years ago, before she was famous, playing the piano in the lobby of the Marmont. I was there to do a party in one of the suites. I had a tube with insects in it inside my jacket, and it fell out as I was walking past the desk, and all these flies and moths flew up, right in front of the man behind the desk, and started swirling around. Sometimes really embarrassing things happen. There's a trick called 'The Telephone Wizard.' You have a friend ready on the phone, and you spread out a deck of cards . . ."

She stopped listening. This was absolutely ridiculous. Bobby was completely involved with the magician, nodding, fiddling excitedly with his hair, twisting the strands into tighter curls. As she was looking around the restaurant, one of her former professors came in and stood at the counter.

". . . so I dialed the number and asked for the Wizard. I had no idea I'd gotten a wrong number. It *sounded* like my friend Bill. Well—sort of. I thought he'd been drinking. I had had trouble talking him into staying home until ten o'clock that night, because his friend Griffin was in town, and they wanted to go down to the Troubadour. But here's the far-out thing: Whoever answered the phone knew the trick! It's not that common a trick. He started counting: 'Ace, two, three . . .' and—" He stopped talking, said to Cynthia, "Do you know this trick?"

"No," she said.

"I didn't think so. I didn't want to bore you. I could just get to the punch line if you knew it." The magician wiped his forehead on a napkin. He went on. "So the card she had put her penny on was the three of hearts. The guy on the other end is counting, and when he gets to three I break in and ask if I'm talking to the Wizard. Now, unbeknownst to me, all the time this is happening, Jack, whose house this is, is trying to get his phone to work so everybody can hear. He has those awful speakers that broadcast what the person you're talking to is saying. I really think those things are offensive. Answering machines are bad enough. Anyway. That was the cue, you see. He knew the card was a three of something. So he started counting again. 'Clubs, hearts—' Then I interrupted, her card being the three of hearts, and gave her the telephone. She dated Robert Evans for a while, before he married Ali MacGraw. I don't know what happened to her. Anyway, she took the phone from me, and I was expecting Bill to say, 'Three of hearts' and hang up and go to the Troubadour, but it wasn't Bill at all. It was some nut. Suddenly he starts talking to her about eating her snatch, and then the goddamn speakers started to work, and she was standing there while he was talking about eating her out. I couldn't understand what Bill was doing. I mean, at this point, I realized it wasn't Bill, but I couldn't believe that I'd dial a wrong number and somebody would not only know the trick, but he'd go along with it! He even told her her card was the three of hearts, then went right on talking about eating her out."

The waitress, lowering a plate in front of Bobby, caught Cynthia's eye. She looked curious. Cynthia looked at her lap.

"*That's* one for Brautigan," the magician said. He looked at Cynthia. "Excuse me," he said. He spread his napkin over his lap. "I'm not like that," he said. "I was shocked when it happened." He bit into his sandwich. "It lost me business, too."

"You said you're staying here with your mother?" Bobby said. "What does your mother think about your being a magician? Doesn't seem like a thing many mothers would approve of. What do you think?"

"She doesn't," the magician said. "She'd like it if I'd put my rabbits in their cage out on the fire escape and let them sweat to death. She's not even sympathetic to the rabbits."

"You know, I'm a college professor," Bobby said. "You can't get more respectable than that. My mother would like it better if I was a priest. She thinks I should be a priest or a psychiatrist, because I have such insight into people."

"People love to think that things can be easy," the magician said. "My mother likes to think the rabbits can just live on air. She was upset when she saw me chopping their dinner. Bad enough I had to disillusion her about rabbits popping out of top hats. She didn't want to see me feeding them."

She sighed. She felt as if she had been pushed onstage during a comedy routine. What was making everything seem even more unreal was that she could not get the real tragedy out of her mind: Only a little while ago Mary Knapp had gotten shot. Their lives must be chaos now. She was sorry for Mary; and, knowing how exasperating Mary could be, she had some sympathy for her brother, who had probably shot her out of the same frustration that had made her want to scream when Mary shrugged and didn't care about something for the umpteenth time. She drank her tea. The magician was explaining a card trick to Bobby, and Bobby was taking notes on a blue index card.

She had met Spangle by chance. Stayed with him by chance. Not entirely. Not entirely true. She had not been cynical enough. One moment, for her, that seemed genuinely magical, had outweighed so much that was tiresome, pointless—even the things that were mean about him. He had not been kidding when he held her hand and said that he wanted to think that it would be that easy to keep her. He was all around her, like the tiny foam-rubber rabbits that had burst out of the larger rabbit the magician had pressed into her hand. Spangle was always springing up when she didn't expect him. Jumping out of the closet at her. But also dodging work to be sitting in the dentist's waiting room, without telling her he was going to do it, to hold her hand for a minute before she went in and faced a root canal. What she had done for him, in return, was to say that there was no fireball when there was.

As they walked out of the restaurant, the magician was griping about too many demands being made on him. "It freaks me out when people think I can cure disease," he said. "I really clam up when I'm asked anything about that. A friend of mine—the friend from the Santa Monica pier—got in big trouble when he said offhandedly that a woman who was having trouble with her night vision ought to take some Vitamin A. She dosed herself with the stuff until she was as orange as a carrot, and dropped dead. She was married to a lawyer." He shook his head. "It's a rotten world," he said. "No wonder people want answers. No wonder they want to have parties and get distracted. Sometimes something nice happens, though. Like getting to spend time with you guys." He turned to Cynthia, who had been trying to walk a little ahead of them. "Even if it happened at the last minute, I made two friends. I know we're going to see each other again. Tell me if I'm not right," he said. "If I sent you a white orchid in December, with no card, wouldn't you know it was from me?"

"You don't do voodoo, do you?" Bobby said. "*That* was something a poet would say: voodoo/do you. No, wait: It's a Frank Sinatra song. I almost pirated a Frank Sinatra song." Bobby shook his head. "Can I see those binoculars?"

"No voodoo," the magician said. "I don't fool with anything messy." He took his binoculars from around his neck and handed them to Bobby. Bobby trained them on a bird in a tree.

"I've *got* to get binoculars," Bobby said. "Why didn't I think

of that? I'm going to buy the most powerful binoculars I can find."
Bobby handed them to her. "This is so amazing," he said. "Look
through these. Look at the way everything jumps at you."

"Here's my card," the magician was saying, talking to Bobby
as she stood still on the sidewalk, looking through the binoculars.
"I know that we'll meet again," the magician said.

"Let me walk you home," Bobby said to the magician. "Do you
ever cast spells, make ladies fall in love with men?"

"Keep the binoculars," the magician said to Cynthia. "Please."
He put his hand on top of hers, and then he and Bobby began to
walk away. She watched until they turned the corner.

The next time she raised the binoculars, she saw Spangle,
sitting on the front step of the building, eating an ice-cream cone.
She stared, pressing the binoculars hard against her eyes. Finally
he looked her way, stood up. He saw her. He was smiling. She
could see that, as he ran, getting larger and larger, until he was
right on her, a blur.

"Save me," she said, half-jokingly, falling against him without
ever lowering the binoculars.

"I was locked out," he said. "Jonathan and I were broke one
night in Madrid, and he made a wish by throwing the key into a
fountain."

"What did he wish for?" she said, head buried in his shoulder.

"I don't know," Spangle said. "The usual, I guess."

ABOUT THE AUTHOR

ANN BEATTIE has taught fiction writing at the
University of Virginia and Harvard, and is a frequent
contributor to *The New Yorker*.